ALEX FISH

Written By

MICHAEL A. BIGGAM

First edition

MMXXIV

ALEX FISH

Cover photography and design by the author.

www.mabiggam.com

Endless, endless, feelings tempest,

on white shore of neck and bare-breast.

D RY TONGUE IN THE MORNING

Dreams of hope this little boy,
Lost forever, left for death.
At the feet blue eyes shall fix,
As raging seas drown on his ship.

W hen I woke up, she was leaving. Concealing my shame beneath sweating blankets I hold my folded genitals and sink into bedsheets that breathed of the same. Laid still, face down so hard that the springs of the mattress began to bruise. Maintaining a breathing pattern that could start a religion. I made sure she could not see me play eye-spy on her, cornea burned with nitrates, caught like a fly in caustic webs of sunlight.

Her lemon-crotched cotton knickers lay balled up on the floor, wrapped acutely, mottled around a faux-Swedish bedpost and hardened by drying bodily fluids. Upon the sheets scored Maybelline contours wondering silently if it had been worth it, and those hardened stiletto heels now providing an unsteady foundation to her feet, instead of scratching down my body as we coupled back on the burnt umber calfskin handmade-to-order Chesterfield sofa.

The girl picks up her handbag and checks herself in the full-length mirror on the wall. Once more she looks to me, playing aloof, yet filled with the pain of longing that cries back for centuries. Hoping for one cursory goodbye, a solitary glance. I peer with one eye naked which cuts as her shame touches mine. Quickly, she is gone.

I couldn't talk to her this morning. Communication is impossible. All I recollect from last night is eating what was left of the bag of whatever it was from some geezer, and then driving home a dirty kebab. Likewise stories fall on the face of everyone with anything to do at those morally forsaken hours.

The glow of solitude forgives me once again. Two blades of light drag heavy across the rug towards my kingdom of cotton, cast by the gaps between blinds, given life by sunlight that fades, as it once again performs the great disappearing act, hidden by the night like cowards playing dead. They forge the trail for my own will to follow.

Before me lay a palette of blues and blacks and greys and green; wandering in to each other, seemingly at random. Shapes come, shadows grow and time attacks like rust against the endless chaos of the universe in which we float.

The bedroom reeks of sweat and come. Windows heavy and painted shut, streaking with married particulates born from the throats of two nameless lovers, just another encounter of drug-fueled sexual-immolation.

Already the edges of an empire crumbled around me, Life thus far being funded primarily by trust fund after funded trust. One dead parent and another now on the marble. There he lies colder than the harshest howling of a raining midnight in winters' last "fuck you".

Torrents wash, hard and petulant from the brushed steel shower head. I still don't know what happened last night but I do have a large bruise on my arm.

I picked up the girl from outside Haji's kebab shop at about 3AM on the walk home, or as I have come to refer to it: The Golden Hour. In this time the streets are pocked with the lucky victims required for a man who walks shadows. If memory serves, we had the same kind of kebab and felt that was enough common ground to chat intimately about the state of the nation. Which nation, I couldn't say, since it lead quickly thereafter to a display of debauchery typical to this existentially aware yet morally vapid generation breeding like a virus through a shanty town of rapists. Smelling my fingers I now remember so much more. At the time I regaled her with nothing but the greatest of drunken conjectures.

"On post-war planet earth, the expectation was that life would not exist past two thousand. Something-War. Your-War, my-war. Neu-War. Passive nuclear paranoia. Bombs will drop at any second." I glare at her soul with a tempest that could sink an armada. "Raise generations of drones without self. Now look at us: we have no fears, no regrets. We walk tall full of treachery and disease, we stand proud at our accomplishments in the era of lies and demanded propaganda. We believe in the story so much, that we will silence anyone questioning the nature of recognised truth."

I remember the playful excitement now, how beautiful she actually looked bathed in the bilious fluorescent glow. How my reflection cajoled and harried her in the glass fronted kebab shops.

"In fact, today we do not fear the end. Our lives have become test cases: humanoid ordnance survey maps. Truth is a concept best left to another lifetime."

Another lifetime.

Here the truth rang out as her tongue awash with Haji's most brutal chili sauce found a friend in mine. I remember licking her teeth and pressing my crotch against her thigh. Before we left the high street my marsala-stained fingers were rooted deep into her once-neatly waxed box.

In the streets a jostling spirit livened all those who worked to make it a nook to be a part of. Contrary to the well-intentioned nature of the few here I stood like the Devil spitting hate against all goodness. Most people it seemed were making do with their lot, giving it back just as good as they got, but for me it was torture, timely and brutal. Trying to count all the walls that had fallen and left my intentions of lurid perversion unchecked and allowed to distort and defile. Henceforth my victims, the sorrowful plague of young souls caught in aged flesh and dreams of the day of sweet silence as children grow fast into mothers and fathers come back after leaving for summer.

Summer. It's embers lighting and hushing away Winters' squalid and bitter fingers. An end to creeping water finding paths through glass to engulf the inside. Windows I always forget to close specked with webs of dried dust after a week without rain.

My clothing reflects the urgency in proliferating a not old yet vibe. A nicked cut on my cheek reminds me of the girl who slapped my face after I suggested eating her cunt at her niece's garden party. Days, perhaps weeks of self-loathing in the looking glass carved upon my head a scornful eye. Scrutiny in the extreme will deny any possible assault.

The living room drunk and swaying with possessions stacked high waiting to occupy the apartment newly-leased. Somewhat of a step-up from the oh-so trendy poverty line I had previously dwelled. Here we have walls of concrete, floors of hardwood, a true manor for a proper modern gent. Double-glazed windows, mirrored for privacy and wall size for exposure, looking out over the arches of train lines coming from the northern counties. East and West converge right here and below that meeting of highways and byways lurked a much different sort of rendezvous. Here lay at rest, yet poised: the dark slumberous urges of a society kept afloat, just above drowning. Enough to satisfy the needs and only just create enough cream to give the kittens. Here was one of their playgrounds, a place at which the very earth reeked triumphantly depending on which way you turned of piss or of come and yet always Amyl Nitrate.

Bags of clothes and moldering boxes gradually split and

rot. The rising of damp already steeped in. In a genuine effort to perform at least one task a day, I sort through the mess. Finally the shape of a lounge can take place. I can insert the ash table with its polished slate innards, perfectly primed for cutting any strain of medication. My varied heirlooms to youth like the crystal blue ashtray I stole from a hotel in Prague, or emblems to Buddhist spirituality acquired through some other likely crooked behavior.

"Let's go for a walk," I said to a crack in the wall where a spider lives. He didn't reply. I headed out of the front door anyway, remembering the half joint from the windowsill and noticed in the hallway mirror I wore a grey T-shirt and a pair of blue jeans and a pair of recently acquired K-Swiss shoes. They felt comfortable, as if I'd just walked eight thousand miles in them and left them to cool. But I hadn't just walked eight thousand miles, I've worn them twice, and once was indoors. With these variables I feel almost in control. On the shelf next to the front door the letter informing me of my fathers timely death, still unopened but for all intents and purposes read and received.

Frenetic blue skies are like visual poison and reward me with moments of iris adjustment. A bird sang briefly and then stopped. I looked around for it but couldn't see anything in the sky except a white line of smoke from a plane long gone. I light the joint and look at the roach end, some form traced through the thin paper, coming back to me now I had roached an old photograph of some trees and a mountain taken so many years ago by one of my lost parents, an inconsequential photograph illustrating some camping trip taken when I was a child. Yet here now I walk alone, beneath vast fields of open sky and paths of men who scratch their initials into the atmosphere above, spitting in the eye of anyone who might care to notice.

Staggering and muted. Parallel, my feet somehow align with the path in the sky as it shatters into a trillion shades infinite with clarity. With burning smoke my path took me to the bus stop and I waited for a ride into town. It was a while until one arrived and I had to endure the sound of an old man wheeze his way to a grave. Nearly there. Mortal shivers and my own fear in self-neglect touch upon my conscious veneer. Visiting a dying relative trapped in a feed farm years ago. Nightmares wrapped in the texture of paper skin and a disturbing warmth in the air that hung with invisible, rotting matter. This moment reinforced my bitter reception of loneliness. Thought born seeds of inevitable decline root hard into my gut, blooming like flowers through acid and darkness.

The bus rattled and a Chinese man sits to the front scribbling notes and peering around at the occupants. When I am confronted with those people of "normality" I evaluate each from a strictly homicidal point of view. Who would I kill first if time came, and how would I accomplish such an act. It is not enough to simply wish death upon your peers and societal colleagues, you must create within the dimension of slaughter, the killing floor on which you may exercise the wills of malice and murder. The museum lingers ahead, another testament to Empire, built upon the broken bones of hundreds of thousands of brown and yellow people and further more of those tones between.

Onwards to the town: the broadly worshipped idol of repetitious design in the idea of a northern-English citadel. Here the shoe-shop, the pharmacy, the two rival record stores. The retired-ladies clothing shop. The eight rival charity shops. Pies-and-cakes, fat and sugar, arrhythmia and diabetes types one, two, three, a, b, c and so on. A million pieces of chewing gum stuck hard to the ground reflecting the night skies above in such a base and venereal language that it screams the drowning realisation that the place is a shithole: purely, simply.

As I smoke a cigarette, a collective ill feeling gathers like storm clouds above my eyes, darkening my outlook until blindness comes.

In the blackness of despair I remember the sun, my skin recalling feeling for a moment as it ripens. For one hundred seconds I remain motionless, silent, and *will* away death as my opportunistic mind revels in the notion of a bullet flying towards me, a heavy blade falling through my neck, a vehicular collision at twenty thousand miles per second, tearing my body and shattering my soul on a molecular level. That moment, so singular, so real, wakes me from a state I cannot identify as conscious or un.

Inside the plastic air-conditioned bar I drank beer while reading from the local newspaper. The barman looked at me in a funny way for a second and made me think I had something written across my forehead. Glancing at the mirror behind the bar I could see I didn't. The most difficult thing about existing in this world day to day seems to be the interaction of people. Not just for me it seems, but according to the newspaper for the whole world. The main story told of a young girl stabbed to death by an unknown assailant. The police were investigating and didn't seem to be finding any good leads. I read another article about Ardian Steinmann, a Polish visitor to the region, who was an author, or Communist, or something.

Beer arrived and it tasted good, as cold as it had to be but not so cold it had to show off. Beer that cold is normally there because the barman has a big ego and bought the publicans' interpretation of a cock extender. This type of barman may have a huge fish tank filled with the most colourful and exotic fish, and you might want to watch him slip down a long flight of icy steps on a cold winter night. But this barman was okay. His beer was agreeable.

My hatred could regress.

The to-and-fro of my inner monologues clocks a glass half-empty, mind smiling as he falls in my projection. I see a girl over at the other side of the bar. Alone, she sits quietly, reading a book. Middle of the road kid metal floated across the room above a light fog of cigarette smoke. I couldn't see what she was reading. As I rise the barstool makes a loud creak that lurches across the room, but she doesn't glance up. I amble over to her like John Wayne.

"Well howdy," I say, obviously stuck on an image of an aging racist with a six-shooter. I sincerely hoped I wouldn't speak like a cowboy for the rest of the day. She giggled and I didn't quite know why. My "howdy" wasn't that funny. Maybe she was an idiot.

"Howdy back". She lowered her book a little. Monbiot. "What're you reading there?" Fuck, cowboy. Her eyes warmed.

"Oh it's The Age of Consent, George "Mon-bee-ott"" She replied, with less of a giggle and more of a smile. Sweet organized revolution. Chaos for middle managers. "Have you read it?"

"Not in a while," I lied.

She continued to talk and I saw her eyes light up as she remembered words, regurgitating perspective and ideology. The conformity in her every aspect belied the works' supposed message, but her effort was in the right direction. She certainly had life in her.

"I haven't seen you around, do you live here?" She perhaps more ruthless than I.

"This is my first time in this place, actually. I'm on day release from the asylum." Another white line had appeared in the sky through the window. It caught my attention for a second.

Her face contorts "Oh, okay, right." Three words that could mean anything actually mean nothing, falling heavy as I grow concerned she may actually believe my playful humor and not allow me to come in her at some point in the next few hours.

"Nah, I live just there- outside, about half an hour away." Gesturing towards a figment of my imagination through the wall and miles out of town.

"Are you a student?" She inquired and I laughed at the idea. Either I was looking young, or they were looking old. I quickly decided to invent each supposed fact for the encounter to come.

"No, I'm a teacher, a science teacher."

"Wow, what age?"

"Seniors. It's all bullshit really. The real learning is earlier. Once they begin puberty there's just a slowly decreasing spiral of hormones and acne." Coupled with incessant erections.

"Yeah," she nods, "school is shit."

"That's what I've always thought."

"So are you teaching now?" The inanity of the conversation builds a sleepy glaze in my eyes. The motions second nature now, I plodded through and feigned excitement, peril, danger, intrigue; all in a day works. She regaled her near perfect scores at university and is the epitome of know-it-all-cunt as she states her grades, top of such, and such, and such, and yet her lack of merit in the real world.

She looked inside for a moment and then to me. "I'm Kim, and you?"

"Ardian. Ardian Steinmann." The lie seemed appropriate for adventure.

"That's some name, where-"

"Czechoslovakia" I interrupted.

"Oh, is that where you're from, Czelescho...?" She couldn't even pronounce it. Dear God, this should not be so easy. If I'm not careful, I'm going to get really bored and have to torment people who matter.

I interject, "What used-to-be Czechoslovakia. No, my parents were but they're dead now." My first taste of half-truth for the day.

"Oh I'm sorry, ah?" She's looking around for a second, I think she likes me but maybe I need to talk about her for a while, if I want to get into her.

"Don't be silly, it's really fine." She was falling towards me; I could see her pupils pooling as I spoke. She began to blush. The moment at hand seemed like a good time for a change of scenery, however I allow a pause to transpire as a kind of calm before the storm. Pause.

"So a first? Don't they say if you get a two-two you drank

too much, get a first you're boring?" I glowered in a sort-of friendly but horny and passionate way.

"They do, but it's not always true." Her responses are tailored to the writings of the wives of readers in a thousand top-shelf wank-rags the world over. She even has a closed-over nose piercing. Just another orifice.

My façade of interest strong and convincing, "So what was your course?"

"Psychology." But of course, what else could it be?

"Now wait," My curtain of deceit thick with velvet and barbed wire. "So you're going to be psychoanalyzing me while I talk to you? I don't want to let my guard down and you have me committed." I let her play the smart one for a time and she seems to enjoy it, while I feign jovial lunacy.

"No, no, no; I'm going to-" She tries to interject.

"I'm sure by the time we've finished talking you'll have the men in white suits on their way. It's okay, I don't blame you."

"What are you talking about?" She laughed, closing the book in front of her. "I like the way you're looking at me. You've got really amazing eyes." I wasn't expecting the comment but I reacted as if I half did.

"My eyes? Nah I wish they were blue, for a while anyway; I'd love to have blue eyes for a few weeks. I might get some contacts. Maybe I could David Bowie it for a while."

"No keep them like they are, what colour are they?" I don't think she knows who David Bowie is, which is inexcusable and more than justification for anything that happens next.

"Depends what mood I'm in. They're usually either green or brown. I think they should be green right about now." As I said this I growled a subtle smile at her to which she responded to with eyes looking at mine. I fixed my vision on the centre of her pupil, and made sure she couldn't look away for a moment. As I captured her sight, my eye transformed into a razor blade and cut into hers, the jellied edges screwing into one another until our collective blindness revealed everything.

"So what are you up to today? You don't look like the type to just knock about in dodgy pubs on your 'tod."

"I was supposed to meet a friend here but she can't make it so I just thought I'd take a minute and catch up on some reading. What are you doing in a dodgy pub on your own?"

"Oh y'know, waiting for vulnerable looking girls, stuff like that." She's laughing and I'm joining in, faking empathy. Nice blonde hair on this girl, long enough to know it's there but not too long. Nice face, perhaps a small scar next to her eye. I reach a hand out towards her face and stroke the scar, she doesn't pull away, just holds her breath. "Where'd you get this?"

"What, the scar? When I was in year nine I got hit in the face with a metal gate during cross-country, it was a lot bigger at the time but..."

"They often are!" Shut up you stupid idiot. She laughs without shame, yet all I feel is the excitement of the impending final act. "Do you fancy going somewhere a bit quieter?" I pawed in, turning my eyes into cotton candy and she began to hesitate. The slight crinkle flinching at the side of her painted lips seemed to be a defensive posture. "I mean, if you like." I soften the approach even more and feel perhaps I underestimated her.

"Yeah okay, that might be fun." Estimations have been reinforced.

In the taxi I kept her entertained by making up stories about politicians I might know, then once I recognised her levels of interest, celebrities. She listened and fiddled on her phone without lapse, nodding and smiling with courteousness. Ordering the driver to my house, the girl bleeds a suspicion that I quell with endless bullshit. Upon arrival she settles down, but during the walk from door to door I have to keep my arm locked around her to stop her slowing and thinking of retreating.

As long as I speak without allowing for shadows of doubt to grow, all shall be good. Consent in the moment that is regretted later on is still legally considered consent in the moment.

The city sky swallows light as the day loses another battle.

"I can't believe I've just met you, I feel like I've known you for ages." She claims, as I stifle a laugh through my nose while wondering if the golf course had been harvested for mushrooms yet.

"I know what you mean, we seem to have like a..." and I pause while pretending to search for the word *connection*.

"Connection," we both say at the same time and somewhere inside my mind a bottle is smashed into my face, gouging out my weeping eyes.

Kim was impressed when she saw my flat half dressed with redundant art and quality liquor. Half of the masterpieces on the walls were my own contrite efforts at faking obscure masters, and I think one of them was the rotted base of a cardboard box turned on its side. Not that it mattered, as soon as she crosses the threshold of the front door I begin pawing softly at the edges of her clothes, finding gaps between fabric and skin through which to probe and play. A good word to describe this scene is: familiar. Cloth wrinkled over the mattress, barely dry, humid air of last night's encounter, body fluids in limbo providing an earthy aroma, sex on sex.

As we pass by the lounge I can see preludes to her choking on my cock, soft-red painted lips rubbed onto the brushed cotton pillowcases and her long, ironed hair wrapped around my fist.

I casually scan over the floor as we enter the bedroom and quietly kick a glossy print French smut magazine underneath the king-size bed.

Perhaps noticing, she chirps "I hope you're not one of these guys who... I hope you're not just going to leave me. I mean, I'm not saying anything but I hope you're not just one of those who just sleeps around with just any-"

"Kimberly, please." I declare, creating a sense of gravity in using what I assume is her full name, almost knocking her over.

"I just," she bleats like a lamb trapped in fishing line.

"I'll be honest, I'm not the best guy in the world, y'know? I've been with a couple of girls, but I..." When trying to convince anyone of your honest participation in a movement, pausing to redress your thoughts and emotions is a good tactic in creating a haze of alliance and empathetic confusion. "Did you ever meet someone and there was just like a-", I gesture my fingers to a clicking position-

"Click." We both say.

"Right." I drawl at her as she melts. "When you feel a click it's just there, don't you think? I don't know where this is going, maybe nowhere, but maybe-" She smiles and we kiss, my hand playing across the downy haired flesh of her neck and over the back of her low cut top to tickle her senses. The depth of her top is justification and as we kiss I make sure to slow down so as to add dramatic tension and make it seem just a little bit more real. In this respect and others I am a truly compassionate contributor to our harmonious purgatory. As we move from place to place on the large mattress, I hit the record button on the small remote control paired with the camcorder placed not hidden, but not on display, across the room and primed on the bed. The visual digest of recorded sex sessions was a hobby at best, but one that provided unique and relatable sex aids.

Her lips were full and tasted like cherry wax, and I used them to lubricate my fingers, which, in the nicest way possible, are inserted into her soaking gash from behind, sliding her panties to the side and mottling them with her own vaginal mucus.

Gently tortured by hunger I wondered on the fridge. There was a bowl of gnocchi with four-cheese sauce but this would not suffice and I concentrated hard to remember on the state of Parmesan.

Lifting her from bed to cock I use my thumb to probe the external walls of her anus from within, a kind of lazy multi-tasking that reaps strong sexual benefits. We cut through foreplay at usual record speed. Her mind on the prize: riding me with clenched lip, focused on reaching orgasm. Over and across my body her fittingly red painted nails, manicured to broken perfection carved pathways to suspended purgatory. I, in a restrained 'out-of-control' frenzy of kissing, accentuating emotion at every heart-beat and tongue lapped. Our hands probed further and it wasn't long before she exclaimed that she can't believe we were fucking and don't even know each other. And I, of course, agreeing wholeheartedly, with references to God and "so-right". I wonder for a few seconds what she is thinking and her teeth clench down on those scarlet smudged whore-like lips. I bet she thinks Ardian Steinmann is a really cool guy, someone she might see for a while and then who knows? Maybe he's really ambitious. He probably has a past, but who doesn't? But he sure seems worldly and just what Kim needs to shake off the funk of her last two boyfriends.

Poor Kim. One would not categorize her as either desperate or devoid of morals, however much her actions defy the statement, yet sunk into this lair of mine those morals become my breakfast, her truth my raging spite. Truly, she never stood a chance.

During those throes of passion I had to snort through my nostrils when she called me Adrian. I could only respond with a hand over her mouth and I suffer a moment of conscience as I consider that neither Ardian nor Adrian nor Alex will ever even see her again.

Ever the salesman, and with this deal more than closed my mind wanders into wondering what I may be missing elsewhere. The clock reads 6:44PM and I watch the readout till it switches to 6:45PM. The sun hangs petulantly low in the sky, preparing the suicide note as it falls into the sea. If seconds slip too quickly I may have to remain in character all night. Time to wrap it up. By now she had been pretty much satisfied to as much of a degree as I cared for, and was holding onto plush downy pillow beneath her head, eyes clenched, with my hand around her throat, just tight enough. I allowed The Beast to grow within me and ushered a conclusion both inside and out, leaving me crouched in stasis, knees red and pointed west and east, with a suitable north-by-north-west compass.

This haze of post-orgasm was more smog than mist. Cooling sperm on skin and hair is not the most romantic gesture for a girl in need of hope, though I have occasionally thought the contrary to be true.

The mood changed swiftly through a spectrum of ideals, from rampant youthful possibilities, to archaic and infinite loneliness. Reality dawns and its shadows creep from maybe to if-only, from ecstatic fable to dreadful truth.

My face plunged into the increasingly stained pillows absorbing shame even now; her exit leered down upon my pimpled shoulder.

She leaned across the bed, I breathed deep into the pillow. Wishing to remain impressive, I turned and held her once her face was dry. My thoughts struggled to find an excuse for her to leave immediately.

"Oh fuck it's Wednesday!" I tried.

"No, its Tuesday." She checked my King.

"Tuesday, of course." I lit a cigarette as she gathered her possessions. Scrawling her number on a scrap. I remained in bed: sealed to the safety and womb-like comfort of the sweat patch.

She placed the paper on my chest and I strained my neck to read it, the scrap quickly absorbing beads sweat and becoming entangled in pre-middle aged spider-leg hair. And so I read:

"Eight three nine-one-nine-one-nine?"

"That's the one!" She burst. Oh God. I took the paper up and slid it onto the bedside table.

"Cool." Sometimes one word is more than enough. "I'll call you soon."

"Fine." She replies, still smiling softly. I try to look more alert; excessively raising my eyebrows in an effort to open my eyes, but she is close to the door so I say:

"Well I'm out of town for a while but I'll call you while I'm in transit. Would you... like to get a meal when I get back?" I heard a dog barking outside, and a can kicked that rattles down an empty street, while she smiled coyly and thought of someone with prospects of modern normality.

"Yeah, that'd be nice."

I paused for effect, "Y'know, I don't- nah."

"What? What?"

"Nothing. I"- the Olivier in me awoke: "I don't want to sound foolish, but- I don't know, I feel like even though I just met you, we almost have..." Oh and she smiles in expectant yearning at each word. "...history, but, almost like history yet to be recorded, you know what I mean?" My furrowing of brow emphasizing beyond words.

She gives a big grin, and shows off her surprisingly white and straight teeth. "I'd really like to see you again." So it's my turn to smile.

I sit up in bed and turn my neck to relieve stress slightly, then look down, and then back up directly at her eye, locking once more just for the emotional torture of it.

She creases and melts, almost whispering her farewell: "Okay I'd really better make a move." She seemed at ease. Escorting her slowly but directly downstairs to the front door, I play piano up and down the black keys of her spine. Sunlight blinds as the doors open wide.

Half-mocking business jargon I jape: "So nice to meet you dear, do stay in touch."

She giggles, replying: "Looking forward to it!"

"Eight three nine-one-nine-one-nine!" I respond ace-like

"That's the one! Use it!!" Her words of positivity reeked of desperation, close to a game-show host ready to spin the wheel once more in search of relevance.

"I will," and slow-winked at her. She wriggles towards a cab rank and I release her to swim south and away. In this moment the joke loses its punch-line as I close every lock tight.

Softly skipping back up the hallway I hear shouting coming from somewhere along with the faint smell of cigarette smoke.

Finally I am able to close the front door to my flat and the towel I wear is dropped to the floor while I walk through the lounge in a moment of tranquility. Standing as Christ I stretch and yawn, correcting my backbone. I myself alone bask in the plenitude of solitary time, praying for this to last forever, for time to stop and death to come.

It has been said that the mind of a woman is complex and impenetrable to mere mortal men. No greater lie has there been told. The mind of a woman is as simple as mans: the urges are the same, only differing in category, motivation. A woman desires security, safety, love and affection. All that the advanced male sexual-being need do is present these ideals as a possibility to the woman in question. She will take the bait like a rabbit takes a carrot.

The sun continues to burn as I bathe. Dressing and moisturizing I stare at my face as it ages in the mirror. Lines grow deep, but still shallow enough to cheat the years of neglect and self-abuse. Those impossibly small hairs gathered over the banks of lines in my skin, peering over the edge into who knows.

Seeking my coat, remember it draped over the bedpost, and laugh almost to tears when I see Kim has used the sleeve to wipe clean her genitalia and my latest deposit. She is more like me than I thought.

I wear something else.

ENTANGLEMENT

That scent so gentle
Caught light on breeze.
Her legs spread wide
As gulf 'tween seas.

Once outside the air had changed to ocean cold. I walked for a while. Had another long-past-coital cigarette while the wind blew my blue Harrington jacket open and trickled up my sleeves to find a shelter of its own. A music store loudly played the first album by Oasis. A more typical Manchester moment there could not be.

I'm making fast moves to get to nowhere, litter chasing me from side and back. The air has changed again to warm, the clouds falling after each other in the sky. An off license lies next to me, and I go and buy a packet of crisps that sit in my pocket. The corner of my eye moves, and I jog over the road to the adult cinema.

I'm not a member, so quickly but calmly walk past.

Mindless motion brings me almost fully down Market Street, and I have to almost force my legs to turn around, glancing over shop window glazings, like mirrors up the embankment, creating an infinite loop at the centre of commerce. It buzzed my brain for a second and I found my way back to the top of the hill, directionless and fluid, here at a spot where the first *Oasis* album was drawing to a close.

I sang it quietly to myself, I would never apologise. As a bus trolled beneath the overhang of the mall it kicked up smoke and dust, and I changed course towards my house, deciding now my eventual end but I don't think anyone noticed. A long walk was typical but this one didn't seem too bad. An air of almost hesitant optimism somehow imbued among the people, yet void here with me. Finding the park I decide to rest and sit on the grass. It was dotted with students from the University and I kept hearing-

"Can he not be?" -Snatches of conversation-

"Paul Scholes, Neville's, fucking David Be-" -Moving-

"So I'm getting four hundred for that," With the wind.

Across the grass I see a friend, one of one. With a hidden sneer I nod at him across the park and he nods back. Standing up I creak.

"As I live and breathe: Sir Peter."

"Lord Alex, take a pew and tell me your sins young man. To what corruptions have you been subscribing o'late?"

"Ah you know: any of the usual bags of shite attributed from known cunts around these woods. All sorts of cunts in these woods, don't you know?"

"That I do, all sorts indeed." Rummaging in a green canvas bag Pete produces a cardboard rectangle, folded into a not-too-discreet wrap that he hands me.

"Ah just a little dab'll do me." I chime.

"Best put it up your snout, fella." Pete suggests.

"Right you are then." And so onto my palm I poured some drugs and snorted them towards my brain.

"I heard the news, by the way, terrible shame." Says Pete.

"Terrible shame indeed." I sniffled as the tiny particulates worked their way like little magicians, performing all manner of tricks-and-treats within.

Pete smiled in sympathy and re-lit a rolled up cigarette

from the grass before him as I examined the cellular degradation inside my brain from the first person, lilting out as I plunged my hands into the ground, turning the world on its axis and tossing the oceans into orbit. As a conscious part of the universe before me it was clear that those things apparent are not always at hand, and those that are near are rarely convenient.

Pete glanced up and turned more prominently when he saw I was shouting silently at him. He smiled and squinted in the sunlight, softly singing Spandau Ballet and substituting the word "gold" for "stoned".

I laugh but my gaze is fixed on a point in the grass where the sky creeps in. What it is like to think of all things over the breadth of as hair, flown past the eye by the tail of a hurricane.

"Hey Fishman! How're you doing over there?" With this man I do not feel acquainted with to the degree that he might award me a nickname, but I let it slide. It may be an hour later but Pete is talking. "Geezer I know, right, he knows this guy who's got a mate from the airline, which airline, I don't fucking know, but anyway, lets him get shit through no worries so they weren't arsed about sending the real high-grade. It's got a good consistency, plus the smell is enough to get you halfway man."

"This?" I asked, lost in confusion.

"No! This." He chuckled through an unkempt sprout of facial hair while displaying a bag of weed and he was right too, this looked and smelled on closer inspection like high quality material. He rolled swiftly and professionally, so much that one might think he worked in a carpet factory, and created a perfectly shaped spliff, loaded equally throughout so to reduce heavy stoner cheating. Some of the other cohorts with whom I was familiar with were often guilty of top loading without consideration for their fellow smoker. But he was a decent guy. A Yorkshireman. Would have fallen on the side of white roses once upon a time but today we are all friends on this patch of verdant acreage. He had the first third and I took an inch or so.

My skin started to consider its surroundings and

decided to take off somewhere, without informing me of exactly what was going on. A wave of magnetism seemed to warp my vision and I watched as the rest of the field moved closer and further away and in and back and forth with rhythmical regularity. Fingers dry and cracked, coated in salt. I smiled as I licked them clean and thought of the idiocy of doing so and the more I thought about it, the more I smiled. My smile quickly became a grin and my grin was fairly soon ear-to-ear.

These were the glory days, the time in life when eyes were supple yet bursting with inquisition. The desire to learn, the urge to pervert from regularity gave each man and woman a sprite, a spark, some vibrancy that despite all the pain and hatred in the world was still a thing to behold; when interest was not just something you accrued in penalty of existence but a genuine facet of humanity and belief towards others.

Pete exhaled, exclaiming: "Hasta la vista, baby." I wanted to laugh, but instead it catalyzed a conversation about the reality of such an idea.

"You've seen it, Alex, the future was just, completely mad, how could people have survived with these rock-hard fucking robots around? If the first robot was almost unstoppable, how in the fuck can the T-800 battle all the T-1000's and expect to win? I mean, Arnie himself said that: *"The T-1000 is more highly advanced than the T-800"*, which suggests that the war is un-winnable. And you're telling me that during all of this running of the apocalypse that some twat decided he was the Krypton Factor after all."

"I'm not telling you nothing." I counter, in deference to thought.

"Yeah well Jimmy fucking Cameron is, and it occurs to me that the very notion of the entire premise is, and unfortunately so, bullshit." Pete waits for my nod to continue, and he receives it. "John Connor, leader of the resistance, born of Kyle Reece, a soldier sent back in time to save Connors' mum before he was born. A soldier sent back, with prior knowledge to his paternity by Conner himself. With *prior-fucking-knowledge*! By *He* Him*self*."

I try to keep pace, "But, how... can... can it be that Kyle is... John Connor's dad, when... he's from the future and he knows John Connor right? So: John Connor's born and rises to his place at the head of the resistance and what-not, then... sends Connor back to rescue his mum- no, wait, *Reece*, sends fucking *Kyle Reece* back, who is his dad, who then goes back in time and he meets his mum and they fuck. How is that possible? Because it's not... because he is.... He's like the fucking, the fucking chicken and the fucking egg: he's not there first, no one is!"

"Exactly, Alex, he is the chicken *and* the fucking egg. The fact is it was never about John Connor, or James Cameron."

"Jesus Christ!"

"*Always believe in your soul.*" Pete had a way about him.

"Wait, but if Kyle had never been sent back, John Connor wouldn't be born though... wait, no, if John Connor wasn't born, to Kyle Reece, he wouldn't be John Connor, so if you look at it like... that, it's a line so, John can only be born if Kyle fucks his mother, but Kyle can only fuck his mother if John sends him back in time. So John sends his buddy in the future army back in time to bang his mum. Jesus-fucking-Mary. But then Arnie kills him. Fucks sake."

"Then comes back in two and saves the kid Connor."

"The fucking ego on that cunt: he's got a fucking time machine and all he can do is think about himself. Fucker should go way the fuck back and wipe out the big banking cartels before the first depression, stop the system even having legs to stand on in the first place."

"Yeah would be a well different movie though, eh?"

Pete grumbles in agreement and I suddenly get the impression that most people around here were looking towards us with interest. Slyly out of the corner of their eyes. Secretly. So much that even the pointed ends of leaves on trees would angle their tips at our dialogue, turning their coils of chlorophyll round and round in spirals directed at my horizon.

All I could see was Pete giggling away at something, and a huge sea of green and blue, shushing alongside and throughout my field of vision. I looked into the sea and saw flecks of matter that reminded me of people I knew; they looked more like seahorses now, though. I swam along in this ocean and was enchanted by the colours and shapes I encountered along the way. I could write the name of this place but never speak it. In a moment I was dreaming.

My feet stood in a firmament of bronze-red chalk dust burned through starlight, impacts so great that rock is pulverized into a powder so fine it could falls effortless through human skin. I thought of a girl I once knew. Outside now, I run alone. Scaling a giant red sand dune that carves itself into a bridge over a deep blue-black river, which snaked across the surface. I reached the peak; the drop was maybe twenty feet, so I jumped without consideration. As I fell, the distance increased by a thousand times and now I was falling fast, and below me the red toned deserts fell away and my body hid in the shade of infinite shadows, leaving my soul exposed to the burning light of self. The infinite battlefield lay before me now. But I didn't feel like fighting. I would gladly feel the cold piercing of steel through my heart, or the thunderous shriek and crack of the tightened gallows rope. All around my hands the sensation of pooling, mottled gristle and the blood of the dead.

"Shit sorry Al!" Exclaimed Pete as he picked up the cider bottle now spilling onto the grass and my arm.

"Bastard." I curse and Pete wheezed, chuckling a girlish laugh that seemed so cold and heavy.

We drain the last of the cider at hobo pace and the dark skies of night return quickly, looming overhead like headlamps' antithesis. Spent roaches and papers hang against branches of grass in a dense micro-jungle. Loaning a generous skinful, I try to make my exit from the park. The boy was right; it was indeed some copious stuff. An old man stared at us and fondled himself as we rose like baby deer, legs unable to coordinate independently.

During my vacant, expressionless walk home, I felt the abundant presence of white lines from jet engines. They created a collage of shapes and impressions in the night sky, a patchwork quilt of smoke and waters of impossible depth. The contrast so high that it seemed almost monochromatic: enhanced by the swallowing colour of the night sky rotating around it. The lines had become the centre of the universe, and all life revolved and subsisted in its tangled elaborations. A spider web so vast it would encompass all things in eventuality. The struggle to get back to my flat was beginning to bear down on me and made me question whether I was ever going to get home. What was around the next corner? Who could say? Who was waiting at home for me? No one. No-one and their neighbour expected me back at any hour, let alone a decent one.

Should I live outside for tonight? Should I live outside for the rest of the week, my life? I pressed my forehead with both thumbs and breathed heavily through my teeth. It couldn't end like this. Life had to hold some sort of goal, some objective, some terminus in which I could reflect upon my wasted youth in precious old age. I was staring my thirtieth in the face. My old friends, or should I say colleagues, luminaries, contemporaries from more studious days had all dissipated into the woodwork. Occasional encounters with figures from the past held no excitement. A few days before this I was in a similar position, drunk and stoned in the same park, staring out onto the street at the cars and people passing by. The symbol of success pulled up alongside me, a particularly lush car. Not being a motor head I could care less usually but something about the driver struck a chord with me, I recognized his face from years before. It quickly dawned on me that he was a kid in the year below me from when I was at school, but his impact was so soft upon me that I could barely remember his name. I settle on Kevin, or Simon. Anyway, Kevin/Simon was fairly dim and certainly not good-looking to anyone but his mother. A slight murmur of jealousy wrapped in fear of my own death was exacerbated when I saw his passenger, a girl who would not look out of place in the centerfold of a magazine and laden with my own come drying between her creases and staples and CMYK beautifiers.

My gawp turned to leering and quickly my tongue loosened but all that came out was garbled nonsense. The girl glanced fleetingly in my direction and then continued listening to a sentence I had failed to even tarnish. In my bitterness I drown once more in liquor and choke on cigarettes, bury myself under drifts of white powder so to embody death in every cell and each thud of my quickening yet drowned heart. That particular night I ended up sleeping under a bench. Some experiences are good for the soul; some just make you stink. Money and possessions cloud the mind easily. It is the object of my id to spend around a quarter of the year living in the wilderness. The other three quarters shall be spent as the devils' bag man, but either way I do like a nice sofa and brushed Egyptian cotton bed sheets.

Just as it seemed my third eye was opening further and pushing me into a world from which I would never return, I was brought abruptly to a state of waking consciousness inside my flat, standing naked in the bathroom, casually pleasuring myself to no end. Both taps were running and I had a large towel wrapped around my neck. I stared at my face for a while; looking into the tiny cracks of my skin and searching a crease next to my eye. A soft, down-like fur brushed the surface, descending the sides meant walking through the valley. My feet yearned to seek shelter deep in the valley. As I stood over it, I could see the walls were safe to slide down. Sitting down I did just this and fell, like feathers, into the valley. The fur was velvety and warm, and got hotter the faster I slid. I rolled and tried to spread my body weight so I wasn't burned. I hit the valley floor and lay in the soft bliss for a while. Perhaps the womb, or what that might have felt like. My body felt a surge of incredible warmth, transcendent yet corrupting. It swam through every pore and knotted bows about my veins, strangling white cells one at a time until my entire body was but a husk of a shell of what used to be. I found it difficult to walk down the valley; surfaces all soft and pliable. The deeper I got the less solid ground, so I slid once again and travelled further into the deep end. Seeing no end to this vast chasm until squinting towards the distance, I start to perceive a solitary blue dot. Hanging like a cobweb against some invisible cranny, it brought a familiar, ancient kind of comfort. Becoming larger and beginning now to take form, it danced through cellular, to insect, reptilian, to beast. From the ordered chaos of evolution comes finally the noble human and detail imprinted itself on it with great attention to the face. It was a female. Her face changed slowly into that of familiarity. It became clear that the girl was around my age, was familiar, although as yet unclear as to how. She had a raw beauty that was difficult to comprehend. Something pure, something long lost. It was a beauty by definition, and she was part of a jigsaw.

As suddenly as I had descended I quickly rose on air as the bridges collapsed and loosened the levee, releasing a slurry that swept in and ripped the heart out of a city full of shit, a place so overflowing with sins and the sinful that even silent prayers were like murder ballads spit through clenched teeth and the choking throats of the young and the beautiful. It crashed down hard, tore even the ground to pieces, devastating and impossible, surging towards me yet the dust came first to suffocate and subdue and I could see it approaching like inevitable death but when it arrived it shrunk down to the size of a ripple of water in the bathtub and I came like a field mouse.

D ISTANT COUSINS

An empty glass is waiting.
For me alone to fill it up.
I have no water, no liquor, no wine,
Just promises empty to pass the night.

A t the graveyard standing in a fine cut half-breasted navy blue Henry Poole two-piece suit and calf-skin Oxfords kissing down on mossy grass underfoot of a "nice turnout" on this dark and bleak day. From high over the rusted metal skies a bitter rain falls, softly punishing the ground below. But the land will not be subdued in its excessive need for debauchery, and instead glows brighter than ever. The slight murmurings of a crowd of mourners were a mere distraction as I stared across the oak casket. Last of a family line, here I stand, not even a dried tear across my cheek. If there were a chance for them to fall they might shatter my eyes, being them made from lead-glass and crystal, harsh and formed under the pressure of ages, of a thousand years in the blink of that very same eye.

Does a dog wandering the desert plains ever cry for his mother? Ever yearn for the warmth of the family set? Here am I now, the dog of all dogs, the raw-tipped hound, sharp toothed, dangerous, wound up to breaking and strung tight as a fishing line between boat and bounty.

My father was a book-keeper. Tallying the accounts of wealthy and cautious alike, he was a firm believer in thorough planning for retirement, taxation, establishment of bonds, war and conflict, those things that generated fluctuations in markets and consternation by investors and such, primarily since he could charge a service fee for it. Here he was laid out before us now. Cold and well-pressed, just as in life.

The vicar droned on, reciting chapter and verse, and it seemed chapter once again. Passing my view from the grave across the verdant plastic turf, over the shoes of the gathered mourners when something suddenly struck me in the uniform regularity of black footwear. A heel: crooked and shiny, penetrating the mossy-grass beneath it and sprouting from the slender legs of a girl I did not recognize as family or friend. Trying to place her, I remember she had been standing with one of my cousins, therefore she must be a friend of the family.

Inside the church the dusty silence broke with her whimpered panting, high and strung tightly, like a small animal trapped in a closing door. She dribbled as my hand pushed her face down onto the pew ahead of us in this, the hour after the funeral. Somewhere in a civic hall mourners ate triangular sandwiches that, in their own way, represent the anti-climactic way that life has of ending.

"*No me moy daddy! No me my moy dad-dy!!*" Went the mantra, snarled in repetitive and unfathomable tones by this now much more familiar friend of the family.

I used all my strength to finish as reverently as possible, working desperately to avoid getting semen on my suit.

The girl continued to suck on my thumb and I felt come start to drip down around her legs, onto mine.

Later at the civic hall, the girl latched back onto the friend from my family, which turned out to be her husband, my now not-so-distant cousin, whose name I always forget.

Only a few piss-head familiars remain and the triangular sandwiches were in terrible form, lending weight to my exit.

An aunt approached.

"Oh Alex: just terrible."

"Yes." I reply "Terrible."

"And so soon after your mother." Her head seemed suspended by a string, her words decided by prescription medication.

"I know, just, terrible… timing." I look behind and notice my playmate glance at me through the gaps between her husband.

"Well of course there's no such thing as good timing when it comes to tragedies like this." I stood corrected.

"Yes, of course not, sorry. Tragic."

"Just terrible. Nice turnout, but just, terrible." She cooshed the words out and walked backwards, as if retreating from an injured boar that could jerk at any moment and impale flesh upon his bristled tusk.

I go to the bathroom and examine my penis, which aches with repetitive rubbing against and inside the fleshy chambers of a healthy range of orifices. The toilet reeks and has the obligatory quarter-inch of piss on the floor. Even in this foul and venal place was there a man in the stall opposite masturbating. Like some Pavlovian hurdle I could not finish pissing until he had done likewise. I am a friend of the low and the depraved.

Returning home from the funeral I have the taxi stop at Fielder's council estate. After relaying usual pleasantries and explaining my mourning suit, he obliges with an extra 'teenth' of 'hi-grade' for 'free'. The night turns quickly and I race against time to drink and smoke myself into oblivion, concealed in the safety of my abode.

Too quickly morning comes. I wake on the couch, face down and legs on the floor, *presenting*, for the want of a better word. Against the heavy plate window reverberates the sound of a train passing through the arches overhead, and I am stirred from slumber.

Through leaden eyes I glanced at the clock: 2:33PM. Another day lost, only night-time to come. Sweet, purifying night. Standing up in the half-light of the room, that afternoon light shines against the floating specks of skin and hair, dust so still and peaceful.

Food is the first priority. Opening the fridge swiftly I immediately made a list of possible concoctions: Scrambled eggs and toast; boiled eggs and soldiers; fried egg sandwich; French toast. I think it'll be scrambled eggs and toast. The milk was fine, only a day after its date. Scrambling eggs offers me the thoughtless escape required to organize myself.

Sitting down in front of an episode of The A-Team I try to remember my dreams. On days like this a quarter burns in no time. Taxi drivers are making a killing. Street lamps flicker giving luminance to crooked corners and sidelong alleys.

However.

B.A. had once threatened Murdock but now I watch documentaries on the plight of sharks and wolves. Atrophy sets and after unpacking and relocating my possessions I considered my options for the remainder of the week. I could stay in the flat and lounge in my ever-increasing filth, or I could go out. Wolfing down the last slices of toast, I checked the cupboards. They were as bare as a nursery rhyme. The fridge too was empty, save for an old piece of fennel splayed like a common whore across the back wall of the ice-box, seems to have been there for weeks. I drank too much tea and felt sickened. If I smoke a joint with each cup I can satiate my hunger. But all it does is grow. Teasing the monster just angers it. I have to find more food.

Grey T-shirt and grey sneakers with black jeans. I go to get my keys from the table, but they are gone. Under the table, not there either. I stop and think. I couldn't even remember putting them down anywhere. I turned the sofa upside down and threw dirty clothes around to encourage their discovery but it was no use. I decided to keep the door open, and close it almost shut. I turned up the volume on the TV to give the impression that someone was home. I opened the front door and found my keys in the lock.

The contrasting soundscape alone is enough to drive anyone to insanity but upon entering the supermarket the truly challenging aspect was the negotiation of people without resorting to a hunger induced display of violence of a tribal and terminal nature. Seeking food with short preparation times, ready to eat, even fucking couscous.

Aisle number 1: Bread, cheese, milk. The lady wearing a long and low cut floral dress holding a bottle of milk and staring at it while her tits peer over the polyester/nylon ribbings notices me looking only as I pass her onto Aisle number 2, for bags of crisps, pretzels and biscuits and to pass by a big fat woman whose cunt is packed so tightly into her elasticated jeans that it might swallow her entire wardrobe, that is assuming she hasn't eaten it. As I picture her gushing hole fraught with splintered cheap offcuts of man-made substitute timber she casts me a look of disgust but I navigate the trenches around her and tread lightly onto Aisle number 5, jam and pasta sauce, and presenting a very well dressed woman, successful, powerful business type with legs wrapped in black sheer stockings and breath strong with the smell of cigarettes, sharp reds, cowboy killers, reading the back of a jar of alfredo sauce, imagining me eating her anus. I give her the best look of all, the one that doesn't involve me mentally spitting in her mouth. By the time I arrive at Aisle number 8 for salad and vegetables my hunger had almost been diffused by rampant projections of sexual brutalization but even the pretty check-out girl was not enough to distract me from my primary task as I paid for the food and left.

Upon leaving the shop, I grabbed a bread roll and began to eat when all of a sudden, the cloudy sky broke open and rain began to pour. I took shelter alongside the buildings but quickly became wet through. I ran as quickly as I could without splitting the bags until a bus came around the corner. It kindly stopped for me after I put my hand out, and the driver was alarmingly friendly. I wonder what he was up to. Just another deviant looking for a friend. I take a seat and place the bags carefully next to me. My grey T-shirt had turned a much darker shade of grey. A man around my age sat listening to a personal stereo in the seat opposite me.

Back at my flat I collected my post and the local paper from in front of the front door, then made ham sandwiches and put some pasta on to boil. It quickly became apparent as I toweled myself dry that the flat had changed somewhat. A different smell lingered in the air, less muggy than before but also less comfortable to me. I looked carefully around at the mess I had left for myself. Someone had been here. I was sure of it. I remembered throwing a pair of jeans onto the back of the sofa, and now they were in the middle of the floor. Someone had been here. Someone had been here? The television was turned off. It was not possible, or, at least not in the realms of my mind was it possible. There would be evidence, a broken window, forced door, signs of a break-in. However, none of this presented itself, instead a feeling of violation lingered in the flat I had so lovingly given a sense of home. Well, almost at least. How could someone have been in without my knowing? Was there a spare key? Alan, the perennial neighbour downstairs and technically the landlord has a spare. His door was rather more expensive and secure than the tenants, but only by a touch. I knocked and saw movement, inverted through the spy-hole. His terrible wife, Fiona, answered the door wearing a cheap satin dressing gown that took me back to pre-pubescent wet dreams of schoolmate mothers in the morning, delivering toast and ample bosoms.

"Yes, what do you want?" she quizzed.

"Is Alan in? I just need to ask him a quick question."

"What about?" Go get your fucking husband, this is important.

"Just need to ask him a quick question, I think someone's been in my flat while I was out. I locked the doors and windows and everything, but I think someone's been in, and Alan is the only other person who has a key." I felt that should satisfy her.

"Been in *your* flat? When?" I was wrong.

"Just now, today. I've been out shopping and I just got back." What is her problem?

She looked at me through sideways eyes, obviously entertained. "It was I!"

"You?"

"Bloody right, aye it was me. Who in Christ's name leaves the telly on full all day? You're not deaf are you?" I relaxed and smiled.

She takes a drag on a cigarette and holds the smoke in her paper-bag lungs: "It's filthy up there."

"Yes, it is." I replied, "I've been meaning to get around to cleaning up soon." She curled her lips and sucked, ash growing longer.

"Alan's buying underlay. Are you not working?" My eyes gleam, and look toward the stairway, when suddenly the players in my mind create a scene from the as-yet unmade low-budget film "Sex with the Landlords Wife".

The frustration and anger building inside her for so many years finally explodes onto the couch as I push her over onto her knees, grabbing huge, swinging breasts and pinching cold and lonely nipples in this softly focused nightmare. She struggles to get a cigarette lit as I pound the living hell back into her.

My private screening was cut off mid-thrust by Alan, rising from the floor in the background. "Who's there, dear?" Her spine snapped back and swung its connecting face to look at him.

"Shut up and get inside!" She snarled at Alan, who scurries back into the depths of the residence, noticing me for all but a split second before seeking lapels behind which to hide. Her thumb is callused with repetitive direction of her husband. Maybe I could get Alan's attention.

"Al- Alan! It- its' Alex, from upstairs, have you got five

minutes? Have you-" I tried to shout through and ask him myself. It was no use.

"If you don't want someone wiping your arse for you then stop walking around covered in shit." Fiona left with those immortal words and all that remained out here in the corridor was the last wisp of cigarette smoke escaped from the tomb of her blackened lungs.

Upstairs I found the pasta boiling away quite nicely. Water gently simmering, I considered the face in my vision. It had a familiarity, a memory within. The rain still wet on the laces of my shoes, my father fresh in the ground, death following me like echoing footsteps.

Naturally, my thoughts settled on Rachel. My dead ex-girlfriend. The bitterness I felt in her life, the hatred called love that burned between us, the saddening relief that came with her passing. Proof that love does not live within the confines of tranquility, but rather between the burning fields of tempestuousness, ravaged by the battalions of the self and resistance to dissolution through unification. Time is never too late for grief, or guilt, or pity.

I picked up my letters and read a bill, a bill, a letter asking me if I wanted to become a member of a book club, no, and the newspaper.

The main story told of the girl who was stabbed; the police were asking the FBI in America about psychological profiling and stuff like that. What shitbags. Can't even do their own policing.

I stirred some sauce into the pasta, served it to myself, and then ate alone again. "Maybe that was it," I thought as I swallowed a mouthful of pasta, "maybe I just miss having someone around." But how can I miss what I never had. I missed the idea of friendship, the idea of family for sure, and just getting through life was difficult enough, but my mode of existence was there to take my mind off all the difficult things in my life. I knew it was something I was going to have to come to terms with eventually.

The spider hadn't been out of his crack in the wall now for a couple of days. I considered his mortality. I certainly hadn't killed him. He might've been old. A many-eyed octoarachnarian. With pasta in my stomach I felt inclined to do something, to at least escape from this place. I took a chocolate bar and put it in my jacket pocket. Upon leaving I made doubly sure my door was locked double.

Descending in the elevator I fantasised about the aftermath of a real break in at my residence. Would I inform the police? Nothing had been taken and entry certainly wasn't forced. I could see the conversation between us.

"Was the house a mess when you came in?" He would ask scribbling notes in a tiny inspectors' notepad.

"Yes, but it always is." Me.

"Is anything missing?" He would ask, looking around the unkempt apartment strewn with belongings.

"No" Me.

"Was the lock forced?" He would ask, examining the splintered frame from another time I was so hammered I kicked my own door in having lost my keys.

"No" I would reply.

"Was the door open when you returned?" He would then ask, looking up at the nooks and crannies around the space, observing the empty spider house, the leaden windows heavy with condensation.

"No" Me.

"Did you see any suspicious characters here in the last few days?" He would ask, now looking at my face, tired, worn, lines threatening to forge their way over once untouched snow.

"No, none." I'd respond, smoothing over the aging skin with dried palms.

"Did your neighbours report anything out of the ordinary?" And my mind would think of the neighbors, of Alan and his

"No, nothing." Me.

"Was anything different? Anything at all?" Him.

"No, absolutely not a fucking thing" Me.

"So why am I here wasting my time?" Him, losing patience.

"I have no idea."

In conclusion, I probably wouldn't bother talking to the police about it. This day was less sunny than the previous. I had no intention of getting high again today, not that it was a bad thing just that I didn't want to.

Depression began to creep into my thoughts. I had been thinking for too long. The same faces appeared around every corner I turned. Every time I saw a person more than once it felt like a slab of concrete had been thrown onto my back and I had to carry them around. My shoulders actually started to hurt from this psychosomatic struggle. I walked and walked until I realised I had been walking around the same three streets repeatedly.

Theft and duplicity are marketable traits in the modern world. I learned early, almost by accident. The wispy old shopkeeper of my youth would take an age to travel from the stool in the back to the stool out front; during which time one could have emptied the entire place. My personal rouse involved the secretion of adult literary material in broadsheet newspapers, then designed to pay for the latter while retaining the former. The majority of time a somewhat foolproof scheme. Except that foolishness seems second in my nature after greed. One such sunny day the keeper seemed to be taking even longer than usual and my rapacious desire for free porn spilled over and I stacked two, three, four and still the shop was bare. Eventually arriving, her stare hardened on me. My heart throbbing and hands shaking, I lowered the newspaper to the desk with a deep thud bringing about an abrupt end to my scheme.

NEGOTIATED TERM

One time I made my heart a prize,
And then I gave it up again.
The second time it was near empty.
One thousand lives later I seek that place.

You can pretend love, you can fake happiness, fear can be hidden behind rows of treated-teeth, smiling white. Hatred can be boiled within each cell of existence; calcifying, tempered harder than diamonds and buried deep within, designated for later expulsion as decades fall like withering skin circled around accusatory eyes.

"I wouldn't bother man, she's after me," Mark growing miffed as my increasing attentions are drawn by a girl he had been spending time and money on. "And anyway, I was talking to her at the bar. She's well up for it." Just another cunt from London, up north to visit friends. Friends being us. Us being Pete, Kerry, Andy and myself. We are in the hotel bar of the Novotel in Manchester. The time is 2AM, and we're all high in spirits among other things.

"Right, okay bud." I placate him as he continues his conversation with Andy. Sounds like a challenge to me, though.

Andy garbled on in Pete's ear incessantly "I couldn't believe he said that, it was like: she gave him that fackin' holiday, least he could have done was fackin' tayke 'er!" Brutish laughter follows between these knuckle headed southerners, far too red and far too jolly for these woods. Pete and Kerry seem to be in a prelude to intercourse, and I try my best to 'fit-in' with this very normal group of people. Across the room came another glance from the contested woman.

"But she just went right back with him, didn't she. Man, she is like, fuckin', y'know?" Andy coined.

"Fuck that man, he's just a fucking, he's a dude. She was coming running that time he fucked that other bird as well." Pete retorts.

"What bird?"

"You know her man, that one who works down at Waitrose. On chicken. Big tits."

"Oh fuckin' hell, tits on chicken: yeah that one. Yeah she's a right dirty schlag, though." His words suddenly fall with greater impact upon a momentary quiet beat inside the room, as Pete leans in to complete the thought, "So I heard anyway. Mate once had her ages ago; she was only like, I dunno, nineteen or summat and like, she says: 'Will you fuck my arse?'"

"Absolute pearler mate." The bullshit in this conversation is almost too much, but my attention is not focused on such matters of ridiculousness.

Through deathly clouds brought alive by international conglomerates committed to the sale and distribution of tobacco, the look comes once more from *the girl*. Tonight's *the girl*, delivering *that look*. As she spoke to her friend at the table the smoke in her lungs would be cradled from mouth to nose, moving in ever decreasing cycles as she draws every last molecule of use from it. In a tight black dress she sits with legs crossed, faux Tiffany silver heart on a neck chain. Not too faux, I hoped. Her brief interchanges with a female friend are punctuated rudely by an older man who may be a colleague, or husband of one or both. We exchange a smile this time, and let it blossom into silent laughter as we both roll our eyes in disdain at our respective companies.

On the television in the corner music videos are played, gyrating teenage girls sitting on top of lollipop after lollipop. Spilled drinks are wiped up by the barmaid, who herself would get one. I lose myself trying to be cool, then notice in the mirror facing me over the other side my hair looks fucking ridiculous. I look like some cuntish actor try-hard, hair all fucked up but too fucked up to be intentional. Need to straighten that up. Kerry knocks a glass over but its empty, and seemed to spring me into life as I raise my hand up from my drink and casually move my hair around using spilled Bombay Sapphire, lowering my eyelids so she doesn't see me looking in the mirror. Then it came again: *that look*. I gave her it back. The special look reserved for those marked for penetration.

On the surface I feign hesitance, and allow it to crumble like sand castle defenses at high-tide, mouthing indecipherable words to her purely to make contact. Kerry sees this and starts to laugh, later telling me I looked like "some twat from *Sixteen Candles*." Whatever that means. The girl beckons me over with a nod of her head. Clearing my throat, I grabbed my Kronenberg and cigarettes, and raise my eyebrows at Pete and Kerry.

I point at the chair I was about to sit on with a quizzical expression on my fucked up and wasted face. Her hand movement told me to sit down. Her mate was laughing at the time.

"Hi." Used a thousand times, but always a good opener.

"Hi." We both laugh at the same time the way that alcoholics do. It was a click, a connection, we had history, future, completely contrived on my part. Her friend had her arm set in a plaster cast, which clashed with the dress she was wearing. Sitting with them was an older man. He looked as if he had a 'proper' job: plumber, builder, joiner maybe. He was in his mid-fifties, and very drunk. *Rum* drunk.

"Who's this guy?" I said quietly and pointed over my shoulder at the man. The girls face changed to mock panic,

"We... don't know, he just started talking to us, we can't get rid of him." she checked her friend "Get rid of him for us?" Seemed like a plan since any lascivious one of mine was certain to be upset by this gentleman.

So I tell her to "Go and get a drink. I will have a... a gin and tonic. Double gin-tonic. Go now and take your friend." I speak softly, yet retaining dominance, like a military commander rallying his troops for one last push for King and Blighty and bloodshed from the dark land. She nodded and signaled to the girl with the broken arm and they both left the table. Left alone with the man now, I needed to talk to him.

"How you doing there, mate?" Be friendly first.

"Aww yeah, ahm great, just fucken pessed, cannae barely ge ma... drenk't'ma-outh y'know?" He laughed belligerently. With the girls gone he almost ran out of steam, the ruddy cheeks flushed a little less and the fatty pockets around his eyes sagged slightly.

"What do you do?"

"What'dja mean? Ahm just heere, drenken, living," he started to speak louder "ahm just being me, y'ken?" he started to point his finger at me "who the fuck're yoo?" This was going to be difficult.

"I'm Mark. I'm friends with... Mary." Suggested the girl with mouthing syllables, to which I raised my eyebrows. "I work in television," I lied. "How do you make a living, um-"

"Ma..." His fat fingers wagged at me, making a point, "fucken name us naen ef yur fucken' business, see..." a pause "and don't you fucken' furget it." He was overweight, had a bad tan that made him very red, and spat when he spoke. He wore a cheap suit, light blue; with white sports socks that lit him up like a cyclist at night. He held more than a passing resemblance to any nightclub comedian from the final third of the twentieth century.

The girls were over at the bar and I looked to give

the signal that I needed more time. Draining my ice of gin I knocked it back and got us both a cigarette, handing it to the man and lighting it for him in a very courteous manner, despite his understandable shortness. He was also looking over at the girls, and got the message pretty quickly.

"Ah fucken' aye." Lets out a long sigh and coughs. "Y'know. S'like, ahm, fucken, the best salesman en the North, nae worries. I cannae just... ahm fifty"- belch, "four, y'know. Hew old air yoo, boy?" His spirit was beginning to falter.

"I'm twenty-nine."

"Jeee-sus Christ. Twenty-nine eh? Gaud help ye when ye get tae ma age. Lohnime 'forahdough eh?" His head was swaying backwards and forwards, he might have thrown up at any time. "Ah sell wendows. Fucken wendow salesman. Ah sell all typesea wen- dows, anahm good aht it anall. Ahm fucken despicable. Werst johb ye cun ahve, sellen double fucken glazen. Wirse then the fucken But iss ma johb, ahm gud ahtet. But s'like, ye cannae talk te folk aboutet. Embarresen. See these slahgs they ken want a fitbawllur or cock fucken' pop-singur or sonken." We allowed a moment of silence before the man held out his hand. "Angus, pal, Gus, plysyr." Gus looked over at the girls, still at the bar sipping their drinks, trying to avoid looking like they were waiting for something. Sighing, he put out his cigarette. "Ah shiete tae-eat. Ahm gonnae go. Gowanea ma room haven a good fucken wank an gowenea sleep." A couple of people looked over as he said this. He went to stand up but slipped and fell on his chair, knocking over the remnants of a drink onto the table and spilling onto the floor. I steadied him and helped him up.

"Woah there big fella, take it easy mate, take it easy." I saw myself in years to come. What a life. I stood him up and helped him into his jacket and out of his seat.

"Year ah gid lad, y'are. Teyll them geerls ah sed goodneight te 'em." He started to walk out of the place then turned and wagged a yellowing index finger at me, "an yoo ahve ah gid neight boy. A'll be seein you roun." I somehow doubted it, but with that he staggered out of the bar. I watched him go and did not notice the girls sitting down until I heard drinks glasses clinking together.

"Well done, we never thought he was going. You're a lifesaver." The girl was still very sexy.

"Oh my god, he just wouldn't shut up- leave us alone!" the friend said the last line to an imaginary Angus. "Dirty old man." We laughed; I felt a little guilty, but then, fuck it. He would have done the same in my shoes.

"So what're your names?"

"Oh um, Heather, I'm Heather" The fit one was Heather. Check.

"I'm Chris" Let's call her Broken Arm.

"Well very nice to meet you both." Customary handshakes and European kisses followed. "I'm Alex Fish." Sometimes my real name slips out.

"Alex Fish." She repeated, very matter-of-fact. "Quite the name." commented Heather. I laughed at her, and took her below- the-belt shot. "What do you do, Fish?" They laughed as did I, and quickly tried to think of a career. I'll just keep the last one.

"I work in TV, I'm the producer for an independent production company. Commercial, idents, graphs. Blue chips, concept development. Dilly dally with a bit of copywriting every now and again but who can be fucked?! Most of my clients I meet a couple of times a year and strategize over a Demi-Sec, it's nice work; I enjoy it." The girls glanced momentarily at each other as I lay out my honesty sandwich.

"That's amazing," Heather said, "Chris is a production assistant at Red Letter M!"

"Red Letter M! Wow!" No idea. Oh fuck.

"Well," Chris begins, "I'm just starting out." I see she is uncertain, and there is no time for half-measures: for the only bullshit that stands is that given with no shame.

"Red Letter M... Didn't you have that client last year, that massive fuck up?" Everyone had a client last year that was a total fuck up. My own being the wank shop that wouldn't take my worn VHS of come gargling whores as part exchange for another.

"I, I'm not sure, do you mean, the chocolate thing?"

"The chocolate thing, exactly." I had enough for some creative development. "And you had all those, uh, what was it?"

"I really don't know I wasn't on the team back then. Oh wait, the chocolate bars! Oh God yes there were hundreds of them! Still are!"

"Exactly, and I was talking to a friend at PCP for Saatchi and that other tosspot in old Berlin and he said "you know, it's typical of this era of commercialism that the most basic concepts of what art is have been bleached out of this thing of ours, and the fucking pretenders are the ones ruining it for the playmakers." And the fucking guy was right: Just because you're a star on You Tube don't mean shit to Nielsen." Anyway, suffice to say he almost dropped his sausage when he heard that."

The girls laugh along with my ludicrously erratic and nonsensical fabrications, both drunk and half-listening.

"What do your friends do?" Heather asks, and shit, they're not in on it, I can't let them talk to them otherwise it'll all fall in.

"All... sorts of... things, just uh, like, normal jobs. None- none of them really have a... career path yet so... Insurance, sales. Wank shit." Which broke the laughter gate and authorized my previous river of lies. "And what about you, Heather, what line of work are you in?"

"She's a pro. Working the streets of Birmingham."

"Chrissy you daft cow!!" Scolded Heather.

"I've heard it's quite a lucrative market. Or is it lubricative?" I quip with lightning brilliance and they both respond with aching laughter at the word play. Truth be told, the secret to conquering your every opponent, is in delaying those moments of time into a solution: dissolving from reality and imprinting them into a singular, observable incident, a series of answers "yes" and "no". The occasional execution of intelligent word play is the modern aphrodisiac. It is, to the woman who hears, proof of the rebellious spirit of society; indicator of a charlatan dancing to the rhythm of his own making, while still indebted to the wisdom of *Roget*.

"She's just jealous cause my fanny costs twenty quid more than hers!" Heather bleats.

"Upping your *own* ante, I see!" Respond I as the two of them grew more at ease, less inhibited, beyond drunk. "I'll see you and call."

"She takes it up the arse for a ride home to Leicester." Offers Chrissy, punctuating the words with a cackle that spills ashes over the table, and Heather responds with:

"Fuck off, y'slag. It's at least as far as Runcorn."

As we tiptoe around the edges of offence engulfed in fits of laughter we share between us a moment of premonition, or at least I do.

"Alex, where's your friend staying tonight?" Broken Arm points at Mark discreetly.

"Mark? Uh, he's staying here of course. He has a room." Little cunt.

"Do you have a room?" Heather asks.

"I don't have a room, I might... stay here though, depends how things... go." Using hypnotism I nod and half-smile throughout this sentence, then take a cigarette in my mouth before offering to the girls, alluding to a blowjob.

They accept readily as I light them up, alluding to swallowing come.

"How things go eh?" They laughed again. "Look," this is Broken Arm, by the way, "I really just... Y'know your mate, um... is he single? Is he here alone?"

"Yeah, yeah I think so," She's eager, "he's um, just up for a couple of nights, um, don't think he's got a girlfriend or, well, *whatever* right-"

"Well?" Broken Arm exchanges knowing looks with

Heather, who returns with overtones of *go-on*.

"Well, do you think...? I just was looking for some..." lowering her tone and body language to a whisper, "...*casual sex*... oh God. Do you think you could, would you ask Mark if he does?" Cutting to the chase but with the rabbit well and truly running she does right.

Hour nearing past three by now, there was no time to waste. "God, I bet I sound like a right slut."

"Not at all, that type of shit doesn't even bother me at all just lets me know you know what you want out of life." Thank you, Andre. "Hang on." I got out of my chair and Mark was in full flow with Andy. "Dudes, how goes it?"

"I'm pissed" Andy's face contorted, affected greatly by the alcohol. "You getting anywhere bro?"

"Quite possibly man, quite possibly" Mark didn't look too happy, seemed to be ignoring me. "Mark, man," he looked over my face and behind me at Heather. "That bird over there with that one I'm talking to, she wants to fuck, man. Just wants fucking, casual sex, uh? Uh? Back of the net, geezer, mate?" Mark just looked away and there was a pause. And so then he to me:

"We're trying to have a conversation here, Alex."

"Fucks sake, man come on, i-it's like, uh, like casual and... Like, easy? It's a bit of a no-fucking-brainer, man." but Mark wasn't listening, Andy just laughed. An uncomfortable silence followed, then I curse him silently "Fine, whatever. Fuck's sake." Mark continued his *conversation* and I went back to the table thinking this was goodnight. To say I was pissed off would not cover even the cherry of my rage. The girls speak closely when I return and motion in my direction as I sat down. I light another cigarette and channel Ray Liotta.

"Well?" asked Heather. I grimaced slightly.

"Oh fuck this is really fucking embarrassing. Shit." Chris wasn't pleased; I had to try to diffuse this situation. "Look, he's just drunk, he's got a girlfriend down south anyway," I didn't think he did, "but, uh, the truth is he... might be gay. Maybe."

Broken Arm started laughing at my efforts to settle her, and I smiled. "I mean, he's obviously gay and all the fanny in the world is not going to change that." The girls giggled as I poked secret fun at Mark.

"It's okay Alex, really." Says Broken Arm.

Behind me now, my friends had all stood up and were putting on their jackets.

"Mate, we're off, you coming?" Pete asked so everyone could hear. I looked and ever so slightly raised one eyebrow, a move I had practiced many times before, at Heather. I was going to chance it. "Nah mate, think I'm gonna hang on for a little bit," nod my head slightly "get another drink... or something." Heather smiled, as did Broken Arm. My friends bid me farewell, except of course for that fucking cry-baby wankalone Mark, who dared not even look at me as he left.

The bar was almost empty except for a table of three businessmen wearing suits. Chris' mobile rang, she answered. As she spoke, I leaned in to Heathers face and she pulled back, teasing me with a smile on her face. I placed a little kiss on her, and she pushed her tongue into my mouth. We kissed for a minute until Chris was finished on the phone.

Chris guffawed as we removed our tongues from each other as she turned back to the display. "Getting acquainted, you two?" I flicked my view from Heather to Chris and back again. Chris groaned and looked at her broken arm.

"How the fuck did you do that? It's not exactly discreet is it?"

"Uh, I was actually moving some boxes, I've just moved house, and I was up some ladders getting one down from the loft and, blah blah, stuff everywhere and a broken arm." Chris then looked at Heather and made a signal, I wasn't really paying attention though, so didn't really see it. "I'm going to the little girls' room."

"I need to as well; I'll come, just be a minute, Alex" I nodded and hummed "yes". The businessmen were laughing and smoking cigars. The hotel bar was certainly a rather strange place. A small bar, long room, with a raised platform shaped as seats where we sat. The walls were typically blood red with cream border. I think they call it a 'dado rail', which I always thought was dangerously close to 'dildo rail'. It was getting rather smoky inside, and there were no windows to open.

Looking around for the first time in hours I noticed the barmaid, in this crowd the definite standout. Early twenties, pretty. Just for a fraction of a second I considered her soaked in sweat, our bodies enveloped, scorched-red lips torn open at my waist, all teeth and tongue. Here she smoked a cigarette, but in my mind it was leaving alive. Around the side of the bar return the girls and I rub my eyes to switch projections, reality here, reality there. Like a safety blanket I run my finger along the corduroy tracks up my blue Bench jeans, ridges courtesy of a *distressed* look. Considering the rest of the evening, I start to wonder where to get coke at this ungodly hour. The girls arrive at the table and sit down closely.

"Alex," They both laughed.

"Alex," and laughed again.

"Alex, have you ever... had a threesome?" I smiled, looked to my left and laughed, they laughed and smiled at each other, then me, obviously embarrassed but horny, so *yes, yes, yes.* Pausing for a second as I ransack the annals of my memory for a suitable leading man to ape and settle on Colin Farrell, so I scratch my eyebrow with the knuckle of my thumb then moved my eyes down and to the right towards nothing in particular but the movement seemed to mean something more than nothing.

"No, I haven't. Have either of you?" I could tell they hadn't.

"Liar!" Bursts Chris.

"It's true!" I raise my right hand and try out Michael Caine to build infallible trust. " Your honour, I never saw the perpetrator. It was very dark that night, and I wasn't wearing my glasses, which I require to read *and* drive." More laughter.

"Well, shall we uh, go to your room?" Given such a rare green light, I decided to return to my normal cadence and be proactive in my approach. They checked with each other one more time, and then started to put on their coats. I stood up and got my ridiculously expensive plain blue Vivienne Westwood Harrington jacket on, collected my belongings and we all left. The businessmen looked at me and as we left I had my hand on both of their arses and looked back at the table, smiling. The businessmen shine green with envy.

As we stumbled up the stairs Broken Arm staggers and knocks a framed picture clear off the wall. Heather giggles and I pretend to shoot a fire extinguisher at the girls fake-shouting *"spring break!"*

To my surprise Chris lifts her top and exposes herself, immediately cursing Heather for not doing likewise.

"Fucking Heather!!"

"That's why mine is twenty quid more than yours!"

A chorus of hushing "shushes" comes from the resident through chained door cracks and we try to bring it down a notch.

"So, have you really never had a threesome?" Heather didn't believe me for a second.

"Really, Christ on the cross, never done it before in my life. I'm," I laugh, "I'm... a total novice at this game." My best Hugh Grant, then I momentarily break into a childish giggle at the prospect of fucking two women at once and then quickly reel it in, then sing *"We're absolute beginners!"* All my Christmas' had come at once and it looked certain to be on.

"I bet you don't go through with it, you'll shit out" Chris was obviously not aware of who I was.

"Oh really. You do, do you? Well, my dear, that sounds like a challenge to me." Oh, it was on indeed. I love and hate it when people bet me shit like that, because in my mind it literally is like a challenge, like at sports day, the egg and spoon race, for example; except, fucking two women is a lot more of a challenge than running with an egg on a spoon. Plus family can't watch. Usually. Falling through the door, someone turned on a light and Chris went to the toilet. Heather made some drinks and gave me something that smelled like cheap vodka, straight. I put my hands on her arse and we kissed sloppily, and then slipped my hands up her top as we licked each other's mouths out and stroked our bodies then the toilet flushed and Chris came back out of the bathroom, where Heather replaced her. Chris and I looked at one another, and then began to kiss, fondling each other in an incredibly personal way. When Heather walked back into the bedroom, we all kissed and rolled onto the bed, we lay there for a second until Chris says:

"So what do we do, how do we do this?"

Lights lowered to a shade and the girls proceeded to clumsily take off their clothes, Chris bumping my hip with her cast. My eyes were adjusting to the pitch darkness so I could see. I am Mickey Rourke and the year is 1988. "Undress each other. You don't touch your own clothes." They hesitated for a minute, but soon got into it. I put my hands on two sets of breasts, two pussies, and started to eat Heather out, while expertly masturbating Chris as she started licking and fondling my rising cock. Three distinct moans is something I will never forget, I thought: "If I am to die, then I'll die right now."

The carefully choreographed yet completely improvised performance-piece continued into the early hours and soon I was able to identify each girl by the taste of her cunt. Heather, like Quality Street strawberry cream had deceptive blonde hair and quite a coarse pussy, shaven perhaps 36 hours previous. Chris, however, with her porcelain arm modification, had a tiny tuft of blonde hair, growing almost purposely from the hilting shade of her clitoris, and tasted heady, like a Californian Cab with a slight cork taint.

From a leapfrog-starting point I rut against Heather and feel a cooling pool of sweat forming in the small of my back, which trickles down as I, simultaneously, gorge on and in the fleshy crevice between Chris' legs. Heather collapses on the floor and, taking a strong arm I swing Heather into a receptive position, opening her legs and entering her in the same stance. A maddening fog of moaning women, cloaking me in flesh and bosom, with battered bedsprings shattered for the briefest of episodes as the bathroom door open in the darkened room, and Heather stumbles from the carnage rushing to fluorescence, turning on the shower and closing the door behind her.

Chris and I stop, rabbit-like, and both peer towards the light as Heather walks in self-loathing.

"Is your friend okay?" I ask, partially concerned at the inconvenience.

"I don't know maybe we should check." Replies Chris. Internally, I grumble.

"In a minute." I offer, finding approval. All good things must come to an end though. Time is a whore of a keeper to tease us so, while ecstatic delights rush by so quickly. The ache and slate of popular shame returns and drags like a continental plate.

After I come in Chris' hair while aiming for her mouth, we tumble into a quivering heap of limbs. I go to the bathroom where Heather is drying herself with lovely towels and as I approach I try to hold her, as I can see the psychological trauma of our romp is something of destructive note in her life. She turns away from me swiftly and I notice in the mirror my face dripping with sweat and body covered in mottled black hair and finger-nail scratches. We go to bed and Heather quickly falls asleep as I casually finger Chris. Within minutes both girls were asleep, and snoring progressively louder. Something told me that perhaps they were not asleep, but wanted to be rid of this perverted stranger. Snaking down the bed and finding my clothes in the dark, I took one more look at the pair with a new secret then banished myself into the corridor.

Walking with a semi-on, I breezed into and out of the elevator on the lower floor, staring at myself in the blackened mirror on the way down. It was six as I walked out, nodding at the black man behind the desk.

My breath fogged and I coughed as the outside air chilled my lungs. A slight breeze cascaded down Portland Street as I made my way towards my flat.

The streets were empty at this time of day/night except for the odd taxi and fast-food wrapper, refuse collectors and old men walking dogs. My flat was a bit of a mission, but I decided to walk as it wasn't raining for once and so a cigarette kept me company. My jacket lifted with the wind around me and air shot up my sleeves around my body. Physical exhaustion began setting in and I just wanted to get home. I patted my wallet then my back pocket, where I always kept my keys, but didn't feel anything. I checked all my pockets, then checked them again, then swore loudly. I'd left then on the table in the hotel bar. Shit. The sun was lighting the sky from the east, not quite up yet but giving half of the sky a yellowy blue tinge, which eventually merged into navy blue then black. This is the colour that shrouded the hotel. I passed back up the street and saw two homeless people shouting at a rock on the street. Time and the elements disguised their genders, providing a hermaphroditic crust of broken teeth and thick yellow skin as they devolve back into what was before. I entered the building, nodding again at the doorman, and walked casually up the stairs to the bar.

It was still open; the three businessmen were still drinking, two completely drunk, and one unconscious. I approached the attractive bargirl.

"Hi, sorry to bother you, I think I've left my keys here, I was in earlier on, um, they're like, bronze and a silver one, and there's a small one too, the key-ring, uh, is, uh, black like a circle or something. Do you have them?" She's making movements which suggest she may have them, and I begin to give her my tried and tested half smile which people seem to like so much.

"Ah, yeah, we did have some handed in before, um, what, a black key ring?" cool, they have them.

"Yeah that's them. I live just around the corner and just

got back, and I'm like, locked out now, it's freezing out there too!" She was looking under the bar as I said all this and then, sure enough, produced a set of keys, and yes, they were mine. "Oh thank God, I was worried I might have to bunk with the hobo's outside tonight." She laughed and I asked how she was doing, then I hesitated and looked down, to the right, feigning meek platitudes.

She was indeed a sexy young thing I wouldn't mind treating you to a night out and taking advantage once intoxicated.

"Well thanks, I'm Ale-"

"Alex Fish, right?" Hmmm.

"Yeah, Alex Fish, how-"

"It's quiet in here, and some people speak louder than others, y'know. So how did you do with those girls?" She's half joking, but cripple me sideways I did fairly fucking well.

"Um, well, y'know, it was... something. I um... yeah, something, anyway." The more I looked at her, the more I saw her beauty. Blondish brown hair, just past shoulder length, big eyes, no, huge eyes, with dark eyelashes that seemed to cover her some- what. Her eyes were so big she looked almost alien, but an alien I would not have a problem with indulging in some vulgar display of intergalactic copulation. Perhaps I wouldn't just use and abuse her like everyone else I've ever met. Strange. "Jesus, I just realized," I lie "what time is it? What time do you work until? How come you work so late, that must be rubbish isn't it?"

"Ah, its okay. I just turn up, make money and stuff. It's not much work at this time of night. I get to pretty much relax." She served one of the less drunken businessmen as he staggers up to the bar. He orders a pair of vodka Martini's, and struggles to get them back to the table unsullied. I stand and look her directly in the centre of the eye, another magic trick that makes girls look away, shyly, if you do it right. Once they do that, you know you have hand. She looks away, shyly.

"Long night, huh?" I say, stating obviousness.

"I actually finish at seven, so I get out soon, thank God."

"Well, I know at least one person who doesn't have to work tomorrow."

"Yeah." A long pause as she polishes remnants of lipstick from the edge of a wine glass. The avalanche of deception continues to fall from my mouth.

"I love uncomfortable silences, don't you?" She laughs and I'm screaming on the inside, but smiling on the out.

"Well, I suppose that was our first." She speaks as if she's in a film. I speak like that. I try to talk in statements, in famous quotes of my own making, or sometimes stolen from obscure films or literature. For months last year I walked around speaking like Proust and whittling away time while contemplating verbally the many indifferences of boredom in the contemporary mode of existence. I never met anyone else who did that. We both laugh at the uncomfortable silence thing, I'm laughing falsely, and so is she.

My legs and arms hung from me like weights, I felt smothered, and I wanted to sleep. But she was about to finish her shift. The counselor in my mind placated: *you have fucked two women tonight, you aren't going to be able to make much of an impression with this one. Take her number, be the cool guy that didn't try to fuck her the minute he looked at her.*

"Look, I'm thinking you're pretty cool," she smirked at my dumb bravery. "I'm really tired right now, need some sleep, but I was thinking I'd like to take you out somewhere, maybe this week. A meal or something. I don't know." A pause. Say something. "Actually, y'know, I think-"

"That might be cool. I think I'd like that." Result.

"Well, um, well... uh" I laughed "okay, cool, can I... have you got a number?" she smiled and got a pen from behind the bar, then wrote her number down on a napkin and handed it to me. I looked it over, folded it, and then put it in my pocket, smiling all the time. "Cool. Well without wanting to sound like a cliché, I'll give you a call soon." I am the God of chatting shit to girls. Then she laughed and nodded shyly.

"I'll look forward to it, Alex." With this, I smiled, nodded, and then laughed. I thanked her for my keys once again, then made my way out of the bar, avoiding the executives, lest they remember me and make a comment about my previous tandem of delight.

I finally made it into the street behind my building. It so late, the sun is well up now, hassling the horizon to attention. Long dull shadows splash across the ground and a prostitute is walking at the end of the road. It stops me in my tracks, and I stand against the wall of the bridge and watch for a second, a few minutes. She is walking in small rectangles and stopping every now and again to look for cars, customers. After about five or six minutes, a saloon pulled up next to her, well, about ten feet away and the electric window, which was already being lowered.

I couldn't hear what they were saying, but after about twelve or so seconds, she opened the door and got in. The car moved away, and disappeared into the morning.

I was standing, left alone as the wind picked up again, spurring me to go home.

Two more fucking homeless people stand near the entrance to my flat. They shout at a stray dog that is hiding across the road.

"Come here!! Hey! Come here girl!!!"

I once received a piece of advice from a friend that the perfect bachelor flat must be spotlessly clean, with a slight hint of masculinity to it; a football, a sock draped over the sofa, perhaps a slightly slanted lampshade. However mine was like a *before-shot* in a BBC *clean your fucking house* programme.

After watching prostitutes for a while from my window I come to understand that they have a system. Like ants in a glass farm, once one is picked up, another appears to take her place. There is seemingly no communication, and I rarely see two prostitutes together. Someone must be watching them. Someone other than me. I couldn't see them. Him, probably. So I just watch and wait; girls come, girls go, get picked up, get dropped off, bow-legged and broken and waiting to be fucked, getting fucked, getting paid, getting picked up, then fucked, paid, fucked, paid, beaten, fucked, fucked, beaten, raped, robbed, spit on, fucked, paid, beaten, fucked and finally they go home, to be fucked, or to cry or to spike their vein or to die alone and once more away, as does the rest of the darkened, rotting edges of humanity. I observe in silence, naked, smoking, freezing, soiled.

S ITTING ON A TALL STOOL

If you would shout my name from high
The birds would fall and clouds turn black.
You think we share a tryst of love
But lies are all I've ever known.

The record player cracks and pops over the grooves of a charity shop purchased copy of Simon and Garfunkel's Sound of Silence, as I tune in and out of a porn video I bought for twenty-five pounds a few weeks ago. A seemingly excessive price given the flares of interference that crop up frequently over the image. It is a German video, looks like four girls, and men to the factor of three. There is a typical structure to the piece: The men fuck the women in the mouth, pussy, arse, then return to the mouth. They then complete by ejaculating on their faces. But there's one particular girl here, a red haired girl who might be about twenty or less and is the designated 'come-magnet'. She has taken at least ten loads in her face and mouth so far, and seems to love it. One thing I have noticed about these girls, though: they might take thirty odd servings of sperm in the mouth, but they seem to have all been to the same finishing school that teaches the time-served methodology of bubbling it out of their mouth so it goes down their chin. Every girl, every chin: without fail, without exception.

The clock ticks northward and I see shadows start to creep across the early afternoon, barely perceptible to most daytime creatures but to dwellers of the night like me, the status of the day was always at the forefront of my mind. I stop masturbating without even realizing I had started, and sigh deeply, noticing the gentle stir of dust and ash around my seat. The eyes of the come-covered girl question me bluntly on my motivation and intent. I am apologetic enough to admit defeat and consider whether I can get a part exchange on this video. There are really only *so-many* times one can feign surprise while wrenching out another civilization onto an ever hardening dishcloth. I decide to save the couch for later, and hurry the night.

The proprietor is a thick, degenerated, white man in his mid-forties with ageing cavities for eyes and leather skin baked hard under the neon lights of his dispensary. The glass counter is adorned with bottles of "bull pills", Amyl Nitrate and the obligatory video/DVD player combo relaying lesbian fisting sessions. *The B-Sides.* He sports a rough moustache of brown, grey and yellow, perhaps to hide the years of neglect or future shame.

"Alright boss," he enquires, "What are you looking for?" His approach almost aggressive, doubtless there is an endless stream of wanking window shoppers, though I am trying to quietly browse, and although not ashamed of my extensive collection of erotica, still do not wish to advertise this fact to anybody. However, this is a red-light, beaded-curtain porno shop, dealing exclusively in hardcore, so I should feel at ease while inside.

"Ah yeah, y'alright mate? Just havin' a look, uh, is this all you've got?"

"Well, depends what you want." The walls before me display commercial hardcore; interracial gangbangs, fisting, gay body-builders, old ladies, light bondage, come-shots galore. Glancing over the available titles I show my loyalty card in the form of the previously purchased European saga of sperm.

"Ah yeah, bringing back this one." I state as I place the cassette on the counter-top, "You do do exchange, don't you?"

"If it's from here, we do, yeah. What kind of thing are you looking for?" This is not a situation one wants to spend all day doing. Despite the stench of thousand-year-old cigarettes that strike fear into my own heart, the real ugliness was all around as shoals of aging perverts enter and browses, playing pocket pool, coughing and hocking lungs like greasy paper bags.

"Well, not sure really, defo get some real hardcore, usually German, Dutch maybe."

"Oh yeah, can't go wrong with a bit of Eurotrash."

He pulls a cardboard box full of loose videos and disks from beneath the counter. I turn my head slightly to ask their origins and purpose. "Stuff on the shelves is all legit, but this is like the 'special' box, all your proper nasty stuff in here." As the word 'nasty' vomits from his mouth he winks his eye, which features at least two small white growths from the very lid, that must be torturous pain in perpetuity, carrying his sins in a Biblical sense.

"Ah safe, nice one." He fingers through the tapes and retrieves one. The label is hand written in German, I recognize the words *sperma* and *arsch*. Seems like a good place to start. The video player whirrs into life and spools the tape. The opening credits roll. *Ficken zu sperma am meine arsch* is the title of this particular opus. The man spins through the opening gambit of clips from the film and into the first scene proper. A woman, thirties, maybe twenties, who can say, dances alone. She is soon joined by two men in matching production t-shirts, who strip her, and choreograph blow-jobs. Spin forward again. Another woman, and three more men join her. The men take turns in defiling the women, the women are paid to smile and say 'yes'. Spinning further through the usual collaboration of come shots laid waste to the girls' faces, all the while being penetrated in the throat, vagina and anus by increasingly large members.

"And it goes on like that." Comments the proprietor.

"Yeah, pretty good. What about American or like, I don't know, French or something?"

"Uh lets see…" he shuffles through the tapes. "Ah, this is actually a British one, but mate, this bird is fookin' unreal." His enthusiasm seems genuine.

"Yeah sweet, l'tsav'a look."

The tape loads and another gangbang situation drama. The woman though, is plainly an aficionado of the whole scene, and relishes every inch cock and every drop of sperm.

"This is a good one because it's not too staged- see you've got the young girl here and then" we're watching in fast-forward, "all these older fellas, on the blue stuff of course but makes for better entertainment, I reckon." She must be around her early twenties, and surrounded by a gang of old men, all paunched guts and tiny stiff dicks, bolstered by erection enhancers and her looking like an advert for government subsidized combinations of coke and heroin. "Not bad eh?" He says.

"Yeah, fuck man, very nice. She obviously likes it."

The man laughs and lights a cigarette "You can tell eh?! Some of 'em are just fookin' born for it." Using both hands on two cocks and sucking another. "She's like; you see her?" He points to the girl in the video.

"Yeah?"

"Reckon when I were your age, what are you, like twenty five?"

"Yeah, let's say that."

"Aye when I was your age I used to see this bird, a fuckin' woman like; anyway she looked a bit like her, or could have been her old mum, was about… fifty odd, prossy eh. She taught me fookin' ev-ery-thing. Honestly mate, nothing like it. Pure filth. She was into her heroin as well like, but she used to do all sorts; dressing up like a school-girl, getting 'us to rape her, slap her face and that, spit in her mouth and that. She was well into her dirt."

"Fuckin' hell, no shit?"

"Yeah mate, she'd be like," he gesticulates that of a head between his legs "goin' for it, deep throating, gagging... she were well into her puking. You had that shit before?"

I cast my mind and come up blank, "Nah mate I think you beat me there."

"Aw seriously, she'd choke herself on ma cock, then puke all over it and keep sucking away, real pro."

One of the old men in the store approached the counter.

"Poppers?" He said quietly.

"Fiver mate." Says the proprietor, handing over a small bottle in a brown paper bag.

The old man leaves the money and takes the bag, shuffling and sniffling away.

"Shit man sounds like quite a girl."

"Aye she was an'all. Died a few years back. I'm fookin' sick of women now like."

"Not the same eh?" We reminisce about a time when women were 'real whores' and the woman in the video bends over and inserts four fingers from two hands into her anus, spreading it wide for the madding crowd.

"Nah, not even close. These lasses today, they're all fookin' *pretty-pretty, don't mess me hair up, wear a condom,* fookin' *like,* come-on, *eh*?!"

"Yeah I know what you mean, man; they've missed the point of casual sex."

"Exactly. Now you know when you're down the pub 'n you get a bird, you know there's gonna be all this shit to go with it. Nothing's simple nowadays. Fookin' CIA mate, spreading this AID's shit all over. Fookin' ruined the field."

"CIA?"

A light inside him switches on as a conspiratorial opinion is required. "Shit, yeah! They fookin' started it, fookin' Yankee cunts. It's population control; it's like the Fourth Reich or something."

He laughs at his own comparison.

"Aye ah reckon you're could be right there, mate."

A moment of silence as our attention gets drawn by the video once again. The woman chokes on a cock and a huge ball of spit slobbers from her lips and onto the awaiting red face of another similarly motivated woman with large natural, almost sagging tits and we both laugh heartily at the shot.

"Aye and then this other time," he continues, "I picked up this lass,"

"What like, pulled her?"

"Nah nah, she was a working girl as well, anyway, and I take her back mine, were chillin' out, having a smoke, she's got a bit of coke, all good eh?"

"Yeah yeah?"

"So then I start taking her clothes off, pull her top off, nice tits, she's like, maybe twenty odd,"

"When was this?"

"Oh not long ago, six month maybe."

"Right, right."

"So she's got her tits out, I'm suckin' her nipples and that, then I put my hands down her pants," As he says this I look at his hands: thick, yellow, coarse. "-and as soon as I'm fingering her like she fookin' stops, starts crying and gets up to leave!"

"What? Outrageous. What was up with her?"

"No idea. She just, like, went the other way, y'know?"
I nod, for some reason actually concerned.

"Yeah. Weird."

"She told me later she used to get raped when she was younger by her uncle or something."

"But, she's a prostitute?"

"Tell me about it! Aye poor lass. She was alright. Got an extra gram off us anyway so it was worth it for her."

"Still, must have been a pain."

"Buyer beware!" He laughs and I follow suit. "I fookin' had it as well though, so no bother there!" The woman on the screen by now has come on her face, hair, and the men purposely ejaculate onto her eyes glazing over like a pair of donuts melting in the sun.

Still laughing I say "Ah, fuckin' women eh?"

"Fookin' women."

"Can't live with 'em."

"Yep." Ending the expression and adding the punch-line of silence.

We both laugh and I feel somewhat purified; knowing there are souls just as, if not more lost and damned as my own wandering the cold streets, and not all can conceal the emotionally crippling social truths as my new friend demonstrates marvelously.

"Yeah, I reckon I'll take this one here." The British woman now sits on the plastic-covered floor, wiping come from her face and dropping it into her mouth.

"Good choice."

"What's your name anyway, chief?"

"John."

"John? Nice one, Alex."

"Top stuff we'll see you again then eh?"

"Aye I reckon I'll be sick of this one in a fortnight."

"Too true: there's only so many wanks you can get out of a vid."

"Such is life." I offer. "Give us a bottle of poppers as well, John."

John hands me the paper bag containing my dubious purchase, "There you go, lad, take care."

An old man enters, hands in his pockets and leers at me as we pass by the door. I look down the street for normal people before exiting through the beaded curtain, leaving the recorded sounds and images of copulation ringing in my ears, providing colours of corruption to these grey and lifeless streets and faces.

L AST DAYS OF THE CIVIL WAR

Lately I have been so happy, the light seems brighter.
But there is still a hole where my heart sits
I hope it will live, because right now
I felt it beat again.

I had first met Pete a couple of months back and for all intents he was a good bloke. Could probably call him a friend. I had spent a Sunday looking for a long out of press record, which was allegedly worth a fair bit. Boards of Canada are an electronic music duo from Scotland. They make music that sounds like a computer game slowed down to the speed of a wheelchair and filtered through a drain, and I like that sound. I'm looking for Twoism, an early release and probably their best. I go into HMV Records and ask the tall, bearded pseudo-hippy behind the counter.

"'Scuse me mate, you haven't got uh, Twoism by Boards of Canada have you?"

"*Twoism*? Nah man, but Boards are awesome though, I know Twoism, they um, they released it when they first started and they were at a gig, I think only about two-hundred got made, it's rare as fuck." Then he glances and checks the Little Lord Faulteroy look-alike manager didn't hear him. "Actually, I know where you might be able to find out how to get it, if you're serious about paying for it."

"Yeah man, definitely," I reply, "I've got a little stash for it." I've heard rumours about how expensive it actually is, so am prepared for the worst.

"Sweet man, well, you need to go to Emu's Eyeballs, it's uh, round the back of that big shop and on this back alley opposite that pub."

"Right, pub? Uh, which one?"

He looks puzzled trying to explain it. "It's um, 'round the back of the Arndale, Ships Arms or White Dog or something like that."

"Right, okay,"

"Actually, I'm getting my dinner in a minute, and I was gonna go there anyway so I can show you where it is if you want?"

"Yeah, sounds good, man, um... I'll just wait about."

"I'll only be a couple of minutes."

"Okay." I just mill around in the metal section and look at the fit little mosher girls, then over to the dance and hip-hop bit and look at the fit young Asian and black girls. Over the other side are all the office workers getting the chart shit. My new friend heads past me and goes downstairs.

"I'll just get my coat."

"Yeah, you've pulled." He laughs and so do I. Walking past him as he heads through the door is a moody looking lanky streak of piss carrying a yellow crate and muttering something to himself. He looks a bit old to be working here and it looks like he knows it so I just look at a *Squarepusher* album while waiting for my new friend to return which he does wearing a huge green Vietnam jacket with a big furry fuck-off hood on the back.

"Alright mate?" He asks.

"Yeah let's go." We walk out and turn left up Market Street, for some reason I don't feel like walking past the girls' clothes shop just ahead but I do anyway and just keep my head forward.

"Yeah man, I'm Pete by the way."

"Oh right yeah safe man, Alex."

"Nice one. Are you studying?"

"The finer arts of drinking, majoring in drugs and chlamydial relief."

"Ah yes, I was looking at that course. Actually, I might have a bit left." Pete is quick and joins the farcical exchange while scratching his crotch as we laugh through our darkening teeth.

"You work in the shop full time?"

"Yeah, I started last winter, it's alright."

"Fuck I couldn't be arsed serving the idiot people in this city all day."

"Oh God yeah, it doesn't end in that place, you've got like, fuck; talk about students, they're dicks, but then you've got these knobs who come bringing shit back for returns every day. I'm like: I know you burned this fucking CD, mate. It's a nightmare."

"Well, yeah, technology ain't what it used to be."

"That's right, never so technical than today. What do you do then?"

"Uh, I'm currently between distractions."

"Ha. Nice." We pass the bookshop crafted from a shipping container and Pete smiles at the keeper. "You live here? In the city, I mean."

"Down in Castlefield."

"Castlefield?!" Pete recognizes the status of the area. "Very nice, what in like a loft or something?"

"Yeah like a loft with big glass and shit, fucking giant corduroy sofa. Can't complain; big walls, big ceiling, good spot, really."

"Mmhmm." Our feet cross the tram tracks heading towards the old red brick buildings.

"This town though, you get used to it. It's not that big really."

"Yeah, gets fucking cold though, eh?"

Pete was one of those asexual people. His manner was gruff and sweaty, but as he spoke he did so with warmth and humour, combined with an intelligent hatred for the trappings of situational drama, gangbang or otherwise, and instead actively listened and contributed to conversation. It was an unusual way of communicating, these days, not simply waiting for a moment of silence to blurt out whatever shit you might remember from whatever magazine or piece of disposable news you might recall at any one second. He told me about the architecture of the city as we passed cryptically constructed churches carved from sandstone thousands of years old, and nightclubs that would host zealously paid disc jockeys and great culminations of light and sound. These days the clubs in Manchester were the church, the disc jockeys like mortal Gods, and the holy words delivered in clear baggies and folded flyers. It was the last signal of the society destined for auto-sarcophagy, the self-consumption and cannibalisation of humanity. It would be so easy to design a youthful, merciless army through the use of hyperdelic drugs sold to the very victims themselves. Pete and I ate hot-dogs from a metal trailer rigged up with boilers out on the freezing street next to the tram lines that lead elsewhere.

The day was cold; it was early December and the only Christmas spirit in the streets was scotch. The frenzied assault of shoppers left the streets looking like a raging river of consumerism. We had traversed the gentler streams and now came to the white water, contorting as we paddled through a swirling pools of limbs and torsos blocking our path. One old lady tripped up right in front of me and we helped her up. She had a bruised eye and was shaking, spouting nonsense through thousand-year-old lips.

Pete had lazy sideburns; the kind that sunbathe on your cheeks. I could grow them if I so wanted, but sideburns are one step from a goatee that screams, "Talk to me". A car follows another down a road that cuts across a pedestrian walkway-without enforcement of societal norms the people become animalistic, disbursing of care and fucks to be given. Read in the paper that some old guy got killed when a bus smashed into him on this very street. I went down to see it that day and you could smell the blood and gore in the air. Big crowds of people gathered to look at this dead guy; there's nothing like a corpse to bring people together. I started to talk about scoring some weed, which I've wanted to do all day. Pete tells me he can help, and I'm happy.

We arrive at this record store and it's down some steps under the road, built out of an old public toilet. I walk in and there's a blue fug of burned Amber Leaf in the air. Thousands of records boxed in some sort of semblance of order. One other customer is in there; he's on the other side of the room with a growing stack of vinyl. The assistant is sitting reading this month's *Wire* magazine, and smoking a self-rolled cigarette. We approach.

"Y'alright mate," I begin.

"Yeah man?" The assistant acknowledges us.

"Just wanted to know if you guys sell a record called Twosim by Boards of Canada. They're a Scottish-"

"I know who Boards are," He looks up slowly from his magazine and starts to give me a stoner laugh, looking at the guy across the room and attracting his attention.

"Yom, Do we sell *Twoism*?" What the fuck kind of name was Yom?

"*Twoism*?! Huh huh huh. Nah man."

"Huh huh" he looks back at us. "Not unless you've got six hundred quid. They only pressed like, I think it was about a hundred, and uh, they sold it at this gig back in something like ninety-six? Rare as rocking-horse-shit." I'm slightly taken aback by the cost, but not so much to let this little fucker win. Pete looks up from some records then over to me when he hears how much it is.

"Fuh-king hell." He mutters it, so as not to sound cheap, but shit, that isn't cheap at all. The guy is eyeballing me, cheeky little fucker, waiting for my next move.

"Well, do you have any in stock?" Come on you mother fucker.

"Uh," he's looking around as if to say 'seriously?' and has placed his cigarette into the ashtray. "We don't stock any,"

"But?" I am the King.

"But, I mean, I actually have one." He's totally in shock, and most probably awe. I just roll my mouth very casual and say,

"Well, is it here?"

"Yeah, yeah it uh, yeah it's here."

I nod and say

"...and I can buy it?"

I conjure memories of winning sports day, coming first in the three-legged sprint. My dad and I entered on a day when the sun seemed like it was never going down. The sun was bright, and when we crossed the finish line, sweating like real men, we collapsed in the heat.

Hottest year on record forever and ever.

I got really sunburned that year when I went to the South of France. That was the first year I ever got drunk. I had been gorging on crepes all week, and this night a couple of us found this huge bucket of Sangria. Nowadays Sangria is nothing, but then, I was so young. So I got really drunk and ended up kissing my friend who I met-on-holiday who was also drunk. I was ten or eleven; she was thirteen, maybe fourteen. I fell asleep in my own little tent, vomited all over the place. At 6AM with dried fruit and dough and bile covering my face, I staggered across the campsite on my own, half-naked with a ten-year-old sleepy hard-on in the morning sun, desperately looking for the shower block.

He sighs but a flicker tells me he wants the money more than the record.

"I wasn't thinking about selling it."

Pete and Yom get closer in anticipation. Who would crack first? "...but I suppose for like... six, I would." I'll offer four and take it for five...

"Six? Well I was thinking maybe four?"

"Fucking hell mate, no mate, can't do it for four, I can do five twenty five minimum."

"What about four fifty?"

"I just, I can't possibly go lower than five for it?

"So, five then?"

"Fucks sake: five hundred quid for my *Twoism*?" Twig Leaf asked himself his true worth and faced with the sale could not resist. I procure a rare record and segment of his soul.

"Done." Everyone cheered then Bruce Willis shot the guy and said "Yippeekayay, mother fucker", and the token black cop came in and smiled ruefully, knowing that races are united then Willis punched his fist into the air but the whole thing changed to a delightful European situation porno where one girl was getting fisted by a guy and another is jacking his cock against her tits and saying German expletives, at which point in time someone did or did not come in somebody else's face.

S TONED WANK

One million years is all there is between us.
One chance at life, caught between aeons.
A second hand turns on the face of the moon.
It has been here since last you were smiling.

The sun has long since dropped, and now burns a smoldered coal in the distance, imploding into what we call "night", now painted across the horizon. I smoke a cigarette and try and exhale against the wind, blowing smoke rings that fail to form time and again.

I don't see him when he pulls up from behind me, only the deep grumbling bass box working in the rear of the car alerts me to his presence and I instinctively turn my head to look in the opposite direction, seeking infiltrators.

As I step towards the car the back door opens for me. In the front, driving, is Pad: short, chubby, a few years younger than me but built up in preparation of being a very strong man, when the time comes. Pad has dilated pupils, which are hard to see in the dark. Fielder looks round and up from underneath his flowerpot hat.

"Easy man, Al, how's goin'?" The light from the stereo shines blue and illuminates only the bottom of his face, revealing a goatee beard and obligatory gold chains.

"Fine, usual shit really. Ready for the next thing."

"Yeah you know we got the ting, fucking safe mate. Yeah we just been in the flat, blazed on this, yo, tap that."

Fielder hands me Pad's joint, and it burns the insides of my chest like firewater. I cough hard as Fielder and Pad laugh. "This one they call Windowlicker. White Widow/Tangerine Dream hybrids."

"It's fucking raw, man."

"True that."

I take another hit. For some reason I never felt comfortable around people in the harsh light of day. It's like everyone has a part to play but rather than approach the performance as an art, it is delivered as a lie. There is a common degradation to humanity that is well aware of the inherent perversion within, and also to that of their neighbor, but still they fight like horses charging through rain, thrashing mud up to their faces that fall towards a thousand wielded blades that slice and cut and dissect and all for the preservation of the common lie, the ridiculous charade to mask our true emptiness.

"What was you after?" Fielder asks.

"Ounce?"

"No worries mate, just on the floor in front of you, s'a bag,"

"Black bag?"

"Black bag yeah just uh, bags are in the front pocket, just go in the main bit there's ones and halves. Have a feel at the bigger ones, they's what you want."

I feel around at a rucksack full of probably half a nine-bar. A nice fat bag with at least two huge juicy buds as big as a baby's head sitting in the middle grabs my attention straight away. Naturally, the immediate thought at feeling such a large quantity of high quality marijuana is to grab it and run in a straight line for the painted horizon, but I recognize Fielders' loyalty test, and play the game, continuing in the common lie.

"Is that what you're smokin' there?"

Fielder looks like he almost forgot the joint in his hand,

"No, this one the next *next* ting, tho' check that." And passes me the bulging spliff.

The draw is like rolling heather. I smoke a few off and taste the intoxicating aromatics, then find the bag I deem to be fullest.

"Yeah mate got a good one right here," I hold the bag and my free hand up to show I'm only taking one bag, then remove the money from my pocket, folded into four-by-width.

"Nice one Fielder man, one three yeah?"

"Prices up yo, recession putting it down at one-four-five."

"Fucks sake."

"Money trap. Some Wall Street shit."

My fondness for Fielder is easily dissipated as I cannot tell if he is profiteering or stupid, and don't even know within myself which I'd be more annoyed at. Perturbed, but without recourse, I palm him the wad of notes retrieved recently from the cash-point and add the difference.

"Safe, have a good weekend." I'd forgotten the weekend was even here. Haven't even thought about it. It's Friday night.

"Uh, shit man I forgot was even the weekend. Probably do something."

"Yeah man looks like a lot of fanny about, fuckin' warm night and that, girls getting down to the good shit an'at, man!" Fielder by now is talking to both Pad and myself, Pad laughing along, though I am unsure as to what exactly.

Like Christmas morning when finally presents smelling fresh and wrapping paper crinkled in the night I rip open the sack of weed once home and safe upstairs. The beauty of an unfettered ounce is almost overwhelming.

I hurriedly shuttle through cassettes and watch a video myself fucking a black girl from months ago, another silly girl bought and sold by poetry and humour.

All Of a sudden I am hard. It grows through my trousers

and struggles to break out of my underwear. It rises and stands like some classically forged Totem pole, and every beat of my heart pushes the blood cells through its tight network of nerves and vessels.

The stillness in the room is only fettered by my rapid and synchronous masturbatory movements, and I notice a tiny fragment of paper floating in the air. I am so high there is no chance of resisting orgasm, not that I know why I should. I seem to be throbbing in time to the Boards of Canada record, sounds that pour from my expensive floor-standing speakers.

I push my trousers around by my ankles, the restraint created adds another element of sexuality to the self-administered scene. Fumbling and rubbing my cock that sports drippings of pre-come making for the perfect lubricant.

The weed has given me a sensation of paralysis or maybe it is partly due to the crouching position I now find myself in, restrictive blood flow and suffocation make for excellent bedfellows. I remember the bottle of poppers still wrapped in a brown paper bag and add these to the maelstrom of confusion and stimulants supporting my session like cock-shaped Greek pillars holding up the Parthenon.

Pulling my cock from inside my Hugo Boss boxer shorts I begin to masturbate at race-horse pace, the skin of the head moving easily over the shaft because I can't feel its tightness and my nerves are completely numb and I can feel every thrust is nicer than the last and I feel it building inside me and I can't stop it but still it takes a long time until that numbing feeling can coax my orgasm into making an appearance, fueled quickly by another hit of Amyl while my balls bang against my perineum and I can tell that afterwards I will be sore but for now none of that matters as the peaking almost reaches its apex and my mind is flooded with a thousand images of sluttification, driven by the video of me now a solo wank video made while spying through landlord Al's window onto his filthy old wife, herself a special kind of pervert and when this is all over perhaps in three hundred years I will ejaculate and it will be an event on par with a royal wedding that tens of thousands of people will swarm to see and write that they were there the day that He came for good and it may be the last thing I ever do but I feel it now and it comes before me, rising, rising, on cue with the count of one, two, three.

Breathe.

Breathe.

Sigh.

Yawn.

The moments of time dripping over my fingers and wrist and pooling around my feet. I feel a chill draft of air coming in from somewhere. The smell of solvents around the room and my feet wet and frozen, as I try and coordinate this uncomfortable position. The film has changed to one of me struggling to bang a hooker I picked up one twisted morning after a session but it is the last thing I want to see right now. She screams like a bird trapped by tightening wires. Post-wank guilt has set in. I struggle to find a tissue while not spilling come on the fabric beneath me and settle for a black sock, throwing it behind the couch afterwards.

T HE REFLEX

When she asks you not to speak
And closes up her eyes,
To seek escape is not her path
But clarity over the visions of sleep.

A decade of sexual trial and error has encouraged my predilection for contact with human flesh to grow like a virus, embodied in my clockwork efforts to further grow my arena of conquests. It has taken me across kink and perversion alike, imbuing them with a misaligned appreciation and direction towards deceit in vainglorious efforts to leave a beautiful corpse.

In the Garden of Eden there was neither the feeling nor meaning of pleasure nor pain, but a tame, beast-like reason. The days and the nights were not sullied nor dusk, and the winds travel south from the closest of mountains and vales. But here we are far from The Garden, having journeyed throughout the deepest pits of what man calls his hell, to get to this plateau that speaks to hidden young children residing in the Winter of Feeling. Surveying the tundra before us we call it a land of great promise. All that we seek truly: the warm and the soft, that memory of crushed violet flowers, petals amassed until the reaping of amniotic fluid. Acting as a membrane of distillation caught round all ideas of faith and of ruin so that even the faintest of hopes would be colored with the darkest of inks. Managed beyond the last gates of regret to the fences of hate and the channels of faith that creep here. To return to this moment for seconds, cut to fractions is the true meaning of life.

When age pursues and the fat settles will you regret the times that you made me your dog? Laid now to rest in the chasm of ice and dust you stay; stained by the starlight and burned by the day. In the case that at once all my memories turned upon face there was one empty vessel that gave me no grace: was a lost lonely soul and a torturous place, given to greed and compulsions of base that drew deep from the red of the ink and would bleed until brinks of the heaviest paper and softest of quills would dance just like the stars held above water, but scatter when winds would caress ripples over the mirrored edge caught in the face of the lake. Mountains grow highly and stranger things happen when trapping a victim caught loose in a net made of wit and of chivalry, tinged with an accent of humble futility. Therein resides the prey for this next triviality. Certain signs you can bank on perpetually: fingers near mouth to indicate readily, syndication of mouth to the precipice, swollen like bee stings inside of the tendon. Was not a God could turn from her majesty. Was a torturous sight made by atrophy, of the darkest of times left with less to feel than the blowing of reeds across rolling green fields.

Over the crest of the crown should a perpreteur rest on his dominant hand in the way of the glorious might brought on by ancient feelings, that weave between histories, bleedings of lies and of death and of spurious teachings. In case of that glorious night that might leave the world reeling, when truth may be told in the legends of being; like light caught in darkened glass bottles that shine and reflect on the end of tomorrow. His heart should be beating to time no more fixed than the sun and of season and gently repeating to intrinsic codes that could spell either death or of life to the soul that gave us the black night so that lines between pain and paradise may be tangled forever in impossible threads. Where the dreams and the flesh meeting, moaning and peeling, for anguish of zeal that all other things borrowed from idiot ramblings and half thought ideas, the very one here that life is consequential. Since truth is a haze it can stand to reason that all things in place are a drowning of easing since this is the time above all those great others, when physical girth breaks on spiritual borders.

No road sign upon this route of desolation that leaves at least one with a question of reason, when tonsils are teased from their usual station and throats are choked without a care for the ending. Stop and give wonder, for this time is given not from mankind but from those Godly beings, surely, without a hair of influence from mortal men blinded. By seeming to purport to dictate immaculate den but instead barely see the consequence of any transgression over field of tongue and on quarries of pink flesh insides that hark twice of the reason and last of the weakness.

To suns exploding can one be endowed, but be warned this is fleeting, since moments of such are made only to pass; instead lays the stench of a consciousness bared to the gleaning eyes of a thousand sullen misers, to peck and to nibble on gentle nerve endings collected in atrophied towers of sinew that fiend from first of the moment of birth and on to the last of the last respirations.

And how we do get there? Through means devoid of a purity. Of the finer arts and sciences many claim to be definitive in their importance, or of their paths to knowledge, but in truth and reality blowjobs are the art, and their procurement is the science. If you are fortunate enough to have received a fully engaging mouth to rampart against then you know already that therein lies God, as the sensation of an entire penis inside a mouth and rutting against the back teeth and intriguing choking points beyond the red cliffs of the throat.

"And that's that whun." John said, rubbing the buttons of the remote control that have now been worn down to tiny rubber raisings, more like braille than functions.

By the life-size cardboard cutout of a German filth-pot with the word "Annette" autographed across the tits, an old man coughs and dislodges something that sounds only just closer to death. John lights a cigarette.

"They've lost the touch these days. Birds can't even suck cock proper anymore. Get a good blowjob; it's'like a gift from't Gods, innit. Bad one, worst fookin' *see ya later*, guilt trip you can imagine."

"Innit?!" I agree using localised dialect as John inserts the next cassette, with the words in black marker over white-sticker "Aldous Farm" and as he does so the tape-head bends as the image corrects on the screen, which shows the eaves of a large barn-looking structure, black and shaded against a murky sky. The screen cuts and reveals the inhabitants of the barn, gathered together in groups of five and six and so on and dressed in a mixture of fetishistic rubber and latex and furs and feathers and teeth and bone. The image was warm and fuzzing, it held a dangerous tone of colour. A poised woman in her forties was getting whipped with grassy ropes and fisted by a younger girl, while three older gentlemen used their mouths like the aforementioned playgrounds.

"It used to be so much better." He moaned again. "I'll tell you something, because it's not completely dead out there, well, for me it's fucked." I listened to this proprietor of filth and fornication as would you listen to any professor of opinion. "But you're a young man, you'll have plenty more and I'll tell you: to get a good one, to really push the girl but in a *nice* way: *fighting* for it will get you to the goods. If you're with some dainty little slag who can't take any pain or even a bit of roughing, chances are you're going to get a crap BJ followed swiftly by an even crapper fuck. Now then, if you're with a girl who can take a knock, reacts well from being grabbed and roughed up, choked an'at, spit in her mouth stick your fingers inside her cunt nice and rough: if she can take that, then you're onto a winner."

The movie continued and a man in a large mask made of an assorted collection of bones and skin, fur, teeth once more but hung low and pointed high. The man stood with purpose.

"You can tell early on, what she's going to be like, it's always a good thing if she tries to hit you in the arm, all playful like, before the act. A gentle hand around the face, maybe neck, from you will get you one of two things: if she's not game, she'll either fuck off or go ballistic. If she's into it, then it's a whole different story. I've been with girls who, at the slightest hint of a bit of rough, go fookin' bananas." Some developments onscreen involving light to moderate pain management.

"Neck's a good place to start if you meet a girl in a club, like, so you'll have kissed her by now, and you should have you're arms and hands stroking her back, then put your mouth onto her neck and just give it a little bite." John mouthed the action, which in itself was grotesque but in the situation would be considered coaching. "She might squirm to move away, but she doesn't mean it, just hold your course, be firm, decisive. Chances are, she'll probably be well into that, so you should take it a bit further. Once she's shaken a bit from the neck job (which might even be enough if she's off her tits on pills), then tense your back muscles and press you groin against her, not in a stupid, over the top way, but just enough to let her know you're around. Don't be afraid to get a finger or two in there either, she'll be ready by now. So you're in the club, she's turned on, you want to fuck her anyway, but full sex is sometimes inconvenient, right? That's why we have mouths. And I bet clubs today you can probably anywhere but back when it were me I'd be in a taxi on't way home, in the toilets, or next to the bins outside, but wherever you are, she should be giving you a blowjob." Johns lecture had attracted a couple of old men, eager to learn from this past master. John notices and tones down just a notch, which encourages the class to lean closer, now the air humming with come and sweat and poppers. "The only problem with a blowjob in a public place is the fact that you can't do everything you would if you were at home. So, let's say you're in a taxi on the way home. This has happened to me a few times, it's fucking superb if you can get a girl to give you a blowjob in the back of a cab. Something about the guy in the front thinking 'yes', seems to turn them on. She'll not be able to do it that well in the back seat; it's just not practical, so you get her home, keeping a semi-lob-on."

The videotape made a grating sound as a wave of electro-magnetic static drifted across the screen and the barnyard fornicators were dissolved into VHS memory. "Fucks sake," mutters John, as he replaces the tape with furthermore filth, this time a compilation of sorts featuring strictly cumshots. The standard static frames of mid-air arcs of semen just for laughs as the film begins and a preamble of soft nudity, hot-pants lowered over white cotton panties, blonde haired girls biting lips and red-faced brunettes taking cock just out of frame provides a suitable introduction as the cavalcade of cumshots begins, each edited to cut just after contact, immediately before impact.

"Once inside, then all bets are off, it could still go either way at this point so it's very important you don't lose your concentration. If it's not your house then have a quick look around- take stock of your surroundings. Make a mental note of where the front door is, where you take your shoes off if you do, where you put your coat. Also, find the bathroom and a chair or surface with a good height for oral sex both ways.

That's the secret really, if you want to get a girl to do exactly what you want just make them come with oral sex. I've found that alternating between hard and soft, slow and fast is the best." The man who previously had been rubbing one out in the private video booth was leaving, mottling white tissues between his orange, thick-skinned fingers that up close would stink of tobacco and semen. He left wondering what fresh insight he might have missed but like all perverts once he has started walking he cannot stop lest the jig is up. "Find the clit straight away, Play with it until she starts to get really into it, then stick your tongue inside her, then outside for a while, be delicate and pay special attention to the clit and arsehole. Your hands need to be moving around her body, try her tits, up her side, her stomach, but don't reach too far up: try to touch her face and you'll look stupid. Once she's come, or at least gotten close, she'll be like a little fookin; pocket rocket trying to go off. At this point, you just move her body off the chair, or down the bed, so you can kiss her. This is the point where you know what you're going to get. If she's a bit funny about kissing you with a load of spit and her come all over your face, then this might be the wrong girl; but, if she gets right into it, starts rubbing the come over her own face and lick it off or whatever, then you're onto a winner. Give a few gasps, she'll be amazed how turned on you are from just *going down* on her, and will want to *please* you *more*. Now, you can initiate a blow job using a very simple trick in the position you should now be in. You should have the leverage and ability to move your body up a little, so that your groin again rubs against her, try and get her crotch, and that your head looks down onto her face. This'll start the natural motion of her body, and she should go down on you. Try to make sure you're on the bottom for this, as I've found this is where you get most control and freedom, although if you really want to get her then going on top is the place, but I'd save that until you know she's game. She should be holding it by the base, what you're aiming for is for her to slip her hand off your cock and play with your balls, letting you get the full length into her mouth.

Chances are, she won't be able to take it all, well, hopefully for you anyway," Some of the old men grumbled silently, "and when she can't her gag reflex takes over, but then she can go one of two ways again. Remember, gagging on a cock isn't too pleasant *physically*, it hurts the back of your mouth, your throat, and you can't breathe properly; it's inconvenient. But as we know, when you're engaged in the act:

rules are bent, tastes are varied. The 'gag' itself, could be just what the girl wants, or it might be the opposite. When she comes up for air, see what she does with her mouth, does she wretch? Does she cough? Does she drop a thick string of saliva out onto your cock and wank it onto it? This is what you're looking for; a cough might just result in an argument due to your so-called 'lack of respect'. A wretch can be a different matter altogether. I've only personally met one who did, but once upon a time this particular girl would go down on me and purposely make herself sick, just to release the endorphins around her body or whatever it was. We did it like that a few times in my flat until I had to stop seeing her- ruined a perfectly good sofa.

Anyway if all is good by this stage, then you can start to do something known as "skull-fucking". This is achieved when you grab her head or hair (preferably hair), and fuck that mouth like it needs it. From now on, you should be in full flow and not a lot more needs to be said. All that is left is to choose where you are going to come. In the mouth is good, I'm a fan of on the face and in the mouth at the same time, followed up with some porn-star-style licking from her, but I'm probably biased but anyway- each way has its own merits." John just coming up for air and giving me the slightest crack of a window to speak:

"Could you not just ask them?"

"Ask them for what?"

"For a fucking blow job."

John's face wrinkled as he accepted the evolved thinking. "I suppose anything *could* work. Have you got a bit more of that?" He asks, and I hand John the wrap of caked off-white powder that oh so greatly drives us forth.

John was wrong though. His whole testimony was built on the foundation of deceit, when in fact that very deception must be so well hidden that not even the perpetrator knows of its existence.

NEIL FINN'S MIDSOMER PARTY

Dance and dance and dream of last
The word you spoke so soft to ears
That took the time to listen close
Instead of holding tongue in pause.

There is an animalistic strut to my step as I walk along a particular route towards the pub. No doubt brought on by the strange tablet given to me by some stranger during another forgotten binge. No more than a tingling for now, but good, fresh poison in the water, snakes climbing ladders.

Skirting the sidewalks and hovering like vultures a scrum of paps- battalion armed with Canon, Nikon, Panasonic and such. Leering towards the rear entrance of the local TV Station where often too those commercially desired quasi-heroes go. In all of its rectangles and muddy tones the building was itself a testament to *grim northernism*. Right angles, right angles. Dirty metal coated in plastic now bleached of colour, cracked by the elements. Stained walls choked black with piss and exhaust fumes from decades-last three.

Not out of place entirely but a reality removed from the collective in this establishment, actors and TV types, all air-kisses and pseudo Southern accents, ever-so-keen on that *London money*. I can't walk exactly straight as I enter the pub.

Music might help, but not here, just a wall of chatter-massive and hard against plate walls of glass, an echo chamber of increasingly hyped proclamations about nothing. The Machine in its organic form. Late summer sun streams through the windows and creates waterfalls of ultramarine cigarette smoke that flow towards all of our ends. I lit one of my own and dive into the pool. Pete should be around somewhere.

As I approach the bar I recognise some TV talent, minor celebrity but all the same. I wait until the bar girl comes over.

"Yes love what can I get you?" she asks in a very Mancunian accent. I pretend to be fancy with crooked eyebrow.

"Oh I'll have a pint of shall we say, Kronenburg, please."

"Anything else?"

"That's all thanks." She starts to pour the drink, takes some money, gives me some money, gives me my pint, and that's that. To my every side conversation incessant. Door opens, Pete's here, thank Christ. "One more please, darling."

Pete gives me a look and battles through the forest of fools between us. By the time he arrives his drink is on the bar. "Mr. P., how goes it sir?" I give the easy appearance of affluence through excellence.

"Yes man, the dick of the day has been well and truly sucked, what's the plan for tonight, then?"

"I don't know, maybe here for a few, then there's the other place fairly close, so that later, then I dunno, how the fuck would I?"

"How the fuck indeed, you probably need a little something to start the night right."

"Or at least pick me up." I say as Pete palms a wrap of powder, I taste it to be MDMA.

"That'll do you."

"From usual?"

Pete looks at the wrap momentarily, "This? Actually got this off a mate who brung it from Amsterdam."

"You're joking?"

"No mate *bona fide* 'Dam gear."

"Amsterdam? Oh quality, that's the place to be. Yeah a long weekend would do me just right."

"Fuck man, I went for a fortnight once, couldn't get back to living normal. I think I'm always just one bad day from moving back."

"Such as life I would say."

"It's the sort of place that gets under your skin. There's something about it that even though it's just a washed up piece of capital with legal weed, there's a courage to them, the people, a blind faith in humanity. They're what makes it Amsterdam. The bridges, the doors,"

"The drugs, the whores,"

"Exactly, so you know what I'm talking about, it's hard to give all that up and settle for Englands-fucking-Glory."

"Next it'll be knuckle tattoos and permanently upset eyebrows crowning over yet another fat-head squeezed through the big hole in a string vest."

"And that's just the tourists."

"Fuckin' natives around here."

Just then, a group of people walked through the door, adding more noise to the place.

"Do you know it's two-for-one on cocktails over the road?"

"Is it really?"

"Yeah, fancy a few?"

"Bit of grog-with-sugar-syrup? I'm up for that. Down these, s'get the fuck out of this place."

Down the beers went and before leaving by the side door bumped into a friend of Pete's, a blonde with big tits, but looking like someone's mother in the hip young crowd. Leaving the bar we pass a group of people and I catch:

"No it's catered for two-hundred, just in case!"

The next place was somewhat different, but had many of the same characteristics as the last, except this time there was deafeningly loud Drum and Bass coming from the walls and bouncing against our eardrums. Nobody seemed to notice and reacted by simply screaming their lines of dialogue louder and louder until a garbled mass of syllables at a deafening level was the other recognizable characteristic of the whole place.

"I'd *like* to like drum and bass, but I just don't think I've got time for it." I scream into silence against the rising tide of decibels.

"Oh yeah?" Replied Pete.

"I mean, I'm sure it's good, but there are only so many hours in the day and I just can't sleep knowing that any of them are for drum and fucking bass music."

"Yeah. It's like wanking to home shopping channels: The girl is there but it's all for the wrong reason. Jungle, on the other hand."

"After wanking to drum and bass I can never be bothered to do jungle afterwards; seems somewhat superfluous."

"But definitely massive."

"Touché, you cunt."

Hours in time and dozens of units pass by and for the next two or three hours we cross off the list of cocktails, smoking endless cigarettes.

"So what did you think of Steph? She was asking after you the other day."

"Who?"

"Steph, my mate, you were just talking to her the other night. Blue dress."

I remembered but didn't want to let him know, "Steph, Steph- big tits? Blonde?"

"Yeah right."

"Oh right? Asking after me was she? She's alright I suppose, uh really, really nice girl. Where's she tonight?" Somewhere in the back of my mind a memory of cheap bleached blonde hair coiled around my fist, directing her mouth and throat onto my cock, layered with saliva and lipstick that may or may not be part of a fragmented memory of the aforementioned Steph. After awhile they all look the same. Either way I am loathe to go over old ground.

"London this weekend, going to Benidorm on Sunday night so she's gone for a few weeks. Works in a bar out there, she'll get fucked six ways 'til Sunday."

"Jesus man, tell me about it, she's a bit like that eh?"

"Ah well y'know, she just loves it up her. Got serious daddy issues."

"Haven't they all? What sh'we have next?"

There are only two groups of people in this place; one, Pete and myself, and a group of about sixty or seventy people commandeering the rest of the space. At first they don't look like they're together, but the way people are moving around, literally talking or acknowledging most or all the others in the group shows that it must be a work party, or some professional engagement. I go to the bar because it's my turn.

Navigating through the tightening crowd I feel like an anchor swaying against a storm leagues above my head, just impactful enough to move me gently left and right, but soft like a bear, dense as the weight of the moon. I somehow win a position at the bar once again and begin the process of ordering drinks. Looking around at the faces surrounding me, swarms of desperate men, hard-ons at the ready, dick in hand, primed to fuck all these girls at the blink of an eye. If only they knew. I feel an impatience that overwhelms the attentive efforts of some cunt across from me and the bargirl comes to me and I order four more. The moment over, I reacquaint myself with the localized members of my current ecosystem, two girls, talking while smoking, vibrating at just the base frequency required while talking yabberous bullshit.

"...but he's been there for about a year now, I don't even know what he does," says one of them to the other.

"Well, he's a dick, a fucking waste of space."

I stand for a moment channeling Sunday afternoon heroes of Riggs and Murtaugh, McClaine and Columbo. But they do not take the bait. I have already lived the conversation anyway. Someone was supposed to do something that this idiot thought otherwise of, and then the other idiot concurred so we decided to just say what-evs and have us a girls night out. Better not to give them the satisfaction. Returning to Pete we sat on plastic chairs salvaged from the carnage of the gathering, drinking ourselves further into the haze of which so familiar. Reaching into my left pocket I find some Xanax crushed in the plastic wrap from a pack of cigarettes. In the right a moistened bag of just under half an eighth of coke. Yellow and wet with sweat and who knows what else, I look at Pete with scientific intensity.

"Two-for-one, you slag," and crumbled the remains of both bags into our quadruplet of drinks, presenting ourselves with a devastatingly off-menu bar selection.

Barely able to find the words I direct my conversation to explain the impossible stupidity of the people at the bar, but instead crumble into incessant laughter as my face grows red and eyes blaze hot, Pete and I sipping at the two alternating bringers of intoxication, now spangled into the hallucinatory edges of Xanax-ville and cranked back to unreality with apparently Peruvian marching powder. Pete cracked too, and we found ourselves concealed around a darkened corner behind an invisible curtain. Here we were safe, the room much wider and spacious, the people muted and almost washed away by tides that drew forth from the walls and ceilings, below us and within us; dissolving all colour, texture and light. Peeling back this fresh surface of existence until nothing remained but the faint hum of a life spent in indulgence. That one dimension that makes all others futile, for without the dimension of existence, where does the house of the soul reside?

It struck me later, much later, that we'd been in the bar for a few hours, and were incredibly fucked-up. The people were still all there, and joining us were more revelers looking for a night out. I had exchanged a few glances with some girl, some waif-looking anorexic girl with long, dusky blonde hair and that dirty skin I'm so fond of. Just glances though, nothing concrete. My hands shake in spot, yet are cold and limp to the touch. I keep hearing the word "party".

"Pete," I try to say over the drugs, "I think those lot over there, are going on about some party, man."

"Party?" asks Pete, slowly, behind glass and formaldehyde.

"Yeah, they all, I think, work in TV or something, I mean, look at them. Fucking TV cunts the lot. I've heard them going on about a party they're all going to, man, that'd be sweet."

"Party would be- nice change of scene, is it like a proper party and that?"

"Can't say, don't, don't know nothing about it. I just think, I've heard them talking about a party."

"Oh right, sweet."

"Fucking right, mate, this could be a nice night, you know?"

"It certainly seems like that."

I somehow got myself over to the bar and ordered some more drinks, making use of the time next to the group. The storm overhead now battering my anchors weighted to the sea floor, writhing like serpents in a cloud of ferrous oxide. As I stood there waiting, I realised they were on a free bar, and some were already shit-faced. This would hopefully be an easy one. Somehow I manage to channel some prelude to Hammer horror gentry-type.

"Madam, have you been drinking?" I mock say to the blonde. she's wasted, so I jokingly play the concerned elder even though I'm quite a bit younger. She staggers slightly in my direction and I think I see her let out a little burp that was only supposed to be for herself.

"Yes, I have been, so?"

"Well, I must say, I really wouldn't be able to tell unless

you'd just said so; that's a talent right there." She laughs, but not much.

"I'll tell you what, I could do with someone like you to get around my parents; they always suspect me of drinking. If I had you there, you could play the sober one, and I'll look straight by comparison. What do you think?"

"I don't know if I want to meet your parents just yet. But in the meantime, what's your name?"

"Finch, Aldous Finch. Like the bird, and like the Huxley."

"Meg Thorne, pleasure."

"Likewise, charmed."

"Fantastic name, by the way!" She exclaimed, already falling towards me like spinning plates on top of cartoon broomsticks. I grin back, mastered and practiced over the infinite timeline of evolution and procreation.

"I'm thinking of changing it. Abalone Montague or some shit."

The girl laughed and I could already taste her dripping cooch.

Drastic waves of confusion carried us to the party and I eventually found myself carving a line of coke onto the back of a CD from someone's handsome collection. Four perfumed and powdered primadonnas stared back through the plastic hard-shell case and I could no longer read the fine print of song-titles. The party was held at a large house surrounded by woodland set away from the main road down a grassy path with a wrought iron gate and brass horse plate over the fencepost. Following the path toward the house a row of trees hang overhead, leering like perverts. As we got to the party we were now with a group of three others. Meg was there with a couple of female friends, one of which was chatting up Pete who looked like he was prepared to engage with earnest. There was a large garden full of trees and a banquet with all kinds of food, which I helped myself to and never touched, then got myself a glass of punch. After dosing some coke I ventured to explore the party. I hadn't realised how cool the party was until

I opened the door and went into a lobby-type room with a ten foot long table covered in bottles of vodka, whiskey, tequila, wine, and lots of other liquor. People were everywhere. All in early to mid-thirties, but Pete was about twenty-six and I look pretty tired so we probably fit into the demographic quite well. At the table, I go to pour some tequila into another glass and my arm gets burned by a cigarette. I flinch away from it and look at the culprit. A girl. Good looking, and saying sorry now. I smile to satiate my urge for expletives and relax, gravitating my gaze and conversation back to Meg who asks:

"So how do you know Neil?" Neil. Must be his party.

"Oh Neil's like a friend of a friend, really. I'm good friends with... someone he... worked with once." I think I'm doing okay.

"Oh, what was the job?"

"The job? Oh man, you know how it is, freelancing. I think it was, it was a while ago, about maybe six months, no, a year ago? God, time flies- So it... was... Oh. What was it?" I faux-curse at myself. "Well I forgot the name, but they we're colleagues."

"A year or so ago? I think Neil was, oh there he is, hang on,"

"No, wait-" Fucking fantastic, Neil's here.

"Claire, darling, so glad you could come."

"Neil, I'd like you to meet someone," the man walks over, an older, rather smug looking man. I think he's an actor. "This is Aldous... Fitch?"

"Finch." I impossibly remember. I recognise a few people from TV.

"Aldous Finch- aren't you an actor?" Asks Neil.

"Aren't we all in this dirty old game? But yes, no, it is the same and I am he! For my sins!!" I take another step down the road of deceit to enable this party to continue.

"What were you up to a year ago?" Meg asks Neil, pointedly.

"God. What? A year ago? Um, suppose working on

Odious Heart, that Beeb thing that never was."

"Odious Heart. Of course." she says, then looks at me, "What does your friend do?"

"I'm not sure, some low hanging fruit gig. Lifts a lot of lights and the such like. Skinny guy, northerner. Always kept himself to himself, a quiet man in general." Surely if I keep making words happen they would leave me alone.

"Oh you mean Andrew, uh... Sandley, Sandbourne I think?"

"That's it, of course, me and Andy are *good* mates, i-is he here yet?" Thinking fast.

"No, I believe he's still in Spain, doing that fucking lion in a box commercial." Say Neil, as he waves at someone else across the room.

"Cor blimey," I pose, "Spain..." Thank fuck, this conversation may be bookended. A woman bumps into Neil and grabs his attention and he reacts with a jump and a hug that makes him walk away to meet some people.

"Lord Finn!" She declares "King of the airwaves!" And gives Neil a flamboyant curtsey.

Neil looks me in the eye as he begins to improvise lines lifted from the stageplay of his own life, unwritten, in production. "Well which is it then, wench? Lord or King? For Christ knows a man cannot be both!"

"By any other word: Queen!" She replies, and they fall into a deep embrace, kissing each other on the cheeks and pinching them pink.

I turn away from the Finn and continue to harry and charm Meg.

"Yeah me and Andy go way back," I speak in safety and relative solitude.

"I might've met him once; he's like a... Scouser right?"

"Yeah, yeah, that'll be him. Old skinny Andy from Liverpool. He's a proper Scouser. More Scouse than a car on bricks." I could thank porno shop John for that one, "I'll probably see him when he gets back; doing a commercial for some car brand or pharma company, forget which. Spain though, all expats and tan-lines."

"For the main part, yes," She says and I have to change the subject since I am running out of generic nonsense.

"So, I noticed Neil called you Claire, what's that, some pseudonymous night-time super hero alter identity or tax loss?"

"No, no, that's my *infamous* middle name: Margaret *St. Claire* Thorne." I stifle a laugh but she's not so we laugh.

"St. Claire? That's a beauty. Aldous Albuquerque Winchester Finch the fourth; that's all I've got."

"Is that true?!" Meg gasped.

"Yes, well, except Albuquerque, Winchester, Dunkirkton etcetera."

"It's still better than *fucking Saint-Claire*." And we laugh again.

"I don't know about that," I counter with merciless charm.

"Oh you think?" She asks, referring to her touchy middle-name and not quite *getting* my incisive dialogue.

"No, I mean: fucking Saint Claire, being I'd much rather be *fucking Saint-Claire*."

Like the first bubbles that break the surface of water left to boil, many more follow as critical mass is reached in the decision-making cubicles that inhabit the office of her mind.

Soon we are pushing each other's clothes aside to reach genitals and kissing with frantic excess. Neil Finns' marble sink is heavy and solid, cold and brutal. She leans on her elbows, pressing against my crotch with her bottom, then produces a bag of white powder from her jeans which she empties part of onto the surface and using a credit card makes four thick lines that reflect double in the mirrored stone. She does one line, then one for me. A streak of chemical burn that fucks my nose, much more painful than last time for some reason, but only still for a second until the obligatory dab-more beckoned. Someone was arguing outside, a couple, one girl was screaming at this poor guy who's just standing there going "what?" but she's looking pretty hysterical. Meg gives me the note we're using to snort the coke and I see she's done more lines so I do two, then she hits the last two and now my brain blasts out of the back of my head and unconsciously directs hands over stomach, small of the back, spine, breasts, throat, ear, hair. She's got plenty of coke left, and I intend on using as much of it as I can.

"This party... I live quite close here, y'know?"

"You want me to go home with you?" Her eyes are wide open and her pupils are dilated while she's looking right at me, but it's not an outrageous question, more of a statement of fact.

"Yes, I do, come home with me."

"Okay, when are we leaving?"

Outside the air fogs with our breath, we still kissing through the garden and see the unfortunate guy with his wailing girlfriend somewhere across under a bunching of fairy lights, mascara running, his head limp and lowered in misery. Looking through the large glass wall I see Pete talking to someone and consider that I should say I am leaving, but then have a cold feeling of doubt and suspicion and conclude instead to simply vanish with something close to not even a trace.

The Asian taxi driver seems barely flustered at my fingering of Meg's juicy cunt on the ragged back seats and as my index reaches a point of no return she stops and looks at me, exclaiming "I know we've only just met but I feel a real-"

"connection." I offer, correctly, and without pause, returning to the preludes of orgasm.

A frozen wind barely touches us as we exit the taxi, somewhat of a walk still from my door giving us plenty of time and opportunity to fondle close to fucking as we stumble up the street. I'm a dog herding a lost sheep, corralled against the red arching brick-work and piss-soaked walls teeming with dark green moss born of that same effluent waste. She's so wasted she can barely stand. Across the canal at the edge of a bridge some hundreds of yards away my eyes meet with that of a lonely hooker, kicking herself and wondering if she is filling her own particular niche with enough *gusto*. I may be contemplating her sucide more than she is. Through the safety of plate glass and magnetic locks, we scale the building in the darkened cherry-veneer lined glass elevator and I eat her cunt ever-so briefly between floors E and 6.

Caught there in that small room, rising up through space and time I drank in her scent, as it coursed through me, cleansing and narcotic.

Finally I open the door to my flat, light flooding the rooms ahead almost like dominos falling in a dream and her clothes are loosened from her body and I chase her into the living room.

Our games turn more physical. She uses her nails to write a discourse over my back, while I tighten the grip around her throat and so on. It's hard to say where she enjoys being grabbed more: the neck, the face, the pussy, the hair. We fall into a coital position, I from behind and coupled like train cars, hanging on the branch.

Across the arm of the sofa we tumble, her bottom shining red as my hand delivers blow upon blow at just the right velocity to achieve a thousand goals at once. We go onto the sofa, over the arm and fuck like dogs, and I lap the soaking cunt again, for more than good measure, my face engorged in fleshy delight.

As we enter abandonment our bodies intertwine, sharing sweat that bleeds and falls like dew shivered from the leaves of a mighty tree at daybreak. Her pussy clenches around my cock as we change positions, my back now rigid against the corduroy arm, her face to mine, as we glean upon each other with a base intensity known only to the truly debauched, a people so rare as to be thought extinct.

Crawling away across the two-grand rug she mock fights and then gasps as my cock forges new channels within her, and so I follow, marching on reddened knees over the same rug and repeating the act while confronted by the mirror image of a raging drug addict, bent on the ecstasies of life, shadowed overhead by the haunting grip of steel wrought bridges and rain soaked brick.

The speakers grumble as the volume has been turned up beyond comfort, drum machine madness very unlike what I normally listen to but that doesn't matter. I climb on top of her grappling with a ridiculously hard cock which she cries out for, as tear-shaped shards of reality begin to crumble from my existence- a reality dissolving before me yet preserved by a swirling mass of flesh and fluids, forever burning and hair gathered like roots flowing in channels like an extraterrestrial Ordnance Survey rendering.

Cocaine spills out onto the table-top and I push her face onto it, then join her to increase my dose and regroup in this reality. There is little feeling left as my knees force hers up over her stomach, contorting into a torso shaped hole built purely for fucking. Her nails drag down my chest hard and I suddenly see my mother closing the door on me, my father barely looking me to say goodbye. They thought I was asleep. I am reminded of them now for what? A face half seen, like dreams but awake, like nightmares but too real. A biting pain as she does so encourages my hand to return to her throat and choke her hard, rocks of salt forming between my fingers and her neck. Muddling the yellowed coke onto my thumb and finger tips I administer it directly into both of her openings, and the ride went on. Fingers are hooked so to dose her deep inside I take her shaking as a sign that she loves it, and I push further and harder until she might break in half. Something inside her opens up and I seem to find even more ground to plunder, turning her again like a rag doll and throwing her to the floor by way of the coffee table which moves only slightly yet spills the ashtray across the face of it.

My soaking wet hair whips back onto my neck and I feel demonic forces rise within, unlike my usual dalliances with sexual integration. A presence of something darker; red eyes that glow through smoke at the tattered edges of my soul.

Her face now pushed onto the floor as her body jerks and spinal cord arches into the corners of a spiral while her words remain locked firmly in tongues. I feel the dropping of bombs from thirty thousand feet onto tiny villages of helpless people, laughing as the tears fire through their paper thin faces and fire tears through the rest, leaving nothing but ashes and smoke.

The writhing continues and I need to hold this angle for just a few more strokes as the bridge opens and my hand locked in her hair feels a pool of her saliva and the sound of her throat scraping innards dancing with my guttural moaning in some psychotic waltz. It coats the walls, pouring from wounds so deep within the soul that you might just walk out of your body. I swell with the last push of a death squad running rampant through lawless lands armed with scribbled orders and heavy munitions.

She must be coming too as her head turns backwards and dirty blonde curls mat print black against the floor. I choke her throat from behind but let the ground do the work.

We unite in a crescendo of screams: horrific tones that belong to no scale, yet in tandem open up realms of darkness unseen to mortal men. Through the gaps in reality step demons of past and future, sharp tongued and carbonized claws. My own hand gestured into this shape and finds the girls face, once, twice, and a third: just enough to encourage orgasm über alles.

Up the walls and across the ceiling creep shadows of the demons, rubbing their scaly hands together in anticipation, teeth gnashed and blooded in preparation of the receipt of yet another lost soul.

At the apex of all things is the release and glorious descent from madness that keeps the king high in the loneliest of castles. My heart races even after the finish line and innumerable beads of sweat dance in the air as they fall onto the floor, catching glimpses of my stomach and legs.

Looking at her body through blood red eyes I can see abrasions and dark patches forming all over. Her cheeks and most of her face has gone red from rubbing against my two day old beard and I look at her eye and there's a blood vessel looking back, leaking inside her eyeball. The coke and ecstasy reduces and heightens any feeling or sensation I have, and sliding my cock into her arse without warning buckles her body and she looks like an epileptic in final death throes. I try and shake my head but end up putting my hand around her throat and holding tight against the floor while my other hand is putting two of its fingers inside her cunt and vigorously masturbating, at the same time lifting her up by the hole and moving my fingertips to stimulate a pleasure response which she gives in the form of screams and sobbing. The poppers are out and I take a big hit, then hold it for her. It takes three seconds for the water to start flooding my eyes so I take another hit and it's like air, so normal, so necessary: and so I take another, then her, and another for me, and I'm drowning fast so need some support and then there's this body in front of me looking back, scared to death or drowning in heaven and my naked sef curses her for being born and take a fiery palm and wash it through her face and there's a noise, some cloudy record or a shout from next door but its her retching out some kind of language but her lucid state drives me further towards the edge then I look at her half-closed eyes again and see the blood pissing all over the inside of it, which I don't know why but slap her again but she's so used to it she can barely feel it anymore. Her body moves in spasms beneath mine and I arch my back, feeling my spine crack and the sweat that trickles forth cooling on a breeze and I still try to hold it back but it's impossible and the girl is coming so much that she can hardly move and I cannot hold it back any longer the valley of burden waiting to fall so I let go and release and feel the hot pinch of knife twisting inside my stomach, releasing black salt bleeding from the memory of an ocean at the final sunset but only just so real as I can imagine it, and the earth dissolves and all things are silent and there is but one moment and that moment is now.

When I wake up she is bleeding. Concern too late as wounds have already started to darken and coagulate. The blood is cold. Jarred into panic I shake her and seek some response. Her neck loose, limp, blood I see now, blood, blood-spilling from a crack in the skull. The coffee table. The ashtray. One. Or the other.

T HE DARK WOODS

You and your eye through webs that rise
On empty breeze. A home so subtle,
Smile within silence, God cries for fear
While the spider lays watching.

You must believe in the good guys if you are to stand a chance in society. Even those with a nihilistic position have imbued within them the notions of good and evil. The dark and the light. It is the only way, and completely built around perspective, as those thought bad by some are considered good by themselves and so on. Like a frog on a hot plate, circular jerking, strained, grimaced, yearning, leaping and dreaming to fathom an impossible practice of life whereby one would eternally contort in a gymnastic act of egregious, despondent, egoistic self-defiance. It is our nature to possess, to conquer, to kill. It is not patriarchy, or societal, not the reds nor the blues, or home or away but simply the nature of we poetic beasts to see to the horizon and desire to take it all. The club is the club. The fallacy of righteousness, a trick pulled on mankind since words were first written. Whoever wrote those ancient allegories for existence, those designs for life, knew that man could not simply be allowed to evolve naturally. Here was his finger, yellowed in age, cautious yet imputent furnished to provide whatever type of guiding touch, a set of reins to direct his feet, a whip at hand to discipline fault. Notions of Heaven and Hell were enough to strike fear until late, however, Hell seems to have been found much upon earth for many souls cursed to live in this age. For this we will weep, the veil of contrition, for God and His shadow, stake purchase yet otherwise hath fallen and we are exposed newborn and virgin, naked against the harsh realities of our own truth, a bitter moment where we become both hero and villain, letting blood flow as if it were rain water to be suckled upon by the natural order, while daggers sharpen, cloaked behind a curtains practiced empathy, duplicity in ending of all gracious palms and of smiles in the sideways part edges of truth.

In keeping Jones with illusions of eternity I decide to play along. My attention caught firmly on picking what looks like a scab from my knee which I soon realise is her blood. As if cued by the chime and sliding action of a set of elevator doors, I look up and there she is, bow-legged, bloody, silent and caustic.

"Great!" I exclaim in her direction. This party has definitely taken a dive. I am inspired to rise and walk over to her, we now somehow separated by almost the length of the room.

The closer I get to her the more my hands begin to shake, to the point where I am standing over her almost retching in spasm.

Around her shoulders I kneel, cradling her head, loose and irregular, like a child's doll. Her skin is clammy, cold. My hands move across her body and I check her genitals, still wet. Her face rests uneasily against the rug, pushing her eyelid shut but the other one stares through a marbled ribbon of bloody, burst capillaries. The pupil is dilated and unresponsive as I check her pussy once more for signs of life. Negative.

The dust now settling, the room is now an epitaph to my increasingly probable incarceration. Focusing through tears that have been falling forever, there is the signature of rape and murder. Clothes torn and strewn about, a broken glass, a broken lamp, blood soaked into the rug, spattered up the wall, across the couch, over the coffee table. Everything must go.

Over the coffee table is a bag of cocaine with the best part of a gram left. Some ketamine left on a book about birds on the dresser in the bedroom almost magically appears before me, and I take all of the drugs I can.

Far from earth I look to the sun for solace, in this place neither risen nor fell. A pure and honest star, tar black against the eye. Her arms are long and with tender fingers she carries me, held aloft like birds over the ocean, jagged rocks splitting oars and the long forgotten ghosts of men that dared to dream they could engage with that elemental temper. The crack and the trickle of water through corroded copper piping that connects the radiators to the central heating system adds another dimension to the stage play before me and I start to cry. The patter of rain against the windows, having loosened themselves from clouds once again, and the sky that looms grey and like tombs in the late-afternoon, a cloudy, blackened air, create tiny taps that perforate the silence and bring me to a light of day even colder than usual. I wake in my own bed, tired, twisted, and yet almost at ease. For a few blissful seconds before full consciousness I remember to forget my problems and breathe. Eyelids closed softly against swollen flesh. Quivering hairs and warm fluid, spacious dreams of something I can't quite remember trickle around my mind but the raindrops are heavy and bring me unease, thoughtlessly kicking away the cinder blocks providing foundation to the edges of sleep, rusted and stolen now tumbling around me like so many ignored bells chiming at daybreak and all of a sudden I am allowed to remember the why and the when. A grotesque blood-orange stain grows across the sheets born from the poorly bandaged wound on my wrist. There is a softness in my eyes and ears. I rub them then refocus to see the girl on the floor. No matter how much I try to blink her away she just lays there, mocking me.

Retreating to the highest precipice of the mattress held

high by Swedish designed cheap bed frame I leaned over the bedroom, searching for hope, in the far distance cold limbs and dark blood, a reminder of the dead girl laying in wait before me. Her face, like one of those old paintings that seem to follow across the room, jawned against the floor, creasing into some ghoulish grin imprinted headward, the thought I cannot shake, caught in the throes of those final dread moments. Heaving and cracked like the smiling half-side of those show-pony types.

The silence is too much. I take a changed look, and find the obscenely expensive record. I have to take stock. I hate to crash the party but I've got some bad news. But first let's enjoy this moment, that one before insanity, that suspended moment before yet another life of duplicity, deception, disguise, deceit.

Curly dark hair, now clotted with blood, making peppered belts of rich crimson that daub streaks on the floor as I drag her across the room. Three times I try to move her body, desperate to hide her, three times she slips through my fingers, rooted in place like a great stone, yet fleeting as an ocean breeze over green fields. I get as far as the couch and stop for a cigarette.

The room looks just big enough for her to be laid out flat. Her head seems disconnected while I maneuver her torso around the door and into the space. On the side of her right eye, a blood vessel has ruptured so violently that half of her eye is now lacquered marble red. I carefully move her down onto the floor, her legs askew in front of me. Across her body dried flakes of a cocktail of bodily fluids, drugs. As I extinguish the cigarette I see one of hers from last night. Matted red lipstick against wrinkled paper, I begin to consider the other evidence laying around. It becomes hard to concentrate as I look around the room, a single half-opened eye staring beyond me. First thing is first.

Across the room near to the front door is a small closet, home to coats and brooms and shoes and what not. I kick them out of the way and make a space on the floor, then lay down the rug as bedding and drag her body inside. The room is barely big enough and her legs are folded up as she is laid face down. There's a point of no return that I think I am long past but a slight consideration of options includes calling the authorities and explaining away the misadventure. "I swear, officer, just another accidental death during sex. Standard day-to-day choking, beating, grievous bodily harm and murder." Consideration over. I can't remember her name. Sandra, Sarah, Sonia; Sah or Seh or Soh sound. Shit. Her purse must be around here somewhere.

Back in the living room I was stopped in my tracks by the sight. A real show full-of-horror. Staggered and retching, I fall to my knees, dehydrated, and catch my breath holding onto the corner of the coffee table. Directly across from me where the rug once was the primary blood stain. They'd likely call that Ground Zero or evidence #1. Tracing backwards in time, across the table, over the rug, onto the couch I find her jeans on the floor, knotted by a shoe. A bracelet embossed in platinum or silver perched between the floor and skirting board. An earring elsewhere. One shoe caught between splinters, a picture frame broken, inverted beneath the erudite coat rack that had held so many wayward girls purses and pashminas before.

No bag, no purse, not even a phone. Impossible. I stop for a second and try to retrace my steps: we left the party, got a taxi, kissed, I paid the cab then she got out and I walked her upstairs then I remember grabbing her arse against the denim, middle three fingers pushing her through the door into the corridor and up to the second floor while we dry humped against the mirror in the elevator, swiftly down the corridor through the door against the wall where she dropped everything.

Margaret. Meg, Meg, Meg. Margaret-Saint-Claire-Thorne. *The famous Saint-Claire*. Not too famous, I hoped. Stooped over her now like a TV detective but naked and covered in blood.

Against a surface of cold skin lining up credit cards, business cards, letters and receipts on her body, dead cell phone by her side I find that she works for the TV station, marketing department. Shit. That means she's going to be missed at work on Monday. She has paper invoices for numerous charity organisations folded into little squares that I lay out on her naked stomach, all bruised and scratched. If I lose her body what else is there to tie me to her? That taxi driver? Possibly. He was... Asian... I think, didn't speak much English as I recall, or he just didn't say. We're just a couple of white people, he doesn't care about us, so maybe he's not so much of a worry. When did her phone die? I don't recall her gaping into it in the cab ride over, one would assume that would be the case should it have been charged. To be sure I put the cellphone into my industrial strength food blender and pulverize it into a million pieces of precious rare earth metals mined by third world children. Her friends? I can't really remember how we left, I think I just left, I was there with... Pete, and I didn't say goodbye. He didn't see me leave with her. Not categorically. Anybody else? I can't think of any. Any at all. Anyone but Aldous Finch. His name arises and I almost forget myself until remembering that I am him and all the same he is me. And so the other, the foil, my liege and my master, my arrow and my quiver. There seems to be time to think of natural questions like where to put the body. My breath is slow and cautious. Beads of salt, dry as deserts and hardened into crystals on my face, back and chest. Suddenly the silence is broken as a tiny tin-can rattle of a cough utters from her throat and my body jumps and scatters cards and paper all over the place but her neck arches and her head drops down into place and I'm back, way back against the wall but slowly I look at her face as a whole for the first time and then catch the slightest movement in the arm. *She's alive!* Christ, she's alive. For the first fractions of a second I smile but then this new reality dawns, more terrifying, more real. She remains motionless on the floor and I go over to her, touching her face with the back of my hand but no reflex. She's breathing slowly, sleepwalking through catatonia, brain perhaps damaged, starved of oxygen, choked beneath the raging waters of my bitter ocean break. I look at the gash on her head, just on the left rear side of her skull and surrounded by a swollen mass of purple tissue. The wound is still wet, with a moat of dried blood matting hair to the skull.

I dial the first two emergency numbers then stop. She *is* alive, currently, and currently I am guilty of terribly grievous bodily harm, rape, torture, mutilation- who can say what else? I would be hung, without question.

Closing the door I gently lay a blanket over her and tie her with extension cord cabling. In the elevator I look at the mirror and see the oily smudge of her face, profiled against glass that I polish with haste.

The canal creaks in the day, insects buzzing, the sun beating down and making me sweat under the stupid mass of clothes I put on to cover my body. We... I, didn't kill... her... I just, she... then I couldn't stop it, it was... it was in the heat, of, the... moment. The only person who saw me was the taxi driver. The only person that saw us was the taxi driver. In the club. At the party. Once she's missing, her friends. Her colleagues. She works in marketing. Her links to television. She's in that little room in my flat. She's not dead. She's in a coma. She's in a coma. She might never come out of it. Should I finish her off? I can't. Should I leave her at the hospital? I don't know what she'll remember. We didn't talk for that long, maybe an hour, on and off, so, we were both fucked, wasted, she might not remember. I could get a car and drop her off. I've seen it in films. Just drop her at the front. She's in a coma, I'll drop her off, and they'll help her and then investigate. They'll investigate and it might get into the paper. The police will be involved. They'll do tests on her. She bit me. She cut me, she has my blood on her body. She has my hair and my sweat and come on her and in her. Her fingerprints, fuck, her blood is all over my flat. I need to make her vanish. I need to destroy any connection between us. I can't find everyone who saw us, but if I just totally get rid of everything we had together in my flat: clean, hide and cover. That's what's important. If the flat is clean, without a trace, then everything is good. I can throw away her bag and purse and other effects, burn them all. Then that's gone. Back into ashes. I need to shampoo the floor, no, get rid of the carpet. I think there are floorboards underneath. I'll just reimburse the estate agent. Then if I wipe down all the walls, check to see if there's any cameras in the lobby downstairs, which I don't think there are, then that's the flat sorted. Alex, she's not dead. I know. What if we took her away and dropped her miles away? I don't know. She's still there, she's still just in a coma, half dead. She might have brain damage, did you know that? Brain damage, yeah, well if she does she won't remember anything about it then, will she? Possible, but there's always the chance she doesn't- and then she remembers. I know. Right. So? So you don't know,

"So, I don't know: get rid? It's your fucking problem, man."

"Isn't it just? It's my problem; I'll do with it what I think. Take her to a hospital."

"She'll fucking remember. If you're going to make your own choice, then at least don't make the wrong one."

"Right, right." "Well?"

An old homeless man looks at me when I kick a can into the piss-filled canal. Clothes, flyers, condoms, syringes litter the place and all I see are puddles of piss and dark blotches from blood spilt in a robbery or someone else's murder, I'm walking on the resting place for probably dozens of people. If she was found here...

"It would just be a murder on the canal. I could dump her in the river."

"You're going to have to finish her."

"I know, just fuck off, alright?"

I can't think straight. The taxi driver, the people at the pub, her friends, Pete, cleaning the flat, throwing shit away, killing her, fuck.

"So you kill her, dump her, the police find her, identify her, then what?"

"Then they go to her family. Her family breaks the news to her colleagues and friends. They start to think about what happened and where she is." The arty house. The stories I told. The old queen trying to inch one up in me.

"Do you think things might be easier if they didn't find her?"

"It... yeah. If the police don't find the body, then it's a missing person. Just another missing person. But then she'll be presumed dead, assumed, perhaps. Anyway, they'll know she's dead. People will still try and remember what happened."

"But if the police have no body, they only have witness reports of her leaving the party absolutely fucked with some random guy. And also, to assume is to be a fucking idiot and get fucked over somewhere down the fucking line."

"Yeah, I am just a random guy. I'm Alderly Dent or something, a man with no name. If they don't find her body, she left with a stranger. But there's bound to be some busy-body nosy cunt or camera we got filmed by."

"True, so what can you do to take yourself away from this problem? Get rid of her, and make sure that if they find her, they don't recognise her."

"Yeah..."

A kindly lady looks up from her crossword over half moon glasses as the bell rings in the ironmongers announcing my arrival. I decided upon the local do-it-yourself depot so as to avoid hardwired security cameras at the larger chain stores.

"Afternoon love!" She smiles and is bludgeoned with the force of my misery, her own smile quickly running like wet paint over ice when she sees my face, haunted by the infinite demons of shame. My body aches and arms feel as if they carry lead weights as I pick and scour the store for useful items, loading many up into a steel trolley reserved for delivery drivers and service professionals.

Ringing up the goods, the kindly old lady enquires:

"Anything else?" And I pause in thought.

"Drain cleaner. About, a gallon I think?"

"A gallon?! My that's a big drain!"

"Huge. And full of blockages."

"Okey dokey."

Returning home the sun had cooled into a glowing coal mirrored off the surface of a vast desert that swallows all mankind. I drop the bags full of cleaning products onto the sofa and place the new hacksaw, ball hammer and duct tape on the table, next to the bloody corner. The flat is rank with the stench of fear and blood. I open the windows and the air sits still, a dead weight. The door is still closed, with the chair still propped up behind it, still stopping it opening. I lift up the ball hammer and hold it half way up the handle. The air is so heavy, my body feels so disgustingly rancid and it's only going to get worse. I walk past her underwear and stand in front of the door and listen quietly for a few seconds. Nothing. Un-wedging the door carefully, I tighten my grip on the hammer and feel my sweaty palms rubbing chalk into the black rubber handle. The door handle turns slowly and a lump in my throat, almost a gag reflex is starting to make itself known but I persevere and shake my head. I open the door and a crack of darkness escapes, and it's still quiet, so I open the door all the way and her credit cards and purse is still there but somehow she's not.

"Fuck."

Just then a length of hardwood smashes me good and well in the side of the face and head and I fall over, hitting myself in the knee with the hammer and now my delayed hearing recognises her screams and she's coming towards me now, naked covered in bruises and cuts and scratches and blood on her shoulder with matted hair sticking to it and heaving my baseball bat in two red hands so I swing the hammer and it cracks her in the shin and it's a hard one and the scream is horrible but I swung so hard the fucking hammer spilled out of my hands so as she falls I scramble to get on top of her but the bat comes for me again and I hold out my arm and the pain takes about five seconds to register by which time I've gotten out of her way and me getting over to the hammer and my forearm fucking kills, it feels broken the fucking pain shoots right up my arm and skewers my spine and fingers and I can't move my left hand but grab the hammer with my good right hand and she's staggering for the door and now I realise why she's still here if she's awake; I dead locked the front door when I went out and now its open, and I'm not allowed to let her leave so I vault the table and run after her but she runs past the small table behind the couch leading to the front door and picks up an unwashed, empty cereal bowl and turns around and goes to slam it in my face but I block it with my right hand but it just smashes over my wrist and a solid shard of porcelain slices open my wrist and all I can see is white skin underneath an inch deep gash with a dark blue vein traveling through it then the blood starts to run and is loud and destructive, thick and black and and cakes over my arm and runs down "YOU FUCKING BITCH!", and my fist hits her again in the jaw this time, spraying blood over her and I but I'm not finished because the pain just rushes towards my elbow and up to my shoulder that would make it hard to move but because there are litres of adrenaline pumping around my body and I can't feel a thing and I hit the girl hard in the face again and this knocks her down. "I'm sorry I'm trying to make this quick!" I try to explain, my best British fop-accent mixed with video nasty scenery and she's face-up on the varnished wooden floor that I use as a tool to try and break open the back of her head and her moans get weaker and weaker and the cornflakes dried onto the floorboards are disguised by her blood, coloured not only red, but purple and yellow yet somehow she continues, weak limbed but hits me in the bottom of the chin with the end of the bat she scrambles from somewhere and then turns me over with a leg around my foot throwing her whole body weight onto me. Ordinarily I'd be able to overpower here but this is not an ordinary day. Her knee pushes down onto my bloody arm and the pain is almost nothing to the fear of blood pissing from my arm, that, too pressed down by her knee as she scratches and claws like a winged bird. My body surges with adrenaline and my right arm forces its way out of the grip and slides against the thick bloody mass but my vision is turning cloudy and somehow this would be the most just ending to my life and my hand is reaching out but it finds nothing so I just clench my fist and throw it into her mouth a few times for good measure and she rolls off me as I roar words at her in attack then it's me to dominate, ignore then pain in my arm and grab the hammer. Our eyes meet for the last time and I remember jokes the night before. The punchline is far too late as the hammer comes down and stiffens her whole body, sending it into spasms and a silent, blood soaked wail whimpers across the threshold of the window, falling flatly onto the grumbling of diesel engines and curse words uttered from beneath the arches. Four or five good connections and she moves no more.

The sun begins to set as the sky turns to glorious umber; a fire in the clouds, ravaging the heavens, smoking the angels out from their hiding place, vulnerable now to the hand of the night.

It seems almost trivial to use the toilet at this point as I helplessly piss myself, barely the strength to open my eyes let alone crawl to the bathroom. The road ahead seems harder now, with sharp corners and death-black edges. I am become Him whose name draws in shadow.

A handcut marble pipe reminds me of an easy blow job at a house party once but as I think it over I remember it only happened an alternative to my eager efforts for penetrative sex. Maybe not so easy. Maybe none of them were. From the kitchen I get a large knife, and for insurance on insurance I drive it through her chest, straight into her broken heart and then turn the blade. All lifeless sinew and bone, muscle and flesh, meat against the blade, Japanese in its origin and costing as much as is needed to ensure that the dead remain dead.

I am electrified, descending now through ethereal

planes of existence, of morals, of law, of purity. Teeth chipped through violent interaction leave me feeling like a stranger. Grains of enamel roll over each other as my mouth slowly lolls from side to side, some sort of subconscious reflex in identity transformation.

With the new plastic sheet rolled out next to her body I sit on the other side and try not to look at her eyes, which I close like a soldier lost in war as I push her dead weight with one good hand onto the sheet.

Slowly dragging her past the table and into the middle of the floor, a train passes and I hear it loud for the first time since my windows are open and I am reminded me that the world is still outside and that it's morning time and that people are waking. Someone is missing, a puzzle is incomplete. If they were to find her body, they must not be able to identify it. Fingerprints, dental records, tattoos, birthmarks. What else? Eyes, hair, blood. Maybe. At first examination she doesn't have any birthmarks but as I inspect her body further I find a blue star tattooed to her ankle, very discreet. It's genericism eases my feelings of wrongdoing. Using a paring knife from the kitchen I carefully poke the point next to the design and wait for a flinch that doesn't happen. It's surprisingly easy to get the knife in, but the tearing of the skin as I saw through it with the serrated edge of the blade is another matter. The tattoo is now in my hand on a piece of flesh about the size of a shot glass rim and I put it on the table that I've covered in plastic. No more tattoos. Time to move on. I take two rings off her fingers before I start. The saw balances in my hand and I ease it onto her wrist. With one knee on her arm, I rest the edge of the saw against her arm. The teeth clinch against her soft downy hair and puppy-fat flesh. Wide and tall, the saw is made to cut wood and reminds me of class. Involuntary vocational training for a hapless generation of would-be manual labourers, expected to accomplish nothing more than a clean mortise and tenon.

The sight of skin starting to fray against the saw blade makes me wretch on an empty gut, devoid of food, water, even bile. I might die if I continue in this state so I decide to nourish myself.

A recent grocery purchase garnished with leering eyes over heavy chested checkout girls and magazine covers brings me to life once again. Starting from the stove I fry some diced bacon and chicken for a spaghetti dinner. Using only eggs and heavy cream, salt and pepper for the sauce, I add spring onions, garlic and spinach and dress with fresh basil and drizzle some much-too-expensive olive oil to finish. Returning to the lounge with the dish and a glass of wine I sit on the couch and throw a blanket over Margaret's body while looking for some appropriate dinner time viewing. I'm lost in the commercial break void, synchronized across many channels. Finally some scripted entertainment in the form of another faceless American situation comedy. The sound of canned laughter is a welcome retreat from the silent screams still reverberating around my rooms. As I gorged on the plate it was as if I was eating my first meal. The taste, the texture, the dance with the wine releasing explosive elements of taste and flavour.

"Cheers." I say, hopefully in the direction of the long-lost spider in the wall. Without response I substitute my salutation with the corpse on the rug. The actors on screen are saying "duh" back and forth, back and forth. It seems to go on for a while. When they finally finish saying "duh" the credits have rolled and the fevered pursuit of sales continues with a commercial break. My plate is now empty, I finish the wine and pour another glass, correct myself for digestion and pick up the saw to continue.

Anyone who says that murder is the easy way out has never had to dispose of a body. Certainly not like this. Blood doesn't spurt out as I had anticipated, first there is a flurry of white skin like pulling apart wooly-tissue with thick blue veins running through it, the muscle fibres breaking apart like canned tuna fish. It doesn't take long to penetrate the bone and blood jets and glugs of thick red honey held around the wound in large lumps that drop and spit against the sheet. I force the saw and get into a working rhythm, the bone making a high pitched squeaking sound as the new teeth of the blade bite through it. When I get through to the other side the hand just flops over, still connected by a piece of wrist. My stomach is in my throat and I'm glad at least that I ate. I hold it in and take a big glass of water from the tap, downing it in one. The introduction of water reminds me how dehydrated I am and I take another glass for good measure. Rebecca suddenly seems a lot deader to me now. I watched her die, I tried to save her. This was a half-accident, and by half-accident I mean this: I chose what I did. Now Becky's really gone, and I'm never ever going to see her again.

I saw the other hand off quickly, but cutting through the ankles proves more difficult. Such a wonderful construction. I gasp at the true might of the human body as I strain to remove a simple foot. Gushing blood from thick veins weeps flaccidly from the flesh and bone screeching a truly awful tone as flakes of filament, so minute, fall like tiny daggers.

As I vomit into the toilet, a thick string of saliva coated in lactic acid and scant morsels of barely digested food and stomach lining hangs from my lower lip as I submit to the terrible sensation of hell all over me, swallowing my entirety into a black darker than any night, on any world.

Some dark solace reassures me as I am stuck with the thought that this girl has only recently died, and so will not smell too bad for a corpse, or perhaps I had just grown accustomed to the smell.

I get the second foot off and sit them all in a square on her torso. I put her hands over her breasts and her feet on her hips. It looks like a Turner-prize winner, or at least criminally overlooked contender. The light just glimpses through the blinds at the side and casts a series of six lines across the room, one of which runs over the girl.

The hammer hangs loose in my hand, poised over her face. Her lips are swollen closed and cut, scarlet red in colour. I open her mouth with my temporarily paralysed hand and see bloodstained teeth, one already knocked out at the side. My nostrils fill with a softly dead air, as I raise the hammer and strike her mouth, breaking out teeth like icy metal pegs then hit again and again, totally shattering and cracking her jaw to pieces with the ball end. When it's over there are sopping holes where nerve endings hang like burned spaghetti. I can't stop coughing, feeling a terrible pain in my throat. I've been smoking too much and I spit a gob of phlegm into the toilet as I stand in front of the mirror, surveying the spatter of blood over my face and arms and hands and stop crying my eyes out for a moment to look through the person standing before me. See the edges, soft shaded and a glow that fades with night-time. See the lines that make him whisper into memory. See the skin shrivel and bones turn to dust. See him blown across the deserts of forever, a lost soul found in favour of oblivion.

My nails thick with evidence, I wipe them on a pair of blue jeans tossed onto a heap in the floor. In the pocket I feel a plastic bag, and all joy rises up inside me as I realise it's an almost complete gram of cocaine. Weeping as I do so, I carve out the three lines on the flat surfaced ridge of the polished bath not mottled with blood or hair or fleshy parts. The first line levels me, but the second and third enables. Armour builds around my eyes and the tears I cry now freeze into diamonds, dropping and chittering across the floor like excited mice. An air of calm descends and a degree of heat rises through this icy place. The bathroom surrounding me shrinks down slowly, the white walls sliding like glaciers through the lakes of tomorrow, carving out space behind them but pushing everything closer to me. The solid edged porcelain walls warp and melt towards me, coming out of the wall, blocking the door with a mass of dark air and smoke. My eyes squint through the fog, carving images in the plume and becoming surrounded by an inverted sphere of exhaust fumes. Onto the floor I'll go, and crawl to the wall, to the toilet. Toothpaste is knocked over and the advancing walls squeeze bicarbonate soda onto the rubber mat I use to stop falling over. I'm at full stretch and can feel both walls crushing either side, but the more I push them away the stronger they push me back, like a battalion of limpets resisting my every will. I start for the door but decide not to, and just curl up in a ball as it all falls in around me, the roof coming down and now I'm trapped like a dog in a cage screaming for anyone with ears to put me out of my misery and just do it then my body is locked into position by the room, and I can feel blood forcing its way around my body but stopping in my legs and head but I can't even think about that when my bones start to break, slowly bending at first drilling agony into my temples but then shattering almost surprisingly and first its my arms, legs, hips, but then my spine curls involuntarily and it's almost relieving to have my back snapped in two but the reality is that my life is ending one second at a time and running out.

My body becomes translucent and I can walk through walls, which I do so into the lounge once more, the dread scene now made just that slightest edge more manageable through administration of chemical alterants.

As clichéd as mistakes can be, when disposing of a body it is imperative to pay attention to the details most often overlooked. Anonymity being primary. The descent from the corporeal and into the spirit realm. Eliminate all belief in the self to the point that you are not even aware of your own presence. Those around you will behave likewise and not be able to see, remember, or place you in a crowd. You will become the face of dreams, the eyes of a nightmare.

The smell of rain in the air comes through an open window somewhere in the place. Carried up from roads tarred with crude oil, spilled and sprayed from the tens of thousands of vehicles that run these streets. Beneath the bridges pools of black tar spew forth the mutations of a society gone sickeningly wrong. People are capable of such beauty yet time and again reduced to the baseness of desire, the claustrophobic airs of age and addiction.

There is a green meadow inside each mind, a place of

peace of wonder. If you stare at the sun in this place it doesn't hurt your eyes, it just opens the receptors more, allowing more light, more information to flow within. Soon, like a stormy torrent rushing over a dry-rock riverbed, the wisdom of self will be upon you, and erase the fear and loneliness of walking alone in the woods.

But that is then and this is now. For the woods have never been darker. The sun quickly disappears, taking with it the warm smell of rain and imparting instead the monoxides and dioxides and trioxides that rise from the ground as unstoppable silent partners in our deal with death.

Entering the lounge I am presented with a torrid sight, but one born from memory of fact. Facts that must be buried, deeper even than this body if we are to survive.

The mottled blood cakings beneath the pile of limbs that is so horrific I can barely believe it is here while still breathing. Each step and movement is like a great axe dragged across my soul, like fire drawn up from hell and left to burn over me. Having taken her to pieces I study the cuts, and place each in an appropriately sized container, bedded with drain cleaner and heavy on Sodium Hydroxide.

Once the whole body is accounted for and held within individual containers I begin filling them with dense chalk concrete, and allow them to set over the next few days of darkness. The sun must be rising soon.

L AST OF THE TEARS TO FALL

Rambunctious youth, give to me your heart,
Shatter its spirit and drain it of hope.
Pass it me empty, and colder than night,
With my shallow reason I feign love again.

Winter was finally here and all the leaves shrivel into cockroaches and scuttle after cars and the sky freezes and the world sleeps. My wrist stings and is bound heavily by medical tape and bandages. It looked like it had been chopped by a blunt axe straight out of the Stone Age and I was at once fascinated yet afraid of the large cake of blood gathering around the gash. It threatened to fill up and spill over the edges into endless blood.

Seven rocks, lumps of concrete, pallid blocks of sand and gravel packed tightly with matted blood, shards of shattered bone, tissue and tender muscle fibre still wincing even in coldest-death.

No one visits during these days. I sit and wait, eating little and watching for the police. No story was reported even a week later. I'm restless, suffering from insomnia, lethargy, lack of appetite, raging hunger, blank spots in my mind appear and new information is uncovered along with old imaginings and partial memories and creations and days and days. My one point of human contact being a brief meeting with a drug dealer to load up on staples. Ahead of me lay a long journey and, as was normal in any case, I waited for night time to carry out my business. Gone were the days of mindless banter, fits of giggles and jokes that could crack an anvil; now the humour had ebbed away from me, like it was never there to begin with. My thoughts became like milk on a hot day, sitting in the sun, once perfect for bedtime, now curdled, lumpy and sour. A cloud hung heavy over my heart, guilt and shame seeped between my every inch. It takes a special kind of person to conceal a horrific truth, and special drugs to help that person stay that way. My dealer puts me on to a friend selling a cheap car. It is a cash transaction and I go to lengths to thoroughly clean the inside and outside of the vehicle in the underground parking garage reserved for my sparsely occupied building. And so, dear reader, for this section of the odyssey I choose to dose myself with small dabs of MDMA and key-ends of cocaine. In defiance of the moment I allow a momentary smile, but swiftly return to the task at hand.

Still air, the smell of oil and gasoline, dust and metal rises from the floor, lit by hanging lamps hushed overhead. Having cleaned the car I smoke a cigarette and hang my arms through the metal bars that provide a prison-like security to the building, a design trend that has proved incredibly popular in recent years. Although I am below ground level there is still the peak of the railway arches, illuminated by orange street lamps and the passing of headlamps. I know that when the headlamps pause for a moment they are stopping to liaise with the working girls peddling their wares. By some stroke of luck I see a small hand truck, just right to carry my load from the apartment to the garage. A few more dabs of the good stuff encourages me to get upstairs and begin the next course of action. In stark comparison to the horror-show in my home I had painstakingly scoured every surface, scraped every edge and bleached every stain from the various panels, upholsteries, materials and carpets. What could not be cleaned was removed and destroyed: sunk into the canal with the rest of the City's problems.

The last of the evidence to remove was the cherry. Four blocks of solid concrete, each containing body parts of the unfortunate Margaret St. Clair. Even encased in rock I could not rest easy, and made sure to cut away fingerprints, gouge eyeballs, scorch away hair. Even the removed-teeth I had pulverised in my food processor. A certain sadness came over me as I loaded the hand truck, carefully stacking each block so as to create a stable tower. On top of the tower I lay the torso. Looking back over my home I knew that tomorrow would never be the same.

I drive for hours, within speed limits, down the motorway for one then two then three hours. Passing services, stopping at one for a cup of soup, sandwich and a drink.

Sitting in a darkened car park outside the motorway service station I eat and recuperate somewhat. The night is cold but there is little wind to speak of. Time for medication and in efforts to increase my awareness of perils and pitfalls I up the dose of cocaine and hold off on the MDMA. A fresh pack of cigarettes serves as dessert as I start the car for another destination.

Giving plenty of distance between myself and the services I leave the motorway, navigating through ever shrinking roads until painted markings are gone, streetlamps darkened. Driving up a white stony trail I am led to a circular patch of gravel surrounded by thick trees. This feels like the middle of nowhere, and the air hangs heavy with expectation. I go outside and open the boot of the car. Inside is rancid, despite my best efforts to conceal. First to go must be the torso, wrapped first in plastic and last in three cotton sheets. The night pressed in on me and I take some MDMA to ease the feelings of woe and dread. Coddled like a baby I take the body over a hill, with a gallon can of gasoline laid on top, and walk for close to an hour. Eventually I come across a small wood, positioned beneath the brow of a hill, both concealed and yet with open passages to act as a natural flue. I had no water on me and felt the sting of thirst. Almost settling for a cigarette I have a nagging feeling of concern over my saliva and so take a key of coke to settle my nerves. Somewhere a wood pigeon whispers his cryptic poetry. Even though I have enough fuel to burn the body I build a wood frame around it, ensuring that the flames would indeed destroy any trace of the body. The fuel is poured over and around the structure and away from the fire for safe ignition.

The trail burns slowly, soft blue flames licking across its invisible path. As it reaches the edges of the torso it rises in a rapturous crescendo, engulfing the body and setting ablaze the sticks and logs around it. Watching for a minute I make sure the fire will stay the course and then leave quickly.

Thirty miles away the night is darker still, yet the stars even more luminous. Time hastening. I pass through a generic English town in silence at this hour. I am the arrhythmic beat of a lost and lonely heart. Only the rattle of the diesel engine polluting the streets with noise and smoke before it moves on. I leave the centre of town after getting lost then drive out into another wilderness finding a reservoir and car park, stopping in the corner and reclining my chair. I poke around my pockets for cigarettes. My tongue rubbing the back of my teeth and I can feel the furry surface hasn't been brushed in a week. I have the taste of salt and bile in my mouth.

As I light a cigarette a car across on the other side of the car park flashes its lights, two times. I do not respond but there is activity in the place. The car is too far away to make out any details but looking through the window I can make out the shadows of people. I wait and watch and smoke my cigarette, exhaling against closed windows and watching the smoke seek freedom. The weight of the night is on me now, and I'm so tired I could fall asleep. Haven't really slept for four or five days. Opening the window for air, another car enters the car park and aches slowly looking for a space in the vacant lot. I just sit quietly, on my own, smoke drifting out of my window and into the trees that surround me. The car finds a place and once again the air is quiet and still. It now looks like there are four cars in here including mine. The new car begins to flash his lights, once, twice. Then a reply from the one who did me and finally a third car, previously unseen and shrouded in mist rolling in from the wide open fields flashes his light. Movement. An interior light goes on as someone opens a door a crack then it's dark again. I see two figures in the car: a white family saloon, which the man gets out of and goes round the back, checking over his shoulder. He opens up the back door and says something to his partner, then the lights flash twice, two definite beams of light blazing and signaling something for sure because now one of the guys is getting out of his car, the one who shone me. It's one guy on his own, sneakily making a move and walking next to the wall that comes just below head height, camouflaging most things. I adjust myself and throw the end of the cigarette out of the window into a puddle, a small hiss follows the sound of the low mumbling coming from the saloon, back doors wide open and the driver now inside. Taking a small key of cocaine I gear myself up for the unknown as I get out of the car and check the road for anything then the breeze catches me as I walk across the car park.

Three voices: two men, one woman. Laughter and middle-Northern English accents swarm around me. I am wearing blue jeans with a small rip in the front, just south of the pocket and a very expensive plain black Vivienne Westwood t-shirt, covered by a trench coat I got for next-to-nothing in a charity shop. Arriving at the car the rear left door, which I approach first, is closed. The other door peeps a crack of dark light through, given off by the bulbs inside on the roof. I can't see anyone but then a leg kicks out and knocks the door backwards to the bite then slowly swings back on a loose metal hinge. I hod my step but the girl notices me

"Typical, you wait all night for a swinging dick then three come along at once."

The men laugh and the girl cackles, and I step forward, loosening my belt and jeans.

Seeing a reflection from the side of my car, all of a sudden the car park is lit up by flashing blue police light. All panic rises up in me and the police car drives softly towards us.

The sound of hushed cursing comes from the van as the muffling slumps of clothing quickly put back on rides over my ears.

The police car winds down its window next to me.

"Well now, what do we have here?"

Startled and completely frozen by the situation my mouth opens and tries to speak but nothing comes out. Suddenly from behind me a woman's voice.

"Nothing officer just out watching the meteor shower!"

The woman steps out of the van wearing a tiny ripped t-shirt and short mini skirt which she pulls down over her naked arse, then struggles to walk on the gravel below in high heeled shoes that she holds, reaffixing the strap.

"Meteor shower? Where?!" Laughs the officer in reply.

"Up in the sky, silly, where else?!" The woman approaches the police car and stands next to the window. The officer shines his torch onto her face, her years indicated by winding lines from the corners of her eyes and faded tattoos upon her shoulders and upper breasts. He moves the light down over her chest, to her crotch.

"Looks like you lot are up to no good." before rubbing his hands up her legs towards her genitals and fondling them with familiarity. "Oh yes, definitely up to no good."

"No love, just out looking for shooting stars!"

The officer laughs heartily. "Well I've heard most but that's a new one for me!" The girl leans down further and puts her head into the window of the police car. The officer in the passenger seat puts his thumb in her mouth and pulls her towards him as she mimics fellatio.

"Alright then, you lot make sure you stay safe watching these rockets or comets or what-not, but if you're still here in an hour we'll be having a different conversation. Do you understand?"

"Yes thank you, officer, is there nothing I can do for you now?"

The officers exchange a brief glance between themselves.

"Well, I suppose we wouldn't be very good servants to the people if we didn't give you a hand of *some* sort, now, would we?"

"I suppose not, sir!"

The interior light on the police car flicks on as the officer opens the door, stepping out towards the woman, who stumbles back to the van towards the silent mutterings of those inside.

"Hold on, here love." The officer instructs her and pushes her onto her knees, her mouth falling open and hands working for freedom as the officer unzips his trousers and leans back, trying to poke his manhood through layers of black polyester and cotton briefs.

Stepping away to the shadows I pace slowly back to my car unseen, with careful steps over the uneven ground as the second officer approaches the pair for his turn.

Watching her turn from one officer's shriveled cock to another I catch her eye for a fleeting second and there is a flash of recognition in my human form, but so momentary she dismisses it as a trick of the light.

On I drive for the coast, onwards to the end of the world. The car, despite its maladroit appearance and sound, takes off quickly from standing, but at this moment I keep the rev counter low and creep silently away from the car park. Passing beneath rowan and silver birch trees a half moon reflects across the waters of the still and silent reservoir. Too close to call. The fear subsides as I reach another highway and journey on towards an unknown end.

Infinite road appears from the emptiness like it was nothing, rolling rock beneath me moving faster and faster. I'm in control but the weight in the back causes the car to drift slightly if I don't provide constant pressure to the steering wheel so I keep my foot down to balance this particular peril.

Despite the regiment of stimulants I feel myself nodding off at the wheel. I have almost an eighth of coke plus a single gram, which I empty into a bottle of water and shake for the ultimate homemade energy drink.

Nothing on the streets now. My driving has increased its pace and the initial bitter taste of the drink has been replaced by metallic richness and tasty morsels. Occasional taxi cabs pruning fares from the walls like limpets. Towns wash my face in yellow light, slowing me as I pass traffic lights and scattered drunkards on the street adorned by bald heads, knuckle tattoos and short skirts. At a red light I take a little more coke and dab some MDMA, light a cigarette. The streets are now buzzing and alive squirming worms and orange glow. I was in a special place, and yet it was filled with darkness. Ahead of me and reflecting my headlamps, a white skirt and top, tightly wound and draped around a heavily intoxicated woman staggering towards an unknown destination, my mind wandering back to perversion.

"Time and a place, not this time not this place," I tell myself, but console myself with a hasty leer through an open window and continue driving as the light turns green.

Time seems to slow down as the night begins to close. Silent wisps of cloud cross through clear air clinging to the ground for warmth. I reach the southern coast before daybreak.

The air changes its smell and salt and strong winds from across the ocean fill my nostrils, blowing against my face and casting the weakest glimmer of light across the land in the new morning. Small signs pointing ahead of me towards cliff top landmarks. A white pub gleamed through the twilight, stood silent next to a sloping piece of tarmac and a small fence dividing the gravel from the field and edge. To the left another pathway, still large enough for a car, leads to a wooden gate, heavy with morning dew and locked with a rope. Across the following field I reach the edge and put the car in reverse, backing up to the furthest edge.

Trying to stand I can't even feel my legs. The sun breaks across the sea and reflects orange across the water, crashing violently below but so far away as to merely whisper at the hint of a wave. A high breeze shadows over the land, scarring the grass and breaking its back. Opening the boot of the car I evaluate the next step, pacing back and forth from cliff edge to car, finding the perfect hiding place. Below a particular rocky outcrop the waves cut inland, and provide a spot to drop directly into deeper water. I look around and survey the early morning rain beginning to fall on the fields as the sun continues its petulant rise, but a comforting blanket of black clouds paint one side of the sky as coal so I use the moment and begin moving the rocks. They feel heavier than they did before, maybe my body is just getting weaker.

The first stone is the heaviest, but falls with ease and lays the path for the rest.

I carry on wandering along the edge, looking for different pools, but returning twice to the first, seemingly the deepest part. After such a long journey, such terrible times, before I know it the last stone falls and vanishes into black water leaving nothing but a momentary stream of bubbles that pop into nothingness, reflected in the morning light.

Here I stand on the edge with the car behind me and rocks and water below me, two hundred or so feet down. Enough. My bones chill but my mind is wide open and my eyes cannot close but all too quickly they do and now I can just imagine everything, everything. It's too late, though. The heart inside me tries to break through my chest, but it can't and pumps adrenaline and blood and fear and remorse and excitement through my body instead.

The rain beats lightly down, but then all sorts of things

start to happen. The sky stops raining, and pushes clouds out of the way to reveal a golden sun that chases a shadow the size of the world away, washing it all in a light so brilliant it's almost pure. A sunbeam moves down my body over my legs and to the bottom of my feet. Gulls squawk but in the field stands only me and now I realise it is this point I've been waiting for, I have a decision to make. It's as if it is the first real choice I have ever had. Below me crash waves, above me soar birds, ahead of me passes a boat in the distance, behind me I don't know. I grind my teeth like I do in my sleep and lick a series of imperfectly grown molars. I think my eyes have started to cry. A harsh breeze catches me and I am startled straight. The tears on my face dry to ice and I see no hope. Staring into the palms of my hands, rubbing dirt into the cracks.

DECREASING CIRCLES

The darkest eyes
See clearer tides
That break away
The lies of night.

The dense, heavy fog of morning cloaks the shivering ground, and I drive with lowered headlamps across uneven terrain, still rushing, still peaking. Far behind me now the edge of the world, beyond the twisting roads and ginnels between here and there. I smoke because I have them, exhaling with gratitude against the pearling glass. All that matters is the road ahead. For the first time in a short while I contemplate recent events, my methods of salvation. The torching of the torso - undoubtedly arousing interest whether from the smell or flames, authorities surely looking at it right now, their feet crossing my path. Who could say what methods of detection would be employed. Did I do it right? Suddenly I didn't think so. The entombed extremities, not as much in rock as in cement. Perfectly cylindrical cement. Easy to spot from a distance and dropped into a raging coastline that would make short work of pulverising them into nothing. Considering the ineptitude of my disposals, I curse my name to the farthest reaches of what men call hell. I should very well call the police myself. But wait. To be considerate and objective is paramount.

No failure, no falter. Do not allow depression and despair to get the better of you.

Yet here I drove in what would be to any intrepid officer a fucking treasure trove of evidence: blood, hair, cement, written confession? Not quite, but close enough. I console myself in thought, although the car *is* strewn with evidence, it is *only* attributable to an *as-yet* unsolved crime, and therefore *merely* circumstantial.

By the time the sun is firmly overhead there must be a hundred miles between me and the latest crime scene. Content, at least for the moment, that I had separated myself from the terrible truth I stopped at a roadside greasy spoon for much-needed sustenance. As I pay for the food I notice my wrist seems skinnier than usual, looking closer in the wing mirror of my car I see bullet-hole eyes, heavy rain clouds threatening to pour beneath them. Meat and bread and fat and caffeine in essential order. My body, having almost forgotten the ancient mechanics of converting food to energy receives the plate with suspicion, being fueled in recent times almost exclusively with drugs and alcohol, bile and spite. With the sound of cars and trucks a constant reminder of the world and its force-multipliers there is a moment of peace, perhaps my first in months, in years, in a lifetime. The white noise of engines in constant flow provides a soothing backdrop and I fall asleep for what must have been more than a couple of hours. No one wakes me, I am afforded rest and recuperation and open my eyes in the early-late afternoon.

A lull in traffic stirred me back into existence. Feelings of relief wait patiently in the wings, ready to step on stage at my signal. I light a cigarette and leave the car for a well-needed roadside piss. A cup of tea replaces the almost empty eighth of coke and more cigarettes help me back to my understanding of reality.

Once again on to the road, heading further north, towards home.

I drive on, taking the trail at a regular pace, no hurry,

not rush. A cup of tea replaces the eighth of coke but cigarettes still help with underlying tensions. The car is a rolling jail sentence. There was only one answer and so I took the car to the most secluded spot miles from anything of note and parked up.

The blackened air chilled and I stepped out of the car and opened the boot. Scraggled edges of rope and chalky cement spread across the velour shell casing. From the back seat I took Pete's coat with the fuck-off hood and stuffed a blazing rag into the petroleum inlet.

As much as possible do I like to inhibit the scenes of films unmade, and to the exploding car at my back this was no different, as the woodland canopy glowed green and vibrant, flames rushing forth from the swallowing inferno, burning all things into ash and air.

I took my walk directly across a series of large fields for several miles. The skies clearer, my feet gradually taking me further from the core of all depth, stars amassed in a chorus, shining overhead as if just for me. The only constant in any story is the North Star, always there to guide you home. It had barely been a furlong before I found myself in standing water, soaking my feet and legs that now crept of rising and perhaps terminal damp. It was a toll I gladly took, acting as judge and executioner of my sins. No jury, just decision. Twisted, corrupt, inescapable, unfathomable. Anchored like lies to the throat of a m(M)essiah: fleeting truths and ingrained deceit. Across the creaking regiment of ancient trees and foothills, as the night hushes down I hear creatures stirring, the mists usually so settled around the various embankments and inclines endowed to the woodland; her crooked streams and steepened hills that rise and fall with a whisper, now somewhat hurried, harried, caught asunder, cast into arenas henceforth undiscovered. Passing through another woodland I stopped upon hearing something out of the ordinary. Here in the pitch darkness and near-deathly silence one notices when something is out of the ordinary.

Climbing up the gleaming crest of a small grassy bank, I cleared the woodland edge and saw at the top of the hill a large country manor, lit and occupied. On the shimmering grassy hill stood a farmers pitchfork with its head upright and pointed to the sky. Exhausted and hungry, I scaled the hill and reached the access road leading to the front of the manor. Outside were many cars, rare, collectible vehicles. I stumbled further through and as I passed the gravel court to the front door it swung open unflinchingly and there stood a woman wearing a communication headset, speaking to some unseen associate:

"Well do what you can, mix them if you need to." And then suddenly halting in her tracks as she sees me.

"Oh Jesus, you people are just the worst; come on." She took my hand and led my through the front door and straight up a huge set of stairs. I glanced to my left through a door slightly open and see people, but the woman scolds me. "Hurry up, there'll be plenty of time to dawdle."

We arrived upstairs and she ushered me into a large room with a series of make-up mirrors and chairs, wigs, costumes, and a table with an assortment of powdered drugs and tablets.

"What is this?" I asked, the woman, who impatiently sighs in reply. Introducing the drugs table:

"This pile is cocaine, this one Hollywood, these are ecstasy, and this pile Viagra, this yellow stuff MDMA, this something like speed, um, here this is valium and Xanax, crushed together." I was completely lost. "I suggest you start with some cocaine and take a few of those pills, and hurry the fuck up and take your clothes off, you're going to get me killed." To which I nodded and complied, while she relayed my actions over the headset. The waves of powder crashed gently over my shores, making fluffy white kingdoms of castles long lost to salt. Castles hardened by thousands of years, sealed in isolation, driven to madness, caught between times so no man may ever venture over her lands. The shores were indeed rocky, and sharpened to the degree that the mere sight would cut the retina from your eyeballs. Bright, benevolent, yet just like the rest: conquered by shadow and disharmony of a corruption on inner mechanisms, of machines that should be operational, should be in synchronisation but that have failed and left the foreman disabled, silenced, and vulnerable to destruction. "Hurry up and put these on." The woman ordered and handed me what looked like a spiders web but ended up being stockings that felt like alien skin around my legs, now naked for the first time. "Here," she said, as she brought cotton gobs of pure white foundation powder that enameled my face. Through settling dust she applied thick painted lines of red to indicate my lips, and sharp black lines to illustrate my eyes.

The hushed sensation drew thoughts that I had killed myself and this was some projection of afterlife, a purgatory of my own making, but either way I did a massive hit of all of the drugs and burst into a laughter that came from the very core of all that will ever exist. The sinking feeling around my face gave way once the woman powdered my cheeks pink and topped me off with a curly wig of blonde hair, then placed a cock-ring fastened around the base of the shaft of my penis. More drugs were placed before me on impossibly mirrored surfaces: so sheer that the very reflection of humanity was greater than the Gods that spawned it. I saw through the snowy glaze an image of my eye, peaked and burning, yet serene and complicit. Devouring them like I may die during the next breath, the continuous intake of sediment was a bluntly traumatic devolution in my physical interactions with the immediate environment. Staggering and muted about, I was eventually led downstairs by the woman, all the while on the headset relaying figures and confirmations while leading me across long, thick carpets and at one point I fall over, soft to ground, stroking the wall. Along the crevice I did walk, as if up on the edge of cliff, but no mighty wind nor terrifying storm came upon me, just the cotton woven wall coverings and lead-glass ornamental windows that shrouded a servant of the highest order: one that asks no questions, one that simply acts, always, and without hesitation.

"Oh Christ." Mumbled she while helping me to my feet. "*This* way, *that's* right." I followed her lead and eventually was aware of a great noise rising, many voices, music, laughter, debate and conquest. The woman opened a large white door and revealed the party, the gathering, one hundred people if it were nothing, dressed impeccably, indulged in a variety of conversations and jovial exchanges. An old man with white hair approaches me as the door closes at my back.

"Ah welcome, young man! Thank you Mildred." He warmly greets, extending his hand, to which I take in greeting. The drugs in my system start to create alternate nervous constructions around my body and the basic operational motor skills begin to fail and falter. "You're just in time, please join the party." He leads me towards a group and I notice in the crowd four or five other naked young people, men and women, all high as fuck on the craft services upstairs, and dressed in an assortment of depraved and unthinkable fashions. One man across the room has his erect penis covered in cake while what look like wealthy society types eat it off, chubby white women wearing endangered plumage from hats and rubbing one out through Victoria's Secret or her rich aunt Methuselah.

The man led me to the side of the dining table, a long, heavily populated length of polished oak with anything a boy could ever want to eat.

"Aren't you hungry?" Asked the benevolent old man, to which I nodded. "Then eat," he said, as he took a piece of smoked salmon and put it in my mouth. "Isn't that good?" He asked to which I nodded and blinked. The old man looked towards a server, standing perpetually at the side of the room. "More." He instructed, and the server arrived, raising a silver platter containing the same piles of drugs as upstairs. "Take all you want!" Said the old man, and I took most of the drugs there, which twisted me into a frenzy that burned for centuries remained for a moment. Black ties and sequined dresses are a blur of ripples before me, posh toffee accents mixed with shrill haughty laughter. I find myself on all fours on the polished wood floor, kneeled before a society woman whose pussy is stuffed with Foie Gras which I eat to a crowd of cheering supporters. My mouth chews at her pink softness and gorges on the intoxicating culinary delicacies. Someone pours an emulsion of port and wild strawberries down her cunt and that only encourages the feast in its voraciousness and soon I feel something in my own anus and someone starts spooning caviar into my mouth and who-knows where else.

One of the rented girls is brought to me and we are bred like mare and stallion, neither with memory of the moment, drugged and disabled. Surrounding us a growing group of twenty or thirty men and women, some masturbating through expensive suits, some having sex where they stood, men using catered dishes as makeshift tools for stuffing into any willing body cavity. Before I can come we are separated. Realities begin to merge with the unconscious world and before I know it I cannot tell what is living and what is dead. A line of gentlemen begins to ravage her I can see them ejaculating quickly inside her and she begins dripping on the floor while I am put to work alongside a few other men on the high-society women, all big hats and long feathers, sequined dresses and stiletto heels, not to mention one or two of the men.

The moon is at its peak, full, shining white down upon the vast grounds of the manor, wearing a cloak of fog and frost creeping across the lawns.

Once again we are drugged, and moved, this time outside, the freezing air invading my body and dragging back the retrospections of death. The people in attendance have donned various masks made of furs and feathers, animal claws and teeth form inescapable manes that seem to encircle completely. The whole place is shaking and the darkness begins to give way to a soft glow as we approach a large barn lit red on the inside.

At the front of the barn a fire burns high, licking the night sky and sending sparks up towards the glassy skied heavens. Here in hell, the madness continues, as the well dressed begin to disrobe, leaving the only difference between them and us the animal masks on their heads. Across the roof and joining the two brick master walls of the barn is a mighty trunk, a polished beam, used I should think for some arable technology. At either side of the room there are platforms, as through a tightrope walker could cross the beam and back again. As I tried to look at the rest of the barn in detail through the drug induced vibrations that ebb and flow in a violent tempest, someone places a mask over my head, and my vision is obscured, though not completely.

They began to chant and on the swept floor I could see lines drawn in wet red paint, forming shapes and symbols. Still we were harried and hustled around, never in one spot for more than a few seconds and then I realized that people were laying down on the freezing floor, arranged on purpose in some construction to please who or whatever. A man wearing a lions head, which seems to have been made from an actual lions head, walks around the group and selects a woman and a man. She is one of us but he I am not sure, at this point everyone looking like they are on some champion grade of psychedelic drugs. I am laid down in arrangement as the Lion climbs the steps with the man and woman before him.

He says some words, an ancient language unrecognizable to mortals but to these demons surely a secret doctrine, a hidden code for total corruption. Replying back en masse, the gathered crowd, laying all around are pensive, wired and agog. The man and woman are bound together and now I see a rope attached to the centre of the master beam, the other end fixed to the couple's bindings and tightly knotted.

The Lion begins to speak again and the man starts to rut against the woman, penetrating her while tied face to face. The woman begins to moan and scream then the Lion brings forth a large double edged sword, placing it at the throats of both, speaks some words of meaning then they are pushed from the platform, blades cutting as they fall, ropes tightening and swinging them from the feet, causing the incredible flow to be even greater and showering the entire group with the hot blood, powered by fornication and death, the last throes of life they can push forth being to fuck and to try desperately to seek that paradise on earth, that nirvana for which the first men were banished, for which only the Creator may enjoy, for the Gods only.

The Lion bellowed the words spoken previously, decipherable now but still unintelligible.

"*An ru-ka-ta Im-lo-ka-da.*"

To which the crowd replies in unison:

"*Oh yay, oh yay. Thy treuthe soul, virgin blood and Negro Gold.*"

Still writhing with animal lust, blood rains down upon them as the last spasms of life send forth-crimson arcs from the gallows, onto the waiting faces and bodies of those below. The Lion watched as the crowd continued to copulate in earnest. As if all racing for orgasm. I myself find a woman in a mask, crafted from hundreds of feathers and with shell of rare egg affixed in a gruesome pattern, yet the hardened fleshy face of a pig beneath. As anyone would I try to blend in as much as possible, rampantly violating the woman before me as she howls and screams in pleasure along with the other members of the brood. Men started to ejaculate, and as they did so would rise and exit the barn, leaving the women on the floor and as the men cross the threshold back to the outside, would remove their masks and throw them onto the fire, which blazed hot and blue flamed, growing more wicked and wild the more masks were thrown upon its blazing heart.

Finally I managed to reach my own orgasm, though it left me much colder than usual. Standing to my feet I stumbled backwards as the woman I leave, laying upon the ground writhes and rubs her genitals, snorting and grunting through the pigs face. Her grotesque display is the least of my disturbances as I step backwards and remove my mask, tossing it onto the growing inferno and leaving the shrieking woman behind in a state of perpetual climax.

My hallucinations are running wild and the darkened path-way before me is a knot of entrails and entangled remnants of a memory in the process of banishment for the avoidance of demonic temptation.

The skies were a pitch black. Heavy and set against a thick forest line that is only broken by the soft orange hue of candle light within the grand house. Walking away from the place, my feet caught on roots underfoot and jarred at my toenails, they themselves broken and ground with dirt. Unseen to me came a figure.

"Sir, this way please." His arm out stretched and ushering me westwards towards the darkest place in the drive way, now crunching gravel once more beneath my feet, if only I had sensation perhaps I might feel pain.

"Sir." Said the man, now I see in grey suit, with Windsor knotted tie and flat hat. He looked at my with a degree of sympathy that was recognizable even now, full of toxins and guided my head below the roof of a vintage car, as I slid naked onto the leather seats in the rear. I took my first breath in what seemed like forever, and the kindly man closed the door softly, walking henceforth to the front of the car and entering, starting the vehicle and driving slowly away from the house into the darkness.

Moments passed as I gazed at the shrinking barn, people still venturing outwards, burning their masks and returning to the house naked, yet hurriedly shrouded by likewise servants of the rich and powerful with furs and silks and other fabrics wrought from the lives of smaller creatures.

"Your things, sir." Spoke the driver, now as we move through complete darkness and looking to the seat next to me I see my clothes, pressed and folded neatly, along with a brown envelope, which I pick up and look at the driver. "For your trouble, sir."

I dress as modestly as possible, however an orchestra of drugs is running like wild animals through my system and composure is an asset I surely lack at this time. Finally dressed, I look out of the window while holding the brown envelope, which I open and find five thousand pounds in fifty pound notes inside.

"Do you have a cigarette?" I ask the driver.

"Of course, sir."

Smoking against the original window of this classic car that, if broken, would butterfly my face to pieces. I watch the smoke break out across the plush interior and drift towards whatever ventilation there may be, intended or no. Onwards we drive and this might be the greatest cigarette of all time, and of course, too quickly comes to an end. A thick fog rolls unstoppable across the patchwork moors and through woodland embankments, peeking like children through the gaps in reality and leaving without a trace of damp presence.

Taken by sleep, or somewhere between dreams, I awake in a fleshy kingdom: a place where my feet slip and spill into a billion worm holes, freckled and invariable, as I tumble my hands feel likewise, but a grassy firmament grown in clumps here and there. The more I rooted within the ground the further I pushed my orgasm to peak, but beyond such, so much more than pleasure, my face now on the ground and the holes devouring me completely. Yet I, complicit, engaging like cancerous cells as I gratify and satiate until a warm rushing creek, soft yet indelible, runs around my feet and below my whole being, forging a delta of pleasure crossing my soul.

"Excuse me sir." Spoke the driver, and I awoke at the slip road to a motorway service station in who-knows-where. "We're here." He said, affirming my terminal. As I reached for the handle the door opened and the driver gave me his outstretched hand. "I'm terribly sorry, but this is as far as I can go." To which I nodded like a mute calf given grass. "Please." he then handed me a zip-lock bag, which contained a healthy variant from the party now so long ago.

Returning to the vehicle, the man does not look at me again as he drives directly on to the deathly-quiet main road.

There are a series of moments that break like errant waves, spilling west and east, under and over, and I take a further nose full of drugs to ensure my continued comprehensive abilities.

In the light I will find my way home. Home is surely where I should be. The deathly quiet road has born raging motor vehicles and gusting winds, coupled with harsh dusts and Siberian temperatures. In a state of utter discomfort, I struggle through, and on to the service station.

The Girl from Ipanema plays on wind chimes in the air-conditioned interior, holding a tandem of newsagent and greasy spoon. There must be a degree of paranoia attached to the side effects of these drugs because even the few people in this place seem to be staring at me. I seek the toilet with haste and urgency, yet never stroll over a canter. Paranoia is not the only unwanted bedfellow in this place, as my stomach suddenly feels a sharp pain, like knives heated inward. My steps like a child, I pushed through the toilet door and floated across the floor, seeing my face in the mirror for a moment, smudged white and black eyes with a mottling of fleshy tribute peeking through and recalling the memories already on their way to a deep chasm within, be buried forever. After lathering water over my face and barely cleaning anything I head for the nearest cubicle on which I sit down after dropping my trousers, releasing a torrent of shit and fuck knows what else loosened from my anus. I let out a crude, guttural sigh of relief, but the pain is still there, just moved slightly. Continuing to push I feel beads of sweat trickle down my nose and I take another hit of crushed up mystery drugs to power through to the other side. The momentary dizzy spell gives way quickly as the pain reaches a pointed climax and I gasp while pushing from a place inside I never knew existed. A trickle of hot liquid followed by a 'clank' of contact in the bottom of the toilet bowl, and it was gone. Head hung low and heavy between my legs I take a breath and look for toilet roll, but instead find a tiny hole through which I see a man masturbating. Tears dripping down my face, sweat and spit curdled together in strings hanging from my lips, I reached down into the bowl, my shaking hands cutting through the floating caviar and feces and who-can-say into the murky depth below where I felt a slight, hardened object. Lifting it up I saw the thing: a one-hundred-year-old caviar spoon, stolen from Russia in 1884, trafficked by Opium traders into the Orient and in 1913 given to a wealthy industrialist being that ancestor of the previous and perverted owner of said-spoon. Silver over ivory, coated in blood and shit.

DRAWN QUARTER

In half the walks of life you may have encountered obscure
Behaviour of those imbued with an air of calm and tranquility.
Those cracks between glass allowing
madness to come through
Can be referred to as the bridges of truth.

Isolation. Solitary confinement is the key. Without disturbance or distraction. Black light holds many secrets. In black light the stars are clearly visible. In black light the world becomes smaller and the lie of your life is apparent. If you stay in black light for long enough it ceases to be blindness and reveals itself as light. Days or weeks or years pass as windows frost then melt over and over again. Hair gets longer; beard grows thick as razor blades wear down to nothing more than dull metal edges. The first time I cut myself with a broken razor I don't cut so deep. It's a small cut, a tester: about an inch long on my hand. As the flesh separates a series of chemical signals pass from my mind to my hand to get it to move away, but I ignore the impulse. The cut gets a little longer, now arcing slightly as if it were moving out of the way of the bones almost popping through my paper skin. Like unwrapping a Christmas present. No pain. I'll make a story up about this scar. Maybe I was riding a bike and fell off. Maybe I got into a fight. You should have seen the other guy. Etcetera.

Fortunately the donated wrap of drugs is still thick with potency and girth and over these days he is my friend and keeper. Self-abuse is much preferred when the weapon of infliction is psychedelic.

A spring clean is in order as the rank pungency that creeps about the residence becomes overpowering. The carpet I strip back first, tearing it from the jaws of nailed down boards surrounding the perimeter of the room. Beneath the carpet the thick underlay, reserved for the exceptional to provide comfort under foot for years if not decades. This too was stained with dark patches of blood here and there, and unexplained yellow patches dotted like occasional flowers on West-ward-facing hillsides.

Using a claw hammer I pull out the underlay, ripping it to shreds of rubberized material, thick and lain heavy with perspiration and fear. Further down onto the original floorboards: wide, oak, and partly tinged with scarlet memories of Margaret. This is an all-or-nothing venture, but one that has a heavy tax on my body. My arm begins to swell and yet I cannot cease to work. The bag of drugs is a constant necessity by now and I can clearly see the blooming of white powder over my nose and face. The affected floorboards are particularly cumbersome, and, of course, in lengths of twenty feet or more. I use the hammer once more, aided by a thick pull-up bar I never used to leverage them from their position, revealing long-steel nails like the tendons of some metallic creature. After a couple of hours of struggling I have the offending floorboards removed and stacked at the side of the room. Now to peer deeper into the abyss, into the belly of discontent, to the ancient pipes like blackened veins running through the floor at right angles. Even here, beyond even the whisper of light there stood a solitary sliver of blood; ringed around the piping and curdled just before the drop into some other dimension or apartment. Like discovering the last of a tribe that knows the terrible secret of the white man, I killed it with bleach and wire wool.

By now my arm is bandaged. Blood stained and slowly healing, a series of lines up my arm. Straight lines. Perfectly straight. The natural lines of my body and of nature are not straight. Over a course of time alone straight lines invade my arm and dominate the once pure landscape. Cutting through vast fields of virgin soil and fixing themselves to the earth, seeping it dry. I've made a lot of mistakes in my life. I feel like I'm saving them up. Holding them in record for use in the future. I'm afraid of the world today. Life is an incredibly fickle existence. Death seems infinitely more reliable. Each day passes and you gamble your life. Television gives you the impression you're about to be blown up at any second. It teaches you that you will never be in control. It tells you that those in control are liars. Those in control are cheating the people who put them there. Making decisions against the will of the crop of fools keeping them in power. I won't be a party to it. They can all fuck off and die. If I reject modern rules and systems, does that mean I govern myself? Does that mean I make my own laws and punishments? My decisions are just as valid as any outdated old man who likes sucking off teenagers in public toilets, who has secret affairs or might expose himself on buses to people waiting on the other side of the road. They might do these things, I might do these things. Their decision and opinions are based on a weakness they cannot control. We all have secrets. Some of those have sway. Most of us have nothing.

It is nighttime and the pitch black skies bathe in yellow fluorescence, bled from lamp lights that dot in regularity up and down the opposing sides of the streets. Perhaps not the best time to transport this large amount of evidence, but nonetheless still the *only* time it could be possible.

Over my head rolled the carpet and underlay, in

tandem like deadly bedfellows, rigid and bony with the three floorboards, and we all traipsed through crooks and alleys towards the piss infused canal, down and down until reaching the quieter ends where reeds and grass grow over paths, tangling up the banks and in a place where not even the fiercely desperate and perverse dare to tread. Something turns in the river, a stinking, brown streak, opaque and pestilent, barely catching my attention.

Coming to a small bridge, I dump the whole lot into a thicket of gorse that releases plumes of pollen destined to be lost in the night.

A calming breeze travels down the canal line from behind me and enters the bridge leading to a tunnel.

My arm heavy and aching, a terrible pain drifting through me, my every dream coming to an end and in this moment as a black and cold future rears its beastly head. From the inside pocket of my thousand pound trench-coat I take a can of lighter fluid, and spray it over and across and inside the bundle before me until empty then toss it into the sodden roll. Channeling the venomous charm of a thousand anti-heroes: from Rickman to Kinski, I light a cigarette with a match, and then toss it onto the carpet, which catches immediately. A blue flame spreads swiftly, licking across the weave in tiny ripples that grow and grow, rapidly oxidizing and creating a golden holocaust of an inferno: banishing memories of whatever forever into the weightless ashes of yesterday.

I go back to that room and begin to fix the missing pieces. Great gaping holes have been opened up in the floor and most of a carpet is missing, along with former furnishings. As the moon crosses the sky once more, I scrub and clean any remaining evidence away into bleach and boiling water. The process takes days and the sun is now risen three times, while I eat leftover pizza balanced on the very edge of penicillin.

My phone rings for what I think is the first time and startles me. I leave it for voicemail then check it. The bank wants to speak to me. My accountant has been in touch and the bank wants to speak to me.

Good afternoon. Welcome to blah blah private banking hurry-the-fuck-up. If you are familiar with our telephone banking service, please enter your branch sorting code. Thank you. Please enter your account number. Thank you. Now enter your date of birth in six digit format, for example, if you- Thank you. Now enter the third and sixth numbers in your banking ID. Thank you. Please hold while I obtain your account balance... The balance of your account is eighty. Five. Thousand. Four. Hundred. And. Nine. Pounds. And forty-seven pence... Overdrawn. If you would like to speak to a customer services representative, press six.

Fuck me. Fucking shit. Eighty-five grand overdrawn? What the fuck? Nah. Not possible. I haven't spent that much money. I haven't. Fuck me. I bought the table. The stereo, that's fifteen. Records and DVD's, probably six grand. I haven't spent that much. Rent's quite expensive. A grand a month. I used some of my savings recently. The other bank account. That's still got some in, second thoughts it's empty. The brown envelope: that's all I've got: five grand and a silver-plated ivory spoon.

E XFOLIA

Looking over
Disco floors
I can see you
Wishing it all away.

A dull pain spreading from my lower back to my hip almost cripples me one day as I awake to a room with no curtains, bright sunshine pissing through the plastic-framed windows. I cough and choke while dislodging a piece of phlegm buried in my throat. Spitting over the edge of my bed having lost anything close to giving-a-fuck. I creak into existence. There's a smell coming from the room, a sickening, mouldering odour, and I accidentally kick an overflowing ashtray over, spilling roach ends of rolled joints and cigarettes onto the carpet next to my bed. My arm pains as I bend over to correct the ashtray. Beneath the bed I can see the foot of the yellowy mountain of tissues and come-lacquered socks. I am living in my own filth and I must stop. A dull air sits all around the room, hampering any attempt at movement, a numbing paralytic. She had hit me hard, deep wounds that are untreatable, barely addressable. I suppose I got what you might call revenge. Sitting on the floor I slice dead skin from my foot with a kitchen knife. A spider used to live here but now there is only I; alone and forever, walking through quicksand. Caught by the tide in a thousand bad dreams.

Through the muted reverberations of silence comes a sound: rhythmic, unnatural, a chime, a doorbell. Someone is at the door. I rise like a piano perched at the top of a flight of stairs and balance even more precariously, sliding across walls and searching, the last blind mouse inside a maze of cheese and tom cats.

I press the intercom button to see the video relay from downstairs but a crackle of radio signals gives away my position. It is Pete,

"Aleeeeeeeee-"

I look at the living room and survey the scene. Fish who live in the mouth of a shark do not see it as dangerous, only as home.

"Yeah mate, push the door." I hear the metallic clunk as the magnetic door releases its lockings and Pete enters the building, giving me scant moments to open windows, throw blankets to circulate air, push piles of clothes towards corners for later cleaning and finally put the kettle on.

Pete arrives at the door, which I have left open, and enters, singing,

"*Christmas time's for giving, presents in a row, anytime the season comes, da da holly in a*" Pete burps the last line of the modified carol and the smell of premium lager passes the threshold, momentarily, at least, diffusing the many other olfactory memories of recent times.

"Bearing gifts I come." Pete holds out a bag of one, maybe two hundred broken pills of assorted colour and shape.

"What the fucki- Jesus mate, come in."

Pete looks to be in a walking state of comatose and his monstrous body lumbers through the door, handing me the bag of pills.

"*Laughing all the way, ha! Ha! Ha!*" Pete sings to himself as he enters and is drawn magnetically to the couch, which he lays on and closes his eyes, falling asleep almost instantly. A pack of cigarettes peers from the pocket of his military green duffel coat, and I take one to smoke from the open window looking down upon the train tracks. A light drizzle has started and the skies begin to darken.

In the kitchen the kettle 'pops' and a cloud of steam hangs over the countertop. I pour water over a Yorkshire Tea tea bag, allowing it to steep while looking for milk, which I find has turned.

Pete snores, his glasses pushed across his face, which I take off and place on the new coffee table just arrived.

I step out of the room and wear my K-Swiss, now ragged and beaten like a hundred men had walked a thousand miles each and taken turns wearing only this well-fucked pair.

In the corner shop the familiar smell of coriander and cumin seeds is strong and heavy, and awakens a beast of hunger inside. I buy milk and eight cans of special-brew.

Pete is a big guy. So big that when I returned to the flat he had replaced the previous smell with his own: unique, and all-consuming. This puts me at ease as I open a can, the sound rousing Pete who grumbles like a grizzly bear.

"Well now, rise and shine!" I say, but Pete is still in hibernation, merely snuffling at the air and twitching his big nose and beard, catching the sweet aroma of premium lager that to him is like nectar to a bee. "Rest up big fella, rest up." I say and relax, sitting on the floor by the couch and placing my back against an overstuffed bean-bag. Since Pete is asleep I play a video from Johns shop called "We Shall Over-Come", a film about black men fucking white women but I have seen it many times already and instead look at the new coffee table and bag of broken pills, investigating the contents. There must be twenty or thirty different types, many I recognize and most off-coloured, speckled and dubious looking in composure and tonality. Laying them out on the coffee table in regimented rows, arranged by shade, investigating individually. I take a deep swig of special brew and lick one of the lighter shade broken pills. Tastes like a cocktail of perfume and petroleum.

From the other end of the row I crumble one of the darker, orange/brown tablets and try the resulting powder. A completely different taste: sweet, metallic, but with similar component flavours. The logical thing now comes quickly and I crush each of the pills beneath my now-useless metal credit card.

Taking drugs orally is fine if you have time to properly evaluate the impact, but if you are against the clock, as I decided I must be now, then lines of powder is a much more effective process.

As with God, I go from darkness to light, sampling half-lines of this and quarter-lines of that, until before long I have tried virtually everything in the bag.

It is hard to say which drugs work at this point, and my room becomes warmer as night encroaches. Pete snores loudly but it blends in with the record I have begun to play, the fittingly entitled Before and After Science by Brian Eno. The bean-bag becomes a part of me as I turn my eyes over and over before I realise the first feathers of breaking waves tickling at my nervous system. I suddenly need to urinate badly, and tense my stomach to rise when all of a sudden the wave breaks, and my living room melts into visions through the secret lens of God. Carried downstream I am barraged and tormented left and right with icy rocks and shale splintering through the air. Suddenly the record stops and the lounge comes back to me, distorted and oak-stained underwater. The floor is hard since the carpet was removed but my knees can barely feel it as I crawl to the record player and retrieve another piece of wax, this one with gold leaf on the cover and shining in the end of day glow coming through the window.

The needle picks up the groove and open space is suddenly filled with warm tones from a piano, and Graham Nash uttering words of lighting fires, placing flowers and cozy rooms.

It lifts me into a world that could have been, where I had made different choices, some other reality where smiles are

not the strange currency of today.
> Everything is fine.
> Everything is...

> just fine.

DISCO RESCUE

Speak to me of your ideas
Sell me now your story,
I am invested only
As far as I could
Ever dream to care.

THE FUCKING CIGARETTE MACHINE won't take my money, as coins fall once more through its network of gears and scales and measures. The display repeatedly reads up to seven and eight pounds added, but the final coin fails to register, stalls the machine, and I have to start over again.

Sweat hangs in the air as a thousand young antelope or wildebeest or some such prey topple round like walking string men, carrying yellow cards and dangling from the edge of a speeding car on this dance floor near the seventh ring road of hell. Faces painted strange and lines between edges like liquefied clay swept and swirled into existence. Squinting at the digital display once again reading eight pounds my chest tightens and I can't breath. A steady focus built between the machine and myself, a biomechanical love built on threats of violence. Finally calmed when a passing girl stops to help me in my infantile state.

"MAN, THIS FUCKING SONG- FUCKING MACHINE'S BROKE- FUCKED!" I scream down her ear. She tries it and it works, *fucking typical*, I think, but she smiles as if she was I, and I here do one for her right back.

North: a typical student club. Known for cheap drinks and people of ill-repute. An upswing comes and my hands on the smokes, I reward the girl with one and go to the dance floor, cheap coke and unknown pills firing synaptic responses that trigger motion through my fingers furiously lighting my own.

A local DJ spins classic Mancunian tunes that have the crowd reeling. To my left a wall of speakers vibrates parts of my eardrum I didn't know existed, as I participate in the vigorous pastime of dancing.

"BOON AR-MY! BOON AR-MY!"

Screams the crowd as the DJ raises his hand, his T-Shirt lifting and beer belly falling out, seen by no-one. Ian Brown whispers the words: *She's a Waterfall* and the revelers all scream.

"Yeah!" Here's Pete and we embrace, drugs doing their job through the tiny nightclubs of our bodies, layers of sweat like sedimentary horizons piling one on top of the other. At the wall of sound there was only one matter: simplistic volume. Volume enough that all other things were silent. The organs in my body tingle and shake, demons cutting through me like lashings of the bullwhip. Pete's eyes turn backwards and I am in a sea of girls, youth and nubility thrust at me from every side. Like a moment of realization as I take gaze upon them. They in their own induced states of varied consciousness, dancing like flames over candles. My hand finds a girl's arse and she presses against it, squirming and biting her lip before we kiss momentarily.

"THIS IS WHY MANCHESTER'S THE BEST FOOKIN' CITY IN THE WORLD!"

We jump and dance upon the floor covered in beer and spit and do our best not to fall. There is a clinking sound in my ears as Pete and I hug the grille of the loudspeaker but it feels almost pleasant, inducing laughter. Hitting the top of my Budvar with his, Pete laughs at the spraying lager. In slight jovial vengeance I pour it over the both of us and we continue to revel in joy. I'm dying for a shit.

Along with Pete we had two girls he knew, one I vaguely recognized in as being someone I had decided to fuck.

We dance all night, bookending songs with drugs, alcohol and smoking cigarettes.

Soaked through, I am aware of the lads in front of me eyeing each other up for a fight. Each member of the two groups had the standard short-back-and-sides, checkered-shirt/white collar/cuffs/cunt combination. I couldn't hear what they were talking about, but all of a sudden, one of them threw a hand into another guy's face, an effort of a punch but not anything in the end. They scuffle but the whole thing dwindles into nothing. Johnny Marr's clockwork childrens guitar sound begins to play and I feel so fucking nice, everyone smiles at me, girls I look at look back and smile, I hug some guy and shout:

"I am a full grown man!" and Pete shouts back:

"Bukkake forever!" and we laugh like the world has ended. I suck my cigarette and blow the smoke into the tubes built into the speaker and can feel the hairs on my arm moving in time to the bass line.

"AAAA-LAAY-LOO-YAH!" the DJ shouts out another one and this feels like the best fucking night of my life and I really truly never want it to end, and the music plays on with the Chameleons and a song I didn't recognise but one that was so fucking superb I couldn't believe it.

I still need a shit, but I'll settle for a piss. I stagger as quickly as I can up the walls towards the toilet.

I bump into the girl and Pete's friend finds us and we all have a dance. I dance into the girl, I think her name's Kelly. She looks at me, and is dressed like a cock-sucking whore, a costume tried and tested near to death by a good proportion of the women inside. She keeps showing me girls, but they seem like they might be hard work, and it's work I can't really commit to right now, I just need to find a girl to fuck and this Kelly seems to fit the bill nicely.

I grab her tits and we kiss, our tongue's cold and inhuman, wrapping around one another as I slide my hand onto her skirt, up her skirt, touching her arse. She pulls away for a second as if she's teasing me but I can't even tell she's doing it and I don't care anyway, I just keep dancing and singing, and then she comes back and we kiss again and my clothes are soaking wet from beer and sweat, but she doesn't seem to mind that I fucking *stink*. Her mouth tastes like cheap vodka and brand-x cola, a thick film of sugar coating her tongue and slathered over the oily base of her lipstick.

The stairs nearly trip me when I go for a piss and walk into a room full to the brim of fucked-up people. The queue hangs out of the door into the hallway where names of ravers past still linger, carved into plaster and painted over so many times you'd have to do a stone-rubbing to identify who. Inside the bathroom, the sinks too, are all taken with people pissing in them. I wait and wait. Nearby a couple of guys are talking about football and the intricacies of the England teams' last royal fuck-up. Finally a spot at the urinal opens next to a cracked sink: overflowing and splashing piss onto the floor as if an earthquake were jarring the structure, wetting through my Gazelles with an assortment of drug-imbued urine samples.

So I stand there in the gap and see a shelf above the sink, which is part of the aluminum construction. I use this for my beer and pop it on top.

"Best fucking invention in the world, this." I mutter to a crack in the wall.

"Uh?" says a guy in a white collar-cuff shirt next to me.

"A fucking shelf for your fucking beer while your having a piss. Best fucking ever." A light goes on inside the man as he tries to talk through what looks like a lot of drugs.

"No way man, I know, I know, but: no man, fuck, I don't know man I once, oh man, once there was a pub I was in, fuck, there, there was a fucking toilet with an ashtray above it, an ashtray. Ashtray! I was fucking-"

"Oh man, a fucking ashtray, a fucking ashtray! Bastard." So I think about this amazing thing for a second,

"I reckon, I reckon the best, man, would be a shelf, for beer, and ashtray, *and an ashtray, man*." His words have me hypnotized as I picture the contraption.

"That's it man, nice one."

"Yeah man." Silence.

"I'd hate to be the poor cunt who had to clean it up, though."

"Aye man, that's a plumbers', uh, plumbers' job that, get stuck down there," pointing down the drain, "They get good money. Good fucking money though, man, for plumbering."

"Yeah but for picking up piss-soaked cig ends and shit up the wall; not enough money man, not enough money." At this, I button my blue jeans and slip out over the urine-rippled floor, cool-as-fuck.

On the way out of the toilets I secrete myself into a small corner and make a couple of wraps of strong MDMA, taken from the brown envelope stashed safely at home. Prior to leaving the house I had somehow remembered to prepare provisions for the night ahead. Orange powder, white powder, white crystals, quartz-like rocks in purple and blue.

Back on the dance floor sonic waves of music are laying waste to all in its wake, the room like scurrying crabs beckoned and destroyed by the turning tide. I bump into a ginger Aussie guy and give him some drugs, and we embrace. Rage Against the Machine sing protest songs for everyone to jam to. My ginger friend and I grinning and posturing like mountain goats, ram and butt heads with no feeling through a thick curtain of drugs and alcohol, one of which we were short of, so I find the nearest bar.

A swarm of student wankers were being served

selectively by a smaller swarm of student wankers, definable only by t-shirts and name-tags. Barely even anything in terms of feminine talent to be seen in this crowd. Once the thought of youth being that of exoticism and wondrous exploration, with the group at hand now there was merely an impression of acne, obesity and anti-social behavior.

"Bo'l of four-ex mate."

"---" can't hear him.

"WHAT?!" I rudely bellow back.

"Can't serve you, too drunk." This strawberry-blond fucking milk-skinned wet bag looks dismayed at my level of drunkenness.

"You fucking what?" I'm staggered and violently drunk and can barely believe my ears.

"You're too drunk, I can't serve you."

"Fuck off you cunt, fucking," Anger builds on insanity like salt under the sea, boiling under magma-crowned plugs.

"I'm afraid I can't serve you if you're drunk."

Gaskets blow in my mind as I reply with disbelief "Fuckin'... every fucker's drunk in here, every cunt's been drinking all fucking night, I just want a fucking beer, now you go and you get me a bottle of fucking Four-X or I'll fucking lamp you, cunt!"

"No can do," and I lunge a hand for him, but he jumps back.

"Right I'm getting security." He's not even listening to me just being a cold fucker and I instantly want to put a hole in his fucking face.

"Fucking do it you fucking knob head, go on then, fucking go on then you fucking wet cunt." He walks to get the manager and then I turn around and see the Aussie, whose name I think is Mike. He's beckoning me over as if something's wrong so I go over.

"He'll chuck you out man, bouncers'll kick your arse." He then puts out his hand and says he'll get them and I give him the money. He comes back with a double vodka and cranberry juice for him and the same for me.

"Little jumped up wanker, man, fucking twat."

"Yeah, fuck him."

It's getting close to two, closing time, and the DJ plays *Born Slippy* by Underworld, and now I can't believe how fittingly good this song is, good, it's such a fucking

"TUUUUUUUNNNE!" screams Boon, and we all yell with him:

"CHHOOOOOOOOOON!" and it's the whole crowd shouting and we're all united, one people, vs. the world and all its torturous love: walking hand-in-hand through raging currents, blurring into the other side where everything is nice and everything is soft and white, and you can sleep and dream and oh, man here comes another fucking beauty *Little Fluffy Clouds* and we're all just so fucking happy because the fucking drugs are killing the fuck out of me but it's so good and then I see Pete and we greet each other in typical fashion.

"Hey man!" Pete screams into my ear, but I can still barely hear him, "Got anymore drugs?" This I recognise.

"Yes bro! Hang on!" Searching my pocket I find I have left all the drugs in the corner across the other side of the club.

"Fuck!" I cry, signaling Pete to wait for a minute.

Marching across the dance floor, revelry quashed inside me as all of my attention is turned to rediscovering my drugs but it's no use. As expected, the drugs are long gone.

"*Fucking shit.*" I cursed to myself. Biting my lip, I ventured back to Pete and the ginger.

"Sorted?" Asks Pete.

"I'm fucking, mate: I fucking lost the thing. Ah, hang on."

I kick myself and spit, furious at my lack of control and coming up hard on the drugs I have already taken.

Searching the dance floor I see someone resting at the edge of the mess, smoking to himself with long hair and stubbled face.

"You look like you're on drugs, got any for sale?" I shout

into the ear of the man who gives me a warm face.

"Errrr, yeah man, what kind of drugs you after?"

"I dunno, like, coke, MD, pills?" A crack of a frown flashes across his face.

"Nah mate, sorry, only got ketamine. Can sell you that though."

"Ketamine, what is that?"

He then explains, with shamanistic tones: "Well, have you ever done coke?"

"Yeah man, of course." I reply.

"Well, you want to take like, a normal line of coke, half it, then half it again: that's all you need."

"That's *all* you need? I asked.

"That's all *you* need." He reaffirmed.

...This night's first taste is a cleansing ritual, as I slump against a wall next to a broken glass and beer soaks through the suede cloaking my feet. A vision unlike anything before, carried through a gathered choir of insanity by a plethora of other drugs, a melting pot that begins to pulsate and flourish along to the varied and muffled musical tones and melodies. Somehow I stick to the man's words, dosing myself with small, child-like-looking lines, one after another after another, after another.

Letting my mind be lost in memories of the past, I run from the demons of the present. Hiding in my deep conscious I climb *Big Tree*, swim the streams of my youth and swing across a modest ravine, that in days of yester had been so large, yet now I grew like a giant, dominating the forest, lurching forth over valley and thicket. I see myself standing at a great fire, swallowed by the flames and drowned below ashes.

An hour or maybe a week later my neck arched in a right angle staring at the sky with my eyes sweating and skin shuddering, sealing my flesh to the plain-black Vivienne Westwood T-shirt purchased for ridiculous sums of money. The sky dissolves into black tiles and coloured lights and I am returned to the club.

I keep my eyes closed, dancing, moving, sweating. Maybe I cried, I don't know, I feel in awe: in wonderland. Then I think I see that little cunt from behind the bar and Mike's still with me.

"Is that that little cunt from behind the bar?" And my fists clench as best they can. The guy looks different now though, he's wearing a jacket, he must be leaving work, so I'm primed and ready to boot fuck out of him if he gets any closer or if the mood takes me. I down my vodka and cranberry and Mike shouts in reply:

"No, it was a different guy."

"Oh! Oh well." I resign and console in flaccid complicity instead.

Beneath our feet grew a swamp of broken bottles, cigarette ends, churning brown liquid and mottled hedges of paper tissue inexplicably lining almost every corner and edge in the place. A common thought passes, certainly through my mind that we may all just die in this moment. The death pact, the suicide club. We will preserve this moment in ice and glass like the fallen warriors of old, that last clench of sword before the heavy hand of death silences man into eternity. Here we will stand, crystallized, so that in centuries to come the order of the future can come and see what a real fucking party was like. This is the name of "a good time". This death fantasy is not the worst I have ever conjured.

I pace frantically around the floor, realizing after some time that I am searching for the offending barman, in an effort to extend my hand in retribution and lamp the little cunt in the eye, although the drugs wouldn't allow me any of that, perhaps just expletives.

Despite the fact that I am just walking around, my head still bobs to the music. Gunfire from *Blue Monday* makes everyone raise their hands and I join them and close my eyes because I can feel the whole room in my ears and it's all turning inside out and beer bottles fly through the air like a kaleidoscope of alcoholism soaking me but hitting some girl in the back of the head and almost knocking her over. Nobody even notices.

Someone makes a hand signal, unseen to anyone but Boon as the chaos increases inside the asylum and he yells into the microphone one last time:

"PARTY PEOPLE, YOU'VE BEEN FOOKIN AWESOME, HAVE A GOOD NIGHT, SEE YUS NEXT WEEK."

And with that the party was over. The music stopped and the lights came one, suddenly everything seemed so yesterday. The urgency to leave the place was on par with any losing-side military exit strategy. Surveying the place I made sure to keep eyes on who I knew and who I didn't. Uncomfortably walking and staggering about in slow-motion towards some sort of structure, I, thankfully, hit a wall and use it for support. Stairs at hand now, we were a few floors down, so I made my way up.

At the top I could see the door for the toilets and needed to wash my face, otherwise I was going to puke to fuck. A metallic taste in my mouth is brought on by the strip lighting. The toilets have emptied, just me and two other guys who were just leaving and caught short. I went to turn on the tap, and the sink's clogged up with tissues, beer labels, beer bottles, and of course, about a gallon of piss. I get a mouthful of the smell and it tests my stomach. I can't use this fucking thing, so make my way out, feeling fucking grim after smelling the contents of the sink, then as the main door opens, a waft of air from the Chinese takeaway next door falls inside, and *fuck me* it smells of pure solid grease, chicken, pork fuck knows what and now I'm leaning against the wall puking down the stairs back into the nightclub and some people are avoiding me and some don't notice and walk through the contents of my stomach which looks like a stretch pizza. A girl gives a disapproving glance, and I tell her to fuck off so she does. I breathe heavily, spitting out bile and saliva that hangs in long, clear threads from my lower lip until it reaches the floor then I am no more. My knees bend and I take a long look at my shoes, drenched and misformed. A hole has started to form between the knuckle of my big toe and foot and a bouncer comes over to me with a fat fist.

A LEX PARTY

Didn't you once say
That we were in love?
Since this time passed
I have struggled with that definition.

Concrete outside the nightclub grazes my hand as I fall into the wall then onto the floor, at the same time dropping my packet of cigarettes and spilling them all over the wet ground. I stumbled and swore, scrambling around, getting my knees wet, salvaging the last of the dry cigarettes. This went back into my pocket after lighting one in my mouth. The air shot down the street with the urgency of fateful death- there was no atmosphere now, just the heady afterglow of thousands of moments of reckoning, fragmented glimpses into paradise or mortified witnesses to purgatory. I stumble drunkenly away from the door, meeting up with Jenny or Kelly or Kenny or Jelly or fuck knows the name. She is wearing the slut-uniform. Variant number one billion and one. Looking more than fuckable. White micro skirt, fishnet stockings, boob-tube, whores lipstick, bleached blonde hair with council-flat brown growing through. If a writer ever struggled to describe a girl of loose morals he need look no further. Smoking Lambert-and-fucking-Butler for Christ's sake. I get over to her and do my best Colin-Farrell with a cigarette-in-his-mouth smile, and she looks at me disdainfully. I don't care, and seemingly, neither does she. We walk side-by-side, hand-on and getting close to in-arse. She reeks of Joop or Eau de Scumbag or Chicken Tikka Kebab with chili sauce and extra everything. I put my hand up her belt, grab her pert and rounded arse through lace half-bottomed panties, and receive no resistance whatsoever. A good word to describe this scene is: meaningless.

People mill all around us and her friends have vanished, so it's up to me to get her home, wherever that may be. So this was the end of the night, the drugs needing topped up shortly lest reality and daybreak may go together.

Behind us a glass breaks and I turn around to see two men punching each other in the chest and face. It is the pair from inside earlier: the white-collar/cuffs/cunts and I cannot believe I can actually remember. Maybe I didn't. Maybe just another pair of cunts beating each other's brains out. A little blood, then some fucking idiot girl steps in trying to placate them both and gets a fist in the face. Like a car crash you can see coming, it is hard to have anything close to sympathy. She staggers back, twats the guy who hit her, right in the balls, then punches him in the nose, her own now bent and bloodied, with tears streaming around it. I ignore the action as does the girl, then we round a corner and bump into Pete.

"Heeeey hello! Where've you two been, uh?" he's being the picture of homosexual indulgence and quite amusing. "We were so worried, thought Steph would've taken advantage of you by now." Steph? Man, I was way off. "What are we all up to now, then?"

"Well, if you want I've got a big bag of weed at home and plenty of skins and party drugs!" If I can get her home, it seems fairly written that I could fuck her and check another pussy off the list, I the perennial slave to duty.

Minor checkpoints such as this dirtbox seem pointless, perhaps, under the harsh light of day. But daytime it was not, for now all that matters is gaping wet hole and hard, grisled cock.

"Yeah man, sounds good. Is it far?" Cheers Pete.

"Oh no, just round the corner." We start to walk.

Following me we have Pete, Mike, and Steph's friend Kelly or Jenny. I walked with the guys, Steph went with the girl. Somehow having the foresight to order pizza on the way, so it'd be delivered soon after we got there. The streets were soaked with black rain, giving off an orange-yellow glow from streetlamps, and a red diffusion from brake lights. I kick a bottle, breaking it against a wall when I get bored of it. Pete and Mike are chatting to each other about fuck knows what.

When we arrive at mine, a prostitute, unseen by all except me, works like a squirrel in my garden. Looks like the blonde I saw the other day. We had to navigate our way up stairs, due to an out of order elevator, the only advantage being we had literally only walked for two minutes.

Opening the front door, I remove my shoes as an invitation, or should I say instruction, to the rest. My living room was relatively clean, despite the echoes of slaughter that still resonate although only within my darkening mind.

I sat on a beanbag next to Steph, while Mike sat on the sofa with the other girl. A large rug covered the oak floorboards and fresh cut pine boards cover the new holes in the floor with only minor discolouration being of notice. Aside from that the residence looks like the picture of promiscuous bachelor credo.

Pete passes out on the floor after one joint. Mike kisses the girl, despite the fact that I later found out that she was fucking Pete. I am confused as to sexual roles and responsibilities: Nothing of matter, nothing of import. Our pizzas arrive, delivered by hand and consisting of chicken and sweet corn for me, pepperoni for two others and nothing for Mike, who stole Pete's.

Not really in anything like a conversation with Steph, I instead busy myself with my expansive CD collection. Nick Cave, Talking Heads, Lali Puna, Ten Benson, Anticon, Aphex, Autechre from a time when I was more organised. The night drags on and more weed is smoked, Mike crushes some pills between us and snorted those, then I break out the ketamine and made a party pile.

It goes straight into my brain. Not helping.

The brown envelope of drugs had been cracked open and four or five separate bags of drugs across the table, including remnants of the black powder sprinkled across the cocktail mountain.

I couldn't eat more than a mouthful of pizza and farted so nobody could hear but everyone could smell me. We blamed it on Pete, who was still vegetating on the floor. Steph's friend was a good looking girl, tits that almost fell out of her top every time she blinked, good figure. This group all in 'early-thirties', which means verging on forty, despite Pete working in a record shop and Mike the picture of foreign backpacker. The girls had lines on their faces like lazy school desk ruler scrawlings, but the guys obviously took care of themselves more. They had handsome faces, good bodies, in fact, the more I looked at Pete, the more he looked like Scott Bakula circa Quantum Leap. I hoped Dean Stockwell would walk in and 'Leap' me the fuck out of here, but it never happened.

I put some music on and Mike asks for really fucked up shit so I put V/VM on, but it's a bit far out for him, and anyone in their right mind, so I put on the much more moderately engrossing Shake & Shakir and it's all good. Then the television comes on without any sound and someone guesses at Coming to America but I say no, pause then think and finally know what it is:

"It's *The People vs. Larry Flint*. I fucking love this film." Then a shot comes on of Woody Harrelson sitting at his desk looking cool-as-fuck with sunglasses and a nameplate reading Jesus H. Christ. We all laugh. Then I put Patrick Wolf on the record player and Mike asks me what I'm into and he seems a little desperate so I say,

"Uh,"

And he says "Like Unabombers?"

I search my mind for the artist but come up blank, perched by the coffee table now racking out lines of ketamine mixed 30:50:15:5 with coke, powderised pink pills, and black powder respectively.

And I go, "Yeah, well, no, not Unabombers but like, *proper cuntish "IDM"* Electronica, I've got loads of it." Then it's silent for a bit except the dude and the other girls are chatting and Pete's unconscious, but I'm silent and can't find the words and it feels deafening, my ego muffling any real words from escaping my mouth.

"Have you been eating Chinese?" asks Mike, somewhat strangely.

"No man, why?" I snort a big line, and the taste is like some new cleaner, shotgunned into my nasal cavity and I suddenly have a splinter of memory as to the events of recent times.

"It smells like Chinese food in here."
Mike says again.

"Does it? Chinese?"
I struggle, mostly because I don't want to smell Chinese food for fear of vomiting.

"Yeah, Chinese, I'm sure."

"I don't know about that; I don't really eat Chinese food."

"No?"

"Wait, no it, uh, it smells like weed."

"That's it, that's what I can smell." Mike eyes the ounce bag with about half an ounce of weed in it, and I lean over the table and grab it, tossing it over to him.

"Smell that; you bastard!"
Mike carefully opens the bag.

"Fuckin', shit: that is strong."

"Make one, man."

"You mind?"

"Shit no, not at all, roll away. Skins are in the drawer."
And I start laughing because he's asking,

"I like to ask man, s'like,"

"I know man, it is polite, but like, you don't need to ask at all man, just do it dude."

"Cheers man, I appreciate it. So do you always 'ave parties like this?"

"I dunno, not really, actually. It's pretty sweet though, I don't mind."

"Yeah. I like your place, too, it's like: not like a home, it's, it's like that's what it's here for."

"Yeah I know, actually, when I first came in here- wait." The music stops and everyone's conversation seems to come to a synchronised stop and the room is so quiet now, I almost feel stupid for just sitting around with a few people I don't know talking about fuck knows what when I could be doing so much more or less. It's my flat so I'll have to get it sorted and be the DJ, then I see Pete getting up and putting Roots Manuva on, fucking good choice, much better than I could've picked right now. Everyone watches him get the CD from the rack and he knows he can't talk either until the music starts and then I remember I need to clean the heads on my CD player because it takes ages to start and he doesn't know how to use it. We all watch and when Pete looks over at us lined up in front of him we all break down laughing for a second and are all mentally agreed that without music we can't talk. The music doesn't start though, Pete needs my help.

"Just... Take it out and put it back in," so he does, "okay now don't touch it, wait for the numbers," it takes time but finally the CD info comes up on the front, "okay, now press play, stop, play," So he does, then the opening clunk and 'yeah' of *Dub Come Save Me* kicks in and we all nod our heads along and it's all serious again and the music gives us a second wind and on comes the next rhapsody.

We smoked a couple of joints, I looked around my flat, not paying much attention to the people around me as I rolled the second one, loading it much more than Mikes first effort. I have an excuse to move when some shit song comes on, a weepy fucker, and I decide to change it. Then I can't move. But then as I sit there listening to it and it actually sounds okay so I just sit back and smile, content that my work is done. Next, I'll put something really good on. Then:

"Are you going to show us around, then?" The girl says so I get up to show her around and Mike actually stands up as well and follows us into the bedroom and sits on the bed. I'm thinking, fuck. Even her friend didn't stand up. I feel about as cock-blocked as I ever have, but I show them around the rest of the flat and they are suitably impressed, especially when the girl looks in my wardrobe, and sees my extensive collection of incredible clothing.

Ah. The music plays to itself and echoes around the flat, the rising piano loops lifting everyone up as they drink their J&B straight, then secretly wince when it goes down. We do more drugs and as I slouch on the sofa it feels as if it is connected to some giant pendulum on a Lazy Susan, occasionally correcting itself on a perfect angle but all too often tethered to clock or counterclockwise five, ten, quarter past. Metaphysical gravel scrapes below me and what feels like bubbles rise before my eyes and between my brain, but staring too close jolts me back into reality on a perpetual loop.

Larry Flint is doing some crazy shit, while Courtney Love looks not at all like what she's supposed to, and I put a Queens of the Stone Age album on.

When it kicks in I hear something; an intro I've never heard before; it's a track I definitely haven't heard before, like a jingle and an echoing beat like duh, duh, duh, duh, and I go to sit down but am genuinely interested, so say to Mike,

"Did you hear that?"

And he responds "Yeah that car starting?" And grins as if it's something good he's spotted.

I smile slightly, "No, no, the echo thing," and start the CD again but don't hear it so I take it out and play it again but still I can't hear it. Fuck it, I heard it. I wonder if I'm the only person to have ever heard that and I hoped to meet the band one day and ask them about it over drugs and metal.

So we smoke the joint I rolled when I got back from the tour and the girls talk between themselves. Mike seems impressed by the shit but doesn't want to say and finally says:

"Right, I better be off," but just sits there, and I'm waiting, but not really, because I'm so stoned. So we sit there for a minute and he says,

"So do you think they'll get it on?" And I think he's talking about the People vs. Larry Flint, but then realise he means the bird, and me and had actually said, "Do you think you'll get it on?" I give a never-had-a-doubt-in-my-mind nod and cocky smirk, and then he gets up and goes for a piss.

Then Pete wakes up and I'm not yet asleep when Queens of the Stone Age start playing Another Love Song,

"This is quite a different sound for this lot," Then Pete and the girls are looking through a digital camera and I think they're pointing it at me and my conversation carries on as I look at the lens and don't so much pose as put on a facial expression that could be seen as cool in an 'I don't care' sort of way.

"Yeah man," I start to tell, "Queens of- they had a few guests on this album, I know from Mark Lanaghan, erm, Screamin' Trees did vocals, and Dave Grohl did drums, of course, but I don't think he done any vocals. I don't think anyway,"

Suddenly feeling I was in some rampant quest for acceptance, I rally back the horse.

"Yeah man," They still look at me and are vacant, pubescent coma-patients, but then I notice they haven't looked at me once, they must be looking through the camera at me. I keep looking back, regardless.

"But the drumming on this album is just fucking superb; I mean, really fucking good. It's like, I guess, I have a tendency, like a habit, of just ignoring drums 'cos they're so standard most of the time, just not that much difference in the world today," Steph and her friend vacated the room to get more drinks for themselves.

"Anybody want a drink?" Asks Steph as she walks out,

"Yeah cheers, I'll have a beer," I reply.

"Right."

I stop looking at Steph and concentrate back on Mike, and am surprised when it's Pete, and not Mike sitting in front of me.

"Yeah do you know a band, well, they're pretty hardcore, but you might have heard of them, Tool. Have you?" asks Pete, "Yeah, Tool, I've heard of them, but not heard them if you know what I mean." Speech is like from a broken spastic robot; formative, yet ridiculous.

"Yeah, they've got this drummer man, and he's like... the second best drummer in the world after this guy from fucking, Rush or something, but he can do like, four different sounds at once, y'know he'll have like, like, bass drum going with both hands and like a cowbell and cymbal, and, oh man. And he like, y'know that bass drum you play with your foot, y'know the one?" and I'm nodding and mhmm-ing, "Well he can do like that like a fucking machine gun, he can do it twenty eight times like dudududududududuh. Fucking amazing man." Pete does a rapid-fire karate chop to signify the drum beating quickly.

"Yeah good drumming really makes a difference, man." He passes me the joint back and I say "Ta."

"Oh man if I smoke that I'll never get up tomorrow," and leaves it in the ashtray.

I ask, "Does that matter?" and I mean it, but he just laughs and gets up and goes for a piss. I sit upright and do another line, then tend to the remains of the joint that burns the fuck out of my lips. He gets back and stands in the middle of the room as if he's going to leave.

"Ah well, fuck it," I say for no particular reason. As he stands there slightly at an angle, his hand on the wall. My legs are tapping away and my jaw chews as if I was losing my mouth tomorrow. Pete starts to shake again, or should I say I start to shake, or my eyes do or whatever but there's two of Pete and the vibrations are fucking me up royally, can't even focus on either image, earlier I could see both images in clarity, both Pete's in perfect vision. Now he's a mass of limbs and laughing.

He's coming up.

I'm coming up.

"Fucking good though like aren't they?" To the drugs I am referring.

"Oh, fucking yeah man, I haven't, I mean this was a lot of fucking drugs I done tonight man, fucking coming up again man, a lot of everything!"

"I can, I am, I'm coming up man, too, fucking" and my expletives tail off as adrenalin and his many cousins rush through my body, as a thousand pills dissolve in my stomach, battled by ketamine and magic black powder scorched from the screaming lungs of sacrificed youth, a thought best not entertained through bubbling plumes and white blood cells exploding on themselves. I can imagine them, turning everything inside me blue, stacking tiny cubes in an archaic assembly, glowing as my internal organs juggle cause and effect in an effort to figure out who's winning. Sweating, chewing gum, wiping my brow and eyes until I don't realise I'm even there anymore and Pete and I just stand laughing at each other, turning the stereo up as loud as it'll go, heavy guitars and bass drums echo through the desert of my flat, as far as the valley of the kitchen and beyond through the front door into no-man's land.

Fuck the neighbours, I'm gonna stand here for a second with my new friend and we're both gonna nod our heads, tap our feet and chew like fuck to this tune.

Behind me on the wall is a picture, a dark art thing to provoke stimulating conversation. The black oils on one side melt and merge into the light on the other but at this time there are two of the pictures to go with the two of everything I see. As I move the paintings move too, sliding up and down in opposite directions on the wall, one up, one down, one down, one up. My face beams a big smile and I close my eyes and imagine the sun rising in front of them. I can feel how sweaty I'm getting. Better drink some water.

Replenish my liquids so I don't dehydrate.

Water is good.

I pass the bottle to Pete who is looking through into the hallway at a sliver of light coming from the crack under the front door that shines right through the dark hallway and casts a beam like a meat cleaver reflecting car headlamps against the inside of nothing.

Here in the place walls kept moving slightly, but then when my head moved, they would move back. Trying to get a clear picture of where the walls lay is no longer as straightforward as simply looking.

My head...

My... head keeps doing that nodding thing when you've taken too much, and I could taste blood mixed with pizza grease and doublemint as I chewed the inside of my cheek and then my neck began to jut out like a rooster when my spine twitches. The time ticks somewhere close to six.

Hours that roll consecutively to one another have been coming and going all night. Each time I am happy in one hour, the next hour comes.

I'm confused, why is time acting in such an odd way?

I thought it was now just then but the more I think about it the more now is the past, and if now is the past, then surely it matters not at all. My actions now have no effect on the past, because, no, my actions now are the past. Any action I take is instantly in the past and of no use. My whole life exists in the past. I don't know how much of it in the future.

Once I'm in the future it'll be the present, which will swiftly become the past. Life isn't difficult, life is strange and life is just what it is.

I recall looking at a stagnant river suffocated in oil and waxed liquid, watching while a water snail floated just under the surface, the point of its shell peeking like a child through the curtains at the back of the hall in Sunday school, to where the priests would be alone, to the curriculum not written on paper. The water snail does not swim, cannot control its path in this medium, instead relying upon wind and tides to carry it to shore at which point it may slither and crawl to some new adventure.

I am the water snail, destined to live my life according to tidal flow and prevailing winds, or perhaps I am the pike: poised beneath the surface, brutal and hungry, and with a mind like a vice, never forgetting.

I glance to my right; Steph was on her mobile, talking to someone, but talking to her other friend at the same time. I looked at her body, and could see her underwear from the angle she was sitting, or squatting at. In my drug fuelled state I somehow got a twitch in my dick and reached out my hand, slipping a finger inside the fabric and into her pussy without lubricating, warning, or anything. She let out a little moan that made her friend jump back, but didn't stop me. She controlled herself, and I continued to masturbate her in plain sight of her best friend and the rest. All those present were so fucked up that nobody cared.

"Wait a second," I said, and looked at Mike. "Go in that envelope there, see that bag with blue powder?"

"What bag?" Asks Mike.

"That fucking bag in the middle, under the flap of paper."

"Oh, hang on." Mike reaches and grabs the bag, fifty grams at least.

"Rack out a few." I delegate, hands occupied by Steph's juicy cunt.

"Okey dokey." Mike Aussie accent comes through thick over his words, and he makes the lines then offers to me first.

"Rackers rights, go on mate." I offer to Mike.

"Ah cheers mate." Mike bangs a line and his face turns. "Oh Christ." Mike passes the CD case to Pete, who does a line without a note, snorting at the case and accidentally doing two, exclaiming,

"Oof, fucks sake Alex, is that Mr. Blue?" and I suddenly realise the Supersect in existence for the first time, those other thinkers, those who live inside the splitting of atoms as a means of transportation and deliberation, dilapidated, shaven, glistening.

"So I'm led to believe."

Steph initially declines,

"What do I need to make my cock hard for?" She asks, before doing it anyway and then giving to Kelly and finally me.

Laughter is quick as a common thought crosses our minds collectively.

Crouching towards the table to construct further party lines, Steph presents for me and my fingers waste no time in finding their way inside. Jenny laughs warmly and walks to the toilet, leaving the room. Pete looks at Mike who too laughs at the sight but soon hushes down when the punchline fails to drop. A snake swims through the walls and startles a school of concealed krill who are usually too small to see with the human eye and as they dart softly in synchronized strokes.

Jenny returns, Mike is at the window, turning from the CD player back into the room and Pete, sweating profusely, catches his eye, both looking thereafter to Kelly.

Her face upon reentering the room is of horror and shock, and just as a song fades to close leaving a gap for reality.

"Oh my God." Her words are solemn and heavy, my own self begins to rear its ugly head in memory and conscience. Her words are like smoke from a rifle, as we wait for sound to catch up with light. "You're not going to believe this." By now everyone is paying attention to her. "I've got this exact coffee table in my house."

"Jesus fucking Christ!" I exclaim, "I thought you'd found the dead bodies!!" I gauge the crowd correctly and hilarious laughter ensues, kick starting the drugs into the next level as I continue to penetrate Steph with various limblets; her head held loosely by my hand wrapped in her locks of bottled blonde hair. The very indolence of the act gives way to great excitement, and all parties start to feel obligation, as clothing is shed and flesh comes together.

Through blazing eyes came my grunts and my snarling, though one could mistake us for livestock in heat. It was a common tongue carried from cross the bare floorboards, as Mike did the Jelly and so did the Pete. Weeks seemed to pass in the briefest of moments or seconds could travel at breathtaking speed and the gurgled cough chokings brought forth from the openings on cavities searching for stuffings with greed, was a delicate soundtrack, a foley mans night work, the things few, if any, call rest and retreat.

Mike slips while standing one-legged and trying to angle his penis in places to please, then he stumbles and staggers, falls into the speakers and jumps the grooved needle that makes the song bleed.

Sexual tension melts down for a moment like chocolate warming on soft summer hands, collective laughter and the tone is returned to the previous beat with some ease. We sit back down, yet remaining close quarters, Mike mouthing Jenny's, and Jenny mouthing Pete's.

A string of saliva joined up with the others seeped deep into contours of the corduroy seat that now Steph faced-down on, my tongue in her anus and her firmly jerking my cock just beneath.

Pete got there first the great shuddering roar as he thrust at her quim with ferocious clenched teeth. Mike followed suit as she turns on a penny to receive his advance before he sinks it deep.

I look at Steph our eyes finally meeting and she shudders over her orgasms peak. Mine is left waiting, last bus in the station but suddenly Steph needs a moment to speak.

"Fuck me its half seven."

"And what of it?" I ask.

"I have to go. You can come with me if you need to complete." Impossible, I thought, blue powder touched.

Inside of the taxi, a black cab, the seating collapsing and

raising as fevers were pitched.

After dropping off Mike and Pete, the taxi took us through the outer suburbs of the city, to her house that from what I could gather was in a rather dodgy area.

Pleased I'm not walking as I look at all the broken windows and phone boxes. The taxi driver drops off her friend and Steph gets out to walk her to the door, talking along the way. I lean in to the cabbie.

"Late night mate?"

"Nah, early morning, started an hour ago, twelve more left."

"Fuck me mate, that's a long time. My mate's a cab driver, he has to work the most ridiculous shifts." I don't know any taxi drivers, nor would I want to. "Worst one he says is when you've to drive fucking miles then the cunt don't turn up."

"Oh I've had more'n me share uh them." Steph begins to say her proper goodbye, and I look at her arse beneath the tight skirt, then I get an idea.

"Here, mate, tell you what, I'll tell you what:" The driver looks at me in the mirror. "Just angle your mirror so you can see up this daft slag's skirt, I'll give you a good tip." He smiles, an aching, decaying smile with teeth like lone warriors after the storm, then starts to chuckle and corrects his mirror. Steph gets back in and sits next to me exactly where my new friend and I want her. The cab drives off and we wave to the girl. Lights pass through the cab windows, washing us in white and yellow and green. I move my hand up her leg and pull her knickers down.

"Wait- the driver" Steph whispers.

"Don't worry," I whisper back "Oi mate, do you think you can get a move on?" Oh we boys and our in-jokes.

"Yes-sir!"

Steph looks at me as if I command the slightest iota of respect from the guy, who I can see is smiling as I go back into her knickers and yank them down around her thighs.

Two fingers later and she's still wet from inside, juicy

plums rubbing together wedged between her thighs. I'm working her cunt like it requires resuscitation, and tensing my arm muscles and stomach in case she brushes against them. Her bush is badly kept; long hair, haphazardly shaven into some sort of shape that once may have been a triangle, with red and white-tipped spots surrounding the field cropped at the centre of her inner thighs. But I didn't care.

We were almost at our destination when a car came around the corner and almost smashed into our front end. Our driver, distracted by the backseat show swerved and hit the kerb, my hand popped out of her cunt and she let out a moan of surprise as I think I might have nicked her labia since I haven't trimmed my nails in a while.

"FUCKING CUNT, WATCH IT!" The driver shouted at an errand road user, when in fact he had been completely distracted by the private back seat show. Moments later we arrived at her house.

I paid the fare, left a five-pound tip. Steph went to stand up and put her underwear back on but I told her to keep them off and put them in my pocket.

The girl jumped out of the taxi and nearly fell when her slut boot heels became too tall for her. I didn't bother helping her up. She got some keys from her bag and made her way to the front door, leaving me to follow. The cab drivers window was down and he was laughing to himself.

"Cheers for the tip mate." I smiled and put my hand in my pocket.

"That was just a taster, have it!" Tossing the moist knickers through his open window, to which he burst out laughing even more.

"Nice one mate, nice one. See you 'round."

"Probably not."

"Yeah, well, enjoy." The taxi left and I walked up to the house smiling, but wishing I'd kept the sullied underwear for my own museum of encounters.

PUSHING THE LINE

Listen to this sound, it speaks in loud volumes.
Here for a second, then fleeting, forgotten.
Grown from a murmur, an idea so twisted
That came to life screaming: Blue murder, rain trodden.

As Steph opens the front door to her house I grope from behind, grubbing fingers prone against naked genitals, hooked inside her she walks through the door and drops the keys quietly on the side table. I, like a pocket dog firmly acquainted and knotted into her cunt.

Inside of the house is a smell of mildew, heavy soil and stale cigarettes. Paper hangs loosely from excuses for walls. Yellowed beige and off-coloured white paper layers rot and peel from the wall. Damp creeps up the stairs and the carpet looks third generation at least. That old maternal smell of hairspray and cigarette smoke. I follow her through a room adorned with pictures of the Empire State building, those guys sitting on scaffolding in New York. What a fucking try-hard. The three-piece-suite has cream throws and cheap cushions dotted about it. She'd obviously been watching those bullshit makeover, redo your house episodic torture shows.

Into the kitchen she goes and I hear a *click*, so I follow.

"What are you doing?" I ask while she's standing there boiling the kettle.

"Do you want a cuppa?" Fuck me. My mind far from this fresh reality, quickly gaining traction and impact.

"No, I don't." I imagine myself as the picture of *cool*, suave, successful alpha male with atomic codes behind my loins but in truth more likely the image of drug addled wastrel, a filthy, lost dog with a broken bone. As I reject the cup of tea I walk up to her and take her top from her, exposing her not-quite all-over tan, which I think is a *little much* for suburban Manchester close to Winter time. She's wearing a black bra, which doesn't match the knickers, now half-way around the ring road and all the way around some taxi drivers cock, and she sports a three-colour tattoo of a leopard trying desperately to change his spots.

"Well, I need a nice cup-of-tea."

"Oh go on then," I submit and lean against an unbalanced faux-pine stool.

I thought for a moment of sunny fields with innocent girls from the Alps running and laughing and leaping. I bent her over the kitchen sink and began to finger her pussy, which despite its appearance all spider legs and mystery white paste was soaking wet and instantly arousing.

She was surprised, and knocked the bottle of milk into the sink, pouring all over the stinking mass of plates and bowls. Smelled as if someone had been cooking fish, or maybe not. Between her legs was a white line on each leg going from the very top of her thighs, right next to her pussy. This is where her fake tan was rubbing off.

Her cunt tasted okay, which surprised me as I chewed, almost metallic, quasi-organic. We moved upstairs into the bedroom and Steph encouraged silent movements so as not to arouse her housemate or whoever.

The various creaks of the staircase felt like knife blades

pushed through my skin. Every step brought with it a chime or chorus of age, of time, of destiny. Inside the bedroom half-empty cups of tea sitting here and there, some with cigarette ends, some not. Dirty clothes and underwear all over the floor, a small bin with at least two used condoms inside.

She plugs her phone in to charge and scratches her groin, while I start to think this woman must've fucked half of Manchester given her lack of lust or excitement. She rolls slowly over to the other side of the bed, making a slight effort to be sexy. Opening the drawer, she removes a small bottle, as big as my thumb, and unscrews the cap and looks at me as if to ask if I want any.

"Poppers? Yeah, go on then." She takes a hit then I do and my nostril burns and I can taste it in my nose but a big wave just comes over me and I can't really see straight because my blood is streaming at high speed into and out of my head and I do another one and my nostril itches and burns and a flash of a smile flashes across my face. I go to do some more but my nose is blocked with an immovable object but I force a hole and sniff up the vapour but spill it on my lip which makes my whole mouth itch and go red from me scratching it but the fumes intoxicate the fuck out of me and my dick, quickly rock solid, is kneaded like hardening dough by her clammy hands. I hold the bottle to her nose and get her to do three in a row which she does, and I follow her with three of my own and the room emphatically fuzzes down and follows my train of thought to her body at which point I take a couple of fingers and slide them against her pussy, all hot and wet, then inside is so fucking warm and inviting so after a few seconds I insert another one and before long its all four inside but her face is all twisted and loose, pieces of her life sticking to the walls and I moan out some words from my intense head rush which seems to make her react similarly, and we roll, my cock inside her into a position which has me bending both her legs behind her ears with my shoulders and doing press-ups to jab myself inside. She's taking another breath of the amyl nitrate, and a second later so am I and my head starts to really fucking lose its balance, wobbling on my neck and feeling like its going to break from being so taut but I hold it and she squirms and moans a bit but mainly because of the poppers. I take out my cock, concentrating the end on her more than likely paralysed clit. She's moaning, which is good. I take the rest of my clothes off and walk up the bed and descend around her face, pushing my cock as far as I can into her mouth and she takes a lot, but not all of it, then chokes when I don't take it out. A big wad of L&B stained phlegm comes up with it and she wanks this over my dick, which is just fine at this point in time. I take my hand and hold her neck hard as she sucks me off, at which point she coughs again. As the battle to get her breath back begins to get easier, I flip her easily onto her knees and spit against her arsehole. Then I grab my cock at the bottom, locking a shot of blood inside the muscle, then push her head against the pillow whilst lining up the end of my cock with her anus now lacquered in saliva, then push through the relatively widened hole. She lets out an almost imperceptible groan, as if she'd just lost a parking space outside a supermarket.

I push deeper and she screams, but I knew she would, which is why I put her face in the pillow. She's still screaming a few minutes later, but now it's accompanied by her fingers, working furiously on her senseless clit.

I'm tiring, so I take another hit and get on bottom to let her fuck me for a while. She seems to be enjoying this a lot more, and now I can see her face looks almost possessed.

Bucking against my flagging penis and her fingers are inside herself now, then on her clit again rubbing like mad. I want to come, but I think she does too so it's fine.

It walks up the stairs to the top and looks out over the world and sees the sun rising quickly over the snow capped mountains surrounded by trees and desert and a lake and a valley and a great canyon and its so cold I'm sweating with the heat but I can take it and it's so tight in here the room it's so small but she's coming and so am I and here I do I can see the bottom now through the clouds and the birds flying past me at the speed of sound chirping and singing like air raid sirens and the floor looks closer but I haven't even stepped off the edge yet, I'm still waiting for the thumbs up and I can hear her screaming she sounds like a demon and now I'm screaming and the drugs are making me call her a cunt slut fucking whore or maybe it's just me saying that and so I continue fucking her with all my might until I let go and I'm falling through the air, dropping, waiting to die at the bottom but knowing all along I won't and I can see her falling with me too then I pull out and grab her hair stiff from hairspray but slick from sweat and spit and yank her down to my dick which spurts almost, out of her arse then the she takes it in her mouth then after a minute or two of deep-as-fuck-throating I pull out, slap her once, then come on her face which I then hold like a lantern in the night. Then I think she comes but it looks like she pisses herself in a sort of fountain way, which makes me jump back and she says:

"I came."

"No shit," I reply and she sits back and I make sure I don't get the wet patch because all I want to do is smoke the joint she's just got from the drawer and go to sleep in a warm bed.

The sun eventually rises and melts away the icy blackness of the night with a fresh, almost youthful kiss that seems to give everything greater depth of clarity and scrapes the dirty surface from the world leaving it shiny and new and smelling like wood chips.

I am still in the room and so is she. Neither of us look particularly good this late-morning but I decide the best course of action is to fuck her maybe once more anyway since I'll probably never see her again. Then I should leave.

So I fuck her once more, which wakes her up. At first I have to prop her up on her side, and push my face in the pillow to visualise some far-off place of debauchery, but once she's awake she gets on her knees and I do her like a dog.

I try to be more than she expects, frantically fantasizing on gangbangs, rivers of come, women rubbed and probed all over with and against will, but my back and neck both feel twisted and uncomfortable and I ejaculate rather unimpressively and she doesn't and then goes back to sleep. My cock falls lifeless and hangs cold.

I'm lying there, dozing, and dreaming about a kitchen. I'm standing in front of a toaster and I put some bread in to toast, but it won't. Every time they pop up, they're still stone cold. I check the plug and the fuse, but it was still not working. The grill itself is actually heating up, but the bread just won't heat up. The walls are made of a kind of jelly, and when I check the plug from the toaster, I have to plug it in by pushing the plug into this wall of jelly. Then there's this noise and I sense the clatter of cutlery and the gallop of a hundred small pairs of feet. I'm back in school. The walls are clean and the teachers all have an air of friendliness since this is way before you start to hate every fucker you come into contact with. No, this was from back in the day, before regret, before doubt, when all I had was impulsiveness and innocence. On the field I run but am too young to sweat profusely. Never being very good at football, it didn't matter since all it took was to be able to run fast; which I could. Where I run the grass is green and familiar faces with no names run also. The ball flies through the air near me and I lunge for it with my foot, missing the ball but kicking the goalkeeper in the head, who also goes for the ball. He is the hardest kid in juniors. He easily pushes me over then kicks me in the head, knocking me out. Or maybe I stayed down to reduce a further assault. Either way we collided yet somehow became friends. Simple days.

"Who are you?" is the voice coming from next to me, which I sleepily open my eyes to and see a ten-year-old girl with blond hair ready for school. Despite its normality, nothing can prepare you when you've spent all night fucking some random slag and waking up with a little girl asking who you are. My upright jolting wakes Steph and she quickly and expertly puts on a dressing gown without letting her daughter see her naked and battered body.

"Darlin' you had your breakfast?" She nods. "Brushed your teeth?" she nods, and mum lights a cigarette while coughing remnants of life into her throat, and as she straightens her daughters coat I see the tattoo on her arm says *Beth*, not Steph.

"Beth?" I say, softly to myself, but she hears.

"Yes?"

"I," I do one of those I-don't-ever-want-to-see-you-again-but-don't-want-you-to- know-that smiles and say "I think like we've really got a..." and I pretend to look for the word *connection-*

"Got to go. Great meeting you too, Alan." After which she redirects her attention to her daughter as I lay back in bed slightly, planning an exit.

"Right, okay," *Beth* picks up a bag from the floor and gets a five-pound note out, then looks deeper and finds some coins, as she pockets the fiver and hands the change to the girl. "There's your dinner money, love, you have a good day now." She sucks on the cigarette, kisses the girl on the cheek, and then blows the smoke away from her. I feel like mercy killing the poor child.

"Bye, Alan." She sweetly says to me, waving white hands and grimy, bitten fingernails.

"Yeah, bye." I reply.

The girl leaves for school and I fight against the urge to close my eyes and make it all go away.

FLOOR SHOW

Those footprints in the sand are left here for eternity.
Earth moving winds left quashed underneath.
They have all gone away, fearful of respite,
Running to darkness and are never coming back.

Another shit day in Manchester, goes the oldest of sayings. For me more than any as all sense of identity bleeds away like milk boiling underwater.

I entertain myself by browsing for smut in the local porno shops, attaining semi-on after semi-on, dangerously close to public exposure and never so alone in all my life.

To be jobless in a city surrounded by slaves to the empires of professionalism and retail alike you start to feel like a square peg in a wet mouth. Something is out of place and my permanent pastime of scouting the streets for ill-prepared girls can become isolating at best.

I hadn't bought anything, and started to make my way back home to get stoned as a monkey in a lab, but then walked past something that brought back a memory. It was the hotel where I had fucked those two girls. Allowing a small, personal laugh I wonder if the barmaid was working today. I paced outside back up, then away, then back, and finally into the hotel for death and pussy.

I approach the bar and she is there, shining glasses just like I last left her.

"Hello there..." I realize in my haste I hadn't asked her name previously, so wing it from here on.

She drops a vacant expression my way as I watch a penny taking a very long time to drop.

"Oh!" Clink, "Hi, how're you doing?" I'm still not sure she entirely remembers me.

"I'm well, I'm good; what's going on?"
She doesn't really know how to respond to this, but doesn't seem as uncomfortable as I first thought she might.

"Ah, y'know, just working, don't do many of those late shifts, I need my beauty sleep." I laugh a little bit in a cool sort of new-man kind of way.

"Well, yeah, I need more than most as it goes."

"Hmm." She sort of laughs the way bartenders do when they're not working for tips and then goes back to wiping the bar down. I wasn't really sure of her reaction, and didn't want to be annoying as I might fuck up my chances of getting her in to bed.

"Well, I just... I was just passing outside, uh, and I was just... uh," get a grip "and I was just passing and just wondered if you were still around."

"Yep, still here." She picks up a glass from underneath the bar and a cloth and polishes away. I imagine her grabbing my dick and breathing heavily on it, causing the end to swell and shine in whatever light was shining. She coughed and put the glass behind the bar. "What have you been up to, anything nice?"

Aside from brutal murder, chronic drug abuse, mind-numbing pornographic binges and fucking anything that moves, "Not a lot, this and that. I was just passing actually and I thought I'd see if you were in, maybe you wanted to get a drink or something."

"Oh."

"I mean, not right now, just whenever you have time." My eye gaze isn't doing much to win her over and I don't even bother pretending to look for the word "connection". "I feel like when we met we had some sort of connection."

"Right. I'm studying a lot at the moment, and I don't really think I've got time. Plus my boyfriend is the jealous type."

"Right, of course, boyfriend, jealousy; well, you can't spell lousy without it."

"That is true, but, well, you know how it is, a girl like me can't be waiting around forever for every guy who wants to take me out to dinner to return. I'd probably starve to death!" She smiles but there is an aggression masked within, as if saying my words previously should have been followed by an act, and not necessarily the act of penetration. I look with urgency for an exit strategy and turn the bullshit up a notch.

"I swear the last few months have been torture for me. Just murder and torture. You haven't seen a board-room until you've seen one in four continents. I've got more air miles than Branson."

She laughs, with warmth and manners, a laugh practiced to entertain clientele, to generate more tips, and to keep at bay the endless procession of lecherous alcoholics. "So what can I get you?" She asks.

Standing on a metal footbridge crossing Oxford Road I smoke a cigarette and rest my body against the fence as cars pass beneath and the streets bustle, filled with people going about what would be called daily business.

My desires peaked, there lay only the goal of ejaculation to contend and yet I had been so set upon wet mouth or orifice to release into. At least a fucking blow job. I get a shiver as I walk on and stumble over a loose paving slab.

I walk on through the streets, hounding for women, and almost leering at some that pass by, using each angle to view every inch of flesh available with subtlety and control. The

Empire would never fall.

Passing under the great red brick bridge, I see another prostitute and as the streets lighten with people I consider using her for my needs. But as I get closer she is more terrifying than previously thought: all red scabs and greased down hair. My erection now akin to her stockings pocked with holes, and the sound of her breathing enough to fill one with fear. The cigarette smoke she exhales hangs in the air as if the wind forgot to blow here, as if nature itself was perverted beneath this bridge. A stray dog eats something from the road and onwards I walk through the same dusty streets. Angling my compass for home I hesitate while considering the lack of entertainment in my castle. And so further I go. Beyond retail, beyond society, into Ancoats, the dead eyed badlands of Manchester, that place where fashion dictates a stab-proof vest. Warehouse-type businesses with open doors selling the bulk supplies that keep the retail environment in operation, I forge a trail further until my path crosses that of a small adult cinema and I decide I must visit.

The worn-in and ancient smell of cigarettes seems to be almost palpable, joined by the supporting and familiar odours of shame, sweat, and come.

I feel my heart rise in anticipation, surely orgasm was not much further. The quest had taken me most of the day as here I scale the creaking red stairs through a beaded curtain and am presented a stuffy room with cordoned off glass-wall section, inside which sits a comic strip of a man, cigarette attached to lip, ruddy cheeks and a stench that penetrates even the bullet-proof glass separating he and I.

"Member?" He asks.

"Uh, no, first time..." I timidly offer back.

"Right, £10 membership for a year, £8 in screen 1, £10 both screens." Far too much new information as I opt for the easiest.

"Ten for both, here you go mate." I hand over some cash and go to enter.

"Wait you need to fill in your membership. Name please."

"Oh uh, John... Clark." His chubby hands scribbled my information into a dog-eared diary. Handing me the card he motioned me towards Screen 1. Outside the screen was a sort of lobby, well, three chairs, a small TV and a coffee machine so old there may be fossils in the filter. *Kind of like a lobby.* An old man sits in one of the chairs, drinking a coffee and smoking a cigarette. He smiles warmly, but I am not acknowledging anyone in this place and simply look through him.

Inside Screen 1 the mood changes. There are perhaps 20 seats, in a cinema style. The room is not quite half-empty.

In an instant I feel the many wandering eyes. Not just is the sound and vision totally distracting, but also I feel the prick of the "Fresh Meat" sign stuck kindly in my side.

I take a seat near the centre aisle, so any exits I make will be swift and without obstacle.

Settling into the seat I find the film to be incredibly arousing. It is nothing special, content wise, and it seems academic to describe the picture because the action is definitely taking place off-screen. With the aisle to my left, ahead of me and on my right sit two men, conversing in hushed tones. Behind them, a couple of other shady characters. My eyes are drawn to the shadowy goings on behind and I see a young man stroking another man's penis. Perspiration falls from me like rain and my heart continues to throb.

I could walk out and mutter about the lack of a "gay" sign between Adult and Cinema, but then that would be ridiculous. So I sit, smoke a cigarette and relax. After a few minutes the smells become normal and the stale carpet feel is homely and welcoming in a kind of way.

Soon enough a man excuses himself to get past me and sits a couple of seats across. I stand to give access and he has a view as it lurches forth from my unbuttoned jeans. In moments I feel a hand snake across the velveteen chair onto my jeans, and eventually finding a place around my cock. I drive my attention towards the screen, now in it's own battle for standing as 'featured attraction'.

Blonde hair crafted and volumized into a perm tops off the woman who sucks on a half dozen dicks all presented to face. From behind she takes another man and he peddles her hard, loosening the drippings of come that layer like tectonics upon her face.

My own erection growing to heights as it is sucked and jerked in this darkened room. I feel a rising and breath it out, standing and leaving the room momentarily, but not before displaying my erection to the congregation. A different man is now sitting in the lobby, and I decide to drink a coffee and smoke a cigarette. Relaxing somewhat I go to use the bathroom and throw my cigarette into the urinal, with its wall covered in come and all manner of dirty tissues and torn underwear on the floor.

Heart still racing, the lobby is empty now. Screen 1 can be clearly heard through the ultra-thin walls and cardboard door, and Screen 2 also emits a rumble of satisfaction, albeit a quieter one. I prepare myself for but just as I am clearing my throat the beaded curtain giggles and a familiar exchange of words takes place.

It is a female. She speaks quickly to the disgusting old man behind glass then walks through the lobby, past Screens 1 & 2 and into a small, thus far unnoticed door next to the men's toilets.

Staring at the door for a moment I stand and go to see the man behind glass, reading the racing form.

"Alright mate, what's the crack with that bird?" Sighing, as if this question is answered a hundred times an hour. "There's three live shows a day: one, four, and seven-thirty."

"Live show?"

"Screen 1, ten minutes she'll be in."

And sure enough the place began to fill. All types came through as I waited in the lobby. Old and young, executive and labourer, perverts and subverts.

Inside the auditorium seats fill swiftly. The front two rows tightly packed with raincoats and suits, smelling strongly of cheap aftershave, piss and come.

I settled in the third row and vigilantly monitored my neighbours. Still the big screen video played pictures of orgy, one champion arc of sperm clearing her head and sullying a blue couch. With a loud pop, the video is stopped and PA speakers crackle into life and The Stripper by David Rose & His Orchestra bellows from an unbalanced system. A fluorescent strip light pointed at the stage pings on and washes cold light over the entire room. Shame and paranoia flows like a broken dam. At the edge of the stage a door opens and through it walks a mid-forties stripper, wearing a nurses outfit and carrying an overused plastic bag, which she places on the floor next to a black stool atop which she places a stiletto-heeled boot. As the music starts she does a striptease.

Silence washes over the spectators and pieces of clothing are removed. If I were asked for words to describe this situation I would use: grisled-sleaze. From the plastic bag the stripper produces a can of the cheapest whipped cream available at any 24 hour garage, which she squirts onto her breasts, veined-blue and mis-proportioned, then gets one of the aging punters in the front row to lick it from her. As her tattered thong comes off she hides her sagging cunt with one hand, and with the other layers cream into the many folds.

I hadn't noticed, but like everyone else, I was masturbating with racehorse focus.

The man next to me touched my cock and getting carried away he falls into my lap, administering anonymous oral sex. Trying to focus my energy on the dancer, trying harder to black-out all I could now see and feel. Shame leaked from the audience, and I felt a surge when our eyes met, feminine contact, however degraded a female, was still just-that.

To ensure my heterosexuality I raised myself slightly

from my seat, giving the dancer a clear view of my member, then came an amount so heavy that as it landed on the pervert next to me all that could be heard were curses.

Post-wank guilt is something of an event at home, but in a stale adult cinema full of the cities' most debauched and wretched folk it is a cross I have to drag from Screen 1 to Golgotha. But drag it I do, at least as far as the coffee machine in the lobby, empty now as the stripper completes her act and a muted, one-handed round of applause ripples through the room.

She exits the side door swiftly, and walks through the lobby placing items back into the plastic bag. As she passes she tries her best not to allow our eyes to meet but she fails and I catch just a fragment of her soul within my trap. A piece of her cheap black net top trails at her side and I silently wipe come from my hand onto it, providing a chemical marker that beastly types may follow. After she is gone there is nothing to keep me here. My objective was complete, my orgasm passed.

At the exit to the cinema I realise that the real problem was leaving onto the empty street without being clocked by anyone. I prepare myself and set off on a glorious run from awful reality back into manufactured paradise.

My legs tire quickly and I wonder where my health has gone. As I put distance between the stuffy room and me, I find the pseudonymous membership card and destroy it, tearing it into small pieces and scattering like the ashes of an enemy.

Up in my flat the dishes smell from a pasta meal I cooked last night and sit unwashed crowding the sink and I walk past them as I drop my jacket and take off my shoes then press 'play' on the remote control and turn on the television, which brings me (back) to hardcore pornography. Slugs of come shine matted into the material of my clothes, which pile quietly into a corner.

Six men stand over a tanned eighteen-year-old girl with pig-tails and lipstick smudged along a white school shirt collar. When the actress looks into the camera I am sickened and turn the tape 'off'.

Silence is like a deafening roar and my mind races with a series of subjective problems, complex and difficult to translate. Surveying the town through my windows I watch the bridge. Here is where the action is. High in my castle I watch the girl, and realise, as she walks closer to my house that she has blonde hair. She's still smoking, or smoking again. When a car pulls up she leans in, holding her cigarette out of the car and talks for a second. Her skirt rides up a little and just above her knee now, quite long for a prostitute. The man inside the car moves his arm and she jerks her head back, leaving the car to pull away on its own. I've seen this one before; this spot is frequented by a number of different girls, but probably the same six or seven.

While I watch, I drink a beer from the fridge and smoke rolled cigarettes.

Time passes an hour quickly, as the girl walks up and down and back and round. I always assumed that streetwalkers were picked up every five minutes or so. A few people walked past her that she tried to stop but they weren't having any of it. At one point I thought something exciting was going to happen when two lads walked past, pissed, and started talking to her, which quickly changed to them shouting obscenities while standing on one side of the road and walking away from her, a sufficient distance in case of emergency.

I began to feel sorry for the girl. As she stood, I counted her smoking six cigarettes, pretty much one after the other. A man arrived, a skinny guy, scruffy as hell. He started talking to her, but when he spoke, he did a lean-backwards-thing that I couldn't quite get my head around. I rolled a joint while watching. He spoke to her for a little longer than you would imagine, then patted his pockets; he was bartering. The girl obviously wasn't being paid that much anyway so had little bargaining power. The sun had long gone down and a half-moon shone dully in the sky with the memory of airplanes past cut across it dark grey on black. A yellow lamp washed the floor they stood in and cast dark shadows below them. Right next to the bridge under which she walked was a patch of wasteland, a makeshift car park. He scuttled towards it, and kept looking back at her, finding himself standing inside the car park, between two puddles that reflected another yellow light up to me and gave him a surreal kind of framing. She looked nervous, but that goes with the territory as he continued gesturing for her to follow him, obviously with the promise of money. Behind her lurked the night, cars rolling silently on roads towards nowhere, water dripping endlessly from the bridge onto the road, forming yet more puddles with two wide lines from tire prints, one going that way, the other coming this. She followed the scruffy man and they walk together, goading, haggling. She takes the deal and reluctantly walks with the man towards some dark conclusion and out of my view to elsewhere. I looked for a better position when all of a sudden they were visible once more, seeming to have found a place out of the way enough for comfort and sordid dealings.

The maze of tunnels and train lines are so a part of the city they are like her fingerprints. From a tiny alley they have access to a darkened, oily tunnel, one of dozens you can reach from the ground. Straining my eyes to be able to see her blonde hair get into position, I wasn't happy with the viewpoint, and the weed was taking hold of me in a very strange way. Suddenly I remember that my camcorder has a "night-shot" function so run to the bedroom and retrieve it, poising it by the window for a suitable vantage. I finally get it targeted on the two and am impressed with how much I can see.

It wasn't the most explicit scene, but I could see her on her knees in front of him, leaning against the rear of a billboard. Her back was to me, but I could see her skirt splayed out over the ground and moonlit hair held against his stomach and between his legs. His hand reached onto the back of her head and began to push it further and deeper onto his dick. As he shoved harder, she pulled back and said something inaudible to him and he seemed to snarl or curse something back at her, then she went back to sucking him off. Numerous cars passed just out of view of the blow-job ditch and a new girl was dropped off at the corner, but she wasn't around for long and the other girl was almost finished in the car park. I couldn't hear what they were saying but I could see everything. His body jerked and pushed forward as he came, and she stood up and spat on the floor, then lit a cigarette while he put himself back into his trousers.

The urge for completion swelling in me through psycho-social engagement as a third party. Lost in the confines of the blurred images and comfortable chair paradox, I cleaned the pipes of the day of baseness at the window in full view.

STONE FISH CUNT

I can pretend just like you
There is no shame inside my soul.
All these things around my neck
Are choking me to certain death.

A beetle crawls from a straight crack in the floor around the pine wood inlets. The television plays a game show hosted by some pretty rough bird. Actually she's okay. It's a numbers game where the answers are behind some numbers and they showed the answers at the start, which I miss due to a lack of giving a fuck. She asks some questions and I see if I can guess them.

The first one I get right, and am surprised, then I get the second one right and think I might be psychic. I get the third one wrong and she goes on to the people at home quiz. I cannot believe the fucking question: There is a dial of eight numbers, spelling out the word pavement. The question she asks is, what word do these letters spell. What the fuck? The question is, I suppose, can you read?

Crouching on my sofa, I wonder what to do with my time. Wrapped to the base of my chin in a goose down sleeping bag, or something.

In a few seconds, I'm going to have a cigarette.

On the other hand, maybe I will have a joint. I just got back home from the cruelest world. Water still pours from the sky and leaves me soaked to the bone. No talent on those grey, dead streets. Naked now, my clothes piled in a corner of the room, proudly sodden with muddy water ingrained into my off-coloured socks. I keep catching my chin against the zip of the sleeping bag, and my feet are stone cold and still wet. I feel sick. Rubbing my toes together that feel like a bunch of wet asparagus sliding against each other in a rubber vacuum. I put my hands on my penis, which is very hot, but flinches against the sweaty cold palms. The drawer in the table is where I keep my weed, but checking inside I can see I'm out of tobacco. There are bits of cigarettes all over the place, and torn up train tickets, cigarette boxes ripped up for roaches. Fuck. I have nothing to do tonight and no-one to do it with, and all I want to do is just smoke myself into a stupor and let noise and light pour out of the TV. Where is that fucking tobacco? Fuck it. I changed jackets earlier on, and left my Marlboro's inside the other one, and was actually caught short when I went back out, so I go on a hunt for the jacket then realise it's sitting right next to me. It's a brown leather bomber jacket that I picked up in a shop on Oldham Street for about twenty-five-quid, or whatever it was. The inside pocket is torn but still has the name "Peter Caruso" stitched on to it.

Got my lighter, cigarettes next. Cigarettes. Cigarettes?
Where are they? Shit. Where the fuck are they?
I check all the pockets, check near my jacket, check the jeans I was wearing, nothing. My other jacket I wore when I got caught in the rain, my denim jacket. No, not there. I run down the long, pure white corridor and into my bedroom. The bed is unmade, with a few pairs of jeans and some dirty underwear, along with a pair of knickers and a thong I picked up from some foolish girl and a washing line, respectively. Not there, either. The rain is drenching the whole city; it's that insane weather, where you can just walk to the other side of the flat

and it changes. Right now, I can see a combination of heavy rain with hailstones. The sky is jet black like trillion-barrel wells of oil tapped deep underwater.

Check the kitchen, check the bathroom: nothing. *Christ.* I anchor down, dejected, into the sofa. I'm naked and my feet still shiver.Think about having a wank over the new porn video, but cannot even motivate myself to get an erection, let alone masturbate. I want a cigarette. The ashtray is overflowing with dead butts, and I bet I can probably make one from leftovers. Fuck that, I haven't done that since I was nine. I had to get some; I have to go outside. Okay, but first...

I only have a little weed left in the big bag, enough to get stoned, enough for one good joint, but not enough to get really fucked. Maybe it's psychological, I don't care. The pipe I got from the head shop is in the third drawer and in my hands before long. I haven't used this thing with weed, only hash. I don't know if it'll work as well, but I'm certainly willing to try.

The pipe is a little thing made out of volcanic rock, and has an Indian symbol or something on it, with a red dot painted over its so-brown-it's-black surface. I drop a good load into the end, which is blocked partly by a bit of hardwood, and pack it down. The clipper lights first time, and I place the end in my mouth, almost lying down to get the angle. The weed catches but a few bits of ash drop into my mouth, making me pull back. My fingers search out the stray bits of black and green from my tongue, and I sit up a little more, putting the pipe at a flatter angle. The weed catches, a good lungful. I hear the weed crackle and know it's hot but keep taking as much as I can. A burning sensation layers the inside of my throat, and I start to choke. My mouth widens and I sit back in the chair, letting out a cough, and then croak the word:

"Woah," cough "woah," cough "woah," cough and my eyes stream with tears I put down the pipe for a second; head resting on my knees. The burn is making my throat feel like I've just eaten a tube of toothpaste, but there was no mint, and my eyes won't close. I'm thinking I want to eat fish. I want to have a fish. The room plays a bass note, which begins an acid jazz live band playing in my ear - and do they ever know how to play - the music is so good. It makes you want to eat a fish, ah, so much. If I leave now I can get to the supermarket and buy a piece of fish, and some vegetables, oh yeah. Let's do it, I'm ready. I concur with myself that I wanted to go shopping for fish and vegetables. So we start to think not about murdered lovers but about moving our legs, so that I'm not late in getting my food. Cough "Woah."

It's cold outside. The rain has subsided since I got from my room to the front door. The streets look paved with gold since the streetlamps are orange. Cars drive by and carve black lines into it. I shove my hands inside the pockets of my jacket and march as quickly as I can to the supermarket. Pretty girls walked by overhead, but it did not matter because I needed to eat. My stomach was empty. I'd only had a Mars bar and a chicken salad sandwich all day. Shit I just remembered, one Coke as well, nothing else to drink. Oh my God. We're close now. I skip over the rubbish in the street, and around the bus shelter inhabited by the usual fucking old ladies and some other fucker business men. There it is, bright lights in my eyes, I walk in with an ear-to-ear grin and skip my way to a basket, then towards the bakery.

Need a loaf of bread. What to get? How about white? Hmm. Nice and soft. No, I won't eat it 'til tomorrow, so I don't want boring old white bread because tomorrow is going to be a creative day. How about a granary loaf? Good, good, small enough so I don't have to eat too much, but a little hard. I don't want hard bread. Big granary? No, I won't waste bread. White it must be. Okay white it is. No, fuck that, I take the granary loaf, small. Okay, to the fish counter.

The guy behind there is a big fatty who is the man with the knowledge on fish. He always recommends the best shit.

"Hello there," He says in a broad edged middle-English accent,

"Hey, well, I - the fish you sold me the other day, what,

the smoked thing, that was just - it was so good, so... I think something along the same lines, pardon the pun. Ah you've swordfish."

"Yeah the swordfish is really good, 'bit like tuna, maybe a bit tougher. Closer to a steak kind of thing, I really like it."

"Mmm, the swordfish, yeah." He goes to pick it up. "Actually, uh, I think, what about the tuna?"

"Tuna's good, fresh, just got it this afternoon."

"Well, I don't want the smoked thing again. How about, do you have smoked tuna?"

"No, we don't do that here." I don't think they do it at all. "We-"

"What about lobster?" I say, for some reason in a very high pitched voice. He gives a little smile.

"We used to do lobster, but it was so small, and so expensive, I mean, it was only this big," He makes a hand gap the size of a midget's foot "and were like, seventeen, twenty quid each, I mean, people just laughed, y'know, never bought it."

"Well, yeah I guess that is expensive." Right. "Actually. What about the smoked? Yeah, I think the smoked, definitely."

"Okay," his big hands get a pair of something's and start to search for a fish among the pile.

"Just get a fat one, mate."

"Here?" The tool is over a big one, but it is too flaky.

"No, just um," I point at one with a fat end "there, that one."

"Just a piece off this one then?"

"Yeah, half please."

"Okay half." The guy weighs it out and gets a price. "Two-twenty-five?"

"Yeah man that's fine." The fish is bagged and sent to my basket. "Cheers man."

Suddenly I'm in the vegetables section. There are so many different kinds. What do I want? I couldn't decide: Sweet-corn-on-the-cob, definitely, in the basket. Now what?

Cabbage? No. Asparagus? They didn't have any. Baby corn? No, that's stupid, I already have corn. Green beans? I let out a big sigh, I don't want anything green. Broccoli? Broccoli? Yeah, yeah, broccoli. It's green but that's it. Let's go.

I walk past the salad bar. I wanted some potato salad. My body stops at the wrong end, so I keep looking past the croutons, the pasta salad, and coleslaw. I finally get to it. Now that I'm here, I really don't know if I want it. I stood there for a while, looking around. I needed something in the meal with juice or wetness to it, potato salad would be fine, but now that I see it it looks like shit. I thought about tasting it, but I chickened out in the end. I just make my way to the till, when I pass beetroot. Yeah, fuck yeah, I have beetroot in the fridge. I'm having that. Feet move to the checkout and I queue at the prettiest girl's till. Load up my shopping onto the conveyor belt, which seems to take forever and then stand in front of the girl. I've been here before, I recognise her face, as per name tag. Syal is her name, and she says:

"Hello there." And I can tell she recognises me too.

"Hi, how're you doing?" That's like my every-time greeting.

"Uh, I'll be better when I get out of here."

"Ah well, only like, what? Ten, twenty minutes 'til you close right?"

"Yeah, something like that, we've got to clean then though."

"Ah, the old clean-up time." What? The food all goes through.

"Do you want any cash-back?"

"No, no I definitely-don't want-any-cash-back."

"Okay," a pause "God I get so sick of asking for that. Every time. All day, it's a nightmare. So bored."

"Ah c'mon, it's not that bad. I mean, how many people get to go to work each day and sit opposite a fish counter?" She laughs at my comedy and I look around for any more fans, but none are there.

"You try it, come and sit here all day and see if you like it." She has that Anglo-Asian street accent that'll probably get her turned down for a mortgage one day.

"Well y'know I would, of course, but uh, I'm always very busy. But I could see myself sitting where you are. Wherever you are." Another laugh.

"Yeah I thought you might." She's bagged up my stuff and I put my hands through the loops.

"I'm not *that* obvious, am I?"

"Only in what you want and how you want it."

I hung on her words and paused for a moment, enjoying the shared imagery we both were surely witnessing, that of her mouth slobbering around my cock and salivating as her throat opens beyond human reaches.

"In fact- here's one for you: I *never* want cash back, I never *need* it, so: every time I'm in, don't ask me, and if you remember, you'll be like, 'Hey that's the guy who never has cash back, so now that I don't have to ask him,' it's like a bit of variety in the day. And if *I* remember that'll be a miracle, but we'll take it one step at a time, how about that?" She's really laughing. I am a God amongst peasant pigs that burn into grisled skin and charred hair.

"Right we'll see next time, I will."

She coyly writes something on my receipt and hands it over.

"It's a deal! I'll do my *best* to remember."

"Have a good night."

"Certainly will do, you too."

At the cigarette counter, there are three people in the queue. The first, an old lady stuck at the front of the line, talking with some other old lady behind the counter about fuck-knows-fuck-cares what, a guy in front with bleached blond hair in a shitty style, and me. The old lady isn't going to move, but the other guy is taking forever.

I shift from foot to foot, resting each leg as much as the other and desperate for the fucking people in front to *please, fucking move.* My head turns my body around and I glance at the magazine rack while I am waiting and look at all the half-naked women with blonde hair and big tits and golden skin and layers of sweat dressed by art department stylists to look like come. The covers look back at me and pout their lips in unison. The queue still stands. I think about how I am going to cook the fish; I'll sauté it in milk, bang some cheese in, boil the broccoli. The queue moves forward a couple of paces. I start to move into the place of the blonde boy, but he just steps right back in front of me with a packet of chewing gum. Oh Christ. Back to the magazines. Nameless celebrity exposed as whore. Other nameless celebrity exposed as gay. Dead celebrity named as God and washed-up celebrity named as island love-rat. Smile for the camera. Don't be shy. You're a star, you're a star. So much money. My mind is wandering now. Gliding across the nightly-polished tile surface next to the cigarette department. Softly slipping across the room. The queue moved, the raging homo departed.

I order some tobacco as my turn comes.

The fat old lady still stands next to me and I can hear her friend saying "maybe, maybe", and all the women are here now and they're all old, then one rubs up behind the other so she can get my tobacco and I can see their fat, naked bodies touching, all clammy and pink. Like hocks of ham rolling down a greased chute leading from the killing room.

"Cash-back?" Fuck it.

"Twenty quid please."

"Thanks."

I'm out but not until I laugh at the security guard dressed like an American mall guard.

A chill breeze cuts quickly past me as I exit the store and see the blond homo casting an over-practiced "resting bitch face" at cars that refuse to stop for his advances across the street. I entertain myself with thoughts of him falling under one of said cars with a great crunching of soft skin and peroxide.

The air, dense with a fine rain soaks me once more to

completion. I shiver and laugh while speed walking takes over. Nobody walks the same street as I do, but his or her lack of presence only seems to make me faster. The door gets closer and the rain subsides, my feet are wet but there is no sense in stopping as I near my house. The road collects puddles at the edge that block me from one side but I skip over them with ease. The usual slab outside my door tries to wet me further, but I evade that too.

Broccoli spills out onto the crumb-mottled and coffee-stained kitchen surface. I take the tobacco and walk into the living room, shedding clothes as I do. Another set joins the growing pile of festering Alex-wear scattered around like reptilian skin.

Onto the sofa and straight into drawer number one to get the weed. A big skin comes out and I bed it flat down on the surface. Where's the video remote? I check the sofa, then under a sock and find a new German or Dutch porno. I turn it on at the part where the thirty-year-old blonde woman is being fucked by a fat man in a very uncomfortable position. She seems to be enjoying it. I load the skin so much; I can't remember when I last had this much in one joint. All evenly spaced, all impotence causing twigs removed and on with the light dusting of tobacco. While my hand goes for the bag, I look at the television and see the blonde now standing, well squatting, above another woman's face and rubbing her clit, then she leaves it and her face is all contorted, the other woman has, I think two fingers in her cunt. A sudden plot twist as the blonde squats frog-like over the others face and begins to urinate like a seven-pint dam has burst. Although the director must have provided a script for this scene the recipient is ill-prepared and begins coughing and choking, rolling over onto her side to catch breathe. This tickles me and a snorted guffaw of laughter escapes through my nose. I felt the air move around me and glanced back to the table where I was rolling. My face dropped. My fists tightened. My eyes widened and pupils shrunk to the size of a grain of Tom

Thumbs' rice. I looked down to my skin to put the tobacco in, and found I had blown away all-of-my weed except a tiny bud.

"Fuck!" fuck "Fuck, fuck, fuck!" What the fuck am I doing? The bitch on TV chokes again and my next giggle blows away the last bud, which joins the rest swimming in a pool of beer.

Fuck it.

I get my dick out and start working on a cure to boredom, but as I remove my wallet from my pocket the receipt falls out with the Syals number sketched onto it. A flicker of excitement as the prospect of new pussy rises into target, like that *most-golden* of geese. Using my phone and still in the throes of half-masturbation, I call the number and she agrees to come round almost immediately.

An obligatory spring-clean is in swift order as pornographic magazines, red top tit-laden newspapers and half-empty cups of tea, beer cans, bottles and over-flowing ashtrays are quickly brushed and hurried out of the lounge until the place looks almost respectable just in time as the intercom buzzer goes *bzzzz*.

"Alex?" Comes the voice through the monitor and on the screen I see her standing, somewhat daunted yet all the same here in this strange place.

"Hey Syal, come on up, 4ᵗʰ floor."

She arrives still in her work clothes, with a fleece over her top for warmth. As she enters the apartment there is a guarded chemistry between us.

"This is so weird!!" She shivers.

"What is?" I ask.

"Just coming round here like this!! I don't even know you!"

"Oh *that*! No, plenty of girls that come round here and don't know who I am!" My words seem to her a satirical construction but there is much truth behind the supposed humour. I laugh at her misplaced rapport.

"Come in, anyway! Do you fancy a cup of tea?" I am

learning the hidden language of the lower class.

"Ooh yes please," She replies in earnest.

"Well make yourself at home. Enjoy the view."

As I walk away from her I trail a finger across the small of her back, just to make sure she understands that sexual interaction is forthcoming.

The kettle takes time to boil and I sink two teabags in waiting.

"Do you take sugar?!" I call through to the other room.

"Two-please!" Comes the reply, followed by: "Can I take a quick shower?!"

"Of course!!" I reply, "There are clean towels in the cupboard outside the bathroom, just go down the corridor, second door on the right.

In the sugar bowl sits the gilded ivory spoon and next to that is the brown envelope, very much depleted, but still more loaded than most. I consider drugging her tea, but as she is now naked in my bathroom using my shower it's likely that I won't need to, but for safety's sake I dose us both with just a little of everything.

In the lounge I smoke a cigarette, drinking tiny sips of hot tea and looking out of the open window. My whore down below, pacing east and west, hidden in black shadows beneath the bridge, then exposed by yellow streetlights and headlamps of her potential clientele.

"Tea's ready!" I call from the lounge, when suddenly she walks, naked and dripping wet into the room.

"Sugar?" She asks.

"Yes please." I reply and go over to her, embracing and kissing passionately, her wet body hard and toned, receives my hands that run and grope over her not so hidden parts. She pushes me down to my knees and wraps one leg around my face and over my shoulder, pushing her soft, clean genitals into my mouth and face. Chewing without teeth she begins writhing on top of me, my knees on the floor and her hand supporting her arched body on the coffee table. This moment, like all others, is balanced in perfection. Her cunt like a sliver sliced through sugary orange peel, the nectar even sweeter. Tiny peekings of soft downy hair like felt tips, almost like velvet on my tongue.

She reaches a certain point close to orgasm then stops, changing position and presenting on all fours across the large brown cushions of the sofa. I start with deep penetration, hard and shaded golden, Godlike. With every thrust we meet in a different moment. A million such lost in the space of one bitten-red-lip.

Pace and intensity quickens and slows like the ratios of tidal flow, gaining force and velocity, ebbing ever upwards. My usual thumb penetrates her anus easily and I taste it moments later. An almost refreshing anal essence certainly unlike many of the preceding assholes I have had the misfortune to eat. Probing her deeply I switch and lift her round, falling between the couch and the hardwood floor. Something about the position and rigidity of the floor builds my orgasm as I push her down onto the floor with my pelvis and my hands reach around her throat. Once more those old feelings of sexual aggression rise but only in as much as is needed to achieve ecstasy. As I begin to writhe she notices my stroke and turns, removing herself from my penis and squatting over my face instead, allowing me to fuck her in the mouth. Lost deep within her I feel the back edges of teeth and fleshy tonsils enveloping and then releasing my cock head like a hummingbird flaps its little wings. The room begins to take on a blue glow that flashes and as I ejaculate I turn my head and exhale, moaning deeply and drooling onto the floor, which I look across and beneath the couch and see a solitary tooth, roots faced up. Regaining some sort of control I suddenly realize that the room is flashing in blue light, pocked with regularity and I rush to my feet, leaving the girl on the floor naked and masturbating to a finish.

Rushing over to the window there are a number of emergency vehicles outside and it all seems to be tumbling down upon me, some forgotten detail, some clue left unburied or unburned or piece of me foolishly stowed along with damning evidence of murder and treachery.

"Get your clothes on." I command and Syal looks up to see me leave the lounge and to the bedroom so to get a better look at the gathering squadron.

She follows softly, arriving at my back as I peer out through dusty windows.

"What is it?" She asks.

I reply in silence, quickly putting clothes onto my naked body.

On the street I can see the police and services entering the building. It won't be long until they are at the door. I decide to take it like a man, no running, no crying, just approach and cooperate. Simple, time served, good behaviour shall be forthcoming. Murder without resisting arrest. That is surely something. Does dismembering and scattering her body across the country and into the sea count as resisting arrest?

In the lounge by the front door I stand, listening to heavy boots and muffled exchanges of words. Male and female, authority and compliance. It is time to face the music as metaphoric curtains fall ever-so-slowly.

I open the door and my eyes naturally close, as if facing certain death. The commotion and clamouring of many bodies in uniform carrying various pieces of equipment is perceptible even in blindness and I slowly open my eyes expecting the hands of justice to be swiftly upon me.

But they go instead to the door facing opposite, the landlords house, where his wife stands crying glass tears and smoking a cigarette, wailing at the officers to be careful of the new carpet and wallpaper.

Alan is dead.

His body slumped in the hallway, next to a scattered bundle of folded clothes headed for the wardrobe. He died doing his chores. Here lies a life spent in cowardice and a death zestfully taken as sweet, sweet reprieve.

Syal stands behind me, head lowered in reverence.

"Oh my God. Do you know him?" A stony silence rose inside the hallway, muting the lumped footsteps and heavy hands of the emergency services crew.

"He - was my landlord. His name was Alan. He was a very sad and lonely man."

"Wipe your feet for Christ's sake!" Yelled the widow, and I prayed for her very own special kind of death while softly closing the door.

R IMMING THE POT POURRI

Time before, there was a man
Who searched for stars, and lived alone.
He made a fire, he cut the stone.
Simply flesh, wrapped on bone.

A bone dried off-white gull feather clings limpet-like to a blackened igneous rock caught like a chewing tooth in the silt-lined coast of England's south-western edge.

Salt and whitefish strain and fall away from and onto the stoic, yet ever changing beach, gathering in pools for a moment of peace before shuttled once more to the infernal sea.

The adolescent sun hides his pock-marked face behind a deep blanket of sweating, grey clouds. There would be no light today: impossible. Over the revolting seas came odd markers; invisible messages in well considered bottles long lost to the truth and fury of all natural terror.

All manner of forgotten worlds meet in this place; oils liberated from the knotted core forming new crusts over shipping rope and candy bar wrappers alike. Here stood the bleached exoframes of warring Gods of the wash, bettered by the tremendous elevations and unforgiving inhabitants of this open, blinding place. There was no favoritism here- no agreeable eye or scornful hand- as the reef finds ascension to the light; as the ice moves and cuts the earth, there lays the real answer, a pure action, a motive without conscience, a consciousness without reason.

As these empires rise and fall their story is recollected through markings and footprint. This day is no different, armies of good and evil, positions of such in constant sway, no one nor thing forgiven nor forsaken since the truth teaches there is no right and is no wrong; only forward.

Lost somewhere between the lines of this world and that shatters an epilogue in another mystery. Its unnatural curves and shades stand stark to an impressionistic wet dream; that spectrum of misery in technicolour. Its edges cracked and broke away, pieces lost and floating into foam or formed with clay into some part of the bigger picture; invisible to all but vital and renewing in its placement. The once perfectly formed casting now lies crumbling, reducing into dust as eternal waves wash back and forth, back and forth. As the world ends the seas will give up her dead, and all souls shall be freed once more.

"Saying, you Muggle cunt, you can fuck right off- get them in."

"Two – one, dickhead: yours."

"Y'fouled on the white, you want to play fuckin' Yank rules, moving white on a foul. Soft cunt." I had won the debate with traditional, bile-filled aggression and candour.

Pete rolls the cue onto the poorly green baize tortured by vomit and Stella and I rack up another session, vainly straining to spin the black, post-triangle. Waiting, I smoke, standing halfway in and halfway out, complying as much as possible with restrictive rules on tobacco consumption.

Pete returns, anchors the ale onto a table and makes one of his own cigarettes.

"Next week when is it?" I ask.

"Thursday, half one. Just make sure you bring your passport and license and tell Fiona that you know Dave- she'll sort you out."

"Fuckin' need it like, I'm brass as fuck. Still can't be arsed with the shit though."

"Ah it'll be alright, just remember to keep your line open after calls, keeps the clock ticking,"

"Yeah but half eight in the morning, who the fuck's even going to answer their phone at that time?"

Pete argues for the negative as he stands at the edge of the garden. "Fuckin' no one, man: bums on seats though; that's what she used to tell me." Pete lights the cigarette, gulping beer, exhaling smoke, smoking again. My tailored smoke is dead.

"Ah well." I line the shot and break the balls, none pocketing.

"Have you seen John?"

"John," I search my mind, "nah, you mean Johnny OD or what's his name? Porno John?"

"Fuckin', Polak John, Yonn, what's his face- with the hat."

I pot a yellow stripe.

"Oh yeah Yan-Yonn, nah man, fuck knows."

"He's over there, working mornings as well, he'll sort you out like he's a good lad."

"Safe." I pot a red stripe then fuck up the next. "Fuck that's it, you should clean up off this."

"I've still got seven- you reverse-psychology cunt."

"I like to play the long bluff, you know me."

"Fucking dick." As insults fall from his mouth, Pete's phone starts ringing and he curses again. "Work." Pete lays his cue down on the table as he goes to the beer garden to take the call.

"Gi's the 'ting." I softly ask, now Pete caught two ways, slips his hand into his pocket and hands me the paper wrap, discreetly palm-to-palm.

Although the toilets were filled with human feces there was still a great deal of reverence for the stalls at the Dog. For years it had been a mainstay of junkies and chronic alcoholics alike. It had a customary surface which the diverse clientele managed to keep relatively clean. Relative, that is, to the footprints of shit up the wall, to the inch of piss rippling like an orange koi pond disturbed by the beating of a mayfly's wing. But we had evolved beyond mere surfaces here, and so I used a key.

The air hot and heavy leaves the baggy caked, drugs slowly liquifying, but then finally regain bronchial clarity and take my dose. Through the frosted bubbles of glass separating the garden from the toilets a lazy sun reminded myself that it was mid-afternoon on a Tuesday, although I am relieved since this is cheap cocaine (seems almost foolish to pay top dollar for a lunchtime jaunt through a few haunts). My face feels dry; almost doll-liked, after a clean razor beat its way across my cheeks and neck. The obligatory missed spots- the teenage acne always threatening to return in definite adulthood. In turn, I do another key, slightly larger than before then check the wrap to see the damage. Not as bad as I thought so I dab some, a good ending to any chapter. Returning the wrap to my palm I run my finger over the usual drug-taking station and find a healthy portion of white powder left forgotten by men with more money than sense, or at least drugs. By now my gums feel nothing, and these teeth feel foreign and belonging elsewhere. It is an amicable separation and feeling of momentary peace before the toilet door crashes open, rattling its hinges and swinging into my sore arm with Pete's boot the motivating factor.

"Fucks sake!"

"How fuckin' long are you being?"

I make a weary sigh, somewhat not of this world and grin in polyphonics as I tap two more lines from the wrap. And in continuation, I am still not sure who won the game of pool, which stood to gather dust as the entirety of mankind burns into salt while we faced it with our backs turned and leaving nothing but memories.

Another wave crashes down: giant, world destroying.

Hermit crabs and sand flies skip and skate for sanctuary, some surviving, others lost. This once perfect cylindrical cast now cracked into many more pieces, some gathered and heaped at its base, others scattered among the many rivers and seas.

From high above, in the swell of thermals glares the rigid frame of a gull, charcoal black tips on dirty white wings and eyes that never blink, dried out and rock-like, taking the place of some creature from hell- yellow and foreign and rigid against the billowing wind. But keen. So keen, in fact that even from this height comes something reflective, refractive. At first here and gone as quickly as a spark, but then, persisting, some light escaping from the rocky decadence.

The gull lands, scouting now for the glimmer that might furnish a nest so proudly. Until the gull senses something else. Food. Hopping and balancing, occasionally taking to flight, the gull makes its way across the many rocks and pools until it comes to a procession of tiny ants, and bluebottles feasting and laying minute eggs. In this place, cracked between two rocks there lay a shape unlike the others, and cracked through the middle. The gull hovered briefly and landed on the top, peering into the crack with his beady eye and crooked beak until once again the glimmer came. In alert the gull let out a cry, and tried to fit its beak into the crack, but the glimmer was too far down. Only the flies and ants could reach it, and they had little interest in things that glisten and glimmer. But still they came, marching and flying into the crack, using the low tide to reach their plunder before night falls and the sea takes back its booty.

I find myself in a two up two down council house with my cock in an older woman's mouth. I sit relaxed on a pleated-velveteen couch in fuschia pink and watch a series of commercials about personal injury claims companies. A man falls off a ladder; he is rescued by a graphical representation of The Company's logo. I then look over the mantlepiece at a number of photographs, some framed, some loose. I put my hand back into her hair, just to remind her I'm still awake.

The cheap drugs will have been cut with who knows what but the effect isn't completely negative, my erection remains but ejaculation seems unlikely. I have to resort to fantasies of past conquests, of situations far beyond the realms of common decency, of subjugation, degradation, humiliation; of tearing the bodies of festering whores into pieces and fashioning new holes with which to fuck. Of knocking out teeth so to promote smooth and bloody gummed fellatio. I have to force myself in a little more, her Yorkshire Tea-and-Regal king-size stained teeth coughing sharply onto me. All of which eventually works and by the time the commercials are finished I do likewise in the back of her mouth and side of her face, cheeks flushed and blistering red veins carved by years of alcoholism. A late-night repeat of a farming soap opera resumes on the television, and I have my cue to exit stage left.

The all too familiar route home falls black as night-time creeps in. I too, skirting to the shadows and overhanging rafters, shadows seeping in endless procession down the street like some part of the human delta. Kathy, my mature acquaintance, had barely grown tired of my appearance, instead encouraging me constantly to see her more often. That was all I needed. She, a 47-year-old canker sore with heffing breasts that slap like mashed potatoes onto a school dinner plate. She, with a caesarian scar from rib cage to pelvis that could have been cut with sharpened sea-shells. She, who chain smokes king-sized cigarettes and coughs like a Volvo estate. Thank Christ for the walk home. Regret is a strong word, one I try to limit strongly. So instead I look to the positive, keeping to the shadows on the way to my little crevice in the city.

In these early twilight hours, street-walking prostitutes are few in their numbers. Only the least desirable, most desperate and down-trodden remain. Even the rain begins to fall upon them with spiteful laughter. I encountered one I had seen a few times before. It is a small community, that of the whores of Manchester, and in time, one could easily defile them all. She accepts five pounds in coins and wanks me off onto her hand while she swears and curses at me. For an extra three pounds she allows my free hands to finger her cunt through stinking and oversized stockings, torn at the crotch for convenience. She starts to complain as I take longer than initially indicated to ejaculate, and I argue that this is no exact science, but soon enough I do come on her hand and we call it even, going our separate ways. Cleaning the pipes after such a filthy skank as Kathy has become par for the course and I am always open to new methods and practices. However these days it feels all I am ever doing is cleaning the pipes.

Sun now well-risen, traffic starts to build and hunger chimes within. There is a short walk down a side street to a greasy spoon cafeteria that serves a range of hot treats. As I sit in the plastic moulded seats there are scant few other patrons, but this steadily changes as all manner of people from various professions enter and sit, eating and drinking tea and coffee. The smell of bacon and eggs heavy on the air and coffee never tasted so bitterly sweet. Avoid as I could the actions of recent times there would only be so long I could remain aloof, before the certainty of punishment fell forth. But it was an academic matter at this point, those notions being buried within myself, there for no one else to see.

Finishing the meal, I take a great swig of coffee and huddle my coat up, braced for the cold outside. As the tail of my coat rises I notice a dried come stain on my upper thigh, and wonder how long it may have been there. Fortunately the coat is long enough to cover.

Cradling my solitude like a weakling child, the streets are awash with fevered people rushing elsewhere, carrying bags stuffed with useless products churned out of Chinese sweatshops and marked up in price by a thousand percent. Loud, ambient music, not at all as to be expected on these streets of commerce fills my ears, something familiar. I turn my head to see and find a symbol, a design, pattern: it is the cover of *Twoism*. Heading into the store my trench coat flaps in the wind as it meets hard early-morning AC.

Pete standing alone at the desk looks at a magazine with the cover ripped off. I approach him in the empty store.

"Fuck is this, Pete?"

"Hey what's going on, you're up early."

"Out late. Is that fucking *Twosim*?"

"Yes! Can you believe it? Just out today."

As Pete speaks some little cunt walks up to the desk with a copy of the offending article and purchases it for less than ten pounds. "Still, you've got a collectible now man, probably worth even more. Or much less."

Arriving home I sit alone and watch horror films I have seen a thousand times before. The earth turns once more and covers the wicked land in darkness. I remain inside, hidden, silent, secreted.

And the sun rises all over again.

I felt betrayed, laughable, idiotic. Without a friend in a world of buddy fucks. A world that shrinks smaller and smaller until it is barely a pebble beneath my feet.

An eerily quiet low tide reveals a myriad of lugworm tunnels and exits, signified by a hole or the coiling of sand. Humans dig, seeking bait. They smoke cigarettes and wear waterproofs, barely even flinching against the freezing coastal winds. Two fishermen in this area: a long, wide beach of sand and rock. Beyond the coast inland lay the small town of Deal. Perched high upon a cliff face, sooner or later surely destined for annihilation.

Gulls circle and land in a common area, squawking and yelping at one another. One of the humans pays little attention to them, but another does.

"Could be a wash-up." He states, flatly. An agreement is grunted by his younger counterpart.

"Well?" The elder asks,

"Eh?" Comes the reply.

"Christ lad, go and have a look- might be a whale."

"A whale? You reckon?"

"Aye mebbe, your mother was out drinking last night."

"Haw haw, you funny auld cunt." The younger sloths toward the gulls, hands in pockets, as the elder laughs at his own joke.

The elder shanks his spade into the shale, and smokes a pre-rolled cigarette. Blowing smoke against the gale he watches the younger labour his wiry frame against the wind and spray towards the cackling sea birds. The elder laughs again, much more quietly.

"Ask her if she's goin' t'Bingo."

The younger mans reply of "Fuck off," is virtually silent in the weather. Still the elder chuckles to himself.

The gulls fly away as the younger man shouts, kicking rocks into the furor. The elder looks out to sea now, blowing smoke against the wind and allowing the clean air to dry salted tears to the sides of his face. He barely hears the younger calling back.

"Jed!"

As he turns the younger is all arms and legs. Running towards him.

"JED!!"

"Fuck's sake," Jed mumbles to himself. "What?"

"Fucking come here!!"

"Eeh Christ." Jed mumbles to himself as he picks up the spade and marches toward him.

"Fuckin' Jed come here!"

Jed's air of joviality fades and he moves much faster to the boy.

"You're fucking; someone needs't phone police!"

"What?!"

The younger holds his head and turns away from Jed's approach, neck craning backwards as Jed nears the spot. Jed gets to within sight of a smashed and battered half-bucket, filled with concrete, cracked down the middle and gaping in view. "What is it?" he shouts against the wind.

The younger can barely reply. "I fucking... Look!"

Between the cracks a glimmer.

"What the bloody hell..." Jed goes to move the bucket for a better view.

"Don't touch it Jed, just fucking ring the police." Jed hesitates but peers ever closer. "There'll be fingerprints n'tha. Just leave it." The younger walks away, pacing up and down, cursing to himself and spitting onto the sand. Jed peers, almost crouching until he sees the shape of fingers and the spongy blooming of bleached and broken skin.

TO THE POINT

In an effort to reach you I climbed this mountain.
In the rain and snow, I moved forward.
There was a moment I considered turning back,
But the memory of your skin would lure me further on.

Showers of sparks breed unseen by any beneath the rattling chassis of the stoically heavy, unstoppable train. The night sky blackens through tinted windows and the polished interior entombs the passengers between parallel mirrors capturing every lonely soul.

Grown, dirty fingernails before me, scraping across the edges of the table, picking away the laminated surface, forming a crude entertainment in destruction on a minor scale.

Looking at my watch I realise the last age was but ten minutes. The only other people in the carriage are a Trustafarian sitting at the table opposite with a laptop, and a tasty looking in her hey-day older woman with stupid Tina Turner hair and a striped bodysuit. She must be going to a fancy dress party, or at least, I hoped she was. Before I left the station I bought some tobacco and skins, except they didn't have big skins, only small, thick, red ones.

On my table in the train, I roll a secret joint, behind a wall I've built from plastic bags, a bottle of water and a Mars bar. The mission wasn't going too well; the materials are really causing me some problems. I make a three-skinner after some careful construction, tearing one of the papers into a shape resembling a triangle with four sides. After some very careful deliberation, I got the shape and the roll down, but my tongue was so dry I couldn't fix the gum. I had to wrap yet another skin around it, then coated it in scant residue from my dried out tongue and a tiny bit of beeswax lip balm, finally poked the end inside the roach and managed to seal it. The ticket inspector enters the carriage and I hurriedly blow and sweep away all the excess tobacco and weed and scraps of paper and cardboard, concealing the joint underneath the Mars bar, and the bag of weed underneath my long coat.

"Tickets?" I bought an open return. The guy next to me is getting off soon and readies his belongings. The inspector is or is not suspicious. He picks up his machine and walks out, into the drivers' room at the front, and locks the door behind him.

I sit in wait for the train to arrive at and leave the last station of Greater Manchester, as the train heads towards the stations of Lancashire, Yorkshire, and north to Teeside. Inside the train I head into the bathroom, sitting on the toilet lid and look at myself in the half-length mirror on the door. It lights up without a fuss, and the smoke fills the tiny room. I'm having fun blowing smoke at myself and watching it get excited when it thinks it's going to get me but then the mirror comes and bashes it away. After a few minutes I see the joint is burning very slowly, I think due to the change in papers and, ah, yes, the beeswax stuff, which may well be making me feel more stoned, making me savour the flavour. Advertising. Man, if weed ever became totally legal...

"Savour the Flavour", I speak in a low-pitched, cowboy-American accent. Hell yeah. I sat there for a while but then realized I'm not very long into my journey and wanted to save some for later. I thought about putting it inside the box of cigarettes I was carrying, but decide against it since the smell is just too much to carry into a carriage of non-smokers. Looking for somewhere to hide it I find only a paper towel box I might be able to prise open to stash it in, but it wasn't working for me. It had to be instantly accessible. I stand up and look at myself in the mirror, this is a toilet. If I came in here, would I be looking for anything? Where would I look for it? In the bin, maybe, in the sanitary towel bin, definitely. Hmm. Ah, what is this I spy with my little eye? A red emergency-stop handle, just above the toilet. It's at head height, but there's a little cubby hole sort-of-thing where one might just be able to secrete a secret spliff. It fitted fine, and I checked that no other wank job could see it without knowing it was there first and was satisfied. I would get it back by blowing it to the other side of the hole, away from the cover of the handle, and then fish it out. The test run goes well except for a piece of ash flying into my eye. I rub it for a minute, and it's okay. I turn around and smile assuredly once more at the reflection looking back.

As I enter the carriage, I wish I'd kept a lungful of smoke so I could blow it out and everyone would know I'd been a bad boy and would think I was cool. Next time.

Flopping onto the seat and I dramatically throw the plastic bag to one side, hoping the guy next to me would just take off his fucking earphones and say:

"Hey, have you just smoked a joint?"

But he didn't look. Didn't even blink.

We get to somewhere and the overdressed and moderately attractive older woman walks past me to get off. Feel relief that the guy next to me couldn't hear, as I make an "ugghh," sound, in a strangely sexy, but probably scary way. Neither of the passengers noticed me.

The older woman gets off and as I scanned the dankly-lit platform approaching us I spotted a shadowy outline of what looked like a very long haired woman picking up what looks like a baby in some sort of travel seat, and moving towards the train. More prey.

Out with the old and in with the new goes almost every Biblical metaphor once you get down to the core. The new girl walks onto the train by the door in front of me and walks into my carriage. Short, black hair, quite cute looking. Her baby has turned into shopping bags. She heads towards me to get a seat, so I stare at her and manage to get the briefest of glances. The ice is frosting, ready to break. She has dark eye make-up on which makes her look like a whore, of which I approve. She sits about five seats behind me and starts talking to someone. Fuck. Probably a friend of hers. I discreetly turn my head round to look at her then try and remember who was sitting there. I didn't remember anyone. I'm sure no-one was there. Maybe they got on at the last stop, yeah, that must be it. She strokes her long black hair back over her ear and shoulder, to expose an almost perfect half of her neck, repeating the action again and again and again. I turn my head to the window and smile at myself, looking at my stoner eyes with bags underneath like hammocks between palm trees. Then try to catch the eye of the guy with the laptop so he looks at the girl as well, but he's too focused on the stupid fucking film he's watching. I throw another look at her and catch her eye, which isn't hard as I'm kneeling up backwards on the seat, far above the seat back. Again, at the window I smile, and then look more closely at the bags, and worry about wrinkles, even though I'm probably a few years away from that. I keep smiling to try and get the wrinkles to come, just for a second, but can't get the smile right, it's too fake, too not-real, then the door slides open and the ticket man walks in, looks at me immediately smiling at myself then I see my real smile, and the wrinkles too. I think I'll look weird with wrinkles and bags, but maybe distinguished if I just wear suits and have a good haircut. I turn back to the girl and she's not talking just staring blankly ahead. The ticket man gets to her and she asks for one to York, which is quite close, gutted. Ticket man goes away after she searches through all manner of shit in her bag to get her purse, then a thousand receipts litter the table until she finds some money and I'm looking at her again. She keeps stroking her hair back, like three, four, five times in a row, one after the other; and it's terribly hypnotic. I can't stop looking at her and wonder why she's doing it. She stands up and flicks it back again, then turns almost towards me, slightly to the left when I notice she doesn't have dark eye make-up, it's a black eye. All of a sudden, she seems to become this new person, and I can't take my gaze from her. She's looking for something in plastic bags, and then she removes some underwear from them, black knickers, a thong, a bra and white stockings. What the fuck? I feel like a rabid dog. I want to rush down the carriage and drag her by the hair into the toilet then fuck her hard up the arse, oh God. I want her every hole smashed in by my bloody member. Her hair flicks back again, and I'm almost standing up and can see there's no person sitting next to her. The seat is empty and there are no bags, nothing. She's talking to herself. I stand on tiptoes, lifting myself slightly on the luggage shelf and there's definitely no person sitting next to her. She looks a bit mental, I wonder if I could get her into the train toilets and fuck her, then maybe give her another black eye. I laugh at my inner monologue of dark comedy and turn around and eat the Mars bar in record time. As I chew on nougat and caramel, and lick the chocolate out of my teeth, my head turns again. This time I'm thinking about going to the toilet and having a bit more of that weed. So I stand up and stagger backwards, then forwards to the toilet.

Inside is safe, and I enjoy filling the room with smoke and watching it linger in the mellow light. My upper torso is directly ahead of me, and I give myself a big grin. In the sink lies half a wet cigarette, I'm obviously not the only one who smokes in here. I again sit on the toilet lid, smoking until I realise I should have asked that girl if she wanted a smoke with me. Fuck. I'll ask her next time. I save the last third, hide it, and walk back into the carriage, my distorted reflection making me look like The Fonz. I smile, and laugh slightly as I walk back to my seat. As I pass, I stare at her and she speaks to me:

"Does this train go to Chester?"

I don't really know what to say, but manage to string together,

"Uh, yes."

"Oh thank God." The way she says it is so strange, but I'm glad she's staying on for that long.

Back in my seat, I scribble the word "Winkler" on the surface with a bookies pen. She starts to make a noise, like a humming, and listening to

a personal stereo dropping tinny chunks of terrible house music onto the floor. It's awful commercial council estate dance shite. As quickly as it came out, she removed the earphones and put them back in her bag. I sit for a while, then the next stop comes and the guy next to me puts his laptop away and goes to the door.

The girl is staring out of the window, but moving her head close to and far from its surface, focusing in and out on the image of herself. Occasionally she'd turn and say something the invisible man next to her. She's obviously a bit fucked. Sweet.

I can't stop my head from doing that nod thing, and keep looking at myself against the glazed-mirror-surface of the window.

"You alright there love?" I warm her with my words.

"Eh? Aye I'm... You what?!" She is obviously confused.

"I was just saying, are you right? You look a bit worn out."

"Mmm, nah I've been drinking since dinner time, I'm fuckin' knackered."

"I've got a spliff if you want a smoke."

"A what?"

"Joint, uh, in the toilets." I offered back.

The toilet walls shudder and rock as we pile into the cubicle and I wonder what I'm thinking. Her coat is black and shiny, with stains that harken to come and gravy.

I ask her if she wants to smoke some spliff but she has

no idea what I'm talking about. She stumbles as the train veers and I can smell about half a dozen cans of export on her breath.

"Are y'not gonna put yer cock in 'us?" She poses, bluntly.

"Ha, um, yeah go on then."

We indulge in a quick fuck, I hold her hair to help me reach erection and climax with haste.

A satisfactory orgasm for me and a soaking cunt for her preclude the termination of our relationship as she raises her leg onto the toilet wall and scoops my come out of her pussy, flicking it into the toilet and smelling it afterwards, asking:

"Does that smell right?" Once back inside my pants and the carriage, she sits at the other end of the train and seems completely bewildered as to what has just happened, though she adjusts herself throughout the remainder of her journey, ushering any remaining come from the depths back out into her well-worn panties and red-veined legs.

The train slows to a halt and she leaves.

Silent voices echo for the remainder of the journey. No one else gets on or off until we reach the final destination.

I needed to get a taxi to the cheap hotel in which I will be staying in tonight. So I ring the taxi man, famous on flyers but suddenly got very timid as he answered the phone, realising how late it was.

"Hello?" his response was sluggish, tired.

"Hiya mate need a taxi from the station."

"Where to?"

"Crown Arms."

"Oh yeah, no probs mate, I'll be two minutes."

This is the kind of sleepy town where taxis clock off around ten and trains are three times a day.

Three minutes later he pulls up at the station as I finish a cigarette.

"Nice car, mate"

"Yeah, I had another yan, traded it, fucking pain in the arse."

I "Hmmm" in response until he cannot but speak again.

"Yeah... So my mate got a new car an'all, got a Skoda Octavia, so we're all taking the piss out of him. I says to him, 'What's the difference between a Skoda and a sheep?"

"What?" I play along.

"It's less embarrassing to get out of a sheep." We both laugh.

SYNTHETIC WATER MELONS

There is no safety net quite like the human heart;
In its beauty you will see your abstractions
Turned like a screw head,
Bitten with clarity.

Reading the Bible while incredibly stoned and it's actually good, not just *good*, but *really* fucking good. Pure justice and full-on slaughter at every fucking corner. I read Acts, chapters twenty-six to twenty-eight, which doesn't sound a lot, but as I am totally fucked and bombed, and reading this much seemed to take an age. I got the Bible from a hotel I once stayed in, I figured: yes the book does say thou shalt not steal, but it also says to share and stuff, so I just suppose the Gideon's will have to come out of the mirror and replace it with a new one. Nevertheless, this book is so fucking good. It's like Oliver Stone directing Russell Crowe, with full on maxed out action. The story goes, there's this mission from Italy to God knows where, and they're all sailing and there's a big storm which catches them unawares and the crew are shattered by the storm which lasts over ten days, but does not cease until the crew cast aside all their cargo, and make for shore.

Once they get there, they come across these natives. The ships crew were shitting one, because James Bond teaches us that natives are not a nice people.

So they are ready to fight but it's okay; the people are a friendly one, and give them hostel and food. So they stay and recover for three months, until they set sail on some ship, which begat some guy and some other guy or girl.

Then off they go and I'm fucking amazed at how many names of countries I know; I thought the Bible was set in a magic land without countries, well, except crazy middle-eastern ones. So they're on their adventure and my mind wanders onto the crazy woman I fucked on the train and I laugh.

Here after I sit in silence for many minutes, rolling coins around my head. The fingers in front of me keep moving and I can feel the air inside the heater begin to breath. The drip is echoing through my ears, my brain, my spine. And then I'm quiet again. But no, I sit at the bar and order a beer, pausing over the menu to see what's on offer. It looks bland and I ask the dirty looking waitress what's big because I'm hungry. She umms and ahhs over some dishes, suggests the obvious, and I decide I will wait. A football game plays in the television, and I get a Boddingtons. Aside from the bargirl, there is the owner, or the owners' son, and a couple of punters. She smiles as she pours the drink and another girl walks over and sits in the seat next to me but not next to me. She's totally pissed, staggering all over the place, swearing, smoking a cigarette, it can't be: Lambert-and-fucking-Butler-for Christ's sake. She plods on the seat next to me but around the corner. I smoke a Marlboro, and then the barmaid comes over.

She begins to talk to the girl next to me. The bargirl is kind of ugly looking, dyed-ginger hair surrounding a freckled face, those supposed marks of beauty entrenched in deceit. I look again at the menu, still indecisive and lacking in hunger for anything from the selection of greasy fried shit.

The girl next to me really isn't that good looking, but she is wasted. We don't much as talk, as I say things to her and she says things to me, neither of us listening to the other. She gives me a look when she speaks, and it's *the* look. We amicably chat for a while, talking about nothing really.

"My bloke doesn't let me drink Stella, says I get too pissed on it, but he drinks it, so why can't I?"

"Wifebeater," I say. She's drinking Bacardi and coke, which I look at.

"I had four cans of Stella before I came out."

"Yeah, well, that'll do it." She was so bad looking; I could've fucked her even if she didn't want to. She'd be appreciative, happy, content. Football played on above us, someone scored a goal. "Do you play pool?"

"I'm shit at pool, uh,"

"Well, I like pool, game?" I directed.

"Yeah alright, do you want me to pay?"

Her words were like that of a child: simple, unafraid, inquisitive. But her whole demeanour was that of rough-slag, and so I treat her as such.

"No, its okay, I've got it." So I get some change and the pool table is free so we play. I always smoke while playing pool in an attempt to look like Cool Hand Luke or something. My impression seems to work. I'm on fire.

She finally pots one when I'm down to three reds left, and shouts "Heeey", and reminds me of a downtrodden miners' wife "Did I tell you I was married?" she asks. She hadn't. Or maybe she had.

"Yeah? Married young eh? How old are you?"

"Nineteen. When was the last time you had sex?"

I keep cool: despite wanting to spit my beer into her face and fuck her cunt wide open over the pool table. "Uh," pause to play a shot, keep it close to my chest and leave me with one red left after smashing the other between two of hers and nailing it in the corner pocket, "yesterday? I think... Maybe today." Girl on the train. If you can call her a girl.

Her finely trimmed and plucked eyebrows rise towards inconsistently greasy blonde hair, "Really?"

"Yeah, why, when was yours?"

"Two years." Then I do cough my beer and look right at her knowing this is so much of a dead cert it almost couldn't be easier.

"Two years?" I ask, and then repeat in a different cadence. "Two years?" She nods. "Jesus. That's a long time." She laughs a little then we pause. I feel as though an anvil has been suspended over my head and is just waiting for me to bite the cheese.

"I know." She says, swilling back another drink as I take a shot and nail a red into the bottom corner pocket, lining myself up for the next.

Trying to give some sort of consolation, "I remember a while ago I went without it for about three weeks, well, nearly three weeks: that was torture. But two years? I don't think I could do that."

"My husband's very self-conscious, he's... quite sensitive."

"Really, uh, right.

"Yeah. He gets mad and uh and, yeah, he's very like, nervous about things. He hates me getting drunk. He'll go mad when he sees me."

"Sounds like a nice guy." With an extra thick layer of sarcasm added just for cuntishness.

"Well he is, sort of, I mean, I've known him for ages, and I can't live with my parents again, but we uh, have, uh problems."

"Yeah, well problems, y'know, everyone's got problems. So what?"

"He's impotent. Just can't get it up." Cool as fuck.

"Really? Well, I dunno, I guess it happens to the best of us."

"Has it happened to you?'

I think for a second and decide I'll tell her it has. "Yeah, sure, I was about maybe your age, yeah, about nineteen, twenty, and I... um basically got totally shitfaced and had this girl and just was like, well, it's not happening tonight is it? You just move on, man."

"He's been like it for a while. Two years."

"Well, haven't you tried like, wait a minute, two years?" the point was reiterated in my mind.

"Yeah,"

"Fuck, I dunno, have you tried going down on him?"

"Yeah, course I have, he won't let me. If it's not working, which it never does, he won't let me try anything. Y'know?"

"Yeah. God, I can't believe two years. And you're nineteen you say? You should be fucking every day." she mutters something then takes a shot that goes terribly wrong.

"Hmmm. Well. Maybe I should."

"So what's he like, y'know, as a person?"

She pauses and searches for the right word. "He's always been very, uh, he gets uh, nervous."

"Nervous?"

"Yeah," she admits and drinks more Bacardi and coke, "he's always... He's very paranoid." We pause.

"Is that why you're with him though?"

"Uh, I suppose-"

"-Because if it is, that's not a good reason."

She thinks for a second. "I don't love him."

"If you don't love him, why are you actually with him?"

"Uh," she moans, "I don't really want to talk about all this."

"Of course, not that it's any of my business."

"So where are you from? Mr. Tall Stranger." She asks, changing the subject.

"Manchester, but I'm on my way to Amsterdam."

"Amsterdam? Wow." She really labours on the word "wow", like a child looking at the peak of a Ferris Wheel or seeing a friend do a wheelie on a BMX.

The fruit machines behind her create a halo of flashing orange and green lights that smear across and punch occasionally through her fine yet greasy long blonde hair. The kind of hair that almost matches skin tone.

232

Wearing a Widnes Vikings rugby league shirt that only accentuates her homely nature and lack of lure, and yet there is something in her that I cannot resist, or maybe something irresistible I want to put in her.

"We have to be quiet, 'cos the girl behind the bar, she's my best mate." Her words are slurred and without context.

"Okay?"

"And my hubby's ex."

"Okay." And I nod. Somebody conceded a goal and a lot of swearing filled the pub.

Still whispering, she confides: "I ran somebody over yesterday."

"What? You ran someone over?" I'm slightly dumbfounded by her whole nature.

"Yeah." She replies bluntly.

"In your car?"

"Yeah. Where else?"

"Shit. Are... are they okay?"

"Yeah. That's why I can't get back in that car, not now, not yet."

"Right, yeah, well." Three words chosen in an effort to bottleneck the conversation towards fornication. "So you live nearby then, you walking home?"

"No I live miles away, but I'm gonna walk it."

"Oh right." And raised my eyebrows.

"You can take me home if you want, I'll pay for the taxi back. If you want, I mean, you don't have to."

The idea of having sex with a married woman suddenly very attractive to me, even if she is the opposite. Almost as if the worse she is, the better I feel. Like stealing the keys to a piece of shit car when you could just as easily ride in a limo. Not that there was any other particular fanny in this pub I was distracted by. A few sorts, majority in tandem with the girls before me; badly made up, cheap looking. But girls none the less, and even less than that were nowhere near as close to opening their legs as the one directly in front of me spilling her drink down her chin while downing the last of a glass.

"Maybe, yeah," I said, cringing at the inevitable.

I won the second game and nailed the black hard to emphasise my intentions. She knocked some pool cues over, and then the ashtray fell onto the floor when she fell into the table, throwing cigarette butts and burned tobacco everywhere.

"Whoops!" She burps while trying to light her own cigarette. I lean over to her since the match-book she's using is too much technology. When I light it I make sure we have a good few seconds of eye contact and feel my heart start to beat faster, a metaphysical key to making her pulse raise too, and I sit on the baize giving her fuck me eyes. Truthfully I don't need to give her any sort of eyes, she will open gratefully at my word. She sits on the chair next to me, looking at me with the glassy gaze of a patient fresh off the operating table. When she speaks they are like lines from a terrible movie in which I am the fall-guy.

"Do you want to come to mine for an hour? Just to talk?" At which the canned audience and I laugh. I stare out of the window into the darkening sky, imagining the rolls of flesh sweating and sliding together, her gestations of sexual imprisonment finally liberated by this conquistador of libido, this lone warrior fighting tooth and nail against the demons of celibacy.

"I could smoke a joint."

"Can smoke at mine. He never let's me have a good smoke."

The more I hear about the girl's husband the less pity I feel for either.

"That's just criminal."

"He's got a stutter. It's really funny, especially when he gets mad and tries to shout at me and he's all ba-ba-ba. Ba-itch."

Cowardly laughter from the pair of us fills the empty chasm of righteousness within us both, two more ghost ships circling the oceans.

Smoking cigarettes outside of the pub the exhalations particularly cloudy due to the freezing temperature.

Simultaneous waves of relief and apprehensiveness coagulate within but the lack of concern truly washes away any real discomfort.

"One more?" I ask.

"Go on then, same again, rum and Coke."

"I'll get them in you, smoke this." I hand her a joint from my shirt pocket and head inside.

"Do you want some money?"

"No it's fine, save it for the cabbie."

Back in the bar I shudder after the cold and approach the bar.

"Yes love?" Says the bargirl.

"Rum and coke and a Boddies."

She pours the drinks and hands them over. "Having a good night?"

"Yeah, so far. I think so."

"Hmm." The bargirl gives a look.

"What?" I ask.

"Nothing, just a joke I heard the other day."

I ignore the bargirl, as surely she is trying to dissuade me from nailing this drunken tart. As I exit the bar I see another one standing in support of her knucklehead boyfriend who wears a white-collar-cuff moron-costume. His short back-and-sides encourage a glassing to the skull or at least the receiving of one, but instead I consider his girl, sheer low cut top, no tits and too much ego in a land of idiots. The near sight of her sex is almost enough to distract from my cause, but I plunder onwards, musty thoughts upon my lips.

Returning to the girl outside and providing much needed alcohol. "Do you smoke?" She asks, and I laugh and say,

"You've just watched me smoke about four cigarettes and half of this joint. Yes I do."

"Oh yeah." Shaking her head at her own stupidity. "Do

you want one?" Lambert and-fucking Butler.

"I don't smoke those, do you want one of mine?" Cowboy Killers.

"I've got a full packet here."

"Right okay, well you smoke yours and I'll smoke mine."

"Okay then."

Cigarettes are lit and I half-smoke mine, then finish the remaining joint.

"I didn't think you were coming back."

"Well, yeah I left my joint here, didn't I? Plus I wouldn't be much of a gentleman if I left you in the cold all alone." Just a drop of class is all I need to tip these scales. I could probably spit in her face and as long as I look authentic when I say "pardon me" would get away with it scot free.

The ocean breaks somewhere, filling the air with salt and wind, and all I can do I shiver and huddle my denim jacket around me, trying to light up.

"We've got a key of weed round ours. If you want you can come round, just to talk."

"Of course, just to talk." And smiled. The word "key" would ordinarily mean kilo. I remain unsure as to me this is a huge amount, and surely somewhere I am mistaken. But I won't find out anything new without enduring mysterious avenues. Certainly, if she flakes out I could help myself for my trouble.

A taxi arrives and breaks the silence muffled over with crashing waves and rounded rocks.

Travelling quickly over a great steel bridge in the pitch dark of night, boats either bobbing in the grey streams left by receding waterlines or partially sunken in the muddy shore. She continues to stagger despite the fact she is sitting down. We take opposing sides of the cab; no foreplay, no fumbling, just a baited pause prior to assumed copulation.

Perhaps years passed before we arrived at her street. Taylor Street reads the sign and I look the length of it and try to memorise the direction of entry for swift exit.

Taxi man fucks off and we enter her house. The door opens into a communal hallway, leading to the ground floor residence.

The carpets bleed thick, worn cotton twills that age the flooring making it seem we had stepped into a mid-twentieth-century kitchen-sink-drama. The gentle hiss of festering existence emanated from the walls that hung a limp paper, stained yellow and enamoured with my old friends damp and mildew.

She stands in some sort of effort to provoke sexuality but comes off instead as strange and confusing. I light the spliff. Looking across the room and saw Osho: El Libro de Sexo. Or it might have been Ego. At this distance and state of inebriation it is hard to tell but either one of those titles is a fitting mask of ridiculousness. The very sight of that book made me want to vomit; I knew from nothing more than guessing that she spoke scant Spanish in the first place, barely an "Obligao" or even a "wepa", but still purported to own books as such. Likely to discriminate against lovers long term who didn't cut the mustard: *Oh well, in Osho etcetera and so on and forth...* Fuck you. Inside my mind my hands grip around her throat to the point of choking; a common precipice, but still I go on, as the plastic vertebrae click and crunch by way of assimilation into something like that of order.

We exchange a brief pleasantry while sitting on the flowered couch. In the middle of the opposing wall stood a fireplace. The room suddenly felt cold and I felt like asserting some real masculinity so suggested:

"Maybe I should build a fire?"

"Oh, it's not a real wood, it's gas."

"Oh, well, should turn it on?"

"Got cut off."

"Ah." I conceded.

We sat in a moment of silence as I examined my breath for steam.

"I've got this." She declares as retrieving a large bong

from the hidden gap between sofas.

"Oh well, that is more than enough!"

We load the piece with mine, a hit so clean it blew the others from their seats. Opening up a river of concussion and indifference to swim about and around us. She produces a large bar of sticky resin, and a completely obtuse and doubly potent high grips us and it wasn't too long before I felt my eyes and teeth dropping onto the floor, scuttling around like marbles on a running washing machine and she asks with an echo if I would like a drink of orange cordial.

"No thanks. Do you have any water?"

"Yeah, ice?"

"Please."

She brings me my drink and I take a gulp. "Just going for a wee."

"Thanks." I say with more than an air of condescendence as I finish the water, to which she laughs.

As she passes I rub my hand across her jeans, from the knee up to the pussy, holding it and pushing around the fatty tissue of her genitals. She stops in her tracks and begins to writhe on my hand. I push her cunt away and she stumbles down the hall towards the bathroom, muttering in pleasure: praise mixed with curses all tinged with excitement.

She leaves the doors between the lounge and bathroom open and the sound of her urinating is loud and beastly. I hear her coughing to spit. When she returns there is neither flushing of toilet not turning of faucets.

"Have I locked the door? I need to lock the door." She thinks out loud. A moment of panic quickly subdued by the locking of the door. Around the edges of floral felt curtains she peered, out onto an empty street. A gentle rain continuously falls bringing a slow, cold death.

As she performs security checks I roll another solid joint, dense and pungent.

"He hates me drinking, especially Stella."

"Sounds like a great guy." I offer.

"Ugh, he just goes mental when I'm pissed, fucking hates it. I can't talk to him. But I can't talk to my parents either, 'cos I left them 'cos they wanted to know where I was every minute of the day. It's exactly the fucking same here. Never ends."

"Where exactly is he now?" I pondered.

"Oh he's working." She turns back towards me, seemingly content with our privacy.

"What does he do?"

"God knows, shitty fucking waiter, some shitty fucking restaurant. Hmm." She walks towards me and presses her pussy towards my hands, which I push away until she is rubbing herself against the arm of the chair, moaning in self-administered ecstasy.

"Right. That's rubbish. What time does he finish?"

"Uh, ten." She replies. I start to think fucking quickly. What time was it?

"What time is it?"

"Uh," she looks over to a gaudy clock on the wall, illustrated with a picture of a cat, of all things, "quarter past."

"Ten?"

"Yeah. I mean, they have to clean up before they leave and that kind of thing, but you know, I case he gets out early. But he never comes home early. Just drinking always." We pause for a second. "So if he comes in, you're my cousin, right?"

"Right. Cousin?"

"What's your name?"

So funny, "Alex, and you?"

"Dawn."

"Okay, Dawn, so I'm your cousin, what, from Manchester?"

"Yeah, and I just bumped into you. Or, you had arranged to come down for work or something." Dawn placed a hand onto one of her breasts and began to rub it, while approaching my chair and using her other hand at the fly of her tight washed-out blue jeans. I glanced nonchalantly around the room, see a few pictures and stood up to look at one on the wall. Dawn there, on holiday, arm around some guy. Looked a bit tasty. Looked huge. Not fat. Looks like a rugby player.

"And you've been with this guy how long?"

"We've been married for two years."

"Right. So it's quarter past." It really wasn't worth it. I took a big toke, and stood upright. "Look, I'm gonna shoot now, I mean, I'm gonna go."

"No, no, it's okay, it's fine, don't go." I am a fucking God, nobody can touch me. She's gagging for it.

"No, look, this really will look fucked up, especially if the front door's locked, it's like "Hey, I'm her cousin," not very likely."

"Oh. I suppose you're right." Her head drops in defeat and I start to walk to the door and she's there with me, seeing me out, bad US sitcom playing in the corner, which she'll be watching when I leave. The guy was home any second, I had to get the fuck out of there, and I didn't know whether this guy was a hard fucker or anything. I got to the door and she unlocked it for me.

Out in the hallway, the lights were off but orange light gleamed through the frosted window. I still smoked the joint and the front door was swung open.

"Well, nice meeting you." She says.

"You too, sure I'll see you again."

"I'm sure not." She leans in for a kiss so I think 'fuck it', and our lips lock, my tongue shoving its way into her mouth which tasted like jam-on-toast then my dick suddenly sprang from nowhere, while my hand groped her crotch through her jeans, touching the fat around her pussy and pushing what I thought was her clit with my fingers. She moaned as our tongues swapped places and our breath was hot against each other.

"Inside." So I push her through the door, one eye on the street to see any wandering husbands.

I pin her against the wall and continue to masturbate her through her jeans, while she eventually thrusts her hands on the bulge in my pants. I want to be 'the man', so I go to undo the fly myself, trying to do it with one hand, because I've still got the joint in the other, but I can't, the button is stuck, and I need two hands to do it.

I curse and toss the joint onto the floor, ripping open my jeans and pushing her down to take my cock in her mouth.

"Inside, inside."

"Right, quick." So we don't so much walk as stumble inside, especially as I still have my dick out and trousers wrapped around my knees.

I throw her onto the sofa and she squirms out of her jeans, revealing a pair of very normal looking white knickers.

"Off." I say to the underwear, and as if by magic, they're soon around her knees with her jeans.

I guess that if she's married to this guy who hasn't fucked her in two years, who's paranoid, and basically is wet, that she probably hasn't even been touched by another person in a while, so I take two fingers and arc them into a slight claw.

She moans, which turns into a groan as I push two inside her, sliding at first then tightening the grip and scraping on the less-than-tender flesh inside her, then I'm wanking her furiously while her eyes close and I touch myself. The smoke-stained cushions fall halfway off the sofa and reveal crumbs and pennies and the satellite remote control.

Rhythmically moving my hand the sound her pussy makes is like a sink hole with ocean waves breaking beneath it, filling, then evacuating with haste leaving a hollow "sloshing" sound in its wake.

The rolls of fat on her neck begin to sweat in beads and her orgasm is here, signified with loud screaming and flushes of blood I can feel pulsating through her pussy around my fingers.

Taking a condom from my wallet I struggle to get the thing on right. The smell of synthetic watermelons distracting and time-consuming in the application. I toss it behind the sofa and penetrate her with skin, reveling in the sensation of her unused cunt lapping up my cock, hugging it from the inside out and streaming her juices around my balls and legs.

I give it to her enough so that she comes once more, then I feel the beast rise in me, driving home the last thrusts up against the roof of her cunt before I pull out and move my position to fuck her mouth, her greasy blonde locks twisted around my hand soaked in pussy.

"Open." I say, using my magical powers of hypnotism.

She dutifully opens her mouth, revealing a pink and white tongue, and I do my best to separate her head from her body as I skull-fuck her.

Moaning and gasping and choking, playing with her clit, loving every second of it, the girl drifts into another realm of pleasure. I feel the end of my cock pushing against the back of her throat; prodding her tonsils, the dark meat of her tongue. I continue, jeans have fallen right around my ankles now and I've broken such a sweat that I see a bead drop from my nose onto my arm. Canned laughter blares from the TV set, but is drowned out by my guttural, beast-like grunts and groans. I'm pulling her hair now, one hand dropped around her throat and porn-star-choking her as a rain shower starts outside and against the window.

My orgasm begins to rise like a slumbering volcano and I mutter in copulation a series of "yes's" and "fuck's" at which point I pull my cock out and slap her across the face then see her smiling in a wave of I've-just-come-for-the-first-time-in-years relief and I grab her lower jaw and force it open as I come so fucking hard; grunting and snorting like a beast and shooting come against her face and tongue.

We both breathe down, pacing our lungs, regulating ourselves.

My eye wanders off to the door and the handle not turning, which I take as a good sign. I put my dick back in my pants, pick up my wallet.

"Right: now I'm going."

"Yeah, good idea." She is all-smiles and glowing as I

reinforce my illusions of greatness with another satisfied client.

I go to the door but notice the weather outside for which I am greatly underdressed.

"Can I borrow this coat?"

"The black one? Yeah."

She replies while straightening the floral cushions and scouting for spilled semen.

"I'll leave it behind the bar for you."

"Right, okay."

I picked up the black coat, one of three hung next to the door, and the half joint from the nursing-home type carpet in the hallway, as she gets her knickers stretched back around her sweating arse.

An icy cold wind blows down Taylor Street The door closes by latch behind me and the numbers two and three nailed in and painted over maybe four times. The place is deserted and in an alleyway a cat screeches and bolts, sending bottles tumbling which triggers the barking of dogs until followed by silence. I would look back but only to confirm the world behind me is on fire, an eternal inferno reducing all to ashes. Ahead of me are lights, and the distant sound of waves crashing signifies true north in my compass. The network of suburban streets eventually widens and I reach the bridge, now vast and never-ending.

Even darker skies draw heavy and suffocating, accompanied by sheets of rain that tumble like the piss from my cock, hanging loosely over the edge of the bridge. Eventually I reach a supermarket and call for a cab. As before, Al pulls up.

"Well now, this is a fair way off!" He says when he pulls up and lowers his window.

"Fair way bollocks, get that fucking heating on."

Al laughs as I enter the car, huddling against the fans for warmth.

"Here," Al hands me a towel and I rub it over my face and

head, wiping rain water from my neck and upper back.

"So are you the only taxi driver round here then?"

"No but I'm the best, damnit." Al says in a low cowboy-like drawl. "What are you doing all the way out here, then?"

I consider the litany of misdeeds engaged upon over the night and begin to laugh.

"Long story mate, suffice to say my balls are well and truly empty."

Al laughs with great gusto and I'm reminded of porno shop John.

"Smoke?"

"I do but mine are wrecked. Soaked through."

"Here lad." Al gives me a cigarette and we smoke while driving through the estates towards the coast and eventually the Crown.

D ETOUR

Send my love to everyone
Right through my gritted teeth.
Your smiles and salutations
Leave me boiling in deceit.

Skirting the edges of the coastline, blackened white tides break over rounded rocks that make the crescent archings of the beach. The Crown rises from darkness and is in its own way a lighthouse for weary travellers and drinkers alike. I pay the man and reenter the pub through the side door, latched but not locked until I close it. A still air settles within the corridor, and the sense of foreboding hangs heavily within it.

In the room I channel hop for a few minutes, and discover the satellite station playing the sports network. Venturing downstairs I find the remote and search for pornographic content. Nothing. The closest I get is the laboring grunts of female squash players but it is England vs. Scotland so nothing to see in particular.

As I creep past the door back to my room, I hear The Stranglers playing on the set of the landlord, locked tight and in unison with a deep snoring sound. The kitchen door is open a crack and I decide to venture inside for a midnight snack.

Inside a large steel refrigerator, a definitive bounty of food lays in wait of the breakfast shift. I make a layered sandwich with every kind of deli meat and cheese and boiled eggs sliced in regiment. I take an overcut piece of creamy chocolate cake for afters and return to my room.

Commercials for knee pain medication and accident insurance play on a seemingly permanent loop before the sports channel returns and brings women's volleyball. Brazil vs. Russia: finally something to work with. I laugh to myself as I consider this base motivation and stuff my mouth with the last morsel of sandwich, whole grain mustard bleeding from the edges.

Somewhat surprisingly my cock is fully erect after just a few return volleys and one grunting face in the sand. Close up shots depict sweating athletic bodies with brilliant sunshine glistening in refraction, conjouring in my mind the countless ingrained images of girls sucking cock, eating ass, drinking come. As I hungrily chew the last morsel of sandwich I see the cake before me and consider my almost chafing hands and this eastern-edge of North Sea facing climate, dry and cold. It seems as good a lubricant as any. Buttercream absorbs directly into the shaft giving a gliding sensation and chilled flakes of chocolate provide resistance enough to encourage climax once again. What I thought may be a timid display takes me by surprise as come jerks from my cock and is thrown across the room, my spasmodic rhythms enabling it to lacquer the walls and Bible, unintentionally on the latter, in some form of sexually motivated territorialism. The cake slithered down in chunks between my legs and gathered around my anus, warming quickly and not at all uncomfortable.

The buzzing in my head and about my eyes slows to a soft vibration and as I open them I realise the sound is coming from the soaking wet black jacket and is in fact some polyphonic house track, playing through tiny on-board speakers inside a cellphone in the pocket.

Clawing my hands to avoid too much spillage of come and chocolate cake, I retrieve the phone.

The word PAUL, illuminated by a green light underneath the screen. Why not?

"Hello?"

"Who the fuck is this?!" A shrieking in the background of the call told more than words could at this point.

"Excuse me?"

"Are you the fucking guy been round mine?" His garbling formed an immediately confrontational and badly composed statement.

"Well, not any more but I believe so. Do you live in a piece of shit house with your wife that you haven't banged in two years? Ah, yeah, that will be me then."

"You're fucking dead!" A definite threat, to which I sigh in total disregard. "You're f-fuckin' dead. I'm g..." The muffled sound of indistinct words toned to violence, "I'll f- f- fuckin' kill 'yer."

"Oh right, you must be *that* guy. Whose phone have I got?"

"You f-fuckin' dickhead, it's my fuckin' wife's- fucking shut up," to a voice in the background, I can hear her shouting at him once more.

"Right, yeah, thought it might be. Uh, so what do you want?" He's speechless; what exactly can you say to a cunt like me?

"You... I know where you are. I know where you're staying. You're at her work, you're at the C-C-Crown."

"The C- C- Crown? You think I'm still at the C- C- C- Crown, you c- c- c- c- cock? *My God,* are you really that stupid? Do you *actually* think I'd have stayed in the same hotel? I left that place as soon as I got back from your house, your *shit-hole* of a house, you stammering cunt."

"Agh, y'fucki—f-f-cking twat, fucking, ah-ah'll fucking get you."

"No you won't, you'll never even see me. I'm miles ahead

of you already. Do you really want to know where I am? I'm waiting at the station for a train that leaves in about two minutes. You'll never get me, you limp-dicked fuck. Now do one and stop wasting my fucking time."

"I-ah, you-"

"Oh and say hello to whatever her name is for me, her cunt was tighter than a mouse's nostril and she was gagging for me to finish inside her but I ended up just putting it down her throat No worries though, cheers pal, have a good night!" Ending the call I sat with a slight sense of satisfaction having destroyed enough of the world for one evening.

As I washed my face, hands, cock and balls, I wondered if there were many trains out of Newcastle at this time, two in the morning. Two in the morning? There won't be any trains out of Newcastle at this time. He'll be at home, arguing with Dawn. Shouting at her. Quite possibly hitting her. What then? After that, she tells him where I'm from, where she met me. He knows where she works. He'll know where she drinks. He's home now with her and they're arguing, likely a huge argument. He told me he knows where I am. She said earlier on about he was driving somewhere. He drives then. He does know where the hotel is. She said he gets very angry with her. If he's got half a brain, he'll check the trains. If he's that bothered he'll be on the phone to the train station asking if any are leaving now, if that's the case he'll be in the car on the way. When he finds there are no trains he'll be coming for me. He knows I was bluffing.

Fuck.

Shit.

What to do?

If I stay here, he'll be round any minute. These Geordie lads don't waste any time when violence can be counted on. He might have a stutter and a floppy cock, but why else would she not leave him? Because he's probably hard as fuck. And I just fucked his wife, came on her face and took great relish in telling him all about it.

I remained deathly still and silent for a few seconds as some key equations were made in my head, then a decision was obvious:

Get the fuck out as quickly as possible.

One of my less desirable habits is that of removing almost everything from a packed bag when I arrive in any hotel. Suddenly the clock was ticking into conflict and my own personal hour of reckoning loomed heavy overhead.

I managed to fit everything back into my bag, plus a couple of white hotel towels as memorabilia and extra weight. I couldn't even find time to properly finish washing my genitals that now were frosted chocolate brown and gathering syrups between the natural folds around my anus and buttocks. Tying my boots up I was ready to leave and did so quietly. I had made sure to pay for the room on arrival so there shouldn't be any issue should someone see me leave. At two-thirty-odd in the morning.

Floorboards creak like tumbling dominos, one encouraging another until it seems the whole house grumbled internally at my efforts of stealth. Taking a wrong turn into an empty room, I consider hiding out but the thought of squirreling myself into a corner until my eventual and inevitable discovery and the barrage of assault to follow eliminated that as a bare concept. Returning through the corridors I go back past my room, down the stairs and into the bar. All exits deadlocked with a key. I remember a fire-door in the kitchen and make haste towards it but the fucking thing has a bulletproof padlock. The odds of this seem staggering; a simple step to gain entry but exit proving almost impossible. As I turn to head back upstairs some plates are almost knocked from a shelf but a quick reversal stops the accident but as I hold the plates steady the sound of soaked road torn up by roaring tyres rises alone with a pin prick of white light that grows and grows and is cast like a shroud over the house, bearing its lines across the entire visible surface. It was him.

Rushing silently back upstairs, I return to my room,

desperately seeking something to defend myself with, but all I find is the Bible, pasted with come and chocolate handprints. Through the window I see a red metal walkway. The hotel is privately operated by a kindly old couple who didn't have time nor budget for luxury hotel modifications such as locking windows, so I opened it up and look down the two storeys onto a secluded area at the back of the hotel. I spit over the edge and a high crack signifies concrete below, far below. The sound of the cars coming to a halt made the decision for me as I sling my backpack across the gap and onto the walkway adjacent, making the loudest of clangs. Behind me the TV plays the end of the volleyball match and I use the near muted voices of commentators and gasping players as encouragement and jump from the window ledge across to the walkway, just about making it onto the platform some thirty feet off the ground. As I stepped from the ledge the window fell closed and latched itself locked, my wheels now thoroughly in motion. The sound of the car pulling up on the gravel outside the front serves as a stark reminder to get a move on and I quickly scan the available descents. First, I kick my bag onto the floor as a last gasp crash mat, and a chill wind blows through my coat as I begin to climb down a short ladder. My hand slips as the palm has a large piece of melted chocolate I hadn't noticed lumped into the middle and my legs hang perilously over the edge while holding my weight with two hands. Around the front I can hear the car engine revving to a halt, and I fear prolonging my escape more than the road I have chosen so release my grip and allow myself to fall, trying to remain loose and calm despite the fact I am falling down two floors onto a hard concrete surface below.

> Rolly coasters
> Corkscrew round
> My head at night
> Sleeping on rocks.
> When light-bulbs shine

Like starry skies,
The Gods reside
In forty watts.

As I regain consciousness I try and figure out how long I have been out. A stinking puddle of seeped potato peelings drifts between my arm and body and there is the prelude to a large lump on my head.

I hear shouting at the front of the hotel and the unlocking of a door, angry conversation and yelling. I scramble silently for my bag and cradle it like some savior, but we are both far from freedom as yet.

I may have cracked a rib as lifting the bag becomes extremely painful. There are a number of voices, he did not come alone. I stay hugging the wall, close and beneath the darkest of shadows. Rain collected on roof top gutters drops down indiscriminately but I have not the time nor luxury to avoid them, instead inching closer to the front of the hotel.

"Ew ga round't back n'case 'e tries te run." My time seems up and I crouch, between a large commercial refuse unit and a rotten wood fence into the blackest of shadows as one of his numbskull brutalizers hastens towards the rear. I hear him as he passes by mere feet away and his breathing from mouth and nose simultaneously sounds like some horse from hell. But being a moron he walks straight past, eyes looking up towards the windows and walls of the hotel rear.

I stop breathing for this time to completely eliminate any sort of noise. A muffled voice from the front triggers the meathead to return hence as the party entered the hotel. As I reach the front I see the dazzling headlamps of an old car, shining at the front of the hotel. Inside I hear his voice, stammering arguments with the patron as to my whereabouts. It is a matter of seconds until they discover I have left and return to the car, which is now empty with its engine left running. My heart races as I approach the vehicle from the side, staying out of the light and checking no one is left within. It is empty and I use this momentary window to full advantage as I throw my bag through onto the passenger seat and leap into the car, silently releasing the handbrake and driving calmly and quietly away. As I reverse through the gate of the hotel the phone starts to vibrate once again, but this time conversation is neither required nor desired and I toss the phone onto the gravelled ground of the car park and hit the main road, driving away at high speed before I could even see the Crown doors crash open and lumbering frames of vengeful, loveless, brutish men grasping vainly at the dust loosened in my wake.

P IGS

Never could I settle lesser
When you wrote it in a letter
That tomorrow will be better
Than today has ever been.

E very corner holds possible death, each streetlamp a potential witness. Driving a stolen car anywhere is typically bad form but driving drunk and in a completely unknown area is even worse. I slow down to the advised speed limit and manage to control my racing heart with deep breathing techniques learned from years of tantric masturbation. There are times when I can go for hours and hardly take a breath, yet manage to continuously stroke out pleasure poised like a mantis bow-legged in solitude while demonizing that of accepted comfort. Clocking up a few miles of buffer and taking innumerable turns from the main roads I get comfortable in my distance from meatheaded revenge. The starry sky is inked out of vision as a large factory looms past followed by a water treatment plant. The smell of shit and piss is almost comforting as I seek refuge until daytime. A small car park opens up beyond a thicket of brambles and thorny bushes, and I park with the nose of the car against a tree, then turn off the engine.

"Jesus fucking Christ." I sigh, as waves of relief and adrenaline wash through my system, finally at ease and able to relax. As I switch on the interior light I see that there is a wallet and packet of cigarettes sitting in the centre console of the car. Remarkably, the cigarettes are my brand, and I light one from the almost-full packet. In the wallet I find seventy-five pounds and a small bag of cheap coke, which too, is gratefully received and taken without hesitation. Upon administration the bite tells me it is not coke but speed, but as I have done the lot in one nostril it seems pointless to care what it actually is so I just hold on for the ride.

I switch off the interior light and as doing so see in the rear view mirror another light flicker. There is another car here, their inner lights blinking on and off. My heart rises once more. This is the night that will never end. Regardless of the shining sun I know it is just an illusion brought upon us by concentric rotation around a star lost in space. That we are just peons glimmered like droplets of water on a leaf drying after an eternal thunderstorm.

I blink my interior light once more and the return volley comes again.

Underfoot the ground is a sodden mud formed by leafy mulch and dead twigs. Inside the car ahead of me I see figures, one being female and fleshy expositions.

Drawing closer the hushed talking within the car breaks for laughter and shy exchanges between the man and woman inside. When I reach the car window my cock is already out and erect, their window wound frantically down and the naked woman spread eagled on the passenger seat, the man fingering her as I deliver myself into her mouth.

"Go on you slag, get on it." Says the man, replied by the woman with indecipherable words clotted by cock. My hand reaches down to her tits and I rubs them, squeezing the nipples and working the breast as I fuck her in the mouth. "Come on now." Says the man as he reaches over and opens the door, the woman assuming a position surely for the hundredth time given her knowledge of just where to swing her legs so to present her soaking wet cunt for my entry. Without hesitation I push my cock inside. Loose and warm, her juices trickle down as if she has been waiting for hours for this, or perhaps it is the collective sperm of another dozen punters. Inside the car she sucks the mans cock, her husband, judging by the wedding ring on her finger, although I could be wrong. He delights in pulling her hair and using her mouth like a lifeless cavity, smashing into her throat his fully-erect penis and groaning in pleasure as beads of sweat trickle down his nose. On the dashboard a pile of white powder he keeps teasing at and and rubbing on his gums or snorting from between his fingers. "Get on it!" He says to me and I partake readily.

There is something about mystery drugs, much like mystery pussy, that is even more impactful than purest of contraband. Considering the situation, the surge of excitement and lashings of adrenaline seem to go hand in hand and whatever the drugs are, they are helping greatly as blood rushes to my face and my teeth grit together until fractures of enamel form a sediment I rub against the back of my grinning smile, lofted above my waist pounding into the woman who moans in ecstasy. The man starts to come and pulls out, displaying his ejaculant which she works out with her one free hand, the other tight and gripped around her swollen nipple and scratching dirty nails down her own chest. Her face now dripping with sperm and my own rising comes quickly too as I come inside her, forcing my erection to the very hilt and trying to break whatever is inside. The man helps her on her way to orgasm by keeping one hand tight around her throat and choking her in time to my penetrative crescendos.

As if the night couldn't get any more bizarre the icing comes as blue lights begin to flash and police sirens from a solitary squad car illuminate the car park. The man quickly brushes the powder from the dash and takes a last hit to the mouth but we three are like rabbits fucking in the headlights.

"Hold it right there." Comes the voice over the police car

PA system. A sinking realization falls heavy and there is only the desire to run and hide in the trees but as my trousers are around my ankles I would not get very far. Narrow escapes I have had more than most, but this surely could not end well. "Police!" He states, as if it could be any other cunt.

"Fucks sake." Exclaims the man.

"Frank you fucking idiot I thought you said this was a good spot!" Blathers the wife.

"How fucking should I know where the bastards are going to be?!" Defends Frank.

They are definitely a married couple and here am I, the third wheel on a quick route to jail. If a lifetime of evading justice has taught me one thing it is silence above all others and I simply raise my trousers, come still dripping from my cock and finding solace within the cakings of chocolate long melted and spread across the inner back of my thighs and buttocks.

The police car door opens and out steps an officer in full regalia. I desperately search for some get out clause in my mind, some route to freedom, but it seems in vain.

"Sir, can I ask you to show me some identification?" And suddenly it hit me.

"Of course," I replied, "it's just in the car."

"Very good." The second officer stands from his seat and approaches to escort me to the stolen car.

The first officer approaches the car.

"Frank, how many times?"

"Jesus fucks sake John, can you lot not just let us be?"

"I can't have you and your missus fucking in every car park in town. I've got supervisors as well, you know?!" Their conversation fades as the second officer follows me to the car where I retrieve the wallet left by the stuttering meat-head from my earlier escapades.

I um and ah as I root in the wallet, hoping for some form of identification to pass off as my own then I find his paper driving license, and hand it over to the officer.

"Hold on a second, let me ring it in." The officer walked some steps away from my earshot, and then called over the radio to check the details with HQ.

A few moments pass and a chill wind whips around the place, high above, dropping crisp leaves down onto the gravel below. A response comes back over the officers' radio and he walks back to his colleague as they exchange words, motioning towards me. The first officer says something firm and definite to the couple, then marches in my direction.

"Mr. Durham. Paul is it?"

"Yes," I reply, "P- P- Paul Durham."

"It seems you are in a bit of a p- p- pickle are you not?"

"Officer, I'm so sorry about this, w-what can I say? I've n- n- never done anything like this before, I, I.."

"Save yer bollocks. What street do you live on?" He is looking at the license with all the pertinents. My mind races and somehow drags from its hollowed recesses the nameplate.

"T-T-Taylor S- S- Street. T-Twenty-three."

"And do you live there alone?"

"N- n- no, with my w- w- wife."

The officer looks at his colleague in partial revelation then back to me, "And so I should think she might not be too happy if we were to call her now to confirm your identity."

"Please officer, we're going through a rough p- p- p- patch at the m- m- m- m- m-"

"Save your breath, Christ. Here." The officer hands me back the license. "See if I catch you doing anything like this again, it won't just be your missus you'll be explaining it to, you'll have to tell a judge why you felt it necessary to be out banging some tart in a car park."

"Oh my G- G- God, officer, I don't know what to say."

"Just drive safe when you leave, if you could. I don't want to spend the rest of the night writing this up, who would?"

"Of course, thank you, thank you." I take the license and get back into the car, and start the engine as the police go back to the couples' car and begin exchanging what seems to be friendlier words.

"Go on now!" Calls the first officer to me and I reverse out of the spot and return to the road by the waste-water treatment plant. Glancing in the mirror I could see the woman still naked, standing to crouch over the bonnet of the car. Interesting as though it may have been, a closer call I did not desire and drove with considered pace away from the site.

WETHER REPORT

Human ideas are infinite
In their manifestation. It is merely
The lack of comprehension
That keeps them from the tangible.

The sound of rain pattering against the windscreen wakes me and I am entombed in the steamed up car parked by the river Tyne beneath an overhanging tree shrouded with leaves and bedded down into thick mud and rock. An incredible pain in my chest and head combines with the lack of sleep and cricked neck after spending the night sleeping in the drivers seat with great unease and feeling the torrid aftermath of dirty base speed. Having left the heaters on as I dozed, the car battery is dead, but I had parked near to the ferry crossing close to the main shipping terminal from where I would make the rest of my journey so it was of no concern. I could just as well push the thing into the river but I decide upon a subtle exit after the previous night of excessive risk-taking.

I don't have long until that point. Finally, after stretching to regain some sort of humanity I don the large bag and head towards the ferry crossing, smoking a cigarette for breakfast. Across the water I see the boat in the distance, white and shining, like some fin skewered through the surface of the water. An hour or more until departure so I take the leisurely walk and enjoy my smoke.

As I approach the gate to the ferry across the river I am confronted with a chain link fence and hand-painted white sign that reads:

ALL FERRY CROSSINGS OFF DUE TO WETHER.

I curse, shout, spit, kick the gates. Fuck. This is just typical. The road across the river is miles in the other direction, and that leads to an even longer round about detour. Tunnel traffic is notoriously shit at this time of the day as reasons the whole point of me being here at this supposed crossing.

Sighing deeply I decide to take the most direct route and walk down the side streets, seeking passage across the water. Empty boats anchored in the dock tell of decline as opposed opportunity. As I walk further and further I begin to run out of viable land. The river broadens and the waves become choppier. The dark green murky waters hinted at a steely fate.

Finally I reach a boat with a shipmate.

"Ahoy, skipper?" Always wanted to say that, but in reply only silence. "Ahoy? Anyone aboard? I need some help, anyone here?" I hear a tin can dropped inside.

"Hello?" A man appears, "Aye aye, arm heeah, are y'lreet leek?" some Geordie guy, dirty clothes, working jeans, a checked thermal shirt and cap.

"Mate, I need to get across the other side," I point "I'm s'posed to be on that boat there, is there anything you can do?"

He weighs me up, eyeballing me and my huge bag, soaking boots, unshaved for a month, haggard faced fuck that I am right now, looking like shit but innocent enough in the cold and steely light of day.

He points at the skinny rope ladders leading from the dockside to the deck.

"Howay then man, come on down heyoh." I kick my boots to knock any slippery mud or oil off them, and descend the rope, thanking him along the way.

The boat is a fishing trawler, something you can sense from the smell alone. "So whodja need, like?"

"That boat, over there, um, I've got to get to it; I've got a ticket, but I can't get across seeing as ferries aren't running."

"Aye, ferries aohnt runnen foah few weeks naw, cannae git shite awor te thom cunts." I recognized "cunts", but that's it.

"Yeah, um, I really need to get over, and uh, I was thinking, like, would there be any way you could give me a lift over there? I wouldn't ask but, y'know, I'm pretty desperate, man." He's not sure.

"Whel ahm a wee bit bizzy, like, but orh, a ken mebbe get yers cross thor, mebbe, aye,"

"Aw, mate, that'd be awesome," he throws an aloof smile my way.

"Whend'si leave?"

"'bout two hours, but I need to get there for an hour b'fore"

"Aye nee problem, ohwl just finish wot i'm deeyuhn an' tek yee owor." He went back into the hold and I followed, "fucken' cohld eh?"

"Fuckin' hell, I'm freezing like mad in this shit."

"An' its just ganin tuh git coldor, sayin that, its elwis starvation this time iv year."

"Yeah."

"So ye's gowan a holidee? Anywhore sunny?"

"Just Amsterdam,"

"Fucken Amst'dahm aye, ass top leeke. Gowan fe lohng?"

"No probably just a long weekend or something. Just got bored to fuck of normal shite, and I can take a break so I just thought like, you know, 'fuck it, why not?'" he nods but I don't see it.

"Aye, whyde fuck nod eh? Shite ahll owah heer ferra young fella, fucken- any fella. Cohld as shite, ney fanny awll dohty as fuck, slags ohwll owah, fuck that." He lifts a bag of God-knows-what. "See ma gorlfren she fuck'd off wi some cunt fro' Lunden, fucken cockney wankah. A tell's ohr if ah see 'im ahll fucken knock he's fucken teeth oot, e'll nevah knaw who e'is affer."

"That's harsh man, fuckin' women can be cunts like, eh?"

"Fucken tellan me, man. Ah well, I spose we ken ahll be cunts time and again. Ahm just like fucken, gitten ohn wi me johb anat. Cahnut be bothad wi it knaw." He moves another bag of stuff. "Fuken Amst'dahm thoh, ahss a top place, me and owhat lahds went owah thur foh a weekendah, fucken boards they'ves goht thor, tha'll suck an fuck fohr fucken 'ardly owt like, pocket cheng." The man has lived.

"Yeah, can't wait to get me hands on those red light girls, dirty slags. No bother about talking and all that shite, just in out, see ya later ya cunt." He starts laughing and I follow suit when I feel in my pockets and discover half a joint from the night before.

"Aye yoh not wrong theah, lad. Easy peasy, wham bahm thank you ma'am."

"Fancy a cheeky smoke, mate?"

"Wye man! Fucken dancer, git ohn yer man oh."

We shared the joint and it wasn't long before the Geordie was laughing and regaling stories of an unintelligible nature. All slurs and syllables and spitting into bullet grey waters below.

Ahead of us sat the great white ship. Flags ripping from taught wires lashed from bow to stern, by way of the crows nest.

Disembarking the boat I shook hands with the sailor, him thanking me and I reciprocating.

The muddy ground below quickly caked my boots once more and served as a reminded to leave the country with haste. Ahead of me an eighteen-hour boat ride, full bar, cabin accommodation and "live entertainment". No strippers I should guess.

Destinations often secondary to the journey itself, most of my journeys seeming to consist of waiting and this was no different. I enter a large hall with old wooden seating bolted to a concrete floor, wild wind coursing through the place and a scant number of staff to keep up the pretense of a thriving business model. I deliver over my particulars to the check in girl, and then join the swollen masses of obese tourists and screaming litters of children. The hall is a smoking one so I do so until losing my appetite. Stacked like battery hens were row after row of stiff-necked bleach-skinned people, lugging 9-5's around with them like heavy chains rusted over with time. Try as the might to present a face of tranquility I could see that inside they were boiling over, a forgotten pressure cooker, almost down to its last drop of water.

Those returning marked by orange faces and ridiculous t-shirts and shorts, looking more than foolish on a stormy day as this one. The afterglow of relaxation was about them but the prelude to Monday morning grew dreadful and stark as they quickly forgot about sunnier climes and after lunch siestas and tapas and wine instead of pies and chips and gravy.

The hall cleared of those returnees quickly, always in a hurry to beat traffic and rejoin stoic decline. Children screamed and parents despaired and I take solace that I am neither. Teenagers staring blankly and sidled to parents wondering if they will ever be famous, considerations of web cam fuck videos to encourage the world to take notice. Young couples in firm hand-grips, smiling through terrified questions of the truth: "Is this it?" Parents wondering whether they should have waited a few more years before having children. Old people regretting entire lives. Here in lies the slippery slope down which all mankind must fall.

All except me. I never want to have dependents: children, wife, bought house, leased car. No loans, no job, no equity. I refuse the government sponsored way of life. It seems impossible to have a happy life while living inside a set of rules and regulations. Not that I ever considered myself anything close to happy, but still. I think I might have enough to do it modestly. As my mind wanders around its corridors, a boy runs into my bag and spills juice over my shoes. Quick damage report: shoes weren't expensive, not that much bad, just a little wet. I think it's Okay.

"Hey" I said to the kid "watch were you're running"

"Fuck off!" he replied. Fucker, he's about nine years old. Little bastard. He gets up and tries to run away but I grab him discreetly by the scruff of the neck and whisper threateningly down his ear, simultaneously squeezing a pressure point to cause immense pain but no screaming.

"Don't be a cunt, alright?" Now he's scared. His struggles to get free are subdued by the weight of my words and his tiny thrashings are nothing against me, like an autumnal leaf straining against the crushing of feet.

"Get off me!" Came the plea.

"Not so clever now, are you? What do you say?" His face began to go red through embarrassment. I thought he was might piss himself, but he didn't, thank God. "If you don't apologise to me like a good boy I'm going to pull out your fucking teeth with a pair of pliers." The kid looks frantically for his council chav scumbag mother, but finds no one.

"Sorry! Sorry!" I release him from my grip.

"That's better. Now you fuck off." I win. He runs straight past his dropped toy gun and towards his accident/insurance/benefit-seeking parents. It matters not that he is a child: he is indicative of a venereal society that calls itself human these days. I'm by no means a saint, and judgment is a viewpoint best left to those of a higher plateau, but death would be a suitable quick-fix to so many living today.

I turn my attention to a discarded newspaper and cradle a book from my bag to add layers of defense against moronic interludes when I hear the whimpering of the boys voice once more, this time accompanied by his feral mother. Her cigarette burns with a fury reflected in the dead red blood cells from her liver staining her rodent-like eyes jaundiced-yellow.

I prepare a story in one second.

"Whadja fuckin' hell d'ya think you're doing to mah boy?" I ignored her for a second, why on earth would she want to talk to me? "Eeey'ar?!" Jesus Christ what the fuck did she just say? I prepared my finest middle-English accent.

"I'm... sorry, what? Do you mean me?"

"What are you doing calling my little boy a cunt?! My lad here- he sez you grabbed 'im 'n called 'im a cunt! Well?" Her eyes were glaring at me as if I'd just told her she couldn't have her dole cheque this week. "Sais'd you was gonna pull 'is fuckin' teef arht."

"What are you talking about? I don't know where your boy heard that from, all I know is I was reading my newspaper, when this young lad ran into my bag and took a tumble. I tried to catch him so he didn't hurt himself on the floor but he didn't seem to appreciate it too much. He fell over and spilled juice onto my shoes, but that is not a problem to me. I can understand your son's indifference towards me, it is rather embarrassing after all. As for *that* word, let me personally *assure* you it is not one contained within *my* vocabulary, and certainly not one I would utter to such a young and impressionable boy. All I can assume is that he heard it from some rather unsavoury types, the port is a big place and popular with teenagers especially this time of the year... I'm sure he didn't mean any harm. Also I would like to say that I am not a violent man, I do not make threats. I sincerely believe your son has me mistaken for somebody else." Dumbfounded, she and had zero comeback for that one. Ah blissful silence. The PA system crackled into life.

"All passengers for the fifteen hundred crossing to Amsterdam, please make your way to the gate now. Thank-you."

"If you'll excuse me, I have a boat to catch." As I walked away, I could hear mother scolding her son. Poor cunt.

R ED INK

Living with malice
And constant regret
Means a person is a friend
You haven't lost yet.

The notion of a cruise is dressed overtly with luxurious features, spotless presentations and a level of sophistication henceforth unseen on dry land. In my dreams, I had held this idea of nautical travel to be true, but here in reality, truth was a sodden wet shade of yellow vomit. The same air I had encountered as a child at a retirement home I found here today. Walking from the main entrance towards the cabins I pass the kitchen, which emanates the stench of soup long in preparation yet short in regurgitation. The carpets pounded flat, marked here and there with blackened chewing gum, spit, and cigarette ends. I had thought about a Jacuzzi, sauna and shower to prep myself for a long journey but someone had already urinated in the coals by the time I arrived at the steam room, grossly packed with the obese. In my cabin a rusty patch on the ceiling glared down at the bed like a wanking stranger. I walked to the back of the ship and saw the last shapes and lines of England disappear while smoking a cigarette. The trials of recent had taken their toll and only here did I sense some opportunity for rest.

I was looking at the best part of a day on the journey ahead, and decided to pace myself. Starting with a vodka martini just to get a good level. I start to wonder if I look cool as I lean my arm into a sticky patch, which happens to run the entire length of the bar. People often look at me as if I am cooler than I actually am, so I maintain the illusion so as not to disappoint anyone.

"Tall, and a- tanned, and blonde and a-lov-e-ly; dee girl frowm Ee-pah-nee-mah djom bal-kin-ay."

The Starlight Bar faces the Starlight Lounge, and meet in the middle at the delta of the "groove corner" dance floor. I drink my first martini quickly and seek service to order a second with a beer chaser.

A grand piano stands unused while a Spanish pianist plays an electronic keyboard and covers sun-kissed classics to evoke the ideas of escape and exoticism. His hair is cropped shorter than he would prefer, lacquered and oily, and his smile is plastered on. This sycophantic nature is the product of a lifetime working for tips. I finally find the waitress with the biggest tits and ask for a menu then order something to eat along with my drinks.

I love travelling alone, even simply being alone. A solitary existence reminds me with great comfort that we are never apart from the rest of humanity, just separated by time and space.

"Does an ayngel- cowntemplaite a ma feyte?"

Wearing Patrick Cox loafers and dark green corduroys paired with a casual tan brown blazer I am the epitome of sleazy faux-euro trash. Eureauxtrash. Infinitely preferable to English scum.

"Vodka Martini and lager." Says the barman, a seedy looking fellow, with a black ring of hair guarding the precious bald spot, shining atop his crown. Hairs like sticks tousled loose from the edges of a crow's nest harsh black against white skies.

Food arrives and looks nothing like he description in the menu, but hunger being what it is I ate it without issue.

On the other side of the room, enter two groups of people: first, two girls, who sit at the bar; second a group of three lads who sit around a table next to this old couple.

In a south of the river cuntish accent the leader of the three shouts: "Oi barman, three points, you cahnt!" and is joined by a chorus of laughter from the other two. The barman glances over and dutifully pours the drinks.

The men start to talk to an old man, whose wife has gone to the bathroom.

"Oim tellin' ya, look a-dis." Says the leader as he pulls a porno magazine folded in half from his back pocket and spreads it on the old man's table. The others have similar smut before them or in hands or pockets.

The old man looks and nods in a friendly way to the lads who point over the naked spread of a girl with fingers on pussy and nipple, seeking confirmation of their position that "You would though, wouldn't you? You would. That missus you would of yours an'all, but this bird," he pauses and burps. "You would like, look at 'er!"

The old man laughs genuinely "Aye lad, you would that. She's nice."

"Nice?! She's more than fackin' nice, geeza, I'd fuck her rotten, tell'n ya. Knowamean?" The leader looks at his team, one tubby with healthy locks of hair but shiny skin, and one person that could fit a thousand profiles given late at night and under intoxication. "Look at 'im," the leader says, referring to his tubby friend "'e's got gay porn! Lessave a look, c'mon you cahnt, giz those cocks over here." The magazine is thrown to him and the he begins to illustrate to scenarios to the old man who has more than a degree of interest in any form of smut, and whose wife remains in the bathroom. I'm sitting alone, but laughing at this scene; the old man seems really happy that the lads have decided to talk to him, and the leader seems like a very likeable cunt.

"Up-side, een-side out, leevin' la veeda loca!"

"Fuckin' hell, look at that cock." The girls who entered at the same time as the guys are sitting almost next to me, but have an airtight conversation. One has a sour face of beauty, but looks sour, like some cunt of a woman who has it all but takes her own inadequacies out on everyone else. One of those preaching yoga girls who blames her boyfriend for her still eating meat but continues to do so while ramming down his throat the plight of little creatures and the evil of all men. I'm still looking over at the guys and laughing to myself. "Oi, haircut," he calls at me, registering my amusement at the situation. "He's obsessed," he comments to his friends, rapid conversational style befitting that of London speed freak. "You want? Here you go, have a look at that!" He throws a magazine at me, teenage girls being fucked by older men, aged around forty. A French magazine, which I've found is pretty rare but one or two I own myself. I laugh and leaf through a few photo shoots, then look at the girls who don't so much glare at me as though me in disgust. I mumble under my breath something about slags and misery.

I get one more drink then the lads table falls onto the floor in front of me, and drinks fly everywhere. I can't understand why the barman doesn't throw them out, and I help pick up a few glasses with the group. The leader is so impressed by me, he gets me a drink: double vodka and cranberry juice. I sit down again, this time with the table of lads as they talk about work and shit like that. Then the mags come out and James starts to read a story very loudly to the entire room. He gets up on his feet and stands up straight.

"Oh, no no, no! Imma Racker mayyyynnnn- Bolognese a foosa limalong!" Croons the pianist.

"Everyone, shut up, I need to say: Men- are-" some people are still not giving Jim their full attention "Oi, I'm telling a fucking story. So: men are always coming up to me in shoppin' malls... and on't streets, and saying... "you looks familiar to me. How do I know you?" fucking hell. So like... I give them a few minutes, letting them try and... to figure out how they know me. Usually they get frustrated and give up pretty quickly." Raising his voice "Then I'll say, just before walking away, "You know me cos you probably wanked off to my photos about a million times." God what a slag, look at 'er, fucken fanny right out spread'n it." James smirks a fully expectant grin at the pictures of the girl. Many drinkers are disgusted by the man, and some seem to be leaving. There are one or two younger people who find the scene funny but in general it is a badly received oration.

"Haw, don't all leave, I'll be quiet, just sit-down, sit down." As he sits down he holds up the magazine with a spread picture of the woman, Andi-Sue, with her fingers placed to reveal a pussy all sodden and wet as the table erupts in chorus:

"*Sit doowoowooowoowaaoon, een seeem-pa-thee.*" Before the midi guitar solo takes over.

People begin to leave the room quietly. In our drunken state we laugh like jackals and berate those not a part of our group. James spots one of the women make her exit.

"Oooh, look, snooty bitch is leaving the building." She glares over at us but we are too drunk to be phased. "What is your problem? You could fucking shag... a-n-y-one on this boat, you could shag everyone on this boat," the table laughs and James winks at us, "so why don't you shag us lot? We're young lads and we'll shag your mate too, no bother. You just come to our room and we'll sort you's both out and then we can all 'ave an ice cream." The girls waste no time around our group, a primed team of animals building steam to fuck and fight.

The old mans wife, who long ago returned from the toilet, is surprisingly receptive to our childish antics and cackles away behind a "super king-sized" cigarette.

A glance is exchanged between the barman and the pianist and he begins and strongly played rendition of a Sinatra song.

"*Oh the shark, bay; has his tee, tear; aind he shows dem,*

belly wait. Just a cha-nyfe, has old mack-heat, yeah, and he keeps it, out-off-sight."

More drinks then a time check, eleven-thirty, early yet. We won't land ashore until eleven in the morning.

I order a pack of cigarettes at the bar.

"That is two Euros." I take a step back.

"How much?"

"Two Euros" he turns his head slightly to the right and looks out of the corner of his eye. "they are cheaper in Europe than in UK."

"No shit," I say to myself.

On the table, a glass is broken and the guys start laughing, then James knocks another glass onto the floor on purpose. I get my cigarettes and go and sit at the table, now surrounded by shards of glass and pools of premium lager.

Our aggressive nature was entertainment for only a certain amount of time before we left and decided to cause havoc elsewhere on the ship. The boat is massive, and we have half a full day left.

James produces two litres of cheap vodka and a carton of concentrated orange juice from some magical hiding place and we continue drinking on the open deck at the rear of the ship.

As we urinate from the edge of the balcony over the edge of the ship and into the churning waters below, to of the younger members of the bar begin to walk past us, two girls, ripe and fresh.

"Oi oi, ladies," I endeavoured. "Can I offer you two a drink? Only half a Rohypnol in each: a walk in the park." The boys laughed as did the girls, but the girls knew not what for. We begin a more muted conversation than we had exhibited in the bar, but all anyone could hear was the deafening roar of the engine room and wind whipped past our freezing ears until it became obvious we should venture inside for quieter surroundings as I did the gentlemanly thing and carried one of the girls handbags, a slim, green leather design.

Some decades previously I had been on the verge of

youth, tantalizingly close to puberty but not quite there. Without the distractions of sexual activity or stimulation I was focused at my schoolwork. Upon arriving home I would proudly display my good grades to mother, who grew more and more distant once my father went overseas to work within fledgling financial industries in second and third world countries. "Money matters," he once said, "so much that even happiness is secondary. Money can always bring a smile to someone's face, and often smiles on the right face can bring you more money."

One morning before school I went into my fathers study and looked on his desk. A great slab of mahogany wood polished and formed into the desk over a hundred years ago. The desk was an heirloom and had been used by his father, and his father before him. My small hands wiped away the settled dust over the green-leather work-surface in the centre of the desk. The inlet drawer held a few pieces of paper and leather bound booklets and a shiny pen that wrote in red ink. The pen seemed like a treasure to me and I borrowed it for inspiration and wisdom in my formative years. At school the usual dullards occupied each classroom, and the students they taught were no better. One particular day we were set a homework assignment to insert ten words into sentences and present them to the class to following day. Extra credit, said the teacher, a spinster alcoholic who stunk of coffee and cigarettes, if you could insert the ten words into a paragraph. The teacher made an extra point that the results would be read out by students in class. Even before I left my desk I had begun to sketch out ideas for the paragraph, since there was no way my ego would allow me to be be categorized with the rest of the people in my class. Great wondrous ideas came and I scribbled them in the back of my notebook using my fathers red pen.

My feet hurried home over mounds of grass that seemed so vast at that time, past trees that were like giants looming down over the sleepy village roads banked with the fallen leaves of October. As I arrived home I ran into the lounge where my mother had taken to darkness and drink and slowed to creep silently past on my way to my fathers desk.

The air had moved slightly in the room. A great tall bookshelf many times the height of my body even now stood proud and firm, forming the entirety of the wall that faced the desk.

Using the notes as a rough guide, I took a clean sheet of paper and began to write the paragraph containing the ten words. I was careful to ensure that each word chosen was just right for the place in the sentence, useful, reasonable, nothing excessive or over blown. Even my handwriting I took an extra few degrees of care with, properly constructing each "g" and "j" and "k" and all those other interesting letters to write. The sun began to hang heavy in the sky and the room was filled with a reddish-golden hue that made even the dust seem to come alive with mystery and expectation.

From downstairs I heard my mother call, and the smell of vegetables and meat cooking signaled dinner. The call came almost on cue as I had just finished the last sentence to close the paragraph.

A picture of my fathers stern face alongside my mother and I looked back from the desk and seemed to assure me of a significant step taken forward.

The next day at school, I sat at my desk and awaited the teacher who came at her usual time some minutes after nine, then sat with her coffee before writing words of discipline and social suffocation on the black board.

The word "prose" in particular was written in large cursive strokes that trailed off at the end as if the teacher had been distracted by matters of greater importance.

"I trust you have all completed your homework assignments as set?" The teacher asked openly, and was replied with a lazy "Yes Miss Messenger," spoken in unison by the class.

"Right okay then, who wants to go first? Who wants to read the first sentence?" My hand shot up straight and tried to reach higher than physiology would allow.

"Yes Alex?"

"Miss, I wrote all the words into a paragraph." I excitedly spoke to the murmurings of classmates still stuck in the solitary-sentence Dark Ages.

"Well then, I suppose you should go first."

I cleared my throat and began to speak, and almost instantly began to realize that my paragraph was not for public consumption. I had, unwittingly, written a series of very descriptive sentences that individually were fine but when read together were verging on erotica. Between the third and fourth sentences I realized my error, but had begun to walk through the flames of exposure until I felt the crushing weight of cruel faces and judgment laid at my gate with great relish. I decided to sabotage my own trial, and began to fumble some words, mispronounce others and finally make the false confession that I could not read.

The children in the class laughed and Miss Messenger shushed them aggressively, ordering me to the desk with my work.

I took her the paper, which she did not read but held up to my face, demanding:

"What is this?"

"My homework, Miss." I stammered in response, fearful for what I did not know.

"In red pen?" she screamed, "Red ink is not permitted in this classroom, whether on the page or in the barrel." The teacher snatched my homework from my hands and tore it into pieces, dropping them into the small metal bin next to her feet.

In our quiet corner we had dissipated as a group as women were sought for juicy holes and warm lips to engage with. My own conversation with the young girl going nicely, a delicious fabrication about my occupation as apprentice to one of Londons' finest locksmiths and servicer of a clientele consisting primarily of wealthy Jews and Arabs resulting in big money for me and therefore big hopes for her.

She asked if I wanted to return to the bar with her for a dance, but I sidelined her with free vodka.

"I'm actually here with my parents." She says, and I quip:

"Well I think it's a little early in our relationship for that, don't you?!" To which she giggles in glee, holding onto the romantic notion of holiday encounters with tall handsome strangers.

Down another corridor I hear the sound of one of the group, Ian or some such name, berating someone with a flock of expletives which only served to enhance my reputation with the girl, who by now had arched her back at the base as we kiss, while my fingers perform another opus in a lifetime of seduction.

I had decided not to fuck her out in the open so could slow down to add dramatic tension and work her up that little bit more. Taking a breather I light a cigarette and begin to channel Jack Nicholson.

"Could I have one of those too?"

"Of course," I said, cigarette hanging from my mouth, eyes squinting in long-set sunlight "here." I said as I hand her one perched out of the box. As I light it for her she coughs, obviously not used to smoking, at least, not my brand.

"Would you like to have another drink in my cabin? I've got a bottle of vodka and there's some orange juice around somewhere."

"Ooh: vodka? Yes please." Behind my smile I think of the countless women who have spread their legs for free hooch and cigarettes.

"I can't promise the jewel of Russia but it'll get you where you're going." Taking the girls arm, I struggled to recount her name but realized that it was of little use anyway since the walk from deck to cabin was so short.

With two people inside the cabin became further cramped, perfect for the eventual removal of clothes. One shot of vodka in and she splutters, coughing up the best part of the serving. The bed was the only place to sit and its hard surface provided little comfort, but I discovered plenty as my hand wandered from her inner thigh, up her pelvis, over her stomach and onto her tits. She was of Indian Asian descent, and comfortably chubby breasts that hung heavy in my hand. Snaking around her back I unhooked the bra through her blouse top with two fingers on my left hand. With another deft movement I removed it completely and turned the blouse over her head with another swing of the arm so within seconds she was semi-naked. I held her face to return to romance, then kissed her deeply, doing all the usual slow-down, speed-up bullshit of systematic fornication. Breaking down her walls, she let slip a moan as I pushed her head back softly at the neck, then I mouthed the lost texts of mankind against her breasts, latching the vowels onto her swollen nipples graced with a close-to exotic lure, standing erect and tight.

She turned away, first at the head, then at the body. I counteracted her wishes by dropping my hand between her legs and pushing affirmatively against her genitals. A tremendous heat and wetness could be felt from the crook of her valley and it was plain she wanted every last bit of it, but something inside her held her back as she grew a moral code in less than three-seconds.

"What?" My forehead wrinkled and she remained silent.

I returned my hand up her skirt and slipped my fingers inside her underwear, teasing close to the clit but barely skirting the edges of her fine pubic hair. She pulled my hand away once more to which I flinched in offence.

"What's the matter?" Fucking bitch. "Come here." I curdled with urges in sugar and syrup and layered with drizzles of pseudempathy and with only a hint of impending copulation. Soft yet drunk, my hand gropes for her chest, before she jerks and pulls away violently. "Jesus Christ." I curse, with impatient lust crashing against my teeth.

Moments prior I could have been halfway inside but all of a sudden the atmosphere has turned cold and indifferent.

"What, j- I don't understand, what's the matter?"

"I'm…" She looked down "…with my parents."

"I know, you said, it's okay, mine aren't around so I think we have a free room." I try to inject some humour into the exchange before I do something regretful.

"I'm… I can't, I'm only sixteen." Oh, Christ on high.

I down another vodka and think about all the other women closer to menopause than puberty I could've picked up in the would-be disco.

"You never told me that."

"Well, I'm telling you now! Anyway I'm nearly seventeen." She had that annoying, south London tea-stained accent that they love so much on flaccid-cocked English soap operas.

"Well… You know what they say, sixteen is the new twenty-one?" I slurred my words, and began to justify my thoughts within.

"I'm not sleeping with you. I'm going to my room." She stood up to leave, and got as far as the door as I follow and turn charm over like butter.

"You know, I was fourteen when I lost mine. It's a natural stage; it's best to be sure. You could make a mistake and give it to someone who is just some… guy out for sex; who knows who he could have been with before you? He could be a rapist, a *murderer* even."

She put her top over her shoulders and began to sob as I reach for her hand to slow her exit, intending softness but promising violence.

"No, it's against the law!" She screams, and rushes out of the cabin door back and down the corridor towards the deck area as she gets her top on right and storms off to another room.

"We're on international waters!" I call in desperation down the corridor, provoking nosy neighbors to peer out of their respective portholes. "In case you're concerned." Her pace quickens and soon she is vanished and probably too far away to even hear me curse. My head drops in momentary defeat when a door opposite opens, there standing the older woman from the bar scene earlier, wearing a faux-silk nightdress and pressing her lips with a cigarette. "Well?" I ask.

The piled blue eyeliner flourishes a shade like the feathers of a peacock as she looks back towards her beyond-drunk, fucked-up husband, then softly closes her door, entering my cabin.

ACCENTED ANGLO-EUROPEAN

She lay before me
Sleeping soft.
My eyes are candles
Burning wax.

The fathomless striking of metal on metal sounded our arrival at port, joined the thumping of blood in my head as the morning sickness following copious amounts of vodka came to my immediate attention.

Thankfully deserted and still nursing a hard cock for breakfast. I try to masturbate to relieve some of the pain and clean the pipes but even the rhythmic jerking of my arm gave more power to the migraine so I stopped and stretched instead, willing my blood to keep flowing. In the dining hall hundreds of people queued for their free apple strudel and piss-water coffee, sweetened with refined sugars and served in poly cups that will live forever in the stomachs of creatures cursed to be alive today. Nothing truly is free. I am reminded of the purpose of my own journey when I see a red-top tabloid newspaper that reads "Manhunt Continues". I sometimes forget myself: that

I am he who takes life, he who has no mercy. Here I would prolong my own moral reckoning, by man or by God, both of whom without significance.

Despite the crowds of people struggling with over stuffed luggage, there was a hushed pleasance to the city of Amsterdam. The air was almost sweet and something odd about the people, a sort of generalized friendship, a collective empathy so unlike the gloomy streets of England with her various puddles of piss and knife-point stabbings. I could not, however, imagine it being something I could get used to, myself being scourge to the happier class and reveling in the pity and misery of grey skies and hearts. For now I would settle for drugs and alcohol.

The majority of passengers on the boat had brought a car, however, I walked on foot, a preferred method of transport for someone in a new place for the first time. Crossing a white bridge onto dry land I joined the remainder of tourists, grey toothed and overweight, complaining already that "nowt's writtin'n Inglish." Representatives from holiday companies stood by fleets of silver buses, heavily glazed in their expressions of perma-joy. I light a cigarette and and use the abrasive particles to loosen phlegm from my lungs, spitting as I step onto the continent.

A busy road ahead of the large dockside car park gave the notion that transport may be a good idea, so I doubled back and climbed aboard a bus bound for Amsterdam, after I had finished my cigarette.

The rattling of stones in my brain accentuated by the Anglo-European accented voice crackling over speakers inside the bus. The only words I recognized were blah, blah and blah.

Remaining with eyes closed until the bus reached a destination elsewhere was a reflexive and necessary action. Feeling nothing close to wakefulness I leave the bus with or without the exchange of words with others. This journey was about getting lost, and lost I must become. As if placed like a mouse before a trap I am confronted with a slight looking man wearing a blue jacket that makes a sound like tin roofing sliding over dry, yellowed grassland. His teeth are yellow-brown and growing in rows like that of a shark. The shaggy beard and reddened eyes only add to his appearance of washed out never-was. He begins to speak to me in German.

"You what mate? Sorry I don't speak a great deal of German."

"Oh, you're English?" He says, revealing a southern accent, Home Counties or Ludlow vales.

"I am."

We talked briefly and he told me of a barge ship I could rent a room on for a night or two at a very reasonable rate. Much more reasonable than the static accommodations I had seen advertised here-and-there.

He led me across the face of the train station, an archaic building with sandstone frontage and modern interiors that crept out of historical gaps in the structure. Further we walked past the heavy iron cranes and shipping containers in one of the many dock loading areas in this part of the city.

The yellow sidings of the barge encouraged a black damp up from the waters peak, and around the front by the dock floated hundred of cans, cartons, cigarette butts and all other manner of garbage thrown from a barge with rooms rented at seventeen euros a night.

"Yeah, this is the place. It looks like a shit hole but it's pretty wicked though, run by a couple of Norwegians. Totally placid casual."

"Fair enough. Breakfast?"

"Yeah, like fruit juice and uh, toast and jam and that shit, continental innit. So whereabouts you from?"

"Up North; you a Londoner?"

"Yeah lived there for about twenty years. Been here though for like, I don't know, Christ: three, four years now."

I smile and shake my head. "Shit."

"It's like that: man can get lost out here pretty quickly. Madness... madness." His memories were almost visible as his eyes slunk over some momentary escape into half-remembered opiatic adventures, catalyzed by trillions of incalculable coincidences yet as expected as the rain over Manchester.

We approached the barge and the man called to the proprietors who reply with muffled tones from within the barge.

"So where you headed? You look like you aren't the usual weekend warrior." He smiled and held a laugh, friendly and soft.

"Can't say in particular. Just one of those times where you've got to get the fuck out of England, you know what I'm saying?"

"Every fucking day, mate." Our feet felt the efforts of walking just for a moment. "Good luck man. Good luck getting out of Amsterdam. Paul, by the way." We arrived at the barge and Paul climbed aboard. "Mind your step it's been raining."

"Safe, man: Alex."

I sloppily plodded on board, my back hurting from the overstuffed backpack over my shoulders and feet lacquered with grease and oil from the long walk dockside. The land here impossibly flat, a strange view having come from the mountainous cities and villages of England. She is carved from rock like the biggest of itches. As if the cock of God Himself felt that Saturday morning burn and dug His great fingernails across the lands of that holiest of unkempt crotch, carving out the British Isles with the rough edged index nail. As my feet hit the deck it seemed to move, and probably did, making my feet get their grip once again. The barge was called "The Pride of Amsterdam" and sat in a deep black water dock also used by massive tankers transporting oil, steel, lumber, coal, coke, whores, weed, stolen cars and who knows what other goods and services in such high demand from the rest of the world. I followed Paul up to the rickety old door while a bullet-grey tanker struggled down the access stream towards the North Sea. Opening the door to the cabin I quickly adjusted to a fug inhabiting the whole room.

"Grüß dich Paul, allez klar?"

"Servus. Dies ist ein kunden."

Stooped over a block of pinewood boards strapped together by the two-dozen, Bridgette, as I later learned her name to be. She questioned Paul with intent. Her blonde hair defied her age though to look at her face the years of chemical and sexual abuse where more than clear. On the other side of the room a woman with no name read a book and sat before a low table containing a plate with a half-eaten waffle breakfast and burning Dutch cigarette, rolled to her own liking and resting in a red ashtray.

A bar built into the hull of the boat served as a centre piece and Paul placed a two-Euro coin on it while helping himself to a beer.

I cough by way of introduction.

"Hallo." Says Bridgette.

"Hi, thanks, Paul tells me you have rooms for seventeen Euros?"

"Nineteen. He didn't work here long; remember nothing."

"Okay nineteen it is then."

Bridgette smiled and lit her cigarette, blowing the smoke against the wood she hoists from the upper to lower deck.

"Come!" She calls at me.

I follow downstairs bringing my sack with me. "You are Australia?"

"No, English."

"Ah, England. Fucking England!"

"Ya: fucking England über alles."

Bridgette nods in partial surprise at my proficiency in German, despite my entire vocabulary coming from hardcore pornographic films.

"You will stay here how long?"

"A few days, three, four? Something like that?"

That's fine, we've got plenty of space." Heavy layers

of a Scandinavian accent poured over a forty cigarette a day undertone, and the sexuality between us flared like fire through dried grass. Bridgette opens the door to my tiny cabin. "Do you want a drink?"

"Not just yet." I replied as we fell into each other, tearing of clothing and gorging all we had of one another with our mouths as we tangled our genitals into one another and grew like swarms of butterflies delving into and out of one another. I came inside her as the tail of the wasp swells mighty over that intense silence.

"Nineteen euros?" I ask.

"Okay fine, for you it is ten."

I hum in reply and push my bag into the room before us, before making my way back upstairs while Bridgette remains below deck washing her genitals.

At the bar Paul sat looking out of the window smoking a cigarette against the glass. "Oh man, it's so cold out there, I think it's nine under right now."

"Ugh, I got nearly blown off the sides this morning when I was washing up the clothes out there." Replied the girl with no name. Her grammar was bad, but she meant well. Paul, on the other hand, had a sort of- twang to his voice, where you might say, "y'know," he'd say, "you-know," so it was kind of like he was saying every word in its own right, giving every word as much importance as the last. Paul's phone began playing an overture from Mozart, or Beethoven, I couldn't remember which, or should I say I didn't know as Bridgette arrived back and lit another cigarette.

"Hello? Ah hello, yeah, I just got in. No, I've been out for a couple of hours. Hmm. Yeah." I seem to want to know what the other person is saying.

"Well, how about the Greenhouse in one hour. No, I just need to eat. Yeah, okay, yes. Yes, love you too." The phone went down and Paul sucked on a Lucky Strike. "Anna says hello, Bridgette."

"Oh, hallo Anna." A brief pause as she raced over the

room to a window and slides it open. "No! It is to be going over there. There!" She shouted orders to a portly man in the model of cuckolded weakling erecting a sign outside advertising the barge as a hostel.

"Bridgette's my girlfriend. She's awesome. She's an architect, you know." Paul told me as if the information to me was useful, or even interesting, but I thought I'd humour him for a while.

"Idiot!" Bridgette cursed to herself hanging over a long 'ee'.

"Really, an architect? That's cool. What kind of architecture does she work on?"

"Oh, all sorts of things like walls, and stairwells, lots of different things."

I placed a two-euro coin on the bar and took a beer, basking in its goodness before lighting a cigarette of my own. "Sweet man, architecture's a great game to get into." The label on the bottle was wet so I peeled it off and tore it into little squares, which I then rolled up into little balls and arranged them in a pattern while Paul lit another cigarette and Bridgette pointed out of the window to the feckless ballast outside. The girl with no name poured my beer into a glass called a tulip.

After the beer and a cigarette I feel like sleeping, and go downstairs to the room. I believe in checking around the room in hotels as a general rule, and beneath the mattress laid booty, a heavily soiled adult magazine, The Bible in a land like Amsterdam. I read around the cracks in the wall articles and partially viewable fisting photo sets, soaked in come both printed and hardened. The minor urge to masturbate ebbs and I fall into a deep sleep.

L ILYPADS

Forget about it. It was never right
In the first place. You only wanted
To receive validation
For your wicked ways.

Night time never truly leaves Dam square. The sound of bells striking tells me that the time is just passing nine. I have been drinking steadily since arrival and have gathered steam over seven or eight continental beers and some cheap cocaine bought from a Nigerian Hot Dog vendor, who assures me the price is much lower for me since we are 'like brothers'. In a coffee shop I buy more weed and smoke it at the bar while drinking a coffee, since weed and beer together is generally discouraged. In the bathroom the scrawlings of a thousand tourists and travellers adorns the walls and in my drug induced haze I get lost among the lines and lyrics. A little cocaine helps but only as far as the bag goes, which is right to this point. I curse myself for not taking the guys number, but as I walk outside in search of drug dealers I find three, all Nigerian and over-friendly. It is a dead cert they are carrying knives or guns, and so a swift purchase arrangement is executed and I collect four more bags for my trouble.

My stomach almost turns and the pig lips ground into

the hot dog meat start kissing my innards, working on a way out. I spit to the ground but it hits my shoe. A tension builds in the street, growing to life as night crawls on, red lights shining and ultraviolets exposing ancient fluids. A sign for "LIVE SEX SHOW" grabs my attention and before I can think about it I have entered the venue and paid the man twenty euros. Half-expecting the same sort of set up as back home, I am surprised when I enter the room and there are a dozen women sitting in the audience of no more than twenty. Liquor is flowing and the shrill interactions they relentlessly dole out almost encourages me to leave; that is before I do some more drugs to calm the situation.

The bawdy brood seems like they half-expect me as they roar a welcome "Wahey!" in unison.

"Pleasure to be of service, Ladies."

Cackling gullets like yodeling seal or breaching sardines schooling round the shark in a twist of the tale.

On the stage a full sex show was indeed taking place, a tall, muscular Native American looking man having full sex with a typical mid-thirties Amsterdam hooker. The venue tried to evoke towards the spiritual, purifying act of sexual congress, as opposed to the decadent whores seated before them.

"Quite a penetrating display." I said to the nearest girl.

"You can say that again, darlin'."

We both laughed, and her eyes told me a story of drugs so pouring a little coke in my hand I hold it towards her face which sounds like a truffle hunting boar as she snorts it from my palm, then drops her head and puts her mouth around my cock. Just as I close my eyes I realise they are open and I am masturbating in front of the girls, who hasten their pace and leave the room. All I needed was a touch more coke before the security guard arrived to throw me out onto the street.

In darkened alleys I see swirls of light enticing and warm, that rise as I stand tall, cobbled stones bruising my legs and knees and arms upon impact.

Industrial steel walls and flooring gave a militarized look to the next place I fell into. Sealed plastic poster frames blurred pink and red, beads from a curtain dance softly like frogs over lily pads during the season of the mayfly.

The sound of euro pop dance music playing independently from at least three video screens as background to clips of hardcore pornographic scenes. The familiar arcs of come inform me of my position as I find the counter of the sex shop.

"Güten abend."

"Ich keine gesprachen zie Deutsche. Ich bin eine Englander."

"Ah England, of course, welcome, how I can be of service to you?" The man had light blond hair, glasses and reddened facial skin from high blood pressure and he pronounced his "of" like "off".

"What videos have you got?"

"For you we have anything you could want. Pretty standard stuff, Americans, Deutsche, negro, then some of the more harder core stuff; fistings, bondage, watersports, shitting, pissing, horses, dogs. Mainly it depends upon what you are in the market of."

"Not sure really, maybe could do a preview of something?" My heightened state of sexual arousal getting the better of me, and the guy had seen it all before.

"If you want to watch videos, we have a cinema with two screens upstairs." I consider walking out but had gathered the best part of a semi-on in preparation and so oblige the man and reluctantly pay some foreign looking currency then guardedly enter though the red gloss painted door as the man at the counter calls "Come and go you can all day!" Then mumbles unheard "Fucking England."

Through the cardboard wooden door seemed like a billion light years away. The atmosphere shrouds up onto itself; speaks in tongues and rhymes every other verse. Muffled groans and repeated orgasms were hiding like mice in the cracks and darkened corners of the room. Ahead of me a red-walled staircase, lit by a single tungsten-charged bulb hanging at the summit.

I was supposed to be getting out of my head, escaping myself in this place; and yet here I go treading familiar yet mysterious routes, blazing trails well trodden.

Two rooms, numbered with rear-lit plastic plates are stained in what looks like varnish spattered from a distance nearly. I take the room on the left, number one.

It is the beginning of a short vignette, timed to around six minutes and ideally so given the requirements of the scene. In my first breathes of the room there was that old pungent stench of sweat and tar with bleach and come. Up on the screen a young woman was getting it, bent over a tree stump but the real action was the floor. Finding a seat here was a perilous journey, navigating between twitchers and jerkers, some sniffing poppers and many in pairs or more. My expectation of the room had been at least a few women strong but there was not, by my gaze, a solitary one. Stalking the rear of the room momentarily I decided to try the other screen.

Here it was a lot quieter, barely half a dozen people, nicely spaced, and behold, one woman sitting with a man at the rear. I take the seat adjacent and settle quickly. The story on the screen a mostly superfluous fisting saga as the light adjusted in my eyes and I look to the back row and see the woman clearly jerking the man she sits next to. Her gaze fixed straight ahead, as though her hand works independently or at least with a great deal of subtlety. I examine the screen for a moment, fistings making a tangential shift into a gangbang scene, one Eastern European looking girl sucking off a row of cocks while getting two at a time in the process. By staring momentarily at the screen I give my head turn towards the woman all the more memorable. To ensure maximum impact I combine the glance with masturbation, as her eyes look back at me she does not look away.

Holding my cock in hand, pointed and throbbing

towards her I move towards her and sit myself one seat away at which point she drops her head and takes me inside her mouth. Rushings of blood pummel through as I grip her by the throat while ejaculating but as my hand gets a hold I feel stubble and her Adams apple lurching back and forth as I finish coming. The realization is swift and my exit even swifter.

The damp patches of come in my trousers make for an uncomfortable walk out of the sex shop. The streets are building with vibrancy and a harsh green neon leaf sign with a coupled beer symbol draws me inside.

I find a spot near the corner of the bar to roll a smoke. A high-pitched Californian accent shrieked from the mouth of a female physical specimen unlike any of my typical acquaintances found down numerous unnamed prostitute alleyways, any street, town or country. She was blonder than blonde, made up like the idea of whorish-party-chick. I reign in my stalker gaze but she spots and smiles, calling something out that I completely miss.

"What? Me?" I reply.

"I wanted to ask you a question, could you take a selfie of us?"

"Of us?" I question.

"No, of me and my friend." Another girl but a less than pale dilution of this thing before me.

"Now, how could I do that?"

"How could you do what? Just point it and take the shot."

"But how would it be a selfie?"

"How? Well, duh, how about because it has my *self* in it and it's on my own *self's* phone?"

"I suppose you have a point!" I concede to stupidity in the prospect of pussy, anxious to accost something to counteract the transvestite saliva still dredged into my pubic hair. Taking the picture I am coerced to capture seven variations containing identical duck-lipped poutings and protruded, pierced tongues, and offer to buy the next round as I am invited to sit with the unmatched pair.

Gazing blankly over the photographs, and yet with the memory of human excitement, the airhead exclaims, while sipping sugared margarita through a thin, black plastic straw: "Totally awesome, uh my God, Tam you need to touch up your eyes."

Her friend snarls like a tethered Gorgon, snakes hissing behind long-since bleached hair. "Oh my God I saw this thing online that *totally* is like me: this French guy's like *"I don't like what you're saying, but you can say it anyway if you want, it's okay: I'll make sure you can say it."* Totally righteous. But actually, it got me to thinking: why would he say it's okay if he doesn't like what he's saying? Why would he even want to help him?" She is the definition of *airhead*, and not dissimilar to a fish in a barrel.

"One can only speculate on the twisted mind of a Frenchman. There is a certain... *malice* to them." I double down on Englishness, channeling the wrinkled brow of Caine and steel-eyed glare of Neeson meets Law.

"Oh wow, your accent is so cool. I love British guys."

"We can be love-able. Heavy-weight on the *bull*."

Spending the next twenty minutes or so setting up classic British sayings just to garner a touch more titillation I started to lose the will to even consider the girl before me, certainly after introducing myself as Atticus Fable, "Addy" for short.

"I'm like a French history major but I want to study Renewables, they're *so* the future. So, like, I'm going to study that and then open like a store selling renewable energy and junk, some shit." My smiles and noddings barely disguise my disgust at the luridly beautiful moron ahead of me. Her ideas are ludicrous but likely to be a huge success due to her appearance and assumed connections. I try to plunge myself into the conversation, to inhabit her every word and make it almost unthinkable for her not to open her legs to me. Pushing hard to ignore her words as every one that fell from her brain was thicker and more leaden that the last. "What's your major?"

"Well, I graduated from Oxford with honours, first in my class of law and science."

"Wow, law *and* science!"

"Gives me a broader understanding of the comings and goings of all sorts of aspects of life. Kind of a master of all trades, jack of none. Plus, I figured that if my scientific research ever fell short I could always rely on my legal practice." Recently I have been lying on every single word, it makes recollection of memory all the more entertaining. Not so much *what did I say* as *what could I have said*? I might as well tell her I invented digital clocks and have a patent dispute over the wheel. Her hand perennially stuck to her cellphone, and her friend aping and yabbering at her every motion. I drink faster and the plague-like abuser in my head rouses from his sobrietic slumber, demanding more intoxicants and frenzies of sexual violence and assorted chaos.

"So you would be what is commonly referred to as a *hottie*, yes?" I pose the question as a statement and layer the words with a heavy, yet totally inoffensive middle-English accent.

The beastly friend chimes: "A *hottie*?"

"Yes, I should think so, don't you?" I reply with instant razor slashes across her stupid eyes. "She's definitely a *hottie*. Which I guess makes you the *nottie*?" The friend makes a sound like a deflating balloon yet the hottie in question is flattered behind her sediments of foundation and sharpened edges delineating lips, eyes, brows, cunt and so on. The *hottie* was attractive in an "I'll take come with that" kind of way, and choking on cock I could certainly envisage her. The barman delivered another tray of drinks I had ordered using a universally understood hand signal for "another round" and I gave him my card, which he returned shortly, declined. Now the fear set in and suddenly my bags of drugs felt weak and incapable of carrying me as far as was required so I get him to try it again, and once more. The third time would be social suicide and the attractive girl pays using her own black credit card, and is left unimpressed and once more seeking *hard cock* with supporting rafters of even *harder cash.*

"Are you guys staying here for a minute? I've just got to hit the ATM."

"Sure, we'll be around." Replies the friend, rolling her eyes at the hottie and both now exposed for the absolute cunts that they are. I cough into my hand and wipe saliva on the Calvin Klein coat one of them has draped over the chair as a marking of territory, just in case I lose them later. Walking through dense smoke and denser people I disappear once more into the night.

There is something pleasantly assuring about a piss-soaked brick wall, especially when one is propped against it to steady a drunken swagger and not drop drugs onto the floor. I pour a nice pile of supposed cocaine onto my hand and snort it through both nostrils simultaneously to ensure maximum impact. I go about my way to find an ATM and do so a few hundred yards through a rapidly growing crowd of people.

I am not sure exactly what the drugs consist of yet the lights of the streets are raised exponentially and the gentle sloping hills and canals become twisted wiry figures and burning streaks across the sky as I finally reach the ATM and try to use its complex mechanisms. If only I could get the numbers on screen to stop shaking I might be able to know what my status is, but I cannot, and so withdraw as much money as I can, around five hundred euros. It is a sickening perversion of mankind that he feels subhuman when not in the possession of money. Perhaps it is Money who is in possession of Him. Either way, we were reunited and skipped forth into the fields of commerce, my particular wish being that of more drugs, and stumble towards a man in an alleyway.

As he produced a hand full of small baggies I felt the great urge to murder him and take everything he had but instead I play the Empirical authority and bark: "I don't want none of your fucking shit, you hear me? I'm not like the rest of these cunts walking around: I am beyond all of them so you give me the fucking good stuff. Money isn't the problem."

"Right on you are, my friend." He looks down the alley. "You want the really good shit?"

"Yes I do." I affirm, already too high to keep my eyes open, but with verbosity and intention I speak my words as he leads me down the alleyway.

"Come with me."

Moonlight peers deathly overhead, and the sounds of joy and excitement from the people are quashed behind thick walls and occasional slender trees and rubbish bins. Even the pilings of trash were relatively well kept, relative to back home at least. We walk until we could be in any street, all signs of commerce are absent, and instead a hidden world behind the neon veil of the city. The dealer leads me to a chain fence and whistles, mimicking the sound of some tropical bird or desert critter. We stand in silence for a moment and I consider my surroundings as being somewhat dangerous, but at this point fear is the last emotion I will show. Much like angry dogs: violent humans are more likely to attack if fear is exhibited in a potential victim. He repeats the bird-call and somewhere in the darkness comes the reply of a kissing sound. "Come on." He says once more as we pass the fence and arrive at a corner with a new kind of gentle hum, soft lights shining like mirrors off the rained-upon cobble stones. The rocks to build the road had been mined from quarries in Northern Wales and brought on ships some four hundred years past, to supply the building of this explosive city that could not and cannot be contained within the mere mileage allotted.

We come across a shipping container, out of place yet somehow hidden at the end of a row of houses close to dereliction. A cloud of smoke rises from the throat of a man in the darkness waiting. He speaks only to the dealer, quietly in his ear, as the dealer explains his presence.

"So you want the good shit?" The man asks in an Australian accent, his tone suggested mid-fifties, West coast but I wouldn't know much about that.

"Yes I do."

"And money is no object?"

"Well, five hundred euros is what I have got, but was maybe thinking three hundred."

The umbrage in his voice made apparent: "Five hundred euros? How in the hell you call that no object?"

"I guess, well I thought five hundred is not bad. But maybe we had a misunderstanding."

"I should bloody well guess maybe so, hey?" Then he muttered the numbers to himself. "I shouldn't even be talking to you. You're a bloody chancer. Get the fuck out of here. Fucking wanker." He spits on the floor and then hesitates, "Actually mate, I'll tell you what, you can have the good shit, the really good shit, for five hundred, and you can keep the money too."

"What's that you say?"

"Oh you heard that hey? No bloody misunderstandings now?! I said you can just have the drugs for free, well, not exactly free, nothing in this life's for free. But no money. All you have to do is fight my boy here."

The dealer instantly starts to moan "Oh come on now, John, don't make-"

"Come on!" Encourages the man. "Don't be such a fucking lilypad you *cunt*."

The presence of many drugs in my system stopped my simple flight reaction and instead I spoke in counsel "Listen, I don't really think I can beat this guy in a fight for some drugs. That's pretty low."

"Oh you don't have to beat him, you just have to fight him." Fear finds purchase and creeps into the cracks around my face.

"Or you can give me all your money and then we fuck you right up properly, instead of in a fair fucking fight." The lines of time throwing shadows across his face cast from in the muted street lamps above.

The dealer sighs and throws the first punch to my mouth, which knocks me with surprise and backwards a half step, I level myself and he returns by punching me in the stomach and smacking the sides of my face. I taste blood and spit.

"You should fight back." Gasps the dealer as he continues to throw punches my way and pauses to regroup and I punch him in the eye and follow with heavy jabs to the cheek and chest.

The Australian laughs only as those type can, generational criminality twisting his comprehension of the normal world until every alleyway is another rape, mugging or street fight.

"That's the stuff lads, get in there!"

The dealer retaliates and so do I and we tumble onto the floor, he with much greater strength than me but allowing me jabs and digs in response. This was not the first time he had been made to fight for the pleasure of what I can only gather is his boss. Strange working practices in this company. He punches me particularly hard in the eye and I pull back, holding my face, The older man at this point guesses we are sufficiently tested, bloodied and beaten to satisfy, and stops the fight by raising his hand.

"There now, do you see? You should never be afraid to fight in life. Couple of scratches. Bump on the head. Barely even notice it. Hesitance in conflict results directly in an increased number of casualties, and the same can be said for one-on-one combat. That said, don't you ever fucking come back here again. Here's your drugs, now piss off."

I walk backwards then turn and walk away as the man talks to the dealer closely, chastising him for allowing such a low yielding bond through the secret door.

Retracing my steps is easy and once I reach a good distance from the hidden place I try some of the powder: as pure as can be. All notions of the garbage awash in the streets is carried away by a silken hurricane spun by some galactic spider, turning and biting through my body, spreading from my bronchial cavity and lifting soft pillows beneath me to help me sail back into the tempest of Red Light District Amsterdam at midnight.

A man dressed as a tiger breathes fire beside another on stilts and clowns marching like pendulums and smiling using waxed impressions tick like clocks tocking across the narrow citadel street. Mystical scenes spreading organically through the different performers and entertainers chorused by a band I only now realise is in reality and not my head. The crashing of cymbals and grumbling of trombone seeming like some infernal wrangler brought on by my already forgotten battle.

Ducking and swinging around and about in my mind but on foot here I stagger and swerve in a daze. Something through the crowd catches my eye and I have an objective to follow. To reach it I must cross the bridge and join the street parallel with the canal and I can see the ultraviolet strip lamp that seemed such a pretty colour so far away but here up close it is used to light a room painted red but lit up dark green. Inside the door I walk through a beaded curtain and find my hand once more around my genitals. There is a fuzzing ache around them, as if the tribulations of recent times have created sharp, amber ridges, not unlike the plates of bone rising from the spinal tracts of a dinosaur. Moving further I find the bag of drugs, roughly ten grams and counting down. I take just a few touches and steady on through the peeling wallpapered corridor into another room while lighting a cigarette.

Here I encounter a girl with long hair, luminous bikini outfit and bulbous features like a comic book whore. The cigarette is the best I have ever smoked and I offer one to the girl, which she receives and waits for a light.

Her eyes find mine as I strike the fire to burn the cigarette and from here it is plain.

"Is fifty euros," she states, and I stare through chiseled cocaine eyes at her freight train lips and globular tits and repeat the interchange.

"Fifty euros?"

"Ya. I give you real good second fuck."

"Second fuck?" Wait a minute. "Wait, I get two for one?"

"Two what?"

"Two fucks?"

"No, no, *suck and fuck*, you know? I suck you cock real nice then you fuck me, all is good, alles klar?"

"I see, perfect. You like drugs?" I ponder, generosity being one of the side effects of pure cocaine.

"Natürlich." Which must mean *yes* since we proceed to devour a heady pile of pure white powder, and she shares with me some blue pills which I crush on the side table to add to the mix.

"These will make the high go low and the low go high." She giggles getting the words out, sniffing another bump of the cocaine "Wow, really nice fucking shit, baby, you must be rock star."

Her words barely have time to leave her mouth before she is between my legs and teasing an erection out of my worn and tiresome penis. But tease she does and before long we find ourselves fucking like those oft-referenced rabbits. Her words are like poetry from some beautiful disease ridden Dickensian tramp. "You cock has so much better than the others! Oh baby!"

Her mouth so welcome around my cock, dissipating the almost forgotten blowjob previous, her sweet spit washing away the memory and I hold her cheek and throat and feel the head of my penis pushing against both. Creating a vacuum she sucks a great erection into my dick and then pivots her ass to allow me to enter her from behind. The sweet invitation like a red carpet and I dose us both with more of the happy powder, the throbbing blood surges like broken levee banks from within, a swelling around my eye reminding me of my previous outburst of street violence and walk over thin ice.

There is something about the working girls of the world that is truly honest, further more than their counterparts in the "normal" plains of existence. They trade sex for money, they suck cock for cash and drugs, but then so does every other person on this rock. Not a woman or man living today does not work for sex. We are all slaves to the master, that being cock or cunt, or combinations or dissolutions thereof. Our chains are wrought from the emptiness left and warmth last felt from our mother; for whom she is forever lost and gone from sight on the day that first sexual dalliances are unlocked. Perhaps not physically, but in a sense, washed away by the turning tides of lust and fever.

As sweat showers from my brow and come nestles firmly within the luminous bikini clad girl I roll off to the side and scramble for a cigarette which she lights and provides a final caress.

"You are very handsome," says the whore, "but your tooth, is rotten?"

I look at her with honesty, lick my broken lips and try to remember to blink.

R OOM SERVICE

Anger at the things unthought of
By your feeble mind. Laughing at the
Moons you've spent
Debating day for night.

I am woken as pillows struggle against the angles of my freshly bruised face with a throbbing pain throughout my mouth and jaw. The teeth hanging from my gum line feel like they may drop any second. As I inhale I hear a creaking sound from my lungs, and a deeper inhalation makes my spine crack, delivering intense pain in the form of relief. I am on the barge. How I managed to return here is a mystery, yet that could be said for a thousand other nights where I happened to find my way home.

I must be woudned as my face sticks to the pillow in a couple of places. Drying blood and saliva soaked into the downy innards. There is a shower at the end of the corridor and I use it for the first time in what seems like weeks. Through a mottled hole water matching the shade, temperature and velocity of human piss trickles onto my face and body. As I massage a bar of soap into my skull I feel bruises and lumps on my head and am reminded of the night previous. Memories I would rather have lost come crashing back. The one benefit of my actions being that they have taken place in a foreign land, and one such that I may never see again, so consequence is of little concern to me, but then it rarely is.

At breakfast (sharp at 3pm), only European lager available and cigarettes on the deck faced into a cold, yet refreshing wind. Great ideas are the same as justice in that they degrade very quickly from the point of conception; when you have an idea it is best to try and preserve it immediately, to crystalize the essence and vibration of the idea so that it may be brought to life at some point. The same can be said for justice. If justice is not swift, then it is diluted, and eventually harmless. True justice must be instantaneous, and the advanced perpetrator knows this is the case and so utilizes moments where he or she knows that justice will be far delayed, to the point of non-start, so to exercise the wicked will of corruption.

Bridgette ties a rope to the sea-facing end of the barge, glancing at me over the end of a burning cigarette and heaving the rope taught and stringent. I nodded backwards in salutation, lighting a cigarette of my own.

"You look terrible."

"Long night, I think."

She finishes tying the rope and makes her way towards me.

"There is a lot of shit on the streets around here you should not play games for." Then, correcting herself. "With." Bridgette takes a seat facing away from me but close enough to touch.

We share a moment of silence where I consider saying many things of an intelligent and spectacular nature but leave it hanging in the wind instead. We are fitted to silence and the cigarette is too good to ruin with conversation anyway.

Bridgette looks at my face and reads me clearly.

"Here, take these." She hands me a bag of pills.

"What are these?" I ask.

"Sleepers. For you know when you have to stop. It's a nice way down."

Bridgette turns away once again and finishes her cigarette.

"Thanks." I say, yet know in myself that I *never* know when to stop. "But *I* don't stop doing drugs, drugs stop doing me."

"Funny." Bridgette says, flatly, as she lights another cigarette.

Hours later, the shadows on the ground cut razor-sharp in their contrasts. My skin seemed a sandalwood brown colour in the overhanging glow of fluorescence. The cocaine was still top-shelf and I now had the overwhelming urge to find a museum to indulge in some fine art, to escape from the drugs and dick-pocked streets of plague, writhing in Sodomesque throws of perpetual orgasm and shameful revelation.

Lost in the milieu of the red light district, I decide that one more beer would help with liberation and so enter a dark yet comfortable looking bar. Inside is warm and cozy, safe from the freezing winds and heckling whores and drug dealers lurking in every corner and alley.

"One beer please."

The more time I spend with European people the more words I drop from my vocabulary. Where once I might say "Y'alright our kid, give us a beer will you now, chief?" now I am short and concise with my speaking, removing intranslatables.

Cigarette smokes touches my eye and as I wince I feel the bruising around my face and swollen cheek. I am approached by a girl with brown skin and straight hair, wearing tightly wrapped spandex with breasts that graze my arm as she sits next to me.

"Mind if I sit here?" Her accent was of African origin, given away by the addition of "y's" in words with "a" or "e" as a first vowel.

"Of course not, please."

Her eyes almost screamed "fuck me" and her lips glistened as if she had not even had chance to wipe the come from them, leaving a porcelain shine and hint of pink tongue within.

"It is so cold out there. My sister and I thought we would never find a place." I look puzzled at her momentarily until I turn and see the seat next to me is being occupied by the girls' identical twin sister.

"It is like the freezing cold of Russia." Spoke the sister.

"Well you know what they say, dress for winter, pray for summer." I am running out of banter and we have barely started.

"Would you like to buy us a drink?" Asks the first.

"As you wish, of course my ladies."

The first sister says something to the bartender and he brings them two not-very Martini looking Martinis and the bill for two hundred and five euros.

I am initially dumbfounded.

"Excuse me, what is this?"

The bartender approaches, his footsteps heavy and movements definite.

"The bill. One hundred euros for each special cocktail for ladies and five for beer. Pay now."

"Are you fucking kidding me?" I turn my head to look at the first sister, and see behind her a hulk of a man standing next to another, staring at me with intent. "I see." Wincing in concession "Two hundred and five." I count over the money and give it up, then leave the bar without saying so much as another word to the hustling girls. "Please excuse me if I don't tip." My levels of trust and compassion reach new depths as I curse my footsteps walking out.

Back on the street and pocket lightened of roughly half of my funds, I stop to think of a plan. Another night in the city and I may well be broke or dead or hopefully both. Escape from escape. Thankfully the crooks in the bar did not know about my remaining drugs and so I found a quiet corner at which to dose myself with a few hits. The fourth leaves white powder plush upon my cheek and nose and just as the powder touches crackling pops up my sinus and bubbles into my brain I hear a cursing from across the road, where outside another bar stands Jim from the ship.

"No fucking way!" I mutter while looking through eyes caught in vices, twisted into strings that are threaded through a billion needles then stitched into place, caught between open and closed.

"Jimmy!" I call through the choking of cavities rinsed with intoxicants and walk with a slight stumble towards the bar front where he stands.

"Mate, there are some fucking slags in here, get yourself in there."

"Fucking right on man." After the cocaine infused intro I light a cigarette to regain composure.

"What's that you got?" He asks.

"My friend, this is the best fucking gear I have ever had."

"What happened to your face? You been fighting?"

"No one wants to see how sausages are made."

Taking Jim by the hand I pour some cocaine onto a depression formed near the base of the thumb.

We go into a bar and I recognize a couple of the guys from the boat seated by the pool table in this sports-themed drinking venue.

"Alex, you remember these cunts, don't you?"

Those from the ship indulge in a 'wahey' in recognition and some hand slaps, shoulder shakes, and Jim gives me the soft introduction to Liz and Karl, the two people I have not met before.

The bar is McDonnels, an Irish pub complete with violin jig music ramped up to overkill, or maybe it was just the drugs.

"Pleasure: Karl, Liz."

"What brings you to this city of sin then, Alex?" Asks Karl, a tall, weathered man with long brown hair and eyes that have seen dimensions beyond our own.

"Ah you know, the drugs are great, culture is nice, got a murder trial to escape from."

"Just another day." Puns Liz.

"What hotel are you in?" Asks Jim.

"I'm on a barge, down by the docks."

"A fucking barge? Like a ship?" Confirms Jim.

"Yep. And before you ask, I've got no fucking idea how I ended up in a barge."

"A fucking barge." Jim laughs and shakes his head. "Did you get into that bird on the boat?"

"What bird?"

"The Indian." Memories of attempted sexual assault with arguable definitions come flooding back.

"Half and half." I shrugged

"Well me and Ian did a double with some old tart. Bumped into her after you trotted off. Found a load of birds on a hen do, and you know what they get like."

"Nice one."

"So we've had something old and blue, her fucking varicose veins, that is! What about you, any joy since you got here?"

"Just soaking the place up really." I felt that revelations about my misadventures in transvestite fellatio and street fighting were best left for legend. Liz looks like she is about to fall over and Karl steadies her with a strong arm. The Irish traditional music changes to Van Halen and his timeless classic.

At the bar I stand alongside Jim, who continues to regale me with cocaine charged stories from the last 24 hours. Over the crowded room I see the Californian cunt and her valet girl sycophant.

"Oh fuck. Jimmy, you see those two over there?" I nod towards their seat.

"The blonde bird with her tits nearly out?"

"That's the one. I nearly got into her last night, she's never more than one or two drinks away from sucking cock."

"Well now, is that right?" Jim examines the pair.

"I reckon so, fancy a roll of the dice?"

"Get the drinks in."

I order two of the same vodka and energy drink piss they were drinking yesterday and as I pay find the baggy given to me by Bridgette with the pills. To keep it fair I put a bit in all four drinks and Jim and I go forth to plunder. "Mate, these two love the English bollocks, so play it up. Oh, and before I forget, call me Addy." We arrive at the table. "My ladies, good evening to you both, how does the night find you?"

"Oh my God!" The airhead is fits of giggles yet her friend remains in a perpetual stone-faced trance, like some wet towel chaperone on "prom night". "I was just talking about you earlier!"

"All good I should hope?!"

"Oh sure, wondering where my hot British guy is."

"May I introduce a very dear friend of mine, this is James of Worcestershire."

Jim takes the idiot girls' hand and places a deft kiss on its top-side. "Charmed, I'm sure."

"Oh wow, I'm Sally, this is Tammy, and yes I am from Cali but she ain't from Tampa!"

"Angels, by any other name, are just as sure as." Jim seems better than me at this game of bullshittery.

"I brought you ladies a drink, apologies for my tardiness."

"Well, better late than never." Interrupts Tammy and is in receipt of a glare from behind Sally's cunt of a smile.

"What a gentleman!" She says as I hold my own drink aloft and instigate the others. Sally had a type of face that duplicitous couldn't come close to describing.

"To the night, and all of her adventures."

"The night." Says the small group in unison.

Over by Jim's friends one of them has vomited onto the bar floor, and the staff seem understandably annoyed. Jim glances over and we exchange silent words. Looking at the group, Jim shakes his head and returns to our microcosm of conversation.

"So what brings two ladies like you to this place? Amsterdam is not the first place I'd expect to find two beautiful American girls." As James questions the girls we are both looking at Sally and she knows it. Tammy is literal ballast at this point.

"Oh well I'm studying French history and I get a semester away, so I've been in Toulouse and this is like my pre-Spring break getaway. Tammy flew in to hang out, didn't you?"

"Yeah," grunts Tammy, "We've been friends forever."

"Forever." I say with warmth. "Have you tried any of the local produce?"

"Oh, I don't smoke and neither does Sally."

"I have a little." Tammy's face turns at the revelation. "Just a little in the morning. I can't just hang out with you all the time and not get bored." Sally giggles and swigs back more of the drugged drink. James and I exchange knowing eyes and continue on with the show.

"Well I have to say that this is not one of the nicer bars in Amsterdam." Says James, setting up an exit shortly.

"Yes, it's not a patch on the hotel bar back in Brussels." I elaborate with falsity.

"Oh Brussels. What a week." James keeps pace.

"Brussels?" Asks Sally.

"Terribly boring place. Diplomatic errands must be carried out in person, however. But there are perks. Brussels Grand is just outstanding and the bar is a place you'd be happy to die in." I create a false smile in "recollection" and James does likewise.

"Our hotel bar is pretty nice." Tammy looks at Sally scornfully as she gives up another scrap of information.

"I usually prefer the minibar!" Winks James and Sally laughs while drinking.

Wishing to accelerate the pace I decide upon a shortcut.

"Well, what do you say we find somewhere a little more

comfortable, shall we?"

"Sounds good." Replies Sally over the silent roar of Tammy's protesting eyes. I raise my glass once more to instigate chaos in finishing our table of drinks.

"Cheers."

With a sense of our status being that of well to-do diplomatic envoy types, Sally had completely dropped her guard and led James and I with Tammy in tow towards their hotel room, a huge suite with three separate bedrooms despite only a brace of occupants.

"Well this is quite nice." Said James. Tammy sat down away from our close group and opened a book.

"Are you going to read us a bedtime story, Tamantha?" I ask and purposely massacre her idiotic name, to the thralls of laughter from James and Sally.

"I'm tired Sally."

"You're just jet-lagged. Hang on." Sally bounced onto the bed towards the hotel room telephone and called room service.

Hanging up the receiver, Sally rolls over the bed towards Tammy and whispers something in her ear. James and I share a moment of anticipation and remain firmly in character.

"Guys, excuse us for a minute while we get changed, we've been in these clothes all day. If room service gets here just put it over by the bed."

"Right you are, my lady." One last smattering of fake British regality before they close the door between us.

I could feel the sleepers working and doing battle with the varied drinks and touches of cocaine I had been taking throughout the night, and James confirmed the same from him.

"Those two must be feeling it."

"Yep. Should be a knockout any minute." We pondered this issue for a moment when the doorbell rang and a voice called:

"Room service."

From the bathroom Sally shouted "Can you get that?"

"Certainly!" I called loudly, and full of pomp.

The room attendant had a trolley with an ice bucket and champagne bottle along with four crystal flutes.

"Anything else sir?"

"No, that will be all." James said and slipped his a twenty-euro note to which he nodded and quickly disappeared. "Jackpot. Season the glasses."

"Nice." I replied and poured a decent amount of cocaine into the bottom of each glass while James worked on the bottle. "Think that will be enough?"

James grumbled as he examined the flutes and finds a pill in his pocket, then crushes it using the base of the champagne bottle and adds it to the concoction. "That should do it."

"Oh ladies, you're going to miss the party!" I mocked as James prepares the bottle to pop.

The bathroom door opens and that is the cue to do likewise with the bottle. Sally yelps as house-kept dogs and stupid girls often do at loud sounds. I provide the two flutes for the ladies first, and then James and I.

Sally and Tammy had indeed changed and were now wearing something close to underwear, Sally in ivory-coloured silk negligée, and Tammy somewhat less provocative in shorts and skin-tight top. Although Sally's body was toned and firm, appearing straight out of the pages of some glossy wank-rag, Tammy had more than the edge on breasts and together both looked more than delectable.

"Oh," moaned Sally, "You guys are still wearing your clothes?" James and I looked at one another and laughed, then began to remove our shoes and clothes. "But wait, couldn't you undress each other?"

"Ah, I'm not sure, that seems a bit funny to me." Said James in hesitance.

"Funny like what?" Asked Sally as she turned to Tammy and kissed her in the mouth deeply, while her hand delved into Tammy's brushed cotton shorts. Tammy relented, clearly dominated and Sally pushed herself onto her, hands roving around her soft body, probing through the gaps between skin and cloth.

"Yes, a little bit like that." I said as we all laughed. James and I clinked glasses and downed our respective drug/champagne cocktails and folded to demand, undressing each other by shirt, belt, and trousers.

Tonguing her mouth deeply, Sally pushed Tammy down onto the bed. Easily big enough for four, James and I take flanking positions over the girls and deliver our erections through jockey shorts and boxers respectively. Sally is first to engage and works us both, while Tammy remains below the action, cupping and stroking in lubricated protest. The best thing for a hesitant partner is gentle coaxing, much like one might try to lure an anxious squirrel with carefully placed nuts and oats, I go to my knees and put my head between Tammy's legs and pull her shorts to the side while I chew on her pussy like stale bubble gum. With another deft move I put a rock of cocaine, the nuts for this squirrel, on my tongue and use it to eat her from the inside out. The wave breaks quickly throughout her body and soon she was writhing in ecstasy alongside Sally, both girls now riding the high crest. Sally has been working James' cock into her mouth and removes it, hitching up the bed and redirecting it into her cunt.

I yank Tammy's knickers down to her knees, folds of puppy fat still gathered at the joints and tiny purple doves fluttered on the brushed cotton crotch. Little resistance could be registered at this point what with the cocaine riding through her from spinal foundation to rooftop idiosphere and sleepers providing oiled-ink for clear water.

Craning my middle two fingers into a hook shape I find Tammy's pleasure centres quickly and work there at pace. Like a beaten dog her cautious enjoyment could turn any second to gnashing snarls of refute so heady involvement was of great importance.

Doubled on all fours above Tammy squatted Sally, cock

in mouth to the hilt until choking, married with slobbering expletives. James pulls her body over Tammys face and I tongue her pink anus, while her own urges push her pussy onto Tammy's face.

"Are you fucking her?"

"Wait."

I produce the drugs and pinch a pile into my palm and rub it onto Tammy's face during intense respiration. The hit is like a truck and the holiest of holy would have no resilience against the purest of the pure.

Another pinch for Sally, all inhibitions now disintegrated and we are captured in a four-way rutting. My hands find Tammy's throat and her moans could be construed a thousand ways but I take for the positive and push on towards the inevitable. Peaks of agony dissolved into the depths of rapture and suddenly Sally removed James from her and presented him to me, while she sat firmly down onto Tammy's face, smothering with her sculpted twat. I take James as per the ritual and find it no less pleasurable than eating out Tammy's onion hole. In fact, James takes the coke and drops a hefty load onto the head of his cock that enables a heightened level of gratification on both of our parts.

Despite her face Tammy had an amazing set of tits. To alleviate tensions Sally took one in her hand and ushered me to do the same. James took the remote and put some music on to soundtrack our session. Tammy's whining soon changed to moaning, and we were all on the right track. James pulls my mouth from his cock and returns the favour, along with a healthy mouthful of cocaine for just deserts. My cock, my foreskin is pulled back so much, solid, right over the top. It grows harder and stronger then it all starts to get really messy: legs, arms, cocks, tits, hair, lips, spit, drugs, all over the place as we fornicate rampantly: me in Sally, me in him, he in Tammy and Sally there too. Her fist working hard into Tammy's fat cunt and so much blood rushing around our brains through our eyes and powering lungs and backbones to fuck and pummel and the drugs combine in the form of a trip while those same sets of bodies merged together in fleshy exhibition while a union of rock salt dried from gallons of sweat soaked into the mattress slowly fills up the room and begins drowning us. Against the wall grimy handprints tell the story so clearly. But it seems impossible to understand until the coke really starts to take intense effect and I can feel my heart beating so fucking quickly, overclocking, at least 180bpm. My head is moving from left-to-right and my hands are slapping first Sally but mainly Tammy on the arse and face and she's loving it too I can see a long thick string of spit and come from James' cock then Sally takes me out of her cunt and puts her mouth, still sopping wet over mine and sloppily fucks her head against my cock while I introduce three fingers to her arsehole which is soaking with pussy juice and sweat, they go up easily, so four fingers and she's writhing in ecstasy against my hand and I think she's about ready, so I take my dick out of her head, and ease my hand from her arse, then put my cock in her arse, and my fingers on her face. James bangs hard home the message on Tammy who whimpers soft and fucking hell, when it comes I can't look to her so I don't and just as I'm holding back from the tidal wave I slap her in the face again with my hands and stick a couple of fingers in her mouth, maybe round her neck, she's loving it and I can feel it coming so I know it's close and I try but fail to slow down, end up going faster and faster, racing James to the finishing line.

Sweat and bedsprings dancing in tandem, Sally directs my cock into her cunt and gives James to Tammy. Our position such that my hands once more find Tammy's throat and are joined by Sally's who pushes them firmly down as she comes. Tammy resists but Sally's orgasm is priority, to be interrupted by no one, certainly since it is joined by the rest of us. As we erupt in a crescendo of strings and organs, bellowing out the last notes in our anthems of depravity and nymphomania we fall like those Amazonian giants, streaked with sweat and spit, come and mottled hair. Our bodies each engraved with clawing nails and lines telling a story of sadomasochism. Sally in fits of laughter, her face deeply nestled into downy pillow. James and myself doing likewise: exchanging eyes and smiles and finding smokes that are lit in haste and savoured in reverence.

James spoke first "Piss."

Sally's face remained firmly down in pillow, and her arching neck revealed streaked eye-shadow and lipstick.

Stretching toward her I passed the cigarette to her and lit another.

It was half a smoke later until we realized Tammy was dead. James made the find, returning from the toilet scratching crotch and shaking last remnants of come and urine onto the executive suite carpet and walls in miniscule droplets. Her unresponsiveness in death being almost indistinguishable from that of life, Tammy was only acknowledged as such when James rolled her stiff body revealing a face locked into the expression of a startled pig faced with the slaughterhouse killing-floor, neck fat grouped like hefting potatoes in a misshapen sack.

A surge of panic rushes through the three of us but James and I know the dictated next step, and immediately turn to Sally, ready to grab her by the throat and I to pounce onto her body and wrestle her into submissive, quiet death. The intensity of his grapple around her neck would instigate choking with purges of saliva and soon blood, her angry protest turned to hopeless beseeching. Lines would been crossed that meant no return and with that thought rose my cock that found a way inside to purchase further domination, and just as we both turned to her to enter the death game she bursts into laughter as so do myself and James. Sally pounces on me, wrapping her legs around me and sliding my erection into her soaking hole, grabbing James too by the hand and laying on the lifeless body of Tammy while we barrage her with intense lashings of cock and ecstatic coupling. Her yelps turn to shrill tongues, mouthed and drooled over the flapping breasts beneath her. Sally removes me and takes James, then barks at me:

"Fuck her Addy!"

Seemingly we are in for more than a pound and so I start fucking the lifeless body of her friend, we three plus one creating a nightmarish vision for the room attendant to come, Tammy giving as good in death as she did in life. Rallying up the pace once more with nuzzlings of cocaine and champagne poured from bottle into our adjoined mouths and tongues we begin a collective orgasm, never before achieved by man, woman or beast; something beyond perfect balance, the brutality of *want*, the clarity of *get*.

Sweat drips like hot rain from the three of us: our bodies unrecognizable save for colourings of hair in swirled mass. Sally and her tattoos of some spiritual nonsense gargles like a newborn and James and I barely have breath to speak let alone move.

It is now that Tammy coughs, startled awake and back to life after who could say how long. Sally, James and I burst into hysterics and Tammy weeps uncontrollably.

Our double all but over, James and I leave the suite and into the corridor where all seemed normal, yet one look in either of our faces would give the entire game away. Both sets of eyes sunken to galleon depths, skin dark with grime, psychosis rampant. James turns to me and we kiss deeply, his hard face rubbing coarse hair across my chin and cheeks. My youth felt risen. A pair of passing guests murmurs the word "faggot" to one another and then they are gone.

"That was fucking close." Says James.

All that had altered was our state of intoxication, which we worked on a remedy to immediately, crushing the remainder of the blue pills in our respective hands and making a brutal cocaine compound to accelerate delirium with likely insanity. The medicine works and we walk in opposite directions, never to meet again.

T HE ITCH THAT BITES

Someone in this world is looking for you.
Out there, just beyond sight.
You have never met,
And inside, hope you never will,
Since the near-memory of their loss
Would remove all control.

W ho lives that is not truly alone? Granite walls of toothy smiles are built solely to confuse and massage the soul alongside its reflection. Those temporary life partners we call Him and Her and mine and yours and everything between give us our relief, provides us our comfort. Safety in arms goes both ways. There is no truth like the unanswered question. There is no cry more primal, more deafening that that which reverberates around the mind of the shadow walker: that entity that inhabits the spirit of man given to strength in weakness.

Pockets light and one shoe missing, the freezing winter cuts a hole and flows ice through my sock into my feet, numbing flesh and sinking through veins while marching tirelessly toward hypothermia. These times of recent have aged further than nature, and despite the pure air and crystal waters I feel I am descended into another circle of torture worthy of lyrical investigation. The drugs are near finished, and the whereabouts of my errant shoe a mystery.

A chill wind scurries dead leaves over the concourse of the train station. A nameless train passes somewhere east of Amsterdam, hushed in a blue winter sunset. Its cargo carried into the wild lands of central Europe, to support those lunatics that might live in such a place. Give me the city, give me the sleaze; it is a quaint yet pitiful fantasy: that of a frivolously muted existence. Life that barely murmurs let alone screams. Coughing lung I spit Black Death onto the oily rocked train track, sunken beneath the footway traversing the platform. A stunningly beautiful girl stands just too far away. We share an eye but it is fleeting at best and more likened to annoyance on her part, the leering subjugation of lies and pestilence carried by my torrid gaze. Her legs take her away and I spit once more.

Investing as I had in the Europe wide train ticket I felt a small sense of liberation, and upon arriving in a remote town plucked with captivating architecture and clear, I was confronted with beautiful people with eyes that did not glare. I felt almost local, despite having no command of language or custom. I walked wide-eyed and entered a forgotten market square, still bustling with people who hadn't heard of the apocalypse all around them. High, stone-walls that hark to times of conflict, although this place seems it may have been impervious to trauma.

The weight of the bag on my shoulders began to creak at my bones: crumbling, ancient ligatures. Entering a smaller alleyway no less awe inspiring than the last I came upon a hotel that was well out of my price range given these frugal times. I decided to say: "fuck it", and checked in without hesitance.

After enjoying a deserved rest on the impossibly twined and unstained sheets, I journeyed back out into that little pocket of paradise. A lack of money had hobbled my recent efforts but my indulgence in the quaint yet expensive hotel room had given me a perfect locale for new pussy. Just off the beaten track, over-looking the cobbled street and quilted with sweet smelling white sheets and embroidered adornments layered delicately and with purpose throughout the room. The falling sun heralds a creeping night-time filtered through the gentle mist that accompanies. I leave and find something to eat at a local bar, enjoying a beer at the same time.

I realized the majority of the patrons of the bar were young, beautiful girls and boys. Half way through my sandwich I looked again, a rising, giggling mess of young people, mainly girls, had begun congregating and drinking in my vicinity. I could still not calculate the happenings.

These were some insanely beautiful and young girls, and strewn about the entire place.

Building my courage with liquor, I eventually struck up conversation with one; a dusky brown haired girl so sweet to look at I thought I might become diabetic. A piercing around the side of her lip, that would ordinarily have me ranking up the whore points was, in this case, more complementary than anything I had seen thus far in my short life. Our conversation was rudimentary but refreshing, covering usual topics, me mispronouncing her name four, five times.

But nothing offensive as my previous records. After three or four more drinks we adjourned to an alternative venue, more of a *pub* pub.

"So what's the deal here? Everyone seems so young." I enquired with genuine interest and confusion.

"Oh, the legal drinking age here is 16, so when all we finish come from school and go to the bar." She replied, very "matter of fact".

"Sixteen?" I held my horses hard and firm. I may retire here. Immediately.

The night continued and we talked and laughed, easy, fun, delicious. I was not feeling myself, there was an impeccable beauty in front of my eyes, so amazing I would gladly kill the entire human populous should she will it. And yet I could not make a move, even a hand on her back seemed inappropriate. My entire self at odds, struggling in the oceans of my soul watching a team of sharks tear my conscious to pieces as it floundered, useless, and in territories virgin.

I won a game involving the hitting of a large metal spike into a piece of wood, and was rewarded with beer. The unpronounceable girl celebrated with me and we shared the resulting prize. Outside afterwards, we smoked a joint, although tolerated, still a contentious subject and one that was best not to ram down the throats of others, so we did this in seclusion.

We sat and watched the fog rising in the gleaming marbled streets, soft waters attaching to sculptures and architecture all around. I felt foreign, lost, and beautiful. We shared the moment and with delicate grace kissed, softly, tenderly, without reservation or judgment. A tear formed in my eye and I eschewed it away with the ice in my veins. A terrible feeling of dread began to creep around my psyche and the forgotten memories of a lifetime ago began to spill over into my reality. If I were to walk in the light my soul would burn like dust falling to the sun, and so hidden in the shadows I shall forever stay. She so pure, I could drink her and dissolve a few ounces of evil within, but it would be a temporary joy at best. Her purity would be tarnished, indelibly and in permanence and would start her on a journey to who knows where, but one certain to be taken alone and sure to end, at best, in pain and regret. With the blood beneath my nails barely dry I face memories of a time when joy turned.

Just a small boy, lost in the woods. Blanketed not with stars but thick, ochre clouds that shine black in the middle nighttime. The touch of the girl carried that old sensation of virtue and life through my nervous system, tingling like the feeling of a spider crawling up my legs and spine.

Family gone, rejected at youth and left wondering what was wrong with a person like me. A time when my heart would beat is all that came to mind and I could recall it like crystals, so clear and vivid. I had planned the anniversary gift of my parents for some weeks, and although it may have been foolish and unworthy of any real praise, it was still a matter that I had poured a great deal of thought into. And then the day the parental units announced they would be parting ways, "taking a break", and bullshit layered upon bullshit. I stood before them as a child once more, my father, pillar of all strength in my world, tearful and shattered; mother, still as stone, smoking a cigarette and emotionless in the face of a great wave of emotive destruction. Spending, as I would in the years that would follow: days here, weekends there, all manner of stresses and internal wrangling not fit for a boy of such tender age to go through. But go through it he did, like many others, and upon reaching adulthood was aware only of the learned truth that he was not good enough, and likely never would be.

Walking through the night-time is easy after practice, and plenty of it, but the induction into this way of thinking was harsh and destructive. Bridges burned with all but a pocket of friends; even those would fade after a short time. Personal relationships built on quicksand and habitual indulgences created only to destroy a heart that had, for one moment, left itself open and vulnerable, and thereafter been torn to pieces by the wild dogs of the mind.

Crippled with fear, I rose and my knees cracked as the cold wintery air fogged with my erratic breathing and stuttered movements. The orchestra tried to warm their harps and flutes but fell upon deaf ears.

"Well, I had better be going." I declared: teeth clenched secretly behind the impasse of false smile and lying eyes.

"You will leave?" She wondered aloud, asking herself of the same questions I had eternally plagued myself with.

"It's just, I have a big journey tomorrow," I lied, "and I wouldn't want to keep you up late."

"I don't mind, I have no classes tomorrow."

Still inside there was a beast growing, wrenching and gnawing at the chains locked around it, salivating pools of heavy liquid onto the ground and throbbing veins flowing with black blood.

Belying the beast, I was quicker to retort.

"You're beautiful, you know?" I complimented her honestly, and looked into her eyes without guise or guile, feeling the fear rise inside and my heart once more and collapsing in on itself. No matter. No matter.

We kissed once more and I left, stealing away into the night and winding my feet down twisting roads into the denser constructions of architecture.

Licking my lips I could taste the salve she used, vanilla notes and sweet to feel. Her face had been like a blinding light, her eyes like daggers into my soul, and the very thought of losing her was enough to kill me. So I did not; instead casting her aside like a broken sword laid on a field of blood and false-glory.

Ashes sparked up from the cobbles as I fired my cigarette into the pearled cobblestones that made up the street, projecting the destruction of worlds, obliterated into unfathomable particles of dust and charred bone. Not a soul left except my own, hollow and dry. The edges of the forest looming like a dark blanket and smothering the even darker night sky.

A beautiful young couple walks hand in hand and I grimace at their joy, turning my head away to look for some solace. The neon light of a head shop captures my attention and I remember some half-boiled theories on hallucinogens and spiritual cleansing. As a chill wind ran through me I found in my pockets some mushrooms from the city. They would sustain me in my journey and so I ate a few and went on to seek shelter within the woods.

The cracking of sticks and creaking of eaves as I venture forward break a hushing silence. Slippery rocks make up the under-footing but a cold autumn has left plenty of mulch around to help with tread. Feet firmly forward I march into the increasing cold and stifle tears, lest they freeze onto my face. Feelings of self-hatred, aged into perfection cajole and taunt me and I find myself facing the edges of a wood, which I enter without hesitation. Climbing over a fallen tree I reward myself with another mushroom and continue the journey. Urban sounds have dissipated and all that remains is the crushing silence of the woodland, seemingly empty at first, but as my ears adjust come across with all manner of sounds. Aching of branches, soft rustle of leaves, footsteps and burrowing of critters here and there, ultrasonic screams coming from bats nowhere near as lonely as I.

A rain must have fallen recently as the earth gives way slightly under foot, and grounded leaves are soft, moist, and palpable. Shapes and shadows linger longer than usual, and I start to blink more slowly. Relaxing, trying to breath in regularity, there is a soft glow from a half moon overhead. Looking into the thickening forest I see a movement behind tree. Recognisable, almost Deitific. I would have risen to my feet to investigate were the adrenal glands inside my body not pumping the hormone around my system, paralysing me from the head down. Placing my arm on a root of a fallen tree I feel the olive green mosses growing over my fingers, hand, forearm. Fear is forgotten in this respect. All things are as they should be.

Behind that tree, there and I see it again, that shape; that, human? Eyes peering back through the darkness cut into my core and yet I do not feel afraid, for there is something real here.

One final journey. One leap into a back hole, a lost pool of never-ending and impossibly cold and clean syrupy water. He looks back again, grinning through the pitch-black air, which by now, I can see much more clearly as a tangible element, not nearly invisible, lucid and captured moment to moment by my slowing breath. A coolness breaks softly through the trees announced by a shrill rustling of dried leaves, falling in time and rising beyond, like sparks from a fire, rising into the stratosphere, cooling, and snuffed out by time. As I merge with the roots beneath me I watch my skin turn from pale flesh to corrugated reptilian scales. A motion so natural I do not second guess or even flinch at the process, instead leaning into the curve and letting the water flow past me, filling my being and purging my intent. There is some peace here. Behind the tree, now the only thing visible in this blanket of stars and silence, I see him again, and recognize all too much. Myself, and me, staring back and forth, one content, the other in collusion. Now the only question was which one was who? Or was that even a point of reason? If both are the same then surely all is identical, everything is apparent. I am the tree, I am the earth, my limbs are the branches and my smile will kiss the leaves that fall in November.

Questions fall into ether and gather as dust, caught by the gravity of situations and satellites. The machine grinds forth, oiled and heavy, yet lighter than moon rays dancing on some distant shore. Time passes completely and circles back around to the present, at which point I rise, shaking off the moss and dirt as quickened footsteps take control and push me further into the swaying mass.

Finishing the mushrooms, I teeter over the edge of a fallen tree trunk; caught like nighttime between the split torso of an ancient oak. The sensation of raindrops falling through my skin permeates and pervades through every vessel of enmity colliding with the next. A colour unseen glimmers achingly through the crowd of trees and acts like some ladder to Everland. Hours I had been walking, or maybe seconds. Perhaps a lifetime. The hush returns as all the creaking branches and rustled leaves and crunching twigs give way to soft green, blue in this light, silver and sheer, silk on water. A clearing opens in the middle of nowhere, a vast space almost foreign to my eyes as I emerge from beneath the canopy and see that half moon, covered quarters by clouds and mists. The field itself, shrouded in a thick blanket of fog and lain thick with grass and little white tipped flowers poking through, straining for the moon light. Acoustics shift inside my ear and I feel as though I am passing through an echo chamber, with walls in constant shift and deformation, cradled somewhere between the here and the now. The insides of my throat flake and I swallow to try and satiate the dry heave, but there is no use. In the middle of the gathering fog I hear the sound of water flowing, some underground stream rising up momentarily. I drive forward, into the fog, feeling the clammy air condense on my face and hearing the sloshing sound of water get closer and closer. Squinting to focus, I see shadows, purple and blue, flashing by my field of vision.

I know I must be hallucinating, and push further in. The shadows gain more traction, greater exposure and the sound of the stream grows into a roar of guttural utterances, caught inside the fog and captive around me now. The shadows growing more intense, seeming to go in circles when all of a sudden a shape is truly defined: a hoof, a horn; the sounds too, concentrated into crystals that now seemed less like water and more in line with rocks falling through a long tunnel to the centre of the earth, bouncing and reflecting around incalculable angles and fractions, broken into pieces by mirrors and splintered heat. Now at the source of the sound, there was no river, no stream, not even a pothole beneath which one might hide; but the shadows remained, intensifying, and the chorus dragged through my very soul until I painfully realise that these visions are not hallucinations, and these sounds are not water. They are wild boar, a large group at that. I have wandered into their domain and now surrounded, suddenly thrown into a deadly primeval scenario.

My haunches are brushed then collided into by one of the boar, jerking back to realities easily slipped I pick up my feet and charge towards the mass of shadows, which now move so fast I have trouble locating them from second to second. Again I am hit, this time more severely, and the warm trickle of blood greets my lower calf.

Stumbling through the forest, dashed into the blackness of the trees, unsure as to whether I am pursued or not, I stumble and fumble through the misty woodland, slipping and twisting my ankle on a rock. My body seems to fall after I do and the weight is something unbearable. A surging spike of pain rushes up my leg and into my hip, making movement unlikely but somehow still, I manage to continue and hoist myself up, escaping through the thicket and away from the sounds of grunting and snarling beasts until the safety of the forest once more consumes and I find refuge by a hollow log. Breathing heavily and spitting onto the floor, I see beetles and centipedes, squirming and swirling about the log, covering my hand and reaching up my arms, and once more I run, tearing my coat on a hardened tree branch spiked through the sleeve.

With great galloping strides and tears frozen hard into the night sky I do not stop to look back. I feel the crawling through my body, my skin peeling and paring itself and then floating like burned paper into the emptiness behind my feet. A voice calls out somewhere, angry, full of vengeance. My feet quicken once more and the voice becomes clearer, screaming expletives and curses to my soul. In the woods a set of lights flashes, headlamps, then another, and another, until all around flashed the lights of parked cars and revving engines. The voice becomes louder, less intelligible, and the trees become people that fold out of the branches and trunks like some childish construction made out of paper.

They gather behind me but for one who stands in front with an outstretched arm at head height.

I wake in the bathroom, clinically assembled. A buzzing light bulb flickers overhead. I am home, home a long time ago. Clare has been here. Her smell, Her soft clothing, lingering and potent. The pregnancy test, positive, still on the sinks edge, all now laded with silvery dust after a thousand years alone. And further, within the toilet, the blood, that first indolence into pure water. The toilet bowl itself begins to pulsate and take on a female characteristic, growing into a massive sex organ which swallows me whole, threatening to smother me and drown my senses within. Through and inside I writhe and crawl, further up over the giant Uterine walls and into the passages of Fimbria until just as the opening seems sure to crush my skull I fall out and onto a solid floor of sharpened carpet. A typical room, dressed with uniform cinema seating and modest projector screen relaying pornography. Practically empty save for a pair of jerkers scattered over the musty theatre. Eyes peered at me as I enter and I feel no fear, just more conquest on this suicide path.

The familiar smell of stale tobacco and ejaculant twisted around my sinus and I gave a crooked old woman some money to enter. She was tiny and staffed a miniature ticket-booth, and when I pay she spits on my hand for re-entry. Even at her I leer somewhat through the stoic tide of tears behind the levees of shame and deceit, expressing and collapsing behind a smile and a wink.

Crawling now, I become aware of the brushings of roof above, it is velvet: red casting black in this dimly lit room. The hissing of celluloid etched with erotica and debasements of the darkest nature. A terrible stench of bleach and I crawl on suddenly under the legs of men in the come dried chairs, fornicating overhead and drizzling sperm from above. The ground before me turns to flesh and I fall through, dropped into some other place and landing in a river of come. Turbulent waves wash me ashore and overhead I see winged beasts flying high, fornicating with screaming, bloodied people and then dropping them from the sky. Rocks shatter around me as one of the great beasts lands, straddled about my head, He is a mountain, who collapses onto my body and grabs at my throat with deathly jaws and He is a man of fire with smoking eyes.

I am lifted above this fallen world, flames rushing across the land, now ashes and molten rock. The sharpened claw draws up my spine, separating it piece by piece until I am turned back into clay, opened and taken, with infinite stamina, relentless peaks with monstrous anatomy. The beast roars until the skin peels from my face. About his own grew sexual organs in permanent arousal and orgasm, brutal, murderous climax.

Red velvet curtains line the walls of a great hall, and I see myself on "date", exuding smart, sexy commentary that loosens clothing with just a word. One eye glance in a particular direction at a particular angle from the girls field of vision and she has already decided to fuck me. I play piano up the steps of her spine and notice the people in the room, high society types, suit-and-tie for-pleasure kind of people, leering and looking here in our direction when suddenly the beast returns, rupturing the plateau of my mind and my nails grow *through* her body, tearing her in half as he has me fuck the spasmodic half-way-cadaver. But even ejaculation could not quell the urge, and another date, much shorter now as she is broken down like dried kindling and entered in one motion, reaching ferocious orgasm and she succumbing in life to twisted arm and throat and yet no satisfaction. Then another, who in penetration I feel *so completely* that my cock swells and she reaches sexual climax, then swelling more, and more, until the girl is screaming, tearing from within. But it doesn't stop, my cock keeps growing, until bruises appear beneath her skin, blooming like black flowers and her eyes mix with the blood that flows through ducts and the pores till she flourishes tumescent, and cracks from within, and still my cock grows, birthing itself through the mouth of the hostess, leaving her bloodied and jaw broken from the inside out, now doused on the floor, split flush open like boiled grapes. Her body in pieces, only my cock remaining, now inhuman in size. It takes the shape of man, the shape of me. It is the keeper of my darkness, the ruler of ideals. It has separated from me forever more, and rises to feet now protruding through fleshy webs that break to reveal pink skin so pure and innocent, so white and full of terror to be yet unleashed. From the bulging chest a head forms bent in eternal prayer, snapping loose from the rib cage and rising, hairless and slick, with tiny eyes that open like springtime flowers. The heart exposed, sinew and gristle in structure and shaded grey. Puking, shaking, and stumbling:

I gaze upon this super-man, and he gazes back at me. This creation of cock and fuck, and hence I weep at its tragic perfection with tears that flow silent for the rest of my days.

A VAMPIRE FOR YOUR LOVE

Do not consider what you are
Running from
Only that you
Must run faster than it.

A bird sings and I am reminded it has been weeks since I last saw one; skies have been blackened with soot and shattered ideas. The forest eaves and tree limbs held aloft by shafts of rising light, caught between between forms cut through the mist and morning sun. From the mossy earth below came creeping damp, a soft water marching steadily northward, leaving toes shriveled and freezing. Before me lies a circular glade, mathematical in its glory and painted green with wild accouchements springing here and there yet wild, and grown completely natural.

Once upon a time I used to care so much. It was important to me that I got where I wanted to go. It taxed me when I felt that another element of my being was not keeping up with me. When I could no longer see the use in that particular facet I would cast it aside like broken armour, ready for the next challenge while seeking sustenance and respite. Years march by forever increasing in their ferocity, and your ardor itself is lost to their battle cries and heavy, iron swords.

Now is the end of these comforts, the knowledge of death, of perseverance in absolute. The great beyond, misty mountain, wonderland, the other place: always so near, but inevitably caught twixt the lashes of the eye.

My soul hung heavy around my oversized green parka. The faux-bone buttons all fell off and now there was an impotent flap mocking my every step.

With all my physical possessions lost to the forest, I tread carefully, discerning direction by will alone and carried by a tide of progression. Something was in this pensive air, some hidden component that was now so close to realisation I could smell it like simmering milk.

The first miles are long, twisting through thick overgrowth, pressing forward with caution and careful scrutiny of my footing, lest my sole receive a lancing. At lunchtime I smoke salvia beneath a weeping willow that draws open like the theatre. Looking out into the vastness before me I am simultaneously carried into tights and leotard, dressed fancily as I portray a character in a Shakespearean play. I am so young, and the shadow self laughs in proud happiness that there was once a benevolent and honest shade of it. As an actor I had little merit: too young, too shy, too honest; and yet it was part of my desire at this early age. For six weeks we toured the play, I, playing a young Prince of the Roman Empire, standing in a pretense of strength, yet leaf-like with my quivering, blunted foil.

Among the company was an assortment of those who were there either by love or by duty. The head, a wise lady with truth in her heart and words, conducted the performances with a skill and dexterity built over decades.

Clare, the beautiful! Clare the enchantress! Clare of my dream, Clare, of my vision!!

She played the faerie and cast spells over all who washed up on that tempestuous shore, both me and myself included. Her footsteps lighter than air and voice like a hummingbird. For the first fortnight of rehearsals we did not trade a word, but when our eyes would meet more than often, electricity charged the air between us. Finally, after weeks of practicing lines, hers being caught inside of a soliloquy, and therefore responded to directly by none, we walked literally into each other on stage. The director cursing us to rise to our feet but we took our time, I helping her to stand and allowing her grace to recompose. We smiled at each other, her eyes so warm, and my face so pure and honest. A few days later, my increasingly disinterested parents forgot to pick me up after practice, and Clare's mother gave me a ride home. We talked happily sitting next to one another in the back seat, and our legs occasionally brushing, titillating the both of us. We would speak on the phone for hours at night, listening to the sound of each other breathing in and out, humming tones and melodies down the receiver into a just as receptive ear. There was the life, there was the peace. But at the time I had not yet experienced war.

Two days before show-time and I arrived at practice early. I began my stretches and vocal gymnastics and entered into the excitement with full indulgence. It was apparent already, but Clare had not shown. I waited patiently, smiling all the while as I knew I would see her face in a moment, any second, any minute. Rehearsals ended and she still had not arrived. I asked the director, and she explained it straight, Clare had moved away, and that she was very disappointed with her.

Dancing briefly with belief, I refused to recognise it; Clare would *not* just leave.

As I arrived at her house I could see the truth was indeed just that. The house was empty, had it ever even been full? Here my mind begins to turn, slowly at first, trying to reconcile truth with life, love with reality. Here the first blushing of the moon cut through as the day sky fell to mourning.

Continuing through the performance, some sort of foolish hope to her presence, which turns into an endless epitaph to be carved into my eyes. I am forlorn, miserable, yet feel strangely alive.

One of my "brothers" in the play was called Max, a wiry

looking man of vermin descent. His presence was that of duty, given for his other activity as an "independent film-maker". I was shattered by Clare, but he told me that he was producing a short that would be entered into a number of festivals and that the opportunity was there for me as the lead actor. I accepted the role with little question, and upon advising my parent received an obligatory and unconcerned "Mhmm."

The first day of production of the two-day shoot, was at his parents house by the sea. A rocky, unforgiving sea, no splendorous beaches or palm trees on this vista save for dark, sharpened rocks and endless tidal surge. The director lived with his parents, him in his mid-late thirties and living in the attic with title more than a slanted window as a doorway to the outside world. My role, that of a rogue government agent at a computer, was not the most complex ever created, but for my verging-on-teenage mind it was more than enough to work with. The street was a buzz with voices playing, children, younger than I, maybe between seven and ten years each, three or four of them.

We seemed to get a lot of work done, lots of camera set ups and close ups of action; I was feeling great confidence and belief in the project. That night I told one of my parents about the events of the day but there was something happening on the television that demanded more attention.

It mattered little, I felt a growing sense of foreboding glory, surely there was a great, golden ceremony for me somewhere in the world. Day two was a little different. The director seemed distracted, like more was happening than I could understand. More camera set ups and now "panicked reactions" were required of me so I could properly evoke the character required. I dutifully, and without question complied.

The hour arrived at lunch, and the director questioned: "Do you want a sandwich?"
To which I replied:
"Yes please, I'm starving!"
"Ham and cheese good?"

"Ham and cheese, yes please!!" I exclaimed back.

The director laughed as he walked downstairs and I leaned back on the computer chair, facing the screen. Downstairs I heard the front door as the kids from the street shouted for the directors attention. He made them sandwiches too, seemed like a nice thing to do. As I sat and looked through the window from the chair I called downstairs:

"Got any good computer games on here?" But my words were lost on the way.

Sighing, I fiddled around with one or two windows until I came to an open folder, containing videos named as numbers.

Opening one at random the player began and showed a grainy hotel room looking space, green couch and off white walls. The camera panned slowly to the left and revealed a bed, with a slight, incredibly young and naked girl, legs spread open, face down on the mattress and the title dissolved onto the screen:

"8 yr old getting rammed." As two distinctly older men entered the frame.

My heart nearly stopped and I closed the window immediately.

Flushed with fear and a million thoughts trying to get parchment but one voice, singular and overpowering telling me to get out of there as soon as possible. The laughing and cajoling downstairs now shriek with reality and pestilence. Heavy footsteps began rising from below with a Pied-Piper-like following, getting closer and closer until appearing at the sunken staircase.

"Lunch time!" Announced the director.

I was left speechless, and simply smiled through the descending darkness. A plate was presented me and behind the director were the three kids, dressed in wind breaker puffer jackets and crystalised snot against their faces.

The first drops of ink fall into my glass and the water is perverted with clouds, never to return to clarity.

Pure tension is now riding through my body, a primal

fear, a desperate need for safe arms.

"Here you go." said the director, as he passed me a plate with cheese and ham sandwiches cut into lurid triangles.

Behind him and downstairs on the second floor I could hear the children play, and the director laughed as he looked from me and then to them and back again.

Here I looked at the sandwich, the perfectly sliced innards holding what, I couldn't imagine. My hands began to shake as I ate a small morsel from the crust, chewing with endless trepidation.

One of the children called up to the director in unintelligible child like words that sound like music. He continued to laugh and I felt the shadow-self rise.

"Just going to use the toilet." I lied.

"Alright," he replied through a sickening, straggly-haired mouth. I pass him on the stairs and as we do he helps me cross with his bony hands. I smell his breath, cheap cigarettes and black coffee, sweetened with syrup to trap wandering insects.

The director begins playing a song about dinosaurs and jeeps and the children yell with glee.

The throbbing of my heart almost too much, I can almost see it through the costume he had me wear, shorts and a skinny t-shirt. "Bedroom hacker". It seems so obvious now. I smile and pretend to laugh as he half lifts me past so I can go to the bathroom. The children in his parents bedroom now, jumping and dancing on the bed. I should scream to them to run, grab a hold of them myself and take them from here, or we should turn and kill him, but I know I can not. I know it is not possible. I am too weak, a crawling insect beneath a falling swatter, ready to be pressed into a dense compendium.

Walking down the corridor I see the smiling eyes on picture frames adorning the walls, and the music penetrates further though I walk away.

The bathroom is left and the ground floor is right. The director is behind me, half-dancing with the children, singing along with his own flat, hissing rendition.

I turn to the left, taking that path, and enter the bathroom with its tiles and murky flooring. Behind me I close the door, locking it softly and face the window. Switching on the taps to disguise my activities, I find he window is safety locked to open but a creak. I try and work out the mechanism but it is beyond me and I return through the door as the song reaches near crescendo.

"Girl I'm just a Jeepster for your lo-oo-ove."

Turning to the doorway I see the directors back, behind the bed and obstructed from my position. I walk silently, without breathing, and step backwards over the loose clothing on the floor and components of dismantled vacuum cleaners, somewhat inexplicably present now.

The children "whoop" to the music as I touch the stair rail, pressing backwards down to something better than this grisly ending. A journey that feels it may take forever is over swiftly and the music muffles in silence as I reach the front door and without hesitation step through and run and run and run up the street, past the post office, beyond the bus stop and across fields that roll into small hills and rocks that rise and are no match for my efforts. I run until my legs are jarred with a dull vibration of base origin.

Almost unable to comprehend my experience, I finally reach a road and a phone box. I have no other options at this time. Lifting the receiver I call the police.

"Emergency services, what is the emergency please?" comes back the voice.

"I've just been in this guys house, I'm thirteen, and I found some videos on his computer, kids, videos: sex videos. I need to report it."

"What is your name please?"

"My name?" I did not want to give my name, for the shame associated would be too great. "I didn't want to give my name, but the videos, he's got loads."

"I'm sorry sir, but if you want to lodge any sort of

complaint of this nature you have to give your name."

"But,"

"Would you like to give your name?"

"I..."

"Sir? We need to know your name."

I am left in silence, speechless, and the receiver is hung up, saving me with an endless tone that begins to echo through the swiftly emptying halls of my soul and I wonder to Clare, where she is, what she is doing, and know that from here on out I shall be alone forevermore.

M INOR FALL

Oh this pity and the shame
You must have hung around your name.
Existence vacant, putrid life
His love that breaks like skin on knife.

It was so cold out there. Only trees were my company for the days that passed and I lived on food from the ground and water droplets gathered about the place. The sun rose and dropped, then rose and dropped once more before it rose and began to slowly dip through an emerald sky. No slender branch, no tender bark; limbs grow knotted, anguished. Bark rotten and dry. Leaves and sprouts not green but black. No fruit but berries hang and drop with poison. The souls of the damned trapped within. A broken branch bleeds red and the stench of death hangs heavy in the thick air. Wiry grass had started to cut my feet from walking barefoot for three days solid. I had no destination, I had no starting point.

Descending a dry rock clearing I stumbled and slid, swearing as my body tumbled over an uprooted tree and launching me onto a pile of limestone gathered by the lower ridge of the trees root system. The pain in my arm resonates and I am reminded of all past sins. Sitting up on the rocks and trying to catch my breath, the flint in my lighter barely working but finally giving a spark to allow me to light a last cigarette. Exhaling and looking out into another dense thicket of trees and roots and bushes straight ahead, to my right I see a slim crevice in the large rock, eight or nine feet high and wide enough to fit. After I smoke I stand and investigate the opening in the rock face and see a cave beyond.

Inside darkness ruled. Black rocks shone green from the tiny glimmer of light and I walked further, stumbling through muddy puddles and darkened pools of water, freezing me to the bone. The only conscious sound was of my breathing, deep and fearful. When the moon rose, I didn't know it; as when the sun came, I was blind. For these days, I walked through the cave, which has no end that any man can reach. No words came from me in this time; I coughed, slept, ate, drank, breathed in and eventually out. Faces from the past and future howl and steal about.

Lying limp in a pool of water, surrounded by rocks and tiny reptiles exploring my body, I heard a deep groan from the cave. I sat up and hit my head on a rock, flinching for only a second then straining my eyes to barely see but feel the blood drip over my face, over my eyes, off my nose and into the water. On I went: hiking as far as I could until I could do nothing but sleep. I was blinded in this time. I didn't really matter, my mind was preoccupied with survival. All I thought of was getting to the other side, for surely there must have been one, of this cave. No-one was looking for me, which for some reason made me feel safer. I was either going to find a way out of this myself or not at all.

Leave me for the rats.

When you wake up in the morning, and your bedroom has thick curtains, especially velvet curtains that block out all the light, your eyes sting when you finally see the sun. When this light came, it was like someone throwing a piece of slate horizontally into my face and turning it to one side before yanking it out.

The light was once again in the sky. I walked in it for a while; humming a tune I heard once but didn't remember and threw stones as far as I could into a lake. My skin was yellow, my eyes were black. My hair matted with oil and dirt. I sat at the opening to the cave. A breeze hushed against this green grass all around me and I could see it moving, like dogs running with each other running after a ball. It changed colour, texture, every second and I watched it for some time, occasionally disturbed by a fly or bee looking for food.

Not deserving light, I vomit and stand crooked. Bones bruised from sleeping on rocks. The rock rolls back against the cave and I retreat once more into darkness. An echoing thunder rushed around the cave walls and filled my ears. There was light pouring through cracks in the door, and I could still see quite plainly. I sat down and acclimatized to the pitch, then looked at my toes. My second-to-little toe was mottled black from dirt and blood, stung slightly and illuminated by a shelf of sunlight creaking through the old door. I remembered when I was a young boy; having one of those plasters made of fabric stuck to my shin and taking it off always hurt as it would pull hairs out and stretch the wound. Always better to just rip it off. I picked up a rounded, fist sized rock, and smashed off the offending nail. Flowers opened and soaked in the sun but it was going to be a long walk back.

I somehow find myself gone from the forest, my bag returned, feet muddied and standing at a train platform in some town outside of Amsterdam. The sun is quiet today and leaves blow down the tracks west towards the sea.

Gaining some sort of composure I take in my surroundings. There are few people, and those who are shudder in the cold. I do not feel it.

There is an attractive girl, early twenties, with blonde hair and tight jeans. Her levels of disinterest are alluring. I try to exchange eye glances but I can feel my beard, overgrown, whiskers wet by my tongue and cut by teeth. My hands, dirty, and fingernails hard with mud.

Her passing look towards me was little more and she seems to laugh and walk away to the other side of the platform. I spit onto the tracks.

As she leaves, I notice an older, attractive and solitary woman, looking at me. Our eye meeting is more prolonged, and polluted not by my shroud of dishonesty but instead a glimmer of true being. The very thought of this almost makes me laugh, and I crinkle smile towards her and we begin to gravitate towards one another.

Smiling now as we enter dialogues:

"You are very tired!" She declares, accurately.

"You're right! I'm exhausted! These legs don't carry themselves!"

"Where have you been?"

"The city. The country. Gets to the point where you don't know when to stop, to the very edge. I just was there for too long, I'm tired."

"Ja, this is true."

During my descent into drug abuse I became convinced that drugs were holding me back from a perfect erection. Before I started doing "drugs", my "drugs" was sex; and I was fucking good at it. I could hold an orgasm on a girl like a metaphysical blanket, lightly suspended in air by an interior dimension, connected to the very core of her sex. But unfortunately, cocaine isn't the greatest conduit of the hard-on. Oh, it will give the facade of pure masculine virulence and muscularity, but in a harsh light and plenty of powder, all you're left with is a cold, paralytic mass. Once I was two days sober of cocaine, and drunk on rum. I took an ex-girlfriend to bed that I'd wined and dined all night, and there was still a certain-demanding sexual charge to us, but in comparison to the night before the night before, that was a different matter on which I shall elaborate upon shortly. But this night was an ex-girlfriend who, I surely did care deeply about, and was actually very happy to see her move on with her life, her having a new boyfriend. But a message

I received from her after I couldn't make a Sunday lunch appointment of "tomorrow you're mine" left me confused, and wondering if the boundaries of engagement had changed. Our initial reunion being surrounded by her more than affable new boyfriend, and me being so excited to be in a new revolutionary sphere as to want to spread wings, to be around, to get out-there, not go over old ground. As we got into bed the memories of coked up nights, both of us fucked off our tits, her choking and slobbering on my cock while I pulled on her hair into matted black slabs of sweat and tears and come and all-that-good-shit came flooding back. They were great memories that were all-consuming at the time, but now mere echoes off of the walls of my mind. But tonight here I am and, yes, I'm trying to put my cock in her mouth but it's falling away; like loose timber from the mill, a fire in the control booth, panic on the store-floor. Closing day, and so: yes, we stopped.

Declaring, as she did, that I *obviously wasn't into it*, I could not argue. I did not want to become a cog between someone's life just for moving to this new city, I simply wanted a second chance of existence, a chance to be someone else, to be new again, instead of the tarnished person I already was. But I could see it wasn't going to be that easy, the darkness within concentrated like too much orange squash in water.

Clare left without incident, and pleasantly at that, and it made me happy to see her go without animosity, a warm throng of friendship blossoming away from the dark sexual blade of my soul. Commenting before she left:

"You can't get it up without coke!" I immediately felt defensive tendencies rise and rebutted and corrected her to the contrary:

"No, I can-not get it up *because* of coke!"

I can only hope that that was completely understood. But it did make me think, to the girl previous, of whom I alluded earlier. I had been drinking margaritas and lager all day; smoking weed and taking coke from around 2pm up until the death. And at The Death I met a very beautiful girl and we plotted in hushed tones to fuck in my abode. As we travelled there I explained that as soon as she entered my door she must remove all of her clothes. And upon entering she did, and I mine. The revelatory pleasure that comes only from engaging new-skin, to dilute ones-own wickedness, to achieve singularity for that briefest of moments, is the engine beneath all-things.

I began to penetrate her with exotic fruits and eat them from her body, savoring the exacting drops of ecstasy hanging from her fleshy horizons. And upon her face I did smother the fruits, and her body and innards were tainted and touched with its blossoming message, and onwards onto me and we created a tumescent display of sexuality that bled onto every surface, and here I wonder what was it that went wrong the night after tomorrow night? Perhaps people just move on; maybe walking backwards is exactly that, the past is mean to be remembered, not recreated or rehashed. Or maybe I can only get it up if I'm eating peaches out of a girls cunt.

I find myself at her house. The older, attractive woman informs me she is a drama teacher at a local school. Small dreams that make big realities. I feel respect and peace when I am with her. Our relationship here seems one of mutual friendship, nothing more, and I am somewhat relieved by this; the lack of pressure to perform, whether projected and external or born from some interior, infernal wrangling.

My bones ache and I sit on a chair for the first time in what seems like forever. She takes her clothes off in the room next to me, in full view, and steps into the shower. Her soft lullabies caress the air and dance towards my ear, receptive and on fire. I stay seated, relax, and drift to sleep.

We make love for two weeks, never stepping past any point of concern, never wanting, never expecting. While she would teach, I would learn. Purely passion, simple sexuality. The way it should be. Working for orgasm. Two animals rutting into tomorrow falling, only, into one another's arms.

It was a dream. It lasted in that moment forever; passing

like an iceberg drifting against the current. My time in this place was short, but so penetrative that I felt the dark shadow-self raped and left dying. The muted murmuring spilling overboard. I would leave this place soon and return to the place I had come.

THE TOAST POPPED

Even at the end of time, when each passing moment
Is presented you like crystal memories,
You will cling on to the moments of degradation
That have turned you into this monster.

Stoned. As the element heats I watch a kettle try to boil for a few minutes. Can't remember why but I find myself in the kitchen wearing only underwear and cleaning. I'm washing up and wiping down the surfaces. I'm thinking, 'this washing up isn't that bad.' Collecting from the coffee table, three-quarters of a long-since reheated pizza left burned on a plate, plates used as ashtrays, some girls panties, a Dominos pizza box, a Chinese paramilitary officer of the world. The song when Jack Nicholson stole the boat in One Flew..., can hear the football on TV in the living room, European match, crowd chanting in bang, bang, bang. I there can hear it and it goes in my head like amazing something green pulsating and a mega handclap by a thousand people.

Wow, wow-wow.

So I wash up and down the surfaces, go back into the living room and empty raining ash out of the window onto the street below. I have a big toke of my joint, then take the remaining three glasses back into the kitchen to be put into an empty sink, get the pizza box and take to kitchen then collect all four bags of rubbish on the floor. I go out of flat, leave inside door open so I can get back in, go downstairs, go out and swing door the outside door shut. What a fuckwit. Ended up kicking a flyer out through the door advertising some trance night at some club.

Sighing, I look back at the building and walk around the side in just a pair of boxer shorts and a T-shirt in the rain. The rubbish goes in the bin, I stand for a while allowing the rain soak me. My building broods down on me and my shadow stands growing taller in the dazzling light of a pair of headlamps from a passing car. It pulls up in the car park and from the driver seat jumps a man, in his late twenties carrying a bottle of red and one of white wine. I start for the door once he gets halfway up the stairs then the great door swings open, opening and allowing me to get in and give the guy an appreciative smile as the briefest of explanations.

My front door's still wide open, football still playing the TV and me soaking wet.

Removing my t-shirt I sit for a while, flanked by the large windows endlessly dotted with rain and roaching another spliff when I hear a noise, must be on TV. I flicked the channel at half time and there's news report now about a little girl killed miles away from here. So I watch on, start to add a major amount of weed, then hear the noise again.

Mute on the telly, ear to the air.

There it is again, coming from downstairs. That's where an Asian guy lives. Moans. So I listen on and on and on. So I listen. All of a sudden lying down against the floor and touching myself. Ear to the floor, listening. Reflexes put my hand on my crotch, can still hear them, be calm, noises go down, can hear the girl moaning to fuck. Shit, I've seen the guy before, he's a right short arse, how is he giving her so much pleasure? I just listen and she's into it. Moaning to fuck, man.

The toast popped up in the brushed steel appliance on the worktop and startled me from across the room. A train passed somewhere that jolted me around when its brakes screeched. I was staggering around my sofa, couldn't keep my eyes open and by now I'd put some pornography on the TV. It was German today, as it was most. Typical scenario: a woman or three, get fucked by around ten men and come shoots onto their faces. My dick was feeling good; seconds away from breaking point: vinegar strokes, and I knew it wouldn't be that long before I couldn't hold back anymore. I had been wanking all day, give or take a couple of hours off for lunch of ham and cheese sandwiches. I woke up at about two in the afternoon, went out and bought a new porn film, a contact magazine, pack of latex gloves and some KY jelly just in case. The sun was long gone as the German woman took another helping of sperm in the mouth. It left a bitter taste in my own and I decided I needed something else.

Human contact, maybe just a blow-job. Perhaps sex. I turn off the video, sick of seeing the orgiastic display already. A gangster movie from some years back plays on the television station to the music *My Life, My Love*. Once I'd finished the joint, I wiped my dick momentarily dry before the next drops of come would fall and got dressed, then made my way out of the flat.

The weather was deceptively mild at that time of night, cars did the usual hurry past to nowhere, and I did the usual get a cigarette out. When I put the Marlboro in my mouth, could smell the tobacco inside the paper. It felt dry against my sticky lips, and I could tell it might pull a piece of skin off. I was searching my pockets for the clipper, not in my jeans, not in my coat, not there. I had no lighter, so put the cig behind my ear and felt a bit like a strong armed worker. This made me laugh, but then a gust of wind brought attention to the fact that I had cut my lip with the cigarette. I fumbled through my pockets and pulled out a handful of scraps of paper. About to throw them to the floor I notice a number written on one. Rachel Robinson God bless you. I make sure I look presentable, then call the number she gave me. It rings out for a few chimes until a monotonous voice chirps:

"Taxi." It takes seconds for me to realise she has done me.

"Taxi?" I ask, somewhat dumbfounded.

"Where you at, love?"

"Um, is this a new taxi service?

"What?

"This taxi, is it new?"

The line goes silent for a few seconds.

"Taxi."

"Never mind." I go and stand at the bus stop into town. Kind of genius by Rachel Robinson, if that was her real name. Without waiting too long at the bus top, one pulls up and I get on. It's late, the sky has been raining for almost five years now and when I sit down, I write "fuck off" sneakily on the back of the seat in front with a red permanent marker. I don't want to go back home for a while, I need to fuck something, badly. All there seems to be at home, all there is, is a bed, a television. Since returning from Amsterdam I have made a habit of trawling the streets late at night for no apparent reason, looking for drama and finding emptiness.

Newspapers and bus tickets are plastered to the floor with dirty water. There are four other people on this late bus, a decent looking girl, student type with style and a big pair of tits sitting next to some arsehole lesbian with the usual short hair dyed purple and various piercings that make her a collective individual. A black guy sitting close to me with the most extraordinary lazy eye I have ever seen and a young girl talking to the driver. The decent looking girl keeps glancing from him to me and smirking in the hope of a reaction. I raise an eyebrow then toss an angled, action-hero smile in her direction, locking eye contact for a second, then pick up a newspaper. Usual bullshit stories, editors filling pages with pointless reporting of a local nature.

I get bored of the paper quickly, after briefly glancing at an article about what bacteria is on peoples' office desks.

Fuck off you cunts. At the front of the bus stands the young girl, a scally aged about fourteen, maybe fifteen. She's wearing Kappa tracksuit (of course) pants, with a cheap puffa jacket on top, and has that dirty-skin look everyone's going on about. Her hair is lacquered to her flaking scalp and is so greasy I can't even tell what colour it is. Her name is probably Tammy, or Mandy or something equally lower-class. She's talking and laughing with the driver, a man in his forties, glasses, stains: the usual, nothing special; but she is flirting. I don't really understand it; she could have any man in the world as long as they drove a Nova and had short-back-and-sides with one earring. A small radio privately plays music from a radio station that stopped buying records when Abba first split.

As my stop approaches, the decent girl and the dyke get up and stand by the front. I flip-flop through my mind and decide I want to observe them further. The girls leave, the compartment fills with icy air and we carry on. I can't hear what they're talking about but she keeps on laughing at him in a filthy way. She turns and looks through the windscreen and I can see the back of a white shirt, wrinkled from her oversized but sort-of attractive bottom and hanging out of the back of the jacket. It looks like a school shirt. She could be from the all-girls school but to be honest I think that's more of a posh place, not where you'd expect undesirables like her to be. She's probably from one of the more inner-city schools, a scummy, run-down institution. Another stop then lazy-eye gets off, leaving me alone with the two, entering territories unfamiliar to me. As we hurtle through the near empty streets, I think about everyone around me, everyone in my immediate conscious crying uncontrollably. There was something that united them all in the grieving: was it a death? Perhaps mine? Then I see myself crying, but stony faced, expressionless, vacant, an empty room. The young girl is smoking now, the driver obviously happy that no-one important is going to get on the bus. I think I see the driver smoking too. I pretend not to have noticed and just stare at them in the reflection of the window, looking for nothing.

We go down the route, then back, which takes about forty-five minutes or so. Then, in the middle of the third trip, we make an unscheduled stop in a run down area, outside a large ware- house-type building. The bus is changing drivers and the two at the front get their stuff together, the driver handing the girl a small rucksack, probably containing her math's book and a copy of Teen Crush magazine or whatever. He and the jailbait get off and walk toward the shadows, away from the bus. In a minute a new driver will come and take his place. I didn't want to wait until then.

Slowing my pace I keep them walking ahead of me. I kept the distance between us at about a hundred feet, a safe distance. He keeps patting the girl on the back and she's responding to his advances, it's obvious they are fucking. I don't have anything against this, no moral objection; I suppose I'm just interested. I walk through a pool of invisible black water on the pavement that rushes through my shoes and curse lightly under my breath.

They go left, into a council estate, and I tentatively follow from afar, only just seeing them go into a block of flats. Waiting patiently outside, I crouched in the tattered greenery and flowerless-flower bed. On the first floor a light goes on and the shadow of a door closing. Movement inside, but the angle stops me from seeing who and what.

I wait for a while then it starts to rain again; lightly at first, then peppering the ground and buildings with icy hailstones that sting my skin like bad acupuncture. My clothes soak through, and my shoes, already wet, take on more water: I'm fucking freezing. At the window there's a dull light casting grainy shadows against the cheap curtains that block any view.

Many years previous when I had just turned ten or so, my parents had lost interest in my activities so much that they would find any opportunity to have me elsewhere. I had few aunts or uncles, and those that I did were terrible company, all spittled handkerchiefs and plums in cheeks. For some time the church was a friend to the family, to my parents, anyway. One particular priest had taken it upon himself to form a kind of "army-of-youthful-believers", or so he told us. We being a group of a dozen or so boys picked from choir practice or detention hall, whichever suited the moment. There were frequent overnight stays for the group, whom the priest had labeled "blessed" and "chosen", picked by the hand of the Lord to spread the good word. On one night after study in the seminary, the priest called e into his private quarters. This was most strange as we boys would all bunk down together, although at the time it did not seem too beyond the realms of normality.

I entered his quarters as the sound of rushing winds struck chords of dissonance throughout the house of worship.

"Father, you wanted to see me?" I asked, looking up at this giant of a man, still adorned with holy robes and removing his various adornments and placing them in order on a delicately carved rose wood chest of drawers with heavy plated mirror standing above. Around the room images of religious icons, verses taken from scripture written in perfect calligraphic style and pictures by some of the boys from the seminary depicting acts of kindness and charity.

"My child, do you love our Lord?"

"Yes Father."

"How much do you love him?"

"With all my self, all I can, Father."

"Would you ever do anything to hurt, or bring our Lord into discomfort?"

"Of course not, never!" The odd line of questioning seeming normal as a gale blew against the stained glass windows and around the priests' quarters.

"So you do profess to love our Lord with all your heart and soul."

"Yes father, I do love him." Boys of such an age are frequently coerced into saying things they don't necessarily believe, but speak to keep themselves from trouble.

"Good." He replied, and sat down on his bed, groaning in pain while stretching his back. "Oh this life, blessed though it is, it is not without pain. Come here my child." I obeyed and presented myself next to his side as he lay on his bed.

"Yes father."

"You know I am next to the Lord?"

"You are?"

"I am. I have spent my life in the light of Christ and learned from the mouth of God those things that mortal men forget. To become a Reverend one must bathe solely in the light of His good grace."

"It's cold in here."

"Yes, my boy, it is cold, and I feel a great pain in my body. God is kind but time has been cruel. Would you do your Reverend a service and massage my stomach? I have such a twisting discomfort."

"Massage?"

"Yes, just place your hand here." the priest took my hand, clammy and cold, and placed it onto his stomach, just above the navel. His shirt was loosened and black hair swirled around his bulging gut, looking not unlike thickets of gorse and bramble. "That's right, and just rub here gently. Oh the pain is terrible!"

"Yes Father."

"Here, the pain is spread across me, move your hand a little lower. Lower still."

He had me work until a moment of obvious conclusion, when a warm liquid appeared like some Godly manifestation, smearing across his stomach at which point the priest excused himself and indicated he was much recovered.

"I feel the spirit of the Lord once more. Now you do remember your teachings, Alex, do you not?"

"Yes Father: pray twice a day, give thanks to the Lord for all things, never say or do anything to harm the Lord and his Kingdom."

"And who is the Lords messenger here on Earth?"

"You are, Father."

"Very good, Alex, very good."

As I walked back to the boys' room my hands were wet and smelled strange.

Hands now that gripped onto a metal fence by my side, dripping with water and freezing in the city night. They were fucking, that was for sure, but I couldn't be bothered waiting around for hypothermia any longer. Over an hour had passed and this had gone on long enough. Just as I began to walk away, something changed; I hadn't noticed they'd been playing music inside and that old tune echoing *the wanderer, hey the wanderer, I go around a ba pa ba pa bap ah.* But once there was silence, it became almost eerie. I could see the girl getting dressed. A door in the flat opened and then the curtains, which startled me into pretending to be walking an invisible dog. It was the driver at the window, thankfully not paying much attention to the outside world. He wore different clothes now; the cheap blue suit had gone, and was replaced with a grey t-shirt with some sort of orange design on the front. I paced back and stood further from the window than before.

My arm dropped back down to my side as the taxi slowed to a stop next to me. Sitting down I asked for the city centre.

"Is this a non-smoking taxi?"

"No, you can smoke." He was Asian, friendly enough and at least let me smoke. I looked for my lighter in my jeans then realised I didn't have one.

"Sorry mate, have you got a light?"

"Yeah." and he searched through his own pockets then gave me a dark green Clipper, just like mine. I considered pocketing it as I lit up, but decided to do the right thing. "Cheers." He said as I handed it back to him.

I stayed quiet for the remainder of the journey, paid the man, and walked on towards Piccadilly train station. Before I get there, I change my mind slightly as to the plan. Piccadilly was the place for streetwalkers; every night, and most days there was someone there, selling their cunt for a few quid. I had walked up there a few times, once I saw a woman, who was so high she could barely walk. It was late night then, too. This woman I'd seen that time had brown scally hair, tied back and big eyes resting on red rings below them. When I saw her, she had her skirt pulled up around her waist and was doing something to her tights. I walked up to her and looked, and asked her what she was doing. She said her tights were falling down, which they were, due to all the rips and holes in them. She was holding them up with a condom she'd customised into a sort-of elastic band. I shivered when I saw it and asked her if it was a used one, as I was feeling the beast rise within me once more after my voyeuristic hour spent in the rain.

But I had a change of mind and walked up Ducie Street instead, which is just next to Piccadilly train station, leading into dodgiest north Manchester.

My feet took me right up this street, not seeing any life apart from a couple of cars and one stray dog I thought about running after. I got up to another main road, the Mancunian Way, and stood still for a second, watching my breath crystallise in the air then disappear. I turned my head and saw a large advertisement for a football match, which changed into a large advertisement for a car, which changed into a large advertisement for McDonalds. I could hear the sign changing, could hear the poster rotating, the Toblerone-esque components rotating, clunk, clunk, clunk. I felt very alone at this point, not really near any friends, not really friends with anyone. I don't know. I just kept walking through the industrial estate and past the huge electrical superstores, the disused factories, the rubbish at the side of the street. It's late but down the road a bit I can see a light attached to the wall, a sign. I get closer, breath still steaming in front of me. It's a massage parlour, and Oriental massage parlour. I couldn't concentrate, I couldn't see what I was doing, but I marched on anyway, across the road and up to the door. I walk three steps up, then four, then stop midway on the stairs. I could hear voices, scally voices. Sounded British Asian. Indian Asian

"What am I doing?" I said to myself, and turned back into the place and went straight up the stairs until I noticed more voices, Asian blokes, street talk, obviously would be the bouncers. This is like being stuck on the fucking bus all over again. I could hear something like four, maybe five voices, two or three girls, and a couple of guys. A security camera at the top of the stairs shows a red light glowing, and I can see a metal grill on the wall, and a large metal gate. Fuck that, I thought. I turned around and walked back away and as I passed through the front door, a buzzer went off, loud as fuck in my ear and surprised me half to death. Upstairs I could hear whores and truckers fucking laughing at me.

I walk on through the night, time ticking slowly away and its getting later and later. I walk past another whorehouse but really didn't fancy it.

It's late, and I was starting to piss myself off. I should be balls deep right now, if I'd gone in that Oriental place I could have a Chinese whore choking on my cock by now. But I didn't. I went further, past Ancoats and through Victoria Station. I'd ended up at the other side of town, quite close to my flat, but couldn't even begin to consider going home, despite the fact it was getting on for four in the morning. I decide to walk back to Piccadilly station. So that's what I do.

Passing Oldham Street and nearly there after the long, boring walk through the town centre, I pass a bus stop where I eye up a fat girl.

"'scuse me," she says, noticing my lecherous eyeball, "'ave you got a cigarette?"

"Uh, yeah, yeah I've got a few left." So I open the pack and take out two, giving her one. "I'll tell you what I haven't got though, a lighter, you?"

"No, oh shit."

"Don't worry, I'm sure someone'll have one." A guy walks past, I ask him but he doesn't have one. "Oh well," and all of a sudden I'm thinking, Yes, I could fuck her, she's short and fat, but she's also young, and drunk, and alone, and probably could be pushed to take it up the arse. As I think this, I actually laugh a bit. Despite this intention, I suddenly feel very out of place, there is no more conversation, and I'm pacing on the spot waiting for her to say something, or thinking of something to say myself. I could ask her where she's been, where she's going, how old she was. Fuck, I couldn't ask her anything. She needs to just ask me if I want to sleep at her house then I'll say "yes."

"Right, well I hope you find a light." is all I can think of as I turn away and drift again up the street, before looking round to see if I get a glance, but instead she's getting a light from a couple. So I go back.

"Got a light." She balked from her very slap-worthy face.

"Yeah, cheers," and I held out my hand, getting the light from the end of the cigarette I gave her, looking at her all the while. The truth is, I could've said more, but I actually *wanted* to pay for sex tonight. It has been said of women of a questionable moral character, or even all that you buy now or pay later. So I fucked off and walked up further, staring at a girl in a white jacket with a furry hood standing in a phone box then make my way down to the overpass where the wild whores wander. Get to the first road where the underclass work, but tonight there is no sign of anyone. So I go further, finally reaching the overpass but even there, nothing. I paced the street and checked the back alleyways but there was nothing, just pigs in cars and dogs on chains. The police are obviously cracking down. It might not be good for me to be here right now. I don't know what to do. Should I go home? I take two steps forward, and then turn around. I'm in the middle of a main A-road that runs through the edge of the city. Massive build up of oil and soot make me stumble as I work out the quickest way to get out of this place swarming with hidden police. I start down a back road that leads into a tunnel taking me right back to the centre of town. The back alley had a small enclosure where a woman was walking out, stretching what looked like half a condom over her stockings to keep them up. She was old, like, late forties and she looked like she'd been working for a very long time. Her skanky as fuck hair dribbled away from her face as she looked up at me with surprise.

"Fuckin' 'ell ah shit one, what d'ya want? I'm not harming anyone, I'm not even working tonight, I'm just walking."

"I'm not the police, so like, calm down." It is half a condom, she's fucking rank. "That's not used, is it?"

She aches a proper scally laugh. "No don't be daft me tights are broken. S'fuckin' pigs all over the place like, fuckin', can't even go for a walk." And I walk away. She's ridden with plague. Just fuck her off and walk past. Be strong. She scatters her brains when she speaks after me. "E'yar you looking for business love?"

She may be the last hooker in the world anyone would want to gamble on, so I decide to make it easy for her.

"I'll give you three quid for everything."
Her face turns in disgust as she mumbles obscenities. I walk away, further into the unknown dark until the next lost soul. She's skinny, with three-quarter length jeans on and a red puffa jacket. I walk past on the other side, heart beating quickly, and make eye contact.

"Have you got a cigarette?" she asks me from the other side.

"Yeah." So I go over, casually, and get within about three feet of her.

"Looking for business tonight?"

"Yes." I say.

"Right, let's go down here." So I follow her down another dark road, leading to some sort of factory.

"It's ten for hand, twenty for mouth, and thirty for sex."

"How about twenty five for sex?" I haggle.

"Have you not got an extra five? Cos for thirty I can give you a blowjob and sex. I'll give you a blow job first, then sex. Have you got the five?"

"Yeah okay, sounds good." Our negotiation over we walk

further down.

"Where do you live?" she asks.

"Just in the city."

"You don't sound like you're from round 'ere."

"Just got one of those voices."

"Oh right. What's your name?"

"Al... James."

She smiles and looks at me for the first time. "You had to think about that one."

"Yeah I know, it's not my real name." she laughs slightly.

"My name's Nikki wi' two K's."

"And that's obviously not your real name either, I take it?"

"No, no, it is; I've got it tattooed on my arse," she laughs again, "just in case I forget it."

"But how can you see your arse to read it if you forget it?" and we both laugh but it's and uneasy one.

"I'll get someone else to read it for me."

"Well I'm sure a lot of people could help you out there, Nikki."

We get to this other alleyway, which is totally pitch black. "Down here."

I can't see a thing in front of me, but she knows the terrain well. All of a sudden, I'm blinded by a light that scares me almost to death.

"Shitting hell." I curse.

"Don't worry, just a security light. So you go to college, I mean uni or something, you a student?"

"Uh, yeah," I lie, "just finished. Two-two."

"Don't they say if you got a two-two you partied too much and if you got a first you didn't party enough?"

"Yes, actually, they do say that." Someone has been stealing all my best lines. We're still walking through a dirty as fuck little area when she stops. I move close and touch her pussy through her jeans.

"Wait, have you got some money first?"

"Yes I do." I pull out some notes, get a five first, then twenty and ten, give her thirty, put the five back in my pocket.

"Right, just pull your pants down." So I do. It's cold, and I don't want my jeans to fall onto the floor and get wet, so I splay my legs a bit, holding them up. I start touching my cock, rubbing it, but it's flaccid for now. She positions herself and her hands reach down to my cock and they're freezing cold.

"Sorry, cold hands."

Laughing "Yeah, Jesus."

She strokes me and I tell her to pull the foreskin back further to get it hard, which works. While I have a semi-on, she gets a condom from her bag and opens it, then puts it on while I get it hard myself. She slowly and methodically rolls the condom onto my dick and makes sure it's on properly, very cautious.

"By the way, if you see a guy walking past a few times don't worry, he just looks after me to make sure you don't do anything to me."

"Well, only what I've paid for."

She begins to go onto her knees, preparing the ground below her, spreading a chip wrapper so she doesn't kneel on her jeans.

"So have you been doing this long?"

"Yeah, uh, about three years."

"Bloody hell, wow. How many blokes do you think you've been with?"

"Don't know," she breathes out and actually thinks about it for a second, blue light from the sky highlighting the bags under her eyes and a scar on her left wrist. "mebbe three, four hundred. Who knows. Not like I keep receipts."

"Of course, not much chance of a tax rebate is there? Christ."

She opens her mouth and gets onto her knees. She has snaffle teeth that grow in a number of different ways, and are quite misshapen. Her mouth is hot, even over the condom, and I can see her back now as I rub the back of her head to make her suck deeper. She's so thin; I can see bones, ribs and spine as she bobs her head back and forth. On her arm above the scar a line of injection marks running up her wrist to the elbow tell me she will do anything for money and I push her head harder, fucking her mouth and building rhythm, which she doesn't complain about.

"So what're you into?" I stupidly ask, to which she pulls out my cock and says:

"Just wait until I've done this." Then takes it again. I bend over and try to grab her cunt, but she squirms away from my hand. My head keeps shooting to the left, looking for the dude. Plan is: if he comes up the alleyway just leg it. He isn't at the moment.

She stands up and my cock is rock hard, then she pulls her jeans midway down her thighs, revealing a tiny black thong wrapping a tiny white arse with, as promised, the word Nikki tattooed onto it.

"So you *are* Nikki." I say to no reply.

I go to pull her knickers down, but she makes me pull them to the side instead.

"Let me touch your pussy." I say as I snake my hand underneath her and stroke it, to which she pushes my hand away so I put a finger onto her arsehole and probe it ever so slightly, then she jumps forward and says:

"Right," as if she's had enough.

"Wait, wait," I compose myself, "sorry, I'm cool, don't worry."

She is facing away from me and adjusting her stance for some reason, then gets hold of me and starts to push it into her surprisingly tight hole.

"Just hold my hips and I'll do it."

"Okay."

Quite soon into the act my hand tries to work its way onto her pussy once more, but she pushes me away with her one free hands, the other used to steady herself against a mossy wooden post.

"No just hold onto my hips." So I do for a minute, then, by which time I'm fucking her pretty hard and she's even moaning very slightly but I don't think it's because she's enjoying herself, probably just hates her life and wants to die.

"You're too tall, you need to bend down a bit." She advises.

I shift my legs apart a bit, "Like this?"

"No, further down, it's uncomfortable." So I look around my feet, see a lower piece of ground and put my feet in it. "That seems fine just there."

The complete lack of sexuality in our dialogue could have been lifted from a corporate training video. I couldn't believe how business-like this actually was. My hands went around the front and onto her tits over her top.

"Just, just put your hands on my hips."

"I want to feel your tits."

"Put them on my hips."

"No, I want to feel your tits. I'll give you ten quid if I can feel your tits."

"Have you got the money?" And stops static while money is produced. I drop a hand into my pocket and pull a fiver out, then hold it up in front of her face, then put it in her mouth. She takes it out and quickly studies it, before loosening her arms and letting my hand roam.

"Just put it up my top and hold my tit. Only one tit for five quid."

"Yeah okay, fair enough." So I did, and rubbed it and squeezed hard.

"You're hurting me now."

"Sorry." But I wanted to squeeze them harder. I carried on rubbing and grabbing her tit, my hands rough against what seemed to be soft flesh. Without warning, or without me noticing why, she turned to the left and shouted:

"Yeah, just a minute, I'm coming." I was taken aback for a second and slowed my fucking.

"Uh?"

"You need to hurry up and come, he's waiting for me." Then again shouting, "Just give us two minutes I'll be right there..." a muffled reply hanging heavy with Mancunian overtones comes through the bushes and Nikki replies: "No he's just finishing off."

This broke my stride a little, but I had to finish quickly so I actually grabbed her hips and speared the fuck out of her until I could feel it starting, then rubbing her shriveled breast, feeling her arse, running my fingers over the tattoo then clenching my eyes, anus, stomach and everything as I pushed and pulled and pleaded, finally reaching climax.

As she quickly dressed the hairs on my legs stood on end, feeling the cold air rushing from train lines across the country. Sweat had formed on my brow and threatened to drip over my eyes.

"Do you mind if I leave first?" Asks Nikki, correcting her genitals and pushing her tits back into her bra.

"Um?" I snap the condom off and throw it down on the floor then think about how many used condoms there are down there.

"Just so we don't leave together." She reasons.

"Oh, uh yeah fair enough."

"Or you can go the back way if you want," points down alleyway, "that takes you out to the main road and just follow that to get back to the train station."

"Right, yeah maybe that's a good idea."

Up came my trousers and I said "Cheers, bye," and wobbled into the alley, finding a corner then the street. My cock is still showing proudly through the denim of my jeans as I adjust myself for walking, tucking the head against my belt and stomach. Around the corner I walk into a pair of teenage would-be thugs with knives.

Without hesitation I step forward and use the weight of my body and adrenaline coursing from my cock around my body and to my fist, smashing it into the nearest muggers' face. He falls backwards, as anyone would, and the second takes a moment to look at his partner in surprise while I swing the other hand around and grab him by the back of the throat, using my elbow to crack into his windpipe. The sound like dry sticks breaking followed by a clunk and clatter of the knife, as the first teen runs away. The second now on the floor choking, I put my knee to his throat and get nice and close for conversation, remembering that one should never be afraid of a little hand-to-hand conflict.

"What was that?!" I ask with menace and advantage, his reply, gargled and unintelligible.

I take the knife and hold it to his eye, pushing the point just below on the flesh, and pierce just enough that he can feel muscle tissue start to tear and threaten his retina. Instead of blinding him I pull the blade down and leave blood trickling from the wound, then release him as he runs into the night, then pocket the knife and step across the heaping refuse at the edges of the path and head towards the main road when a taxi stops for me and lowers the drivers side window.

"Alright mate where you off to?"

The taxi starts up the road and through the centre of town into a bit of traffic.

"So you been out tonight?"

"Uh, yeah. I've been out."

"Where you off to?"

"Head down Castlefield."

"Right oh. So where you been tonight?" As I rub blood from my knuckles, his line of questioning seemed all too personal.

"Just around."

"Oh, uh, right." He drove quietly for two seconds. "I only say 'cos round here there's not much to do except the local slags."

"That's true."

"Yeah man, I mean, I've done that as well, me and my mate was working, right, in Birmingham, and like, we was the only ones there who knew our way round, so like, we went clubbing and that and pulled these birds but then they went home, so we was like, we went to this place right, and there was these girls man, prostitutes, so we had one each man,"

"Right." Let's pause, "Well. It takes all sorts."

We arrive at my bridge and I look up at the building, suddenly confronted with my own loneliness and prospects of solitude for one more night.

"Actually mate, can you take me to Salford Arms?"

"The pub? Be long closed now."

"Yeah, a mate of mine lives round there."

"Right you are then."

We share the remainder of the journey in silence. Darkened grey skies looming broad and suffocating over the Manchester skyline, tall glass buildings giving way to squat red bricked pillars of office blocks and prefabricated 1970's housing estates. The wordless sign above the Arms missing the "A" and "S".

Leaving the cab I stretched my back and corrected my posture. If anything Pete would have some drugs I could use as a route to distractionism, for the time being at very least.

Daylight breaks across the city. From a distance I see the shadows scurry off into their hiding, making haste across the clay-brick houses and structures of old, light kisses onto the modern and polished glass and steel structures thrusting skywards in defiance of the city's true nature: that of soil, that of dirt.

As I traipse up the garden path strewn with plastic bottles and shredded newspaper and my hand touches down onto the door leaving a loud 'thud' sound I am suddenly aware of the time, and a distinct shuffling inside. It doesn't sound like Pete and opening the door and tearful older woman with questions in her eyes.

"Pete?"

Her shaking head and hands gave way to full-blown sobbing and tears, as she falls towards me, my arms catching but only just as the reality of the moment dawns. Around the corner of my own eyes come tears, softer than ever, true in their nature. My only friend, here no more. Gone, gone. I would often dream of isolation, the thought and prayer of true solitude and loneliness. A cold wind blows and I shudder at the reality that this may finally be true.

NOT NIKKI STREET WHORE, BUT NICKI SUPERMARKET GIRL

The differences about my heart
As frequent as the tide.
The sun reflecting endless
In the corners of your eye.

I sit on my corduroy sofa lost in empty thought, next to someone rolling a joint. They remove something from the roll and leave it on the table. I move to look but can't see anything except a small piece of brown bark-like substance. We listen to the collectible record with its limited edition pops and crackles. The recent cash in on rerelease forms a foundation of bitterness and I grow to hate it. The soft, underwater piano sounds grit against my teeth and the hypnotic rhythm I once basked in becomes like the drums of death in the tightened leather back of my soul. My heart feels as though I have been running, tightness gathers about my chest and my mind is plagued with memories long since buried beneath secrets and lies. The idea is to create so much myth within that eventually even I will be lost among the forests of deceit rising from the seeds of lie after lie after lie.

Drugs are a wonderful distraction from depression, and when combined with alcohol, are close to prophetic. However, food is also a shortcut to happiness, a welcome diversion, and required fuel for substance abuse. I may be an directionless addict, but at least I can be a responsible one.

I cough fiercely at the joint, catching tiny pieces in my throat, which spurs on the need for food even more. I run through the supermarket in my head: baked goods, pasta, vegetables, meat, fish, cans of beans and magazines adorned with barely clothed women in endless expositions of genitalia, just hidden enough to keep from the top shelf. All around people clutch and grab for sugary treats and alcoholic drinks, and the sound of collective breathing is torturous: that being through the windpipes of a thousand heavy smokers, wheezing and coughing, phlegm spattered flooring starts to over flow with bile.

The joint comes back to me and I realise the album we are listening to is not the ultra-rare vinyl copy but the newly released compact disc. The clock hits eight PM and I rise in my dressing gown and socks.

"I need to go to the supermarket."

"Oh the supermarket, yeah, you going now?"

"Yeah I need to go right now."

"Okay, well finish this first, right?"

"Yeah. I'll be two seconds."

In my bedroom I look for clothes, which are seemingly everywhere and yet nowhere. I haven't been sleeping recently, and stand naked for a few minutes while I find a pair of boxers, which I find are still stained with a combination of come and saliva from a recent blowjob. My jeans have that cuntish ripped effect haphazardly strewn across as part of the "design", but my knowledge of the audaciousness of this fact makes it seem acceptable.

I put on my pink t-shirt and think about putting on my blazer vest but then decide that's stupid so I don't. I walk back into the living room almost ready to go.

"That was fast."

"Yeah." I reply.

My fingers are moving and I can't stop them. I want to go to sleep. But instead, I need cigarettes. We walk to the front door and stop at a mirror and I see I am the only person there.

Once outside I feel truly alone. A deathly silence hangs over the city, only the distant sound of traffic passing somewhere. The gentle patter of rain delivers something close to life but there is nobody here but me. No birds, no dogs, not even any whores at the usual underpass. I kick a can to break the monotony. Looking to the sky there are still lines carved across it, pointing now in opposite of my direction.

At the market I buy liquor: Stoli and J&B. At the checkout I look for girls, but find only a typically flirtatious homosexual man with what I would describe as a the hair cut of a cunt. The lights burn brightly overhead and yet instill a harshly cold sensation across the waxed floors. The magazines are as my vision: pseudo-celebrities dangerously close to full exposure, anything for a few more column inches. The queue moves slowly, and finally my turn comes. I am served by one I haven't seen before. Curly hair, held up in a bunch, librarian glasses and the hint of perfume over the rubber conveyor belt onto which I drop my groceries. The milk falls over and I leave it, shrugging silently and channeling "who-gives-a-fuck". On top of the butter I balance two tomatoes, no bag. She looks at me, while serving a guy in front and I squint into an imagined spotlight while she passes his celery and detergent over the scanner then pulls out a bag.

"No thanks, I'm good for a bag, just put them in here." He says as he holds up a large sports bag. What a cunt, I think silently. He pays and leaves and it is finally my turn, the conveyor belt moving and rolling my twin bottles of booze like some icon of the night to come.

"Did you find everything you were looking for?"

"Well I'm always looking for something…"

She laughs and a slight crinkle in her nose delivers an instant fantasy whereby that same crinkle sits just over the head of my cock as she tongues around the head and chews on the shaft.

She starts to pack a bag and I interject, feigning refinement "Don't worry, I'll pack it."

Her eyes are sparkling, beautiful; youthful, energetic, positive. She could water down my poison well.

"It's okay, it's in my job description!" Her humour is still fresh and there remains much virtue within as she bags the milk, juice and spirits. Better give her some jokes in return.

"Just letting you get the heavy stuff out of the way first!" To which she does actually laugh. Excellent. I pack away my things but there's not much so hardly any silence.

"Do you want any cash back?" Familiar territory?

"No thanks, I… really don't." Another little giggle from her.

"All these lot round here think cash back, y'know, it's like free money."

"Yeah, cash back is a killer."

"Forty nine pounds seventy three please. Yeah, they just sign for it, like give it to me!" she makes wild-ish eyes and I know I desperately want to fuck her.

"But this is free, of course?" My bill, sarcasm.

"Oh yeah. God I wish I got free food, and I work here."

"Yeah, I heard you guys only get like what, ten, twenty percent off or something?"

"I don't even get that yet, haven't been here long enough."

"Oh right, how long you been working here?"

"About three months now."

"And they don't give you any money off? That's a bit tight, isn't it?"

"Yeah but I suppose they have so many new starters

people would be cashing in then quitting so I suppose they have their reasons."

"To be fair I do so much shopping here I'm pretty jealous of anyone who gets discount." My card goes through and I smile at her. Her name badge says Nicki, Christ, same as the whore I fucked.

"It can be handy."

"Oh sweet, well," choosing my parting words carefully, "I'd better be off," pick up my bags and check in front of me so I don't fall over something obvious, "I'll see you next time!"

"Yeah, see you, later." Great response, and I walk off into the newspaper section, but really want to go back and talk to her.

I should've said something incisive; I should've been funnier, or at least spoken more. I should've said, "Well I hope to see again soon." No, "Well, here's hoping I see you around somewhere, maybe get a drink?" No that would've been wrong too. I should've been funny. "You're not gonna just send me away like that, are you?" She would've laughed. Or maybe, "Well, I hope the next time I see you it's not in the confines of work." Fuck that, "Well, have a nice night and I hope to see you around some time." Too wordy. She wasn't even the prostitute I thought she was. Much different. Although if the supermarket ever did start doing prostitutes I would be very interested in some sort of staff discount or loyalty scheme.

Walking home from the shop, still very stoned, staggering over the street and trying to time my walk with a young lady but failing. I have half a mind to go back to the market and pretend I have forgotten something, but know that that would be far too desperate. I cross the road on green traffic lights but there's a Land Rover in the middle of the street not moving. I walk around the side window and he is looking at a map, a middle aged white man who you'd expect to have been driving for a fuck long time but for some reason didn't notice the lights. As soon as I reach the window, he drives off, doesn't even look up, just put his hands on the wheel and his foot down. Which was weird so I shouted "Oi!" I crossed the next part of the road and it was on a green flashing man but I thought it was a green traffic light and I crossed and saw a car coming and then bounce towards me not a lot but seeming very close.

I ran across the road and burst out laughing and tried to look in the car to see who nearly killed me and it was these two girls, both looked like students and one was looking at me to which the other one looked at me. I just smiled and turned my head away, looking cool enough that they might turn around and follow me to mine. I smiled all the way home, letting my grin vary from intense, to friendly, to demonic to psychotic. When I finally got home, I put some bread in the toaster and went to the fridge. Opening the fridge I see that I have come on my sleeve, and wonder if it was noticed by the supermarket girl. No matter. The shopping was analogous to a life of solitude as sperm upon my jacket. I pour a vodka with orange for colour while unidentified music plays on the living room system and look out of the window onto the train tracks and below. The whores are back, the streets once more washed yellow and rising with piss and blood. There is no one for me to call, no one to love. My friend is gone, my parents, with me now in memory. Wanted to be able to say: "I really appreciate everything," and mean it. Want to be able to say "Do you remember that time I met that girl and you said, "well you be careful 'cos that girls' been around a bit, you can tell. Lovely girl, but be careful," I want to say, "God, you're such a Mum." To my Dad I wish I could say you've been my best friend for my whole life and guided me through the hardest times and never given up on me.

But I can't, and they can't, and I wouldn't if I could. Idiot fuck Alex Fish where death will be your greatest prize. Walk into the living room and turn the music up really loud so everyone in the world can hear it and a lonely tear forms in my eye.

C EREAL

The stranger seemed so full of fear,
So filled with wonder at things near.
His is not a lonesome path,
For it is walked by all who have.

I t had been years, almost a decade since I had found my way
back home: that place where my youth was spent, where
my eyes were first opened. I couldn't have been more bored.
Night time was falling and I had escaped my aunt's house,
with her perfectly rigid rectangular children, now grown into
terribly obtuse, hard-right adults, the house of opulence right
down to scented airs and deep pile carpets so comfortable one
might confuse it for bedding.

In an effort to distance myself from familiarity, I walked
at pace around the maze of residential streets, past the old
wood and onto a large hill with a disused telephone box
overlooking the bay. I recall the telephone box, and the view
below, a church. So much has been taken from me, from the
world, so much good substituted for torment, for wickedness
beyond compare. Those justifying moments of blood beneath
nail rushing back and on to their birthplace, the first drops of
ink in my water.

Miles are heavy underfoot but I feel no weight. My jeans soaked through rub against my legs chafing sores that spur me onward until I reach my destination. In the night sky no moon shines, earth shrouded in a black night. Arriving at the building the great stained glass work glows from dim candles within and a cross on the roof gives the sign of place of worship.

The front door is open as I enter, creaking framework announcing my arrival and I make no secret of it. My breath fogs before me, and the faces of saints look down onto the greatest of sinners.

Passing the alter I blow out the candles and leave the hall in darkness, then make my way through the side door, past the seminary, onward to the reverend's private quarters. It has been almost two decades but the place has not changed. From within I could hear a soft sound, breathing, gentle murmurs. As I open the door, He is startled, yet decrepit and old, unable to protest or even question.

"Father, is that you?"

"Hum ah hum, yes, who is it?"

"One of your students, father, your most loyal student."

"My m-" His words are short as drop my coat and loosen my belt, allowing my heavy, water-logged trousers to fall, then remove my t-shirt, stepping from them and now naked, stroking my penis into full erection.

"My God, what are you?"

He tries to reach for his glasses from the side table and as He does so I pounce and tear the sheets back and rip his nightwear from him. He moans and protests but I turn him over easily and line my cock up, penetrating with caustic brutality and frantically whisper over his screams:

"I would never betray you Father, never you, you have shown me the way, the light, there is only one path, light in darkness, truth in deceit. You are my keeper and my creator. I come to you now, I come to you now, I come to you."

You may think an ancient child molesting rapist such as

he may have enjoyed my reentry into His life but through His inspiration I walked a path of knowledge in the secrets of the sexual arts: how one may bring pleasure and ecstasy and in the same mode deliver torment and agony. His countless acts, for sure I was not alone, now returned to Him as I pounded and hammered and fucked until He resisted no more and let out not even another breath as He passed away into death.

A time there once was when death did not come with such regularity, when *life* was the thing, and death a distraction for much later. But things change regardless of our wishes, and change is often harsh.

"I have missed you, Alex, despite your being a total cunt."

Each weight was lifted, each wound was healed at the very thought of her, of our last moments. It was as if a sun had burned through me and used my body for the planets and my blood for the stars. I see a tear within despite her fury, and despite such we embrace and share a breath's worth of contact.

Clare was giving me a ride home after having seen my relatives some years back. They with picture houses and perpendicular lawn arrangements. Escape from that torture had been with malice of foresight but the meeting with Clare pure chance.

Over the stereo Morrissey laments the listening class, pondering his own place in society forever.

"I wrote. I used to love writing to you. At the slight hope you might even fucking read it. I wouldn't see you or be near you for so long, I didn't know how you were doing. Writing was..." Sigh. "I felt, next to you all the time. I never wanted to move. I had to. My Dad, you know, anyway." I nod "I don't know how you felt, I didn't know how you felt. I still don't. But I felt something; and it sounds silly cos' we were like, young, but, I haven't met anyone I could talk to like I did you, not since we broke up. So just, I don't know, take it for what it is, I don't even know what that is."

The car rolls further on down the road and all of a

sudden, a good word to describe this situation is: regret.

"I never meant to stop writing. I... my intentions were-"

"-Oh fucking shut the fuck up. Jesus. *Your intentions*. You just didn't think. You were just too busy having a good time; which is fine, I don't mind, I want you to, for fucks sake. It's just; there wasn't ever room for me. Dn't pass the blame onto-"

-"but my friends,"

"I hold you responsible. You're to blame. Do you know how many letters I wrote?" She sobs, "I used to sit, when I should have been going out, and think about you all night. The occasional phone call from wherever you were living, a text message here and there. I know we were breaking up, but, but I thought what we had deserved a... deserved more than that. I'd get home from lectures and hold a pen in my hand to do some work, but end up writing your name all over a piece of paper." I flounder under squinting eyes that squeeze out liquid some might call tears. "I just couldn't see you ever doing that, or feeling that after you ignored me."

The environment changes from man-made to organic, from digital to analogue and we're driving around woods and hills surrounded by lakes and rivers and forests. I want to burn them all down, just to get me out of this car.

"I didn't ignore you I didn't-"

"Alex, I sent you letters to which you didn't reply. That to me, sounds like you're ignoring someone." The car rounds a bend and drives over the remains of a hedgehog long baked hard in the white-hot sun. Tragedy over a two-floored public transport echoes from the speakers.

"Clare. It's not. I wasn't ignoring you, I just couldn't... write. I mean I could write, I just couldn't... think of anything to say. I mean, I hadn't seen you in ages, we were always supposed to meet and we only did once or twice: I never saw you. I don't know what you're doing on the other side of the country."

"I'm telling you in my fucking letter, for fucks sake." Light comes at an angle, blocked by the trees and making bars of yellow streak across the road. A single white line divides the otherwise perfect sky.

"Yeah, but you can't just... can't see someone in letters. It's not natural. For fucks sake, who has a fucking relationship through letters?"

I let out a deep sigh and so, subconsciously does Clare. I've missed her so much after we moved away from each other; she'd never believe how much, and perhaps neither will I. It could never have worked, us moving so far away after she went to University.

We should have split up and called it a day. It'd be easier if we broke that tie.

The car weaves through the deep woods on one side and the lake on the other. I remove my seatbelt to get a cigarette from my bag on the back seat, when a deer runs across the road in front of the car and freezes.

"And I am a living sign."

Clare did not have time to scream, but swerved, going straight into the recently built wooden fence blocking off the edge of a cliff leading to the lake.

L OST IN THE WASH

And I once got caught
In a landslide, safe to say
Your eyes were
Last on my mind.

I was taken to hospital and admitted for four days while they ran tests. I had been breathing in water while I was under, and found that if my lungs had filled any more I would surely have drowned. I couldn't eat for a long time. The hunger was there, but the desire to eat had vanished. It was like; I could feel my stomach was empty, I could stand up and totally relax my body and still my stomach would just sit inverted to the rest of my torso. Since I'd been unconscious a lot in the first two days of my admittance, I didn't know that my leg had been broken, well, fractured, below the knee. When I finally came around properly on the third day, I start- ed screaming I was in so much pain. The leg wasn't so bad itself, but it was because when I woke, half asleep, I tried to move it, but couldn't. I thought it was just trapped between sheets or something, so I tried to yank it, throw it out of bed: then I felt it.

I was in and out of consciousness in this time, but I remember a psychiatrist talking to me after they put me on a drip for food since I refused to eat. She asked me about Clare, about what we'd talked about that day, about my parents. I spoke a little bit, not real- ly helping, though. I didn't want her to help me. I didn't know what I wanted.

On the forth day, I made my parents take me down to the lake. They were concerned as I was becoming more and more detached from them, not just since the crash, but altogether. "We're here if you need to talk to us, Al." I wasn't listening. "You've been through a lot, we want- y'know, we want to try and be there for you, to help you?" My Dad meant well. I just couldn't bring myself to speak to him right now.

The cigarette lighter clicked and my parents lit their cigarettes and blew the smoke out of the half opened windows. I opened my own window and took out a Marlboro, lit it, and smoked in silence.

"Didn't know you were smoking now, son?" My Mum got a bit concerned, but I think actually she was okay because it kind of alleviates their responsibility if I breath second hand smoke. "We don't see you anymore, son, we ring and ring, but you just nowhere to be found; wouldn't you like to talk to us? You can talk to us if you want to, we're here for you if you need us."

We drove down the same sunny road as I had barely a week ago. Passed the trees with the same shafts of light, in roughly the same place, passed where the deer had run out, which I hadn't realised we'd actually hit. Stopped at the hole in the fence; temporarily repaired using wire fencing, the kind you see on farms. My Dad stopped the car and I got out.

There were two tracks leading straight off the edge; two tire tracks. They displaced some rocks and left a dark pair of thick lines jutting off the edge. Alex. The water was gone, replaced by rivers flowing from the North, down through valleys, mountains to here, where it flows onwards forever. Alex. Clare had moved again and I once more alone. I smoked half, and then dropped the remainder off the edge, unable to hear the hiss of fire against water but watching it float on the surface.

"Alex?" They called but instead I watched the only girl I've ever met float away from me. When I turned around they were gone and then I remembered they couldn't be there in the first place and remembered everything and finally my eyes open and there's a nurse shaking me and shouting:

"Alex! Can you hear me? Alex, Alex, move your hands if you can hear what I'm saying, move your finger, Alex, Alex can you move your finger?"

"I can hear you." I reply then stay quiet and go back.

Over head stood two white lines, cutting open the sky, but now I go down onto the beach, kicking rocks, roots and sticks, looking out onto this impossibly smooth mirrored surface of the lake, not a dent, not a scratch. I walk to the edge of the water and very carefully put my bare feet on the shallowest part of the shoreline. Then I move out and out and on top of the water I can walk, I can walk. The world below me is crystal clear and I can see fish and wonderful things moving below all the time and I just keep walking until the centre of the lake gets closer and the edge of the cliff appears overhead and then the metallic shadow underwater shines in the afternoon sun and I can see very plainly the bonnet and the roof and the broken window that flooded in and I try to look further down but I can't get into the water because it's too hard, I kick and stamp on it but it won't break but I just carry on and try to punch through when I get on my hands and knees and thrash against the surface just hitting out in spasms trying but not even rippling the surface until all of a sudden it breaks and I'm underneath but the surface is still hard and I can't get out and I can't breathe so I scream and the air just floats out of the water but I can't get through it, I can see the sky and everything so clearly but I can't break out of the water and my lungs are losing bubbles of air quickly that I have nothing to replace with so I swim down, down towards the monstrous vehicle below, the hatchback tomb holding her inside and down I go and here it comes I can see it clearly and I swim past little fish that wiggle when they move, and swim away from my disturbance but it's okay because my hands reach out and touch the metal of the car and pull myself down with it then all of a sudden I realise I can breathe underwater so I take a big breath and exhale, throwing a hundred bubbles into the water and watching them rush upwards. If I can breathe in here, I can stay here.

If I can breathe under here, maybe Clare can, maybe she's down there waiting for me, so swimming is what I do quickly and swiftly towards the door, the windows blackened and impenetrable but the door locked shut and I can feel something behind it beating to get out, I can feel the handle, must be full of water, it won't open, so I try and hook my hand underneath and I try and try but it's no use the door just stays so I kick at the windows and as I do the car starts to turn and sink lower and deeper and I follow it down and try to stop it dropping but its no use I just sink with and drop to the bottom, trying all the time to wrench the door open but not getting a grip on the thing which becomes like a huge sculpture and the doors weld themselves into place, metal joining metal and the panicked movement inside just get more pronounced and the screams seeping from the inside out into the glassy deep just trickle away because there's nothing I can do despite everything and I find my lungs totally submerged in water and floating out of my mouth as my own movement becomes more frantic and my organs inside become waterlogged and start to move and change place but I have to open it I have to open it then the car burns and the water flash boils to steam and my face sears and my hands fuse onto the metal and the whole lake and everything surrounding it just vaporises and I'm here now, back in that place of before, back where this terrible journey began, stuck between nightmare and matter.

CLEANING THE PIPES

Sadness makes
For beautiful pictures.
The issue is they exist only
In your mind.

The fields have grown tall, unkempt, ravaged by time yet lush and thick in stature. Evening dew soaks through my shoes and into my socks, weighing me down but by no means discouraging. I arrive at a wall, made from loose stones hundreds if not thousands of years old. This place is timeless, as is murder, as is vengeance. Hours have passed and I have only this final task to complete before I leave this place forever.

I stand for moments at the door, shaking, not from cold, but apprehension. The thousand-year-old rock in my hand and the street behind me dark and silent, and I once again feel like that little boy, lost in the woods, cast out and alone, left to fend for himself, and fend I shall with great malevolence. Beyond the tiny hamlet broke waves onto polished stones spit out of the sea by the angry Gods.

The knocking from my hand seemed to echo, and for a time I felt I was too late, but then from within, a clicking of gears as the director opened the door with a question. He was much older, and so was I, he on the descent I on the rise.

And so to confirm, I say in hushed tones:

"Max?"

"Yes?"

At which cue I smash him in the face with the rock, knocking him backwards and into unconsciousness. I am bigger now, much larger than before. My muscles developed and my frame beyond its capability yet playing "catch-up" quickly.

"Hello, boy!" I snarl and march through the door frame, closing the door behind me. Max is a broken mess already and struggling to even half-stand. I kick him in the ribs hard like Alan Shearer in front of goal and then grab him by his straggly, balding hair, still looking like a hobo after so many years. "You alright there, chief?" I ask, screaming in his ear and then slam his face against the floor a few times until he goes limp.

And then I see a great beast, a dragon: fly up above ahead of me and split the sky with fire. It breathes acid all over the ground and everyone, thousands of people fall into ashes and die over and over again and their bodies burn and blood flows like a river but they're left screaming, in pieces, their mouths open so wide that the blood explodes from them and they multiply in number by ten and I'm standing there covered up to my chest in blood and walking around in it and it seeps inside my shoes then my trousers now my shirt and the bones under my feet roll over and over and I can't see anything in front of my except the blood foaming into a red cloud that covers all the walls that are moving in and getting tighter around them and as the walls move in the blood boils and churns and boils more and red grows further up the shaft that looked like a huge ocean a thousand miles wide but now shrinking down and blood flows out of my eyes now and floods my brain and I'm trapped inside it and its pushing me up and out and over and over I go I drop I slip through the acrid air into a big ocean of crimson waters that churn into crude oil and I've fallen a hundred feet into it and start choking but then I get out and find a sexless torso and break it in half like a stick and then my heart's on the outside of my chest and I can see it beating but it's no good because the light's are on so.

When he woke up he was bleeding. The wound on his head aching and his eyes crusted shut with sleep, despite his coma lasting little more than an hour.

His words come through muffled against a sock taped to his face, and falling on deaf ears as I turn up the music in the other room, as Marc Bolan coo's and shoop's.

I recognize a "fuck" and "bastard".

"I'm sorry, Max, you caught me on a bad day." His writhing almost embarrassing. The chair I had tied him to rocked and creaked against the hard floor below. On the arms of the chair I had taped his hands, flat and gripping the hardwood supports. These broke easily as I, again used the rock to pulverize his creeping hands into pieces, forming blackened and bloody holes splintered with bone and nerve endings.

His howling stops as I raise my finger to his mouth and hush him down like a trapped animal.

"I've seen the good torn out of this world, the evil coming in. Allowed to thrive and feed on the tears of children. I'm as much to blame as you, but I'm doling out the justice for now, so take this as long-overdue-diligence."

Max tries to say something but I allow my fists hardened by the rock to break his face into as many pieces as I can, until his movements are shuddered, words monosyllabic. "How many?" The life still gurgles within him. "How many did I miss? How late am I? I should have killed you before, but I was too weak. Too small. Just the way you like 'em though, eh?"

Sounds of sobbing and pleading beneath dripping blood and torn flesh.

"Did you ever finish the film, by the way? I'd love to get a copy, you know, for my showreel." Like a cruel master I cradle his face, lifting broken jaw from broken cheek, slowly pushing collapsed face into itself and against the force of gravity, catalyzing the last wheezing of this particular monster, the shadow of the beast veiled within my nightmares.

In preparation for this moment I produce a full can of lighter fluid and spray it across his face and body, trickling into open wounds and twisting the knife of pain once more before the big one.

His tears and sobbing barely audible now as his mouth filled with blood and lighter fluid, and the song reaching its conclusion as I step closely to his ear and hold his bloody face and sing softly:

"Ohhhhh, I'm just a vampire for your love."

Before striking the match I kiss his forehead, then drop it flaming onto a trail of vaporous spirits leading to the front door, which I close behind me. I do not wait to see him engulfed in flames but the muffled shrieks announce the moment, and I walk to the sea across a small field bookended with jagged rocks.

Night time is well and truly upon me, the only light from a slivered moon that gives just enough reflection to show the furious white peaks crashing down onto the rocky shoreline. At the waters edge I sit, my hands plunged into freezing water and suddenly realise I am still holding the rock. Releasing it to the sea, I allow the water to rush about my body, washing away the blood from my lips and memory gives a feeling of relief: all-consuming, world-ending relief.

Back in the village the fire rages through the house of the monster, slain by a beast that grew bigger than he could dream.

Dream.

It brought me to my own, forgotten. I rise from the edge of the sea.

Now it's late in Autumn.

Sometimes the leaves that fall are wet and clog up the streets like a fat man's arteries.

Sometimes they're dry and are blown around like a thousand pages from the book of my life that will never be written. I'm walking down King Street, having just purchased a six-slice brushed steel toaster, evening meal.

I could smell early evening smog from the day, a Saturday, drifting and silently creeping down streets and into people's lives in the form of blackened phlegm or an unshakeable cough. I light a cigarette and make my way home.

Yawning, I march and smoke. Torn flesh and twisting steel banished far into the recess. Tears and laughter of children and that old familiar smell of sweat and come and Bible pages, released instead of buried, set adrift into the open seas of my conscious rather than sunk into the firmament and hidden until great upheaval. There is a way of living that is not particularly nice, but that works on certain levels. My true ideals are a mystery to me. Love is a sensation that comes and goes like a twisted ankle. I exist in a perpetual state of recovery and remission.

Rocks hung around my heart and drag me deep within the ageless earth. It had begun to sink a line that tied around each vein, every sinew. Returning from the edge left me hollow and burned out. Simply eradicated as a spirit, destroyed as a human, and yet alive as never before.

S TAGGERED LINES

It was me!
I cried, alone.
Pounding walls
That held no room.

I t's not quite past dark but I feel good. I woke recently and my spine wasn't as sore as it had been for weeks, so I gave a big stretch and heard the orchestra warming up to performance. As the string section geared into existence and started fine tuning, there was a dusty matter in the air in front of my eyes. Focusing, it disappeared just like it always does.

Weeks and months torment after minor periods of happiness. In an empty room I sit alone and descend once again into my own self. It is becoming increasingly difficult to balance my numerous states of want and existence; a turning point will soon come that breaks all things I know. Cocaine has become expensive, or weak, either way, the ends aren't meeting any more. As the stars began to close and a new sun rises, my feet find brown loafers and take me to the train. As is usual I skip the fare, playing dumb and patently aloof. It works.

Once in the office I receive the usual array of calls from disgruntled members of our opportunistic credit-providing club. Predictable and negatively absorbing. At lunch I smoke and find my supervisor, a fat woman with a pigs face and trotter lips.

"Diane, I need a word," I formally introduce.

"Can it wait? Tim's up my arse with the FRG's." She blathered back.

"Not really, it's a bit of a problem." I reply.

After quitting the job I wander aimlessly, feeling like a teenage girl at the national broadcaster: raped, worn and shattered. Upon arrival at my own apartment I purge the place. I decide upon a new version, ridding myself of mental impurities and tossing the lot into the high rise drop passage leading to who knows where. There are an array of moments that give me a feeling of peace and happiness, but the overall sensation of fear and self-loathing lurks heavily overhead like so many black clouds in Winters' evening. Pushing through, always into distances unseen, I collide with myself on a rocky shore-line.

The journey lasts through weeks and weeks, and on a clear day the television recites topics of news.

"A man has committed suicide after being arrested under suspicion of a series of murders, including that of missing Manchester woman Margaret St. Claire. The man, aged 45, has a history of mental illness and previously suspended charges of molestation of a minor, while in his previous employment as a hospital maintenance worker. Police are investigating his known associates and locations he was known in. The suspect, who cannot be named at this point, was a resident of Preston, and was taken in by Manchester police after an apparent confession during an emergency services call last week. Investigating officers are said to be confident of a swift resolution."

I sit in stunned silence, unblinking for what might have been years, dust gathering over my eyeballs and spiders crawling through my face. There is relief, echoed by guilt, hanging like a dead dog from a tree. I receive a letter confirming my resignation from the call centre, and find that I have been rewarded with *six* months of bonus pay, after working little over three weeks. Jarring ridicule, I tentatively fritter out the cash into cocaine and ecstasy. It seems trite, but natural influences are what they are.

Sitting on my chocolate dusky brown corduroy sofa stroking my cock until a crowning glory. The girl sits aside, squirming as I grapple with her clitoris. We fumble for a time until she comes, then I excuse myself to the bedroom. Frantically trying to eek another breath out of my body I crush the blue hard-dick meds into increasingly staggering lines of cocaine. Sensations being what they are I fondle into glory before long. Returning to the lounge I strut in a navy and iridescent blue dressing gown, or at least under the influence of these drugs seems iridescent. Slaves at dock and hands on oars, we stroke out towards the horizon. I feel the corduroy judder on my bristling chin while I eat her stubbled cunt. I peer upwards to her face and see she has dyed pink hair. This surprises me but only as such that I hold her with a little more disdain than before, and that prior to this point I hadn't even noticed. There She is nothing, but here, She is everything. I kiss her deeply and press myself against her on the sofa until I feel her wetting her neoprene panties.

Lowering onto the bare thread skinny mattress we exchange kisses attuned to Roman-Greco orgiastic indulgences, but always on the edge on conscience. Sweating droplets, we touch and feel and truly love into oblivion. It isn't anything serious, and exchanges of look and lark and laughter smatter over the whole experience, but in a sudden my cock is fully erect and I feel everything teenage working again. I penetrate her and she writhes in dissuasion. Staring into her shaded eyes I ask her with pupil diameters whether we can fuck for normal, but the answer is negative.

"No! Please! Put a condom!!" She grates into my ear, fighting away my advances as I wince and grimace, complying, as a gentleman does.

Luckily the additives are conducive to my erection and it is no issue, in fact, she experiences an orgasm almost moments after penetration. The sensation tears though her and I and we both feel where we are in that certain time and place and she begs:

"Spit in my mouth, please daddy." The pleas coming like the yelping of a puppy dog, and as a gentlemen, I oblige.

Reaching orgasm once again, she and I trickle down into a gentle arc, somewhat aligned with the golden ratio, somewhere like an ouroborosian crochet. A dark mist drops over us both, and even a red Marlboro is not enough to preserve the epic.

I give a tentative kiss and she leaves in a flurry of cheap black velvet. We crumble like apples onto the sofa, so recently indulged with its potential, now retreating into shadows and ideas. Alone, I watch the window and seek a bounty, unfounded. There is naught but sweat and tobacco littered across my couch and chest, little more than a distraction at this point as I stare into the remaining five grams of cocaine and four viagra tablets stacked onto my mirror that seems now more an ornament than placeholder. My bank-card almost cracks over the compacted powders as I blend the quantities into suitable measures. Things are good. I smile broadly, soaking in the magnificence and benevolence of the moment, but try not to look dirtily into the light.

She leaves in a flurry of perfume and silk. I sit smiling, but empty, looking and grinning to the window like some sort of lost fool. A plane crosses over my window, carving a white line, imperfectly straight, but effortlessly solid. I look to the table, holding great mountains of drugs. Absorbing a hearty dose, I sneeze and cough, almost vomiting onto my excellent sofa. There is a moment of safety and peace until things start to fall into place. I split the bounty into mirror evens and take two. Before any real time can pass I find I have two laptops and a TV regaling all indecent manner of pornography siphoned from the internet into my putrid, base eyes.

In some sort of logic I decide that shaving my pubic hair is a good idea, and get a razor from the bathroom, which I place next to my hand, ready for when the time is right. Something to remove the loathing blanketed upon myself. We watch the proceedings, and drop a fat line into a joint to smoke that makeshift crack. Its almost working as I strain focus onto one or more of the screens regaling hardcore pornography and the screens are becoming more and more blurred as I try to understand what this thing is.

In a sudden change of pace and ideals, all videos stop, air conditioners break, and trains creak to a halt. I clamour onto my browser and try everything I can to remedy the situation. It is in futility and I almost break into tears when I realise I cannot stream smut into my world at this time. A phone call to the ISP does little except destroy my confidence in the system, and I am left alone, without stimulants barring drugs, in a dusty room above the end of my world. The answer was simple. A quick replacement. I check the time. It is 7:16 AM. As a good soldier does, I cradle my shoes onto my war-weary feet, gripping my toes into the holes and rivets carved over these few months. My green suede shoes feel good and I wonder about the spider. Looking onto the wall I see nothing but dust and cracks, no living creatures abide, but a wind blown web that may score my existence, or may grow across my dead body. Using a hammer I break a hole in the wall near the spiders' house, searching in the cladded inners of the wall but only wires and chalk like plaster, crushed and now scattered over the floor. I feel the throbbing in my arm and memories of murder come back clear as that accursed day.

The loss of pornographic input is of great concern. I exude great concern over the series of lost screens, and forget nothing about the last time all these things happened. All my analogues have been discarded, lost in an atlas of nightmares and mercy, dropping into the end. Struggling into my shoes I leap from door to elevator. A sweaty, oil filled forehead collides with the metal glass in the elevator and we descend, both physically and metaphorically into the depths.

Hitting the street I almost get crushed by a passing car, which seems reckless in momentary consideration but in actuality traversed correctly and right. I mark a point in my brain, the shop opens at 9 AM surely, and I walk that same road to reach that same place.

In the shop it is not my usual friend, and I buy what I need to achieve what I think is platitude. Back outside the red sand stones seem foreign and dangerous, and the people even more so, but I walk all the same.

A can is kicked and I spit on my shoe. Laughing, I drop into a corner and delve into the cocktail bag and partake a number of keys, changing from spare door to front door, to memento car key almost without thinking.

I reach the view to my house and I feel a sudden emptiness. The shop owned by Pakistani's face the blind view across the road from my house space and I eye it up like a Geordie hooligan before entering. The woman is slow, so I slip a copy of Razzle and Readers Wives into a generic newspaper that holds all my necessities. Without issue I walk from the shop, happy that my purchase has been for free. A smile streaks across my face and my feet stumble and falter, looking back over joy shoulder I see a face, something like familiar. I crevice into a wall and shoulder the bag as I snort what might be called a "hospital line", and crumble into the clay rock construct, with an ever extruding hard on and slight of eye that deems to mystics.

Leaning on my wall I try to compose myself, staring into the red brick arches of the city I suddenly see a face. So familiar. The thrashing of shadow on that barn wall, the curdle of blood. It is Neil Finn, and we lock eyes for a crippling moment. The thoughts of my Margaret, drawn and quartered and for all merits sent to the four corners of the kingdom reeled about me and rushing back to prevalence, like thrashing serpents bent on puncturing flesh and breaking bone. My penis draws to erection and my legs give way as my body sinks into numbness and the cocaine and ketamine and viagra cocktail of insanity forms the raping orchestral surge that breaks me like salt in water. Our eyes meet across the breaking waves that batter my brain, his is a double-take, that which is needed to make recognition and then a smile dances across his face, easy to see but quickly hidden as it defies his current nature of "truth". I take a breath and gather myself, hand gripped around the newspaper filled with lies and smut in equal measures, creating a makeshift handle on which to balance. He pauses for a moment as we revise our collective intention, and he glances towards a short alleyway that leads to an industrial intersection of railway lines that link the east and western edges of the country, guarded steadfast by bridges and tunnels.

My feet begin to move and a puddle makes way for my leather-clad feet. I spit into the cloudy water and take a fraction of a second to appreciate the golden ratio once more exhibited in my drug-imbued saliva. The path ahead of me marked in red now, with the edges of vision disintegrating into corrugated scenics close to Lowry at his best, stick legs and pencil people rubbed away by the great eraser. Quickening pace, and turning into the alleyway he is already at the other end, beckoning me further. My feet are more steady now as a cloud opens and lets fall the light droplets of rain that seem to be slower to impact than usual. Beyond the alleyway a short wall before the cobweb of train tracks heavy in oil and that catch the mottled sunlight glow creating brilliant lines that come from here and there and lead to anywhere. He has found his way across the tracks and beneath a tunnel covering two tracks, one bound east, one west.

With a destination in sight and the rain increasing its haste I do likewise and quickly pass over the tracks into the tunnel. Once shrouded in darkness the fog of inhibition is lifted. We are, in a moment, unchained; I provide a handful of drugs for us each to dose upon and to envelope this reality as our bodies collide and reach inwards for comfort.

A rising thunder from the perfect darkness of the tunnel

as a train approaches and passes us at tremendous speed, we are invisible before it and never seen. Belts are loosened and his is the aroma all too familiar, of furtive patriarchal essence. I find myself on my knees, lost in narcotic blindness and ignorant to the spirits of judgement all around. Perhaps reaching a peak of my own making there is a sudden calm, as the rain begins to shatter the very ground on which it falls, opening cracks in the earth that provide a window to below, where raging fires consume wicked men, my own reflection caught within and dragged by the claws of my own enemies, of those I have wronged and wronged by, for in His eyes we are all sinners, and like the dutiful son of the sinner I cradle before me and all full blood rising our veins intermingled two black hearts pushing forth the tide of blood, each on a shore far away across worlds and the thunder once more rises, as does our veneer, scorched open by the heat of the sun, falling down and the chemical overture has in its employ every string man, each wind machine and skeletons of percussion, meeting at the point of chaotic resolution and dread symphony as he reaches his own peak and finishes as expected. My own song is closing,released at its moment of purest endeavours but here to the west comes the thunder once more, risen and deafening, the headlamps white, blinding, and we, the invisible, shrouded by shadows and him stood before me my mouth full of memories my hands made of murder once more pushing onward, Finn stumbling backwards if only an instant, mind blank from climax yet given a moment to consider the next forward motion: the train is the hard place, the rock *and* between, and it breathes not a whisper in futile addition.

The ruthless front coupling makes short work of Finn now dispersed into cloud, turned into mist, a powder-keg shipwreck, a great mushroom sporing, here for an instant then gone into the morning. Shredded and spit across slick, oil coated walls of the deathly black tunnel, blood scattered in a fine layer across my entire body, my jaw left agape as the dust tries to settle.

Thunder ebbs far through the subterranean landscape, pitched eastward and unaware of its last engagement. The heart in my chest beats at coronary limits and I grow dumbfounded and over and over jerking forth the last whisper of monarchless kingdoms before the night of my eye falls into each cell of my being and all of my moments of fear and of fret go softly to sleep. Laid down in peace after moments that come through a cycle so damned and precise, avarice emptily turning with lies, make a plate for the savage redeemer in tryst that the good die in hell and the wicked live twice.

The last thing he sees before the final dread coupling, the red arching brickwork, piss stained and liquored, coated in stickers and more with wet posters from weekly encounters on cigarette-pocked dance floors. Naked, to chance whores, where easy romance laws drive forth hordes of bastards for whom make the new wars and pick locks on back doors.

THE END

ALEX FISH

Written By

MICHAEL A. BIGGAM

First edition

MMXXIV

www.ingramcontent.com/pod-product-compliance
Lightning Source LLC
Chambersburg PA
CBHW021427240626
47153CB00001B/53